HERE IN AUSTIN, Norris didn't want to join a band of misfit rascals, overthrow the social hierarchy, go to Sectionals, upend the bully, or kiss the prom queen. No, what he needed to do was *endure*. Seven hundred thirty days with room for summer vacations, Christmas breaks, and the occasional long weekends: that was the number. He took solace in that fact, really. All he had to do was make it through this day for the giant counter he kept in the back of his mind to update to 729. Easy.

THE FIELD GUIDE TO THE NORTH AMERICAN TEENAGER

BEN PHILIPPE

BALZER & BRAY
An Imprint of HarperCollinsPublishers

Produced by Alloy Entertainment
1325 Avenue of the Americas, New York, NY 10019
www.alloyentertainment.com
Library of Congress Control Number: 2018014221
ISBN 978-0-06-282412-7
Typography by Ray Shappell
19 20 21 22 23   PC/LSCH   10 9 8 7 6 5 4 3 2 1
❖
First paperback edition, 2020

TO MY MOTHER, BELZIE.
I WOULD HAVE MADE A TERRIBLE DOCTOR, MOM.
PEOPLE WOULD HAVE DIED.

THE FIELD GUIDE TO THE NORTH AMERICAN TEENAGER

1

AUSTIN

IDENTIFYING CHARACTERISTICS: Abundance of food trucks, strip malls, and concert T-shirts worn by grown adults.

HABITAT: 104 degrees. Generally inhospitable to human life.

OTHER FACTS: Observed slogan "Welcome to Austin: Please Don't Move Here." Hypothesis: environmental insecurity masked as pride.

Twenty-three minutes after landing at the Austin airport, Norris Kaplan could confirm that life in Austin, Texas, really did come with "a unique flavor," as had been aggressively promised by all his mother's tourism pamphlets. Unfortunately for Norris, and just as he'd predicted, none of this flavor, tang, zest, *piquancy*, whatever you might call it, was hospitable to your average Canadian.

No, to your average Canadian—black French Canadian no less—Austin, Texas, blew baby chunks.

From the moment he left Montreal, people had been squinting at Norris's T-shirt. Only one little kid, back at their first lay-over at JFK, had appeared to approve of the insignia, giving Nor-ris a big grin. Since then, it had been a sea of neckbeards whose glances went from confused to hostile at the fact that a sports team logo had stumped them.

This was offensive to Norris on multiple levels. Specifically, three:

1. The white-rimmed navy C with an *H* in its mouth left no doubt to the team—especially against the red of the worn-out shirt.
2. These people were way too comfortable gawking at a teenager's chest in public.
3. The Habs—or Canadiens of Montreal—were an iconic, nay, *historic* team. These people ought to be ashamed of their ignorance.

As Norris had learned over these past few hours, one of the ways in which Airport People interacted was by recognizing each other's self-branding. College shirts, home state visors, high school rings. He'd witnessed nods of approval, high fives, and fist bumps occur without the two parties even slowing down from their respective paths. His mother, Judith, was less skeptical.

"Honestly, Nor, even you can't write off an entire state—"

"Country."

"—country because your T-shirt didn't get recognized in an airport. You're being ridiculous."

"I wasn't writing off anything," Norris had grumbled, pulling up his headphones. "I'm just saying it doesn't bode well. Like seeing a white dove before going to war."

All his life, Norris could count on his ability to strike up a conversation with anyone—French or English speaker, black or white—based on this sigil. Hockey was a third language back in Montreal. Where they were headed now, it would apparently only be a third eye in the middle of his forehead, as would most things about him. Black. French. Canadian. Based on sitcom jokes alone, Norris knew Americans were predisposed to dislike all three of those things. Why his mother couldn't see—or at least acknowledge—that was beyond him.

Now that they had landed, however, the biggest offender was unquestionably the Texan heat.

". . . I mean, *good God*! This is inhuman!" Norris groaned loud enough to be a bother to bystanders as they exited the airport and entered the taxi line. The heat hit him like a wall. "Who did this?!"

"Norris . . ." Judith sighed, fanning herself with some *Wonders of Sixth Street!* pamphlet she had grabbed somewhere along the way. "Please don't start."

"No, Mom. I want a name," Norris said, pulling out his phone and navigating to the Wikipedia page for Austin, Texas. Sub-category: History. "*Who* decided to build a city here? What sick wagon of explorers stopped here and went: *Guys, the surface of the sun is looking a little out of reach for the horses; let's just settle here.*" Norris pinched the fabric of his shirt and fanned himself. They were naturally sweaty people, both of them. Norris knew he could get his mother to break on at least this one point.

"'Stephen Fuller Austin'!" He read aloud as the page finally loaded. Even his phone hated him here. "'The Father of Texas. 1793 to 1836.' Burn in hell, Stephen Fuller. Or, actually, he'd probably enjoy that, the degenerate. I hope you're in heaven, enjoying a cool breeze. How's that, Stephen?" Norris asked. His last hope was annoying his mother to the point that Judith might throw her arms up, turn them around, and book two direct overnight flights to Quebec.

"It's not that hot," she said, earning her a deadpan glare from her son.

It was the lying from one's parent that really offended Norris.

"I will take a vow of silence for forty-eight hours if you raise your arm right now," he said, nodding to the pit stain rapidly spreading under the arm of his mother's blouse.

"That's—I don't—" Judith sputtered, self-consciously tightening her grip on her armpits. "Do you know what my mother would have done to me if I talked to her that way back in Haiti?"

He smiled. "Now, Mom, don't joke about that. They take child abuse seriously here in America," he said, steadily raising his voice with a smirk. "Right up there with beer and the second amend—"

"Norris!" Judith snapped, a whisper of a scream delivered through gritted teeth. Of all the things Norris disliked about leaving his life behind, his mother's paranoid insistence that they become apolitical while living in Texas had provided Norris with the most enjoyment. *It's not that you can't have an opinion,* she had told him. *You just need to have less of them. People won't always know when you're joking.*

Norris was just wondering how far he could go into an off-the-cuff firearms reform rant when they made it to the front of the line and a taxi miraculously appeared.

"About time!" Judith exclaimed. "I'll grab the left one, you grab the right," she said, hauling the suitcase into the trunk.

Maybe it was the new country, the new job, but Norris had to admit that it was pleasant to see his mother so . . . peppy, after months of watching her refresh her inbox every morning with too much hope. Creole and Patois scholars weren't in high demand in North America, as it turned out. Her smile would dim with every inevitable rejection of her candidature for adjunct vacancies, but as soon as she noticed Norris watching her, she'd turn it back on. A full tenure-track offer was a rare stroke of luck; Norris knew that too. It's just, *God, why did it have to be freaking Texas?*

From the back of their cab and through the blanket of waving heat, Norris took in the city that was now their home. Everything really was bigger here, as it turned out. The buildings, the highways, the trucks. It made sense, really. With this much heat, you needed shadows. He didn't spot warehouses of spurs and other cowboy accessories, and there weren't any stagecoach collisions on the highway, but he did count no less than four Keep Austin Weird signs and one Welcome to Austin: Please Don't Move Here tag. Austin was definitely a city with a very imbued sense of self, Norris thought. Maybe the rest of America had praised it too much as a child.

"It's an amazing city, Norris," Judith continued, intent on selling him on the city even now. She pulled another pamphlet out of her bag and foisted it on him. "They have movie festivals, music festivals. . . . That South by Southwest thing? . . . Ooh, Elijah Wood has a house here!"

"In what universe is that a selling point?"

They drove past a high school—or rather, a ridiculously massive football field and a square building in the background flanked by yellow buses that Norris assumed to be a high school. The grass on the field was so green compared to the rest of the brown patches of lawn that Norris would bet his life it had to be plastic. For all he knew, this might even be his high school.

"It's not," Judith said, doing that thing where she read his mind like it was just part of the ongoing conversation. *Mother's intuition*, she called it. "Your school is Anderson High, near Pflugerville, I think? It's ranked very highly."

"What's with all the orange?" Norris continued, eyes on his window. Every banner, every convenience store archway was in the same exact shade. Truly, an upsetting amount of orange. Was there even any orange left in the rest of the world?

"Burnt orange," Judith said, already in the middle of a different pamphlet. "The Longhorn football team's official color!"

"Austin blood!" the cab driver suddenly exclaimed, reminding Norris of his existence. He was skinny and the back of his neck was peppered with brown freckles. *Burnt orange freckles*, Norris thought.

The man's eyes found Norris through his rearview mirror. Going by his mother's glare, it was clear that Norris had done that thing where he scoffed without realizing it. It wasn't an altogether-rare occurrence.

"You a big sports fan, son?" the man asked, squinting at Norris's shirt from the rearview. Norris frowned. When was the last time the man had used a verb?

"Oh yes!" Judith eagerly confirmed. "Boys and their sports. Some things don't change, wherever you are."

The driver chuckled. Norris could swear he'd detected a hint of fake Texan already slipping into his mother's grossly heteronormative statement.

"What is that C on your shirt there, son? Colorado?" the man asked with a furrowed brow.

"*No.*"

"Hmm, well, I know that's not the Carolina Panthers," he continued pensively. Norris had apparently entered a nonconsensual game of charades. "Not Charlotte, is it? What do you call 'em, the Charlotte Hornets? Is that what the *H* is?"

A man can only be pushed so far.

"Actually, sir, the C is for cock—"

"*Canadiens!*" Judith exclaimed as she simultaneously pinched Norris's arm. Hard.

"Habs," Norris corrected for the millionth time. Canadiens might be the team's official name, but any fan that had ever called Montreal home knew to call the beloved team by their alternate moniker: the Habs. Short for *Les Habitants.*

"Uh. Weird name," the driver commented without a follow-up. The fun for him was apparently in the guessing.

Norris continued to stare out the window as they cut through the University of Texas's campus, an entire neighborhood of girls in loose ponytails, baggy T-shirts, and orange short-shorts. Austin had legs going for it, Norris could concede that.

"Fifty-one thousand, three hundred and thirty students," Judith said, eyes on the white tower that seemed to mark the center of campus. "Can you imagine?"

It had taken a few years for Norris to understand why, to his mother, Montreal, New York, Boston, Vancouver, and even London were simply points on a map when she'd been applying to positions. Deep down, she was a complete nerd. She made a living translating on the side, but being in a classroom was where her first-generation nerdy heart lay. So: Texas.

The cab took them to what appeared to be a residential area. There was dead grass everywhere. Dead and wet, as if it had been sweating. "We just had a rainstorm. It was a doozy," the driver said. "Now, I myself like the rain. Always have! Especially after the drought we had through Christmas."

Norris thought back to the mountain of snow left behind on their old apartment's balcony, to the two sets of keys left behind on their old kitchen counter that morning, and something rang in his chest. He hadn't realized until just now that he would never see it melt come spring. Nor would he be ordered to begrudgingly shovel it after weeks of putting it off. Right now, one hour ahead, in a different time zone, his best friend,

Eric, was probably practicing his puck on the ice rink behind their building—a flea market parking lot that the city iced every winter for kids.

"I am not forgetting about Whistler," Norris said apropos of absolutely nothing.

Eric's uncle had a condo in the town, and his belated gift to his nephew had been two week-long early spring passes to Whistler Blackcomb, one of the largest ski resorts in the world, for him and his friend to enjoy during the upcoming spring break. He would be away on business and put a lot of stock in being his only nephew's "cool uncle." He had a man bun, for Christ's sake.

Whistler had been one of the carrots his mom had dangled in front of him when Austin had first crept into their dinner conversations. *You can absolutely still fly back for that!* Judith had said. *Canada is not disappearing, Norris. Neither is your friend.*

Another wrinkle that made returning to Montreal for spring break a necessity was that Eric was now gay. Well, had always been gay, obviously, but had only now started telling a select few people, which, as far as Norris knew, consisted only of himself, their friend Stephanie, and two of Eric's cousins. The revelation that the best friend who'd showed him how to get around Judith's porn blockers had been gay was a bit of a shock. Not because Norris had an issue with it, but because with two words, a thousand conversations now would be remembered in an entirely different light. They'd finally begun to settle back into their groove when Norris was whisked off to America. And now, here he was, two thousand miles away.

Of all the casualties of this relocation, Eric was undoubtedly the biggest one. Well, second-biggest one.

"We should call Dad tonight," Norris added.

"Of course," his mother answered with a controlled smile set to "motherly." "I'm sure he'd like that."

Norris looked out the window. The rest of the drive was mercifully quiet.

2

GUIDANCE COUNSELORS

APPEARANCE: Tricolored plumage, "stylish" glasses.
FEEDING HABITS: Half-eaten containers of Light & Fit yogurt known to linger on desk past eleven a.m.; copious amounts of caffeine.
MATING HABITS: Thankfully not observed.

Anderson High looked nothing like a school. At least, not like any that Norris had ever seen. It was a big monstrosity that reminded him of a mall, another one of Texas's looming brick boxes with long, vertical windows running through it. The sight of it made him sharply miss the cathedral-like exterior of Collège Français secondary with its old brick finish and Gothic archways, remnants from its earlier days as a monastery to Quebec pastors. Norris imagined it now, under piles of bright January snow with a few shoveled entrance points, as their car pulled up in front of Anderson High's cement exterior the next morning. Distantly, he wondered if his locker, right over Eric's, would stay empty through the rest of the school year or if it was scheduled to house some new student's hockey calendar and grimy ice skates.

"Time's a factor, sweetie," Judith said as patiently as she could, waving for another unnecessarily large burnt orange pickup truck to drive around them.

"I know, I know," Norris said in a huff. His mother did not seem to get that this was a decision that could come to define his next two years of existence. Dad being in Ottawa with Janet, the baby, and "no real room for a teenager to stay more than a few weeks at a time" had closed that door pretty quickly, meaning he now had to clock two years in Texas—or 11.7 percent of his total life experience so far, not that he was counting.

"Norris."

"Fine, okay!" Norris swiftly removed his Canadiens T-shirt. As their flight in had proven, a bright red T-shirt with the letter C on it was not the best way to fly under the radar here. The fabric was already damp against his skin; he had only been away from conditioned air for that short walk from their new front door to the car that morning. God, what if he was dying or something?

"I'm buying you some medical antiperspirant on the way home today," Judith said. Mind reading: today of all days.

"You know, you could stay home if you wanted," Judith said. "Just today. Nothing happens on the first day back."

Norris paused, shocked. In response to this clear ripple in the reality matrix, he imagined a violent car crash suddenly taking place on some distant highway somewhere. School was *never* optional in their household. Colds, swollen gums from dental surgery, hockey playoffs, divorce court hearings: unless there was a discernable fever, Norris couldn't remember the option to skip a day ever being on the table. If he needed a sign that she was as nervous as he was, this was it.

"No point in putting off the inevitable," he answered with a shrug. This wasn't simply to soothe her nerves; tolerance for new faces was probably as high as it would ever be on the first day back from Christmas break. Tomorrow, Norris would be even more of an intruder to the school than he was now.

"That's my boy!" Judith answered with a smile.

Norris pulled a fresh, label-free black T-shirt from his backpack, bundling the wet mess of his 1993 Habs tee and discarding it in the back seat. With prayers and offerings, the hockey gods would hopefully forgive this betrayal in time for the Stanley Cup.

"The other parents are going to think my kid gets dressed in the car," Judith said with a chuckle that conveyed she would not particularly care if they did. As if on cue, Norris pulled his head out of the shirt just in time to catch a Texan mother in white capris and high red hair stunned by his momentarily exposed nipples.

"We're black foreigners in a rental car, Mom," Norris said, pulling the shirt down. "They probably already assume we live in this Toyota."

"Now, honestly, you shouldn't—"

"I know, I know," Norris said. "I shouldn't go in expecting to hate it."

"Well, no," Judith scoffed. "Of course you're going to hate it!"

"*Reverse psychology. Controversial but effective parenting strategy, researchers say.*" Norris smiled.

Judith continued as if he hadn't spoken at all. "You're going to hate it the same way you've hated absolutely everything from the moment we got here. From the ice the new fridge makes . . ."

Crushed, not cubed.

". . . to the smell of the grass here . . ."

Artificial and plasticky.

". . . to the layout of the grocery stores . . ."

What respectable community put Cleaning Products between Fruits & Vegetables and Canned Goods?

". . . Even the fact that people here like football!"

Okay, that one was an exaggeration. It wasn't the fact that Austinites liked football. There was nothing philosophically wrong with the practice of football itself; Norris had been known to catch the Super Bowl here and there back home. It was that there were seventeen fantasy football leagues in their zip code alone.

"So, yes, you're going to hate it at first," Judith concluded. "And that's fine. It's not ideal—Lord knows it can be trying—but I understand that's how you're processing this, which was . . . big. *Is* big. It's a big change I sprung up on us, this *Texas* thing. So, it's okay if you need to fuss through it for a little while."

Norris gave his mother a look that could curdle ice cream and swallowed his five-prong reply lest it be classified as "fuss."

"Anything else, *Mother?*"

Judith drummed her fingers alongside the steering wheel as if trying to remember a specific chapter of an old parenting book. Behind them, another car gave up on the honking and took the hint to go around. Burnt orange minivan with a Longhorns sticker on the bumper.

"I love you," she suddenly spit out.

Norris paused, shocked. Another ripple in the matrix.

"I love you too? Jesus—why are you being so weird?" he asked.

"I love you," Judith repeated as though the first one had been for Norris's sake and this one was for hers. "So if you really can't stand it"—she nodded over to the school—"if you give it a real shot, your best shot, and being here away from your friends and hockey and Montreal makes you truly miserable, as opposed to just regular teenager miserable, well . . ."

"Well?"

"Well, that will be a conversation. Canada isn't going anywhere . . . but you have to try, okay?" Judith said. "I mean it, Norris. *Try* to make friends, *try* to get along with teachers. No international incidents on day one because you couldn't control your, y'know . . ." she added, moving her palm haphazardly.

"My what?"

"Your mouth, boy!" Judith said, stopping short of poking Norris in his chest. "Your fricking mouth. This is a new school, and these people don't know you yet. So watch what you say to them. There are no such things as second impressions. And if we're going to pack it all up and go back home, which I'm putting

15

on the table, then you have to actually try."

Ugh.

Just like that, "not trying" was no longer an option. Because Norris knew she'd meant it all. The way his mother loved him was occasionally vexing in how overwhelming it could be. Like the sun or some other celestial body; facing it too directly might kill him.

"Fine," Norris conceded, one foot already out of the car. "I'll try."

"Bienvenue, Norris! Bienvenue!" exclaimed admissions officer Laura Kolb. Through the glass door, she'd looked like one of those impossibly compact elderly women who only managed a single city block every day to stave off death. But as soon as she'd spotted him, Laura Kolb had sprung to life.

"Welcome to Texas! We are so happy to have you!" she said, vigorously shaking Norris's hand from across her plexiglass desk and pulling him down onto a chair in a single motion. Her cheerfulness went right past caffeinated to medicated.

Like everything else in the school, the office itself was sleek and modern, at complete odds with the framed photographs, teddy bears, and stacks of mugs that had been added in to suppress this cold, contemporary look. Going by the photos lining the walls of her office, Laura Kolb was definitely a lifelong Texan. There was a lot of posing in front of various landmarks in sunglasses.

"*Nous sommes* thrilled . . . happy? *Joyeux? Joyeux*! *Joyeux de te*

16

recevoir ici," she said pointing both index fingers downward. "*Ici,* Anderson High!"

Norris widened his eyes. Just what fresh hell was this?

"You're from Montreal, right? Oh, *j'adore* Montreal! I visited, gosh, what, fifteen years ago? What a time, I tell you!"

"Yeah, it's a grea—" Norris started.

"Wait, *are* you from Montreal or, like, a nearby town?" she asked teasingly, as if she'd just caught him in a lie. "Like how everyone from Round Rock says they're from Austin because ain't no one outside of Texas knows what Round Rock is?"

"Um, no. Montreal."

"Sorry, am I going too fast? Of course I'm going too fast," she asked and answered in the same breath. "Don't feel bad, I'm a fast talker. Since I was a kid, they tell me! Right, right: I . . . *parler . . . rapide*! Since *tout petit*? *Toute petite! Oui!*"

She squeezed both hands together to emphasize that *petit* meant "small."

"I—"

"Not to worry: we prepared for just this eventuality!" she continued, reaching into her drawer. She wiggled her eyebrows at Norris in a conspiratorial way and pulled out a yellowed translation book. *English 2 French & Back Again!!!* was splashed across the cover.

"We're actually a very international school," Kolb explained, paging through the book. "Why, in my time here, we've had students from Beijing to Latin America, and—"

"I speak English," Norris interrupted on what he erroneously

17

thought might have been a pause for breath.

"Yes. Very well, Norris!" she said distractedly as she continued to page through the book. She made sure to pause between each word. "You speak English very well!"

"Ma'am? Ma'am? Yes, hi," Norris said, waving his hand to emphasize his existence. "These weren't three memorized words just now. I speak English fine . . . *well*, some might even say."

"Oh," Mrs. Kolb said, looking at Norris. She seemed disappointed.

"Plus, my mom's a linguist, so I'm probably one of five kids here that know the difference between *who* and *whom*. So, there's really no need for . . . that." He gestured at the manual.

Kolb blinked furiously and very slowly closed it.

"'Course this is a good thing!" She began to rapidly flip through a stack of papers that had been preemptively placed at the corner of her desk. "Guessin' you won't need these!" She swiftly removed three sheets from the stack, one of which, even upside down, Norris could read to be labeled *Translator Request Form*.

Kolb stopped and looked back up to Norris, her expression still perplexed.

"I don't mean to be rude here, it's just, I was told a French Canadian was coming in and, well—" She motioned to the whole of Norris as if the demand for an explanation were obvious.

"Quebec is bilingual." He shrugged. "*Je parles les deux langues depuis la maternelle.* I've been speaking both since preschool. It's pretty common up there."

"Well, ain't that a thing!" Kolb exclaimed. "I knew that hoity-toity waiter could understand English! I knew it! I mean, look at you: y'all barely have accents at all!"

"*Merci beaucoup, madame Kolb, l'urètre du clown me semble amplement vaste,*" Norris answered with a smile, making sure the cadence of his voice in no way reflected "ample clown urethra."

Kolb laughed as if Norris had just paid her a compliment. Incredibly childish, yes, but he figured he could take some liberties on his first day.

Norris's starter kit to Anderson High included his locker assignment, a folded football pennant for Anderson's team—the Bats—and a sizable stack of pamphlets on everything from "pregnancy scare" to "bullying" with pit stops at "homophobia" and one that was simply the outline of a shotgun with a red *X* overlapped onto it. Norris was beginning to suspect that most of Austin's city board was in the pocket of Big Pamphlet.

"I was going to alphabetize all of this for you, but I suppose you can do that yourself now." Kolb laughed, handing it to Norris with two hands.

"Start with *A*, end with *Z*, and there's an *N* in the middle, right?" Norris mumbled.

Kolb let out a wry cackle that seemed to signal that it was time for Norris to take on the rest of his day.

"Ooh! One last thing," she added as she saw him getting up to leave. "We had this initiative for diaries . . ." she began, reaching into a drawer.

"I'm not much of a diary keeper, ma'am," Norris said, taking the proffered notebook. It was small and inoffensive-looking enough.

"Try it! You get to see the school, the city, the state, the entire American experience from an outside perspective!" Her voice had gone higher with every new perspective she'd listed. Jesus. How was this person in charge of children again?

"That perspective—that's a rare gift," Kolb continued. "And definitely something worth chronicling!"

"Right."

"If the urge strikes you!"

Norris nodded a final time, hastily removing himself from view lest she be struck by any other brilliant ideas.

Outside Kolb's office, he caught a reflection of himself in the metallic doors of the elevator. Generic black T-shirt, forehead glistening with sweat, and looking so out of place with the passing blur of the other students behind him that it was almost comical. He wouldn't want to be friends with the kid who was staring back at him either.

He had only ever attended two schools in his life—Holy Spirit Elementary and College Français secondary—and had seen enough of Judith's old movies (she was a bit of a collecting junkie and he had a lot of free time) to grow up with a healthy fear of the American high school. *Back to the Future, The Breakfast Club, Dazed and Confused, Can't Hardly Wait, 10 Things I Hate About You, Mean Girls, Napoleon Dynamite, The Karate Kid* . . . Not to mention the ad nauseam TV reruns of *Freaks and Geeks; Beverly Hills, 90210; Gossip Girl; Friday Night Lights;* and everything else in between. If the flavors were different—pack of quirky outsiders here, ruthless-borderline-feral popular girls there—it all mostly amounted to one thing: *in* versus *out*. And Norris Kaplan—black French Canadian Norris Kaplan—had no delusion about where he would fall in that demarcation.

Here in Austin, the point was not to enter the field at all. Norris didn't want to join a band of misfit rascals, overthrow the social hierarchy, go to Sectionals, upend the bully, or kiss the prom queen. No, what he needed to do was *endure*. Seven hundred thirty days with room for summer vacations, Christmas breaks, and the occasional long weekends: that was the number. He took solace in that fact, really. All he had to do was make it through this day for the giant counter he kept in the back of his mind to update to 729. Easy.

3

JOCKS AND CHEERLEADERS

IDENTIFYING CHARACTERISTICS: Muscular, rarely spotted without a water bottle, athleisure wear.
HABITAT: The jock table, football stadium or other athletic field, keg parties.
PREENING HABITS: Extensive.
MATING HABITS: Frequency of copulation typically overexaggerated.

It turned out that *enduring* wasn't so easy after all. For the next two days, Norris couldn't seem to stop drawing attention to himself.

Exhibit A: Norris's very first class in his entire tenure at Anderson High—Advanced Chemistry with Frappuccino fan Mr. Donovan Goade—where three tall and interchangeably large guys all wearing the same dark red sweatpants had entered the room, making as much noise as possible in the process.

"Why am I here again?" one of them complained as he

slammed himself into the seat to Norris's left. He had a literal red neck and close-cropped hair hiding a prematurely receding hairline. It was a strong recession too. Like Obama's first term.

"Because you failed last semester, dumbass," the one who moved to his right said, wafting the same scent of protein powder pancakes and shower gel.

"He could have passed me! Goade just hates me for no reason!"

"Well, you did take a dump on his car," said the last one to enter, casting Norris a dark look. He grunted and moved to a window seat, one row ahead.

"*Allegedly* took a dump on his car."

"Allegedly sent around a selfie of yourself smiling in front of the steaming pile."

The other two laughed. They didn't need varsity jackets for Norris to recognize them. Jocks. Subcategory: unquestionably football, each of them a six-foot-five outline that would inevitably tip from "beefy" to "neckless" halfway through college.

And though Norris had not meant to look, had fully intended to avoid eye contact with the jocks, he made the fatal error of doing just that. He would now pay the price for weeks to come. (See Exhibit C.)

Exhibit B: In English, he made the mistake of volunteering a correction when someone was at the board during a truly random round of dictations. Which was apparently a thing, as Mrs. Gallo did not believe in keyboards.

"There's no *s*," Norris had simply said. "The plural of *moose* is just *moose*."

"Well, there you go, eh!" someone answered right on cue from the back. The unending snorts that followed signaled to Norris that it was best to stay away from all things deer- and elk-related.

Exhibit C: It didn't help that someone kept playing a ringtone version of "O Canada" from their phone whenever he was at his locker.

The one thing Anderson High had going for it was an average student body of 658 students per class year. Six hundred fifty-nine would not drastically change things, Norris continued to remind himself. And yet Receding Hairline, Hairy Armpits, Protein-Shake-Crusted Upper Lip, and the rest of their brood—Norris went out of his way not to learn their names, as the ones he assigned were better—had clout at this school. Whatever the jocks talked about or mocked, so did their girlfriends and those girlfriends' carfuls of friends, along with the wannabes and hangers-on. Somehow he'd rattled the top of some horribly cliché pyramid. As he suspected, Original Thought had died in the desert on its way to Texas, baked under the sun for a few miles, and been slaughtered for sustenance when provisions had dwindled.

Judith's constant nudges inquiring about how things were going at school and if Norris had made any new friends did not make things any easier.

Finally: the freaking *heat*. He'd started bringing new T-shirts to school and changing whenever one got soaked through. The prescription antiperspirant worked but barely. Any hint of stress and the pits were back. Austin's was the sort of heat that had left him three pounds lighter in less than a week.

"We need a T-shirt budget!" he had told his mom, throwing his bag into the back of the car after his first day.

"We definitely need a T-shirt budget," Judith had agreed after the fourth laundry load.

Norris still hadn't made it home without a wet T-shirt bundled at the bottom of his schoolbag.

His lunch breaks were spent meandering around the school, getting the lay of the land and avoiding the hassle of figuring out where to sit in the cafeteria. Plus, being car-less with only a foreign learner's permit was a deterrent to travel. Soon, he'd have to sign up for some extracurricular time sinkhole. No way would Judith let him go on for too long with anything less than a top-ten-college-worthy schedule.

The school's layout was one of the few things it had going for it. Norris actually enjoyed roaming the oppressively oversize halls when they were empty. He knew that if he walked confidently, no one would question where he was going or think he had nowhere to go. In a few days, he had figured out the best, coldest water fountain, and the bathroom where if absolute need be a quick, emergency flush-after-every-drop shit could be taken. Really, this building was less of a school and more of a series of contingency plans needed to make these eight-hour stretches tolerable.

He wasn't lonely, just tremendously bored. The biggest fear was that three days in, Anderson High had already run out of anything new to offer.

Norris was just making his way from the second-floor bathroom by the school's dance studio when he saw it. *Him.* He was cut off at the neck and worn down from years of facing the harsh sun of another floor-to-ceiling window, but it was definitely him.

"J'accuse!" Norris snarled. Okay, fine. The French had a way of slipping through.

Stephen Fuller Austin, 1793–1836, according to the bronze plaque. He was, as expected, an even uglier man in 3D, with a wide forehead that pulled into the wide expanse of his baldness and a pinched, offensively crooked nose.

"You . . . asshole!" Norris raged, extending a middle finger at the man to whom he owed his cursed existence.

No reply.

Norris considered kicking the pedestal, but the ridiculousness of his anger—because he really found himself irrationally angry at this prick frontiersman—caught up to him, and he couldn't help but chuckle, imagining what his mom would say right now. *Fussy, definitely fussy.* Instead, Norris took out his phone and snapped a picture of the bust. It was the perfect reply to his mother's earlier text wondering, **How is it going 2day??**

The first photo came out blurry, so Norris repositioned himself for another. Just then the door to the adjacent dance studio swung open, slamming directly into him. He went flying, then sprawled onto the floor.

"Excuse you!"

Excuse him, because apparently the side of his face had greatly injured the metal door.

What was looking down at him—in every sense of the word—was nothing short of a gaggle of cheerleaders. A haze? A miasma. A miasma of cheerleaders.

Unlike the jocks, cheerleaders in Texas weren't what Norris had expected. No pom-poms or red miniskirts, for one. Norris had classes with a few of them and they all wore a variation of the same getup: high-above-the-knee mesh shorts; huge, baggy T-shirts rolled up to the shoulders; and ponytails that started at the center of their skulls. They were athletes in their own right, only switching from gym wear to sequined prom dresses with no in-between. As far as Norris could tell, the key requirements for membership seemed to be flexibility, a dash of self-importance, and extreme displeasure with his existence at the moment.

"Is that—" one asked.

"Yeah, the new Canadian," the first one answered.

If it weren't for the fact that she herself was black, the subtext of "Canadian" might as well have been a racial slur.

"You were in the way," she continued, her hand still on the door.

"So what?" Norris snapped, rubbing his thumb along his phone's screen as he got up—no cracks. "You bump into someone, you apologize," Norris said.

Two of her friends scoffed in faux outrage as the rest of them filed out of the studio.

"What were you even doing behind the door, pervert?" the angriest-looking one asked. From the four clashing shades of pinks she was currently wearing—sweatband, sneakers, top, and nails—Norris could tell there was a particular strand of viciousness in her heart.

"Ew, were you spying on us?" another one asked.

Norris glimpsed into the mirror-walled dance studio behind them.

"You're kidding, right?" he couldn't help but ask with a scoff.

One of them darted an accusing chin toward his phone.

"I was taking a picture of that!" Norris said, waving a little too manically to the bust. The last thing he needed on his bio here was Village Pervert.

"Yeah, right."

"As if!"

"Do you want to check my phone? I guarantee you there are no pictures of you on there."

"She doesn't want to touch your phone, freak," Pink Alpha answered. "Who knows what it's covered in."

Just what the hell is wrong with this school?

The black one next to her stepped forward, hands now actually on her hips. Her fingertips were perfect squares and shiny white at the tips. "Guys, c'mon. He's probably never seen marble before," she said, pretending to stroke the Stephen Fuller bust, her eyes wide with fake wonder. "Y'all just carve things out of ice up there, right?"

Her friends started to laugh behind her, pretending to pretend to hide it.

"Eh?" one more added.

Norris had had enough. Biting his tongue hadn't helped one iota, and the *eh* thing bothered him more than he cared to admit. If he was going to be known as "The Canadian" whatever he did, he might as well be an honest Canuck. Bridges were easier to burn down than to build anyway.

"Hmm, a bitchy cheerleader," Norris said with a sigh. "You definitely get points for originality there."

The girl instantly stopped fondling Fuller.

"*What* did you just say?"

"You can't call her a bitch!" Pink Alpha all but shrieked.

"Actually, I called her bitchy," Norris corrected. "But I guess it does track that a bitch would behave in a manner that can be described as 'bitchy.' Aren't words fun, Madison?"

Norris decided then and there that all their names had to be Madison: the brood of some Queen Mother Madison pushing out egg after slimy egg of mindless cheerleader drones somewhere in the Texan desert.

"That's seriously so sexist," the black Madison said.

"I read that's called a microaggression," Pink Alpha Madison added.

Norris clicked his tongue, exploring every facet of the notion. "I don't believe you read," he eventually concluded. "I really don't."

"Look, you little hick—"

"Now, now, Madison—" Norris began.

"My name isn't fricking Madison!" she snapped.

"At least *one* of your names is Madison," Norris said, moving an encompassing finger across the half circle they now made around him. "Or Brittany, or Kaycee with two *e*'s."

"*I'm* Madison, actually," the blonde on the far left volunteered, sounding more amused than angry. She was even skinnier than her friends; probably high on the human pyramid but low in the social hierarchy. Norris suspected that she got thrown a lot but not always caught.

"Ha! I knew it!" Norris exclaimed. "We've got ourselves one Madison. Do we have an unplanned pregnancy next?"

Norris could swear he saw Madison—the one actually named Madison—stifle a smile.

"Do you have a death wish or something, Canada?" the one who had accused him of being a pervert asked.

Norris tried to appraise the situation as best as he could. Up close, their upper arms all had definition where his didn't, and they were probably already prone to rage blackouts from all the low-calorie meals; he seriously might be on the verge of getting his ass kicked here. "Guy Pummeled into a Bloody Pulp by a Cheerleading Squad" was at least more interesting than "Peeping Tom Canadian."

Just then, a camera flash went off.

"What the *hell*?" the angriest one—Hispanic with a long single side braid—shrieked, causing Norris to wince.

"Calm down, Meredith," their mysterious photographer said. "It's a camera flash; not the rapture." She was dark skinned, Indian or Middle Eastern maybe, with artificially dyed dark red hair that showed black at the roots. "It's not just false advertising: you girls really do bring that school spirit." She snapped another picture; the flash exploding in their faces.

"Stop that!" demanded one of the girls.

"No." The girl gripped her expensive-looking camera with her left hand, holding it over her left shoulder as she looked around the hall, scouting for angles. Norris had never been to Paris—Montreal's skinnier, chain-smoking cousin—but there was definitely a worldly, Parisian thing about her.

"How about minding your own business for once, Aarti?"

"But your business is so much better choreographed than mine," she answered with a pout.

"Shouldn't you be off going down on Ian?" a girl with expertly curled brunette waves asked with a sneer.

For a moment, Aarti seemed taken aback by the swipe.

"Excuse me?" she asked coolly.

"You really thought he would leave me for you?" the brunette asked. "You're pathetic."

"I have no idea what you're talking about," Aarti answered.

"She's not going to admit it," Meredith scoffed. "What, are you going to blow my boyfriend next?"

Jesus, Norris thought. *Texas cheerleaders really are just laboratory-engineered little bags of evil, aren't they?*

"Hmm, I don't believe I'm on the schedule today, no," Aarti answered with a bright and earnest smile that Norris had to remind himself was completely fake. He didn't know who they were talking about; from the roll calls alone, he'd found this school had an astounding number of guys with three-letter names. Tim, Joe, Dan.

"But you should really have access to the master schedule,

Meredith, since you're technically his girlfriend and all. . . . Or, is that just an ornamental title? Like cocaptain."

She brought her camera to her eye and snapped another picture of the outraged look on the brunette's face.

"All right, claws in, people," the one actually named Madison chimed in. "Mer? My dad needs me at the restaurant and you're my ride, so can we please wrap this up?"

Meredith cast Norris and Aarti one more dismissive glare.

"Yes, please," she eventually said with an eye roll. "And if I see one picture of me online I'm reporting a complaint and suing. My dad's a lawyer."

"Really? A real one, with a briefcase and everything?" Aarti asked distractedly, adjusting her camera's settings. Oh, Norris liked her.

"Ugh, whatever! It's called an antiperspirant, by the way," Meredith said, eyes locked on Norris's stained pits as she walked away. "That's freaking disgusting."

Before Norris could think of a comeback, the cheerleading phalanx was already in retraction, too far down the hall to even hear him.

"Well, that was interesting," Aarti said, sidling up next to Norris.

Her nails were painted dark red and chewed at the top. Between the leather jacket and short dress, she looked better prepared for a Friday night in New York than a day at Anderson High.

"I aim to entertain, I guess. . . . Thanks for stepping in,"

32

Norris said, arms self-consciously clutched tight at his sides. "And I really wasn't trying to take a picture of them."

Aarti shrugged, as if to convey that she wouldn't care if he had been.

"I wasn't!"

"Okay, okay! Although, fair warning: I don't think you're going to get many invites to the Sadie Hawkins dance after this."

Norris went through his inner lexicon of American high school customs.

"Is that the one where the girls ask—"

"—the boys out in some patriarchal tradition because a woman making a decision about who might get between her legs as opposed to the reverse is a magical once-a-year event that requires taffeta?" Aarti said as she put her camera away in its stylish case. "Yup, that's the one."

"Gross."

"Not what us 'bitches' deserve, then?" Aarti said in a tone that implied she'd heard the entire exchange before stepping in.

Crap.

"Okay, I really wasn't calling her a bitch," Norris said before he could stop himself. "I said she was being bitchy, which is, y'know, more of a gender-neutral adjective these days. I mean, I'm kind of bitchy sometimes. Often, actually."

Norris imagined his parents, Eric, and really everyone he'd ever met simultaneously rolling their eyes across the continent.

Aarti only smiled in response, eyeing him up and down again

33

in an appraising sort of way that did not, definitely not at all, give Norris the tingle of a boner.

"Look," he continued, finding himself oddly flustered. "I'm really not trying to, like, mansplain away problematic language, I swear. That was an assholic exchange you just witnessed, yes, but I'm really not an asshole."

"Relax," she said with a slight shrug. "They're total bitches. Although . . . shouldn't you say 'the *B*-word' instead of 'bitch'? I thought Canadians were supposed to be polite?"

"Yes, we're all overly polite, forage for berries in the summers, and craft simple wooden objects of great beauty around the fire at night."

She laughed, and Norris immediately wanted to hear that sound again. "Good to know."

A series of questions flooded Norris's brain. *Why did that girl say you'd serviced her boyfriend? Is there an actual schedule? Do you have a boyfriend?*

"What was your name again?" Norris's brain thankfully spit out instead.

"Aarti. Two *a*'s, one *i*." She sounded like she was used to spelling her name out for people around here. "Aarti Puri."

Something new, Norris thought.

"Indian, right?"

"Indian parents. You?"

"Haitian parents."

"Cool." She nodded.

Norris was impossibly grateful that her nose hadn't started to bleed at the concept of Haitians moving to Canada and that he wasn't subsequently asked for a chart of his family's migration patterns.

"See you around," she added. And with that, she walked away, still mostly focused on her camera's settings.

"Um, okay," Norris sputtered. "Bye."

Norris couldn't help but stand there stupidly, watching her walk away. When her jet-black hair had finally disappeared from view, he reached into his pocket for the journal Kolb had given him. She had told him to write about his experience in Austin, hadn't she? Well, for the first time, Norris had had an experience he actually wanted to catalog.

Aarti Puri might just be the most interesting part of Texas so far.

4

LONERS

IDENTIFYING CHARACTERISTICS: Headphones that aren't necessarily playing anything. Sad eyes. Stand out just enough to let you know to stay away.
HABITAT: Basement-level lockers.
MATING HABITS: Weird porn. Like, German weird. Leeches and electro-rods. Stuff that gets your laptop blinking on a registry somewhere.

The Sorting Hat of Anderson High had spoken, and Norris Kaplan was to be a Loner, which was fine by him. Better than Hufflepuff, by all accounts. Two weeks in, Norris had discovered object permanence to be one of the many things the American teenager was still struggling with as, for the most part, he'd simply become furniture around the school. Not trying had paid off, and the novelty of the New Black Canadian Kid had dissipated. He was now the guy who didn't do much except go to class or take strolls between said classes, which again was fine.

His new school philosophy was "Out of sight, out of mind."

Being a loner mostly involved a lot of walking around. Guidance counselor Kolb had officially turned Norris's missing language requirement into a free period.

"This is actually a great opportunity for you to get some content for your diary! Getting involved in school activities is important here!" She had gesticulated during their second meeting in a way that led Norris to believe that "here" meant the 3.8 million-square-mile expanse of America. Judith likewise agreed, and as far as she knew, her son was joining clubs left and right and ate lunch every day with a small but meaningful group of wacky new friends that dressed in black and white and danced with umbrellas in the school fountain.

Fortunately, Kolb had framed it as a suggestion, which meant that Norris would not capitulate until "strongly encouraged" turned "mandatory." For now, he spent that hour browsing the emptier corners of this megaplex high school and not at all hoping to run into a certain Indian girl with a camera, who had disappeared without a trace after saving him from certain death via beheading-by-cheerleaders.

Ever since their encounter in the hall, Norris had categorically *not* been stalking Aarti. For one thing, stalking required prey, and Aarti was nowhere to be seen. If Aarti was actually a student of Anderson High and not just some cheerleader-vanquishing mirage, attendance was not a priority.

Whatever: it really would make sense that the only interesting person in Texas might have been an apparition. At least that's what he thought until one week in, when the algebra teacher managed to confirm her existence.

"Aarti? Ms. Puri?"

"Absent," someone near the front volunteered. "She wasn't in art class either."

"Of course," the teacher whose name Norris had forgotten said with a sigh. By her tone, it wasn't an uncommon occurrence. Norris hoped she would finally make it to algebra at some point or that he would run into her again but, ten days in, that did not seem to be in the cards.

His locker was thankfully away from the douchebaggier corners of the school. No Madison had been spotted yet. It was a particular breed of students that ended up in row N in the sloped basement, by the pool. He'd taken to nodding "sup" to the tall Asian kid who had the locker right above his. There was a certain safety in *sup*. *Sup* wasn't some feral Canadian or the newest entry to the cheerleaders and jocks' crap list. He could go a full day exchanging nothing but "sups." If nothing else, it made for an easy yearbook quote.

The first skill an only child learns is to be alone and completely satisfied. Norris had fourteen years of experience under his belt; having someone else to talk to was nice, sure, but it had never been a necessity. So he spent his free period and his lunch hours walking around. The earbuds were mostly for show, to externalize his desire not to engage. Besides, he really did like walking for walking's sake. Back in Montreal, he used to leave his hockey equipment at the rink overnight and walk home instead of trekking it back and forth on the bus. Aging into an old man with a collection of pimped out canes did not frighten him one bit.

He was wandering the halls between classes and had glanced into an empty classroom when he turned around and came face-to-face with a very long torso that turned into a mess of curly brown hair at the top, staring down at him with uncomfortable intensity.

"Jesus Christ!" Norris yelped. (Actually, not *yelped*: screamed. It was a Viking-like scream of virility, not a yelp.)

"Are you a ghost?!" Norris yelled, his heart beating out of his chest.

"No," the guy under said hair answered after a moment, as if he'd actually taken the time to consider the question.

"Liam," the strange boy continued. He had light brown eyes, sharp features, and the gum over his left top front tooth went down a bit, giving him the mouth equivalent of a lazy eye. "Liam Hooper."

"Sup." Norris nodded through a throat clear.

The boy showed no sign of moving out of Norris's personal space. He really was quite tall, which probably explained his slouch. At the moment, he ranked somewhere between a close talker and good old-fashioned creep.

"You're the super-rude Canadian, right?" he asked with a deeper voice than expected.

Was that how the Madisons were marketing him to the public at large?

"All right then," Norris said, sidestepping this strange human pole. "Don't take this the wrong way, but I'm going to have to ask you to screw off, Liam, Liam Hooper."

"Yup, it's definitely you," Liam said, sounding satisfied—the first thing close to an emotion he came to displaying.

"Me what!" Norris snapped, pocketing his noiseless headphones because this was clearly going to be a whole thing.

"Sorry, I wanted to be sure," Liam said. "I'm game. Let's do it."

"Dude, what are you talking about?"

"Well, I'm a beginner," Liam said, shifting his weight from one leg to the other. "A nonbeginner, really. Haven't begun yet, y'know."

Why was he fidgeting?

"I don't really know how to do it exactly, but I've seen plenty of videos online," Liam continued. "It doesn't specify beginners or, like, advanced, and I figure it can't be that hard, right?"

"Um . . ." Norris mustered. "I'm eighty percent sure you're talking about porn."

"Ice skating," Liam finally volunteered. "I've always wanted to learn. It just seems cool and—"

"Liam, Liam Hooper," Norris interrupted as a ghastly picture was starting to form in his head. "*What* are you talking about?"

"The ad," Liam said.

The boy reached into his messenger bag and pulled out a crumpled sheet of paper that he proceeded to flatten by pressing it against his flat torso before extending it to Norris. A glance was all it took for Norris's mind to collapse into itself.

"At first, I thought it might have been some old dude look-ing to fondle, but then I heard there was a new black Canadian kid here, and it's blurry, but the guy in the photo is black, so, y'know . . . Connected dots and all."

Credit where it was due, Norris did not scream.

Nor did he instantly burst into a long, protracted scream, strip naked, and walk out of the school, all screams and nudity and heading straight into traffic, which was a very close second choice.

WANTED: HOCKEY ENTHUSIASTS & OTHER FRIENDS

Nice, charismatic young man, new to the area, seeks new friends who share his interest in all things hockey. Has lived all over the world!

Most offensively, the flyer was written in Comic Sans. At the bottom of the glossily xeroxed sheet was an email address that Norris knew to be Judith's spam account.

"That's you, right?" Liam asked calmly, which was how Nor-ris suspected this boy did most things.

The picture under the text was definitely Norris. He didn't have enough photos of himself floating around cyberspace like most teens to lose track of one, let alone that one.

The red Canadiens hockey jersey. The dented black helmet. There was probably some irony in seeing one of his proudest moments on the rink coming back to gnaw him right on the

41

penis—and in Texas of all places. If one of the jocks from chemistry saw this . . . or, worse: Aarti.

"Where did you get this?" Norris whispered, instantly crumpling the sheet into a ball.

"You're a very intense person," Liam noted, watching Norris's hands.

"And tall men are at a higher risk for prostate disease!" Norris snapped back, continuing to crumple the ball of paper until his palms were red. That sucker would never be crumpled enough. "Where did you get this?"

"It was by the turtle pond."

"Dude! I don't have time for pothead poetry here," Norris said. *"Where?"*

"I don't smoke weed," Liam said solemnly, sounding almost offended. "And I'm serious. It was on this billboard on the UT campus. They have a sweet turtle pond in their quad I like to check out sometimes." After a beat, he added, "My dad works there."

Norris shoved the now warm and perfectly spherical ball into his pocket and walked away. He made it halfway down the hall before giving in to the urge to look over his shoulder. Liam was still standing there, eyeing him perplexedly from fifteen feet away.

"Do I follow you or was this you walking away from the conversation?" he asked. "I'm not familiar with your walking tempo yet."

What the hell?

"S—stay! Go! Whatever you want, dude. I—I have class now!" Norris sputtered. "This was a mistake. I'm good on both friends and interests, thank you very much."

"Why did you put up the ad then?" Liam asked.

"Does this *really* look like the reaction of someone who put up the ad, Liam, Liam Hooper?!" Norris tried very hard not to shout back.

"It looks like the reaction of someone that needs the advertising," Liam mumbled in reply.

Norris pretended not to hear it, plugging his headphones back into his ears with such power, he might have perforated something. Norris did have class, albeit in another hour. He could not deal with this weird, affectless, tall boy, and his turtles, or whatever the heck he'd been talking about. There was matricide to prepare.

Norris did not fuss that night. Instead, he patiently and maturely waited until it was dinnertime and he had a stomach full of oven-baked mac and cheese to confront his mother with the undeniable proof that it was, in fact, her deepest wish to ruin his life.

"Were you a dancer? Is that it, Mom?" Norris casually brought up while loading their plates into the fancy dishwasher built into their new kitchen.

"What are you talking about?" Judith asked distractedly, glasses already back on and laptop open. The apartment almost felt like home now that their pristine new kitchen had slowly turned into a landfill of grocery bags that had been emptied but not put away, thick dissertations held by rubber bands, and the near-constant buzzing of the printer coming in from the living room. Judith was a quick nester.

"Did I ruin your body in some unforgivable way on my way out? Was that the start of this mother-son grudge?"

Judith finally looked up from the screen with that half-perplexed, half-confused frown that Norris had come to call the Norris Frown.

Norris reached into his pocket and tossed the paper ball at her.

"I don't think two cities qualifies as me having lived 'all over the world' by the way."

"Ah."

"*Ah.*"

"Why is it so crumpled?" Judith asked, trying to pick the ball open with her fingertips.

"Because I don't own a lighter!" Norris said.

"I don't understand why you're upset," Judith said, putting the unopened ball down. "It's how I met my Old Movies Club."

"Your what?"

"Oh, I must have told you. I put a notice on a faculty bulletin board, and a few people reached out," she chirped. "It's just me and a couple of gals during our long breaks on Tuesdays, but it's growing."

"Neat. Sounds fun. Do you blame me for dad leaving?"

"For God's sake, Norris."

"Well, it has to be something! Because this, this is just mean, Mom. High schoolers are not university faculty members. Why would you do this to me?!"

Judith closed her laptop on a slow exhale.

"Because I know you, Norris," she said. "I made you, quirks and all. You haven't been eating lunch every day with Phoebe, Ross, and Joey. Honestly, do you think I live under a rock? We had that show in Haiti too."

Crap.

"You say that you'll try to make things work here, but it will be just enough to throw your arms in the air and say 'That's that!'" Judith continued. "I'm not letting that happen."

Did she have cameras in the school or something?

"You remind me that you made me way too often, by the way," Norris noted after a beat.

"I'm mostly reminding myself," Judith answered dryly.

"Have you never watched a teenage movie in your life, Mom? This thing could have so easily been photocopied and left in every locker in that damn school!"

"Language."

"Darn school," he mechanically corrected. "Some kid came up to me with it!"

"What's wrong with that?"

"I don't know, Mom." Norris sighed. True, Liam hadn't seemed too bad as far as dwellers of Anderson High went, but . . . "It was weird. He had a real leather-trench-coat vibe."

"He was wearing a leather trench coat?"

"No, but I could tell he would if the weather permitted it, y'know."

Norris knew how ridiculous that must have sounded.

"Well, as long as you know," Judith said, eyes back on her screen.

"Was it—"

"Yes, yes, it was the only one I posted in my unending cruelty," Judith said. "Now shoo, I have a lecture to plan."

Norris paused. She only ever mentioned specific lectures or panels when she was nervous about them. This was something Norris was not even sure she knew about herself. "When is it?"

"February fifteenth."

"Let me know if you have any questions you want me to ask," Norris offered.

Judith looked up at him for a good, long moment.

"You're in high school, Norris," she finally said. "You don't have to attend my boring old department lectures."

"I know. But there's not much to do around here, Mom." Norris shrugged, taking the ice cream bowl with him into his room. "I've got an online appointment to get to."

"All right, babe," she said with a smile. "Say hi to Eric for me."

Of course Norris had to attend her panels. The idea that his mom might one day give a speech to an empty room was something that made Norris incredibly sad for some reason. These events, well respected as they were, were always sparsely attended, but Judith could at least always count on a one-man round of thunderous applause from him. His dad's absenteeism would not extend to him. Somewhere along the way, he had decided that he would be the first Kaplan man to appreciate how incredibly smart and occasionally kickass his mother was.

At least when she wasn't a busybody monster with unsupervised access to a printer.

@Eric53 is online.

@Norrtorious—Finally!

@Eric53—Sry, man. Busy times

@Norrtorious—No kidding

@Eric53—You have 10 mins before I legit pass out, so skip the whining, Kaplan. It's past midnight here. How's Austin!!!

@Norrtorious—Groan

@Eric53—I'm gonna need more than that

@Norrtorious—G-R-O-A-N

@Eric53—Lol, man, I miss the Norris Kaplan drama

@Norrtorious—I could literally keep typing "Groan" all night and it wouldn't lose its meaning

@Eric53—It can't b that bad

@Norrtorious—You have no idea. AND the Penguins are wrecking my fantasy league stats, which only adds to my long list of sufferings

@Eric53—Haha, I know! You're at the bottom of the league. Perfect GPA aside, u really do suck at stats. Btw, you left your biology notes in your locker. The new guy found them

@Norrtorious—It was a gift for your ungrateful midterm-failing ass.

@Eric53—Aww, shucks. Thx.

@Norrtorious—Wait, who has my locker?

@Eric53—Marc-André. New kid from Sherbrooke. He's cool

@Norrtorious—Wonderful

@Eric53—Are you fucking pouting, Kaplan?

@Norrtorious—No

@Eric53—Omfg. Did I say "cool"? I meant he's my new best friend, a killer hockey player, and 2 inches taller than u

@Norrtorious—I'm not pouting. Enjoy the romance.

@Eric53—Lmao I don't have a crush on him. He's just a new guy that's all. Probably straight anyway.

@Norrtorious—Is he really taller than me?

@Eric53—Narcissism: The Story of Norris Kaplan.

@Norrtorious—Starring Taye Diggs

@Norrtorious—Seriously, dude! Everyone here is out of a bad 90s teen movie, it's insane. Douche jocks and nasty cheerleaders as far as the eye can see!

@Eric53—Mm

@Norrtorious—What?

@Eric53—Just wondering who the "misunderstood outsider" is in that scenario lol

@Norrtorious—I really don't like you

E@ric53—U love me. But I'm passing out. Off to catch some ZZZs. Lata

@Eric53 is offline.

Norris shut his computer off on his third yawn and slouched into his bed, which was already in disarray. He hadn't actually made it more than a handful of times since they'd moved in, and his new bedsheets still smelled like an unfamiliar detergent brand. Lavender still, but from a different field. Most things about Austin still felt temporary, like a road trip that had stalled in the middle of unknown terrain.

Norris couldn't even remember how he and Eric had become friends in the first place. It had been at school, yes, but he couldn't connect it all back to a single interaction. Hanging out with Eric was just a fait accompli of life back in Montreal. Staring down the barrel of hundreds of new strangers every day here—strangers who either didn't know him or already only thought of him as the "Rude Canadian"—was something he preferred to opt out of altogether. That weird, tall stoner guy might be nice—very, very weird but perfectly nice—but Norris would still be out of here in two years, 716 days, to be exact. *What is even the point?* he thought, closing his eyes.

It was not a great sleep, all things considered.

5

THE PART-TIME JOB

IDENTIFYING CHARACTERISTICS: Occasionally demeaning work that one would never choose to pursue save for a specific financial goal.

HABITAT: Typically occurring in places with sticky floors.

"Welcome to the Bone Yard!" the midday hostess said with a bright smile. She couldn't have been out of college and was wearing the same signature white tee and red apron featured on every page of the BBQ joint's website. Norris had done his research, and the Bone Yard was by far the least offensive of his options. The staff seemed young and diverse enough (by local standards), and the restaurant was within walkable-ish distance of their apartment complex. He had to start somewhere. Tickets to Whistler were not cheap, according to his online searches, and he wouldn't let some last minute "money's tight after the move, Norris" argument keep him here for spring break.

"Hi, yes, hello! I'd like to apply for the server job," Norris said.

"Great! You need an application and—"

"I downloaded it from the website," Norris interrupted, handing her a manila folder containing the application, filled in in his best handwriting, along with his one-page résumé.

"Well, aren't you prepared!"

His résumé amounted to his name in a thirty-four-point font, along with his email, cell number, school, and the seven "additional skills" he could think up that morning: *Microsoft Word*, *Microsoft PowerPoint*, *Microsoft Excel*, *typing speed of ninety words per minute*, *on-foot stamina*, *bilingualism* (soaked in yellow highlighter), and *people-person*. Four truths; three lies. The last one had been the biggest stretch, but whatever, he could fake it if need be.

"Oh, great! Thank you for your interest in joining the Bone Yard family."

And just like that, the folder was already out of Norris's hand and under the worn-down wooden booth.

Hell no. It had taken Norris fifty-five minutes to trek the two and a half miles that separated their apartment building from the Bone Yard. He wasn't leaving without a goddamn job.

A few seconds passed, and the hostess, name-tagged Tracy, looked up from her phone to Norris again, now with a concerned frown.

"Um, did you need to use the bathroom? Are you okay?"

"Overactive sweat glands. It's fine." Norris fanned himself

with his T-shirt. "But could I get that folder back, actually?" Norris asked. "And see the manager?"

"Is there a problem?"

"No, no!" Norris quickly answered. "It's just, well . . . my mom worked in the service industry for years, and she told me how other waiters would sometimes throw out people's résumés because they didn't want to have to train somebody new, or share shift hours and all that. She said it's always best to hand your résumé to the manager yourself."

"Well, I wouldn't do that," Name-Tagged Tracy said, sounding way too insulted. Oh, Name-Tagged Tracy absolutely would do that. By the needlessly affronted tone, Norris could tell that Name-Tagged Tracy had probably done it twice that morning already.

"I know," he said. "But if the manager is around . . . In fact, I think that's his office up there, right?"

Norris nodded to the staircase by the gift counter that seemed to lead to the only office on the premises.

"He's very busy right now."

"I'll be quick, I promise."

"Look, I *think* he's in," she said. "I'll go ask."

"Thanks, Name-Ta—err, Tracy. I appreciate it."

Name-Tagged Tracy sighed and handed Norris his folder back slowly, as though reaching under that booth was the most grueling task imaginable. She made sure not to roll her eyes, though there was a twitch there.

Tracy disappeared up the stairs, and Norris was left standing alone, fidgeting. It was a good résumé; Norris had even sprung for the fancy beige paper stock. He'd be damned if it was going to go into the trash with a bunch of misprinted receipts.

Most of the actual restaurant appeared to be around the back. Waiters moved between picnic tables and large fire pits of smoking barbecue under burnt orange patio umbrellas and an extensive network of Christmas lights currently turned off. Giant industrial fans encircled the area, making it surprisingly cool. Norris had to admit that it had a certain feel going for it.

"Jim is upstairs and real busy," she said.

"I just—"

"But I told him you insisted," Tracy said with another smile that didn't betray a hint of her annoyance. What was it with Texans and this apparently innate ability to fake the most genuine smile while also obviously telling you off with their eyes?

Norris followed Tracy's nod up the creaky wooden staircase.

"Hello?" he called ahead, taking the partially opened door as permission to enter. "My name is Norris Kaplan, and I—gah!"

As soon as he entered the small, wood-paneled office, Norris was instantly handed a pink infant by an equally pink man he could only presume to be the manager.

"Jim McElwees," the man said as he handed Norris the . . . being. "Can you take him for a second? Thanks."

Okay, so maybe Name-Tagged Tracy hadn't been lying about Jim's hands being full at the moment.

"Yeah," Norris started as diplomatically as he could. "I'm not great with—"

"Nonsense," Jim said as he crashed into his chair and immediately got to typing on his desktop. "He already likes you."

"Um . . ."

The baby looked to Norris as if it did not seem to know if the change of hands warranted a fit but clearly had one in store, just in case. After a moment, it settled for slight spittle onto its already-stained blue sweater.

"I love him, I do," Jim continued, eyes on the screen and fingers going at way over ninety WPM. "But when did grandparents become a twenty-four/seven babysitter fill-in? Hmm? His dad is on the golf course right now. This one's already my least favorite of the two, tell you the truth."

"Two?"

"Behind you," Jim said, finally giving Norris a glance from behind his glasses. Lying on a blanket was another, mirror-image infant, this one in a green sweater and sleeping soundly on its back.

"Yeah, that one deserves the better Christmas present," Norris conceded.

"Sorry, I had to send this order two hours ago," Jim said, still typing, nodding for Norris to sit. "So, you want a job, right?"

"Um, yes, sir," Norris stumbled.

"I suppose I can skip the part about this being a family joint," Jim said, smiling at his least favorite grandchild on Norris's lap. The baby smelled equal parts dirt and baby powder and seemed fascinated by Norris's chin at the moment.

"Um, y-y-yes," Norris stuttered. "I'm a hard worker with an impeccable work ethic an—" Wait, was this the interview? "I'm sorry, is this the interview?"

"Ain't that what you wanted? Tracy said you were pretty adamant."

"I just wanted to introduce myself and give you my résumé in person today," Norris said, wiggling his shoulder to highlight the manila folder that had been stuck under his arm when he'd been handed a child.

Jim raised an amused eyebrow. "It's a busboy gig with occasional fill-ins when one of our servers is out. How many steps did you expect this process to take?"

"I brought a couple of number-two pencils for the written portion."

Jim smiled.

"You're still in high school, right?"

"Junior year, sir," Norris said as he moved his chin away from a deceptively sharp fingernail.

Jim clicked his tongue. "We typically try to get college kids."

"Oh."

Norris knew he shouldn't have shaved last month. The shadow of a shadow of facial hair that began to appear after twenty-two days had a way of killing some of his face's prepubescence.

"I mean—" Jim started but didn't get to finish because just then, a wild Madison appeared.

"You!" Norris couldn't help erupting the moment he recognized the cheerleader. It was the skinny one, the one legally named Madison.

At the moment, she looked thoroughly unimpressed by the sight of Norris.

"Me."

"Friend of yours, Maddie?" Jim asked, fingers finally off the keyboard and pressed under his chin, watching Norris like a hawk. Did they have hawks in Texas? Regardless. The point was that Jim was looking at Norris like some bird of prey that enjoyed the taste of meat. Norris got the impression that most boys within a mile of Madison got the same look.

"He goes to my school," Madison said before throwing Norris a dismissive look. Diplomatic.

It was only then that Norris noticed her white polo and red apron.

"Um, her *high* school?" Norris emphasized. "Meaning, she's the same age as me and she has a job. Not to make a federal case out of this but . . ." Norris pointed to the uniform Madison was wearing.

"Family joint." Jim simply shrugged. "All my kids have worked here since they were yea high."

"*That* you could probably make a federal case about," Madison added.

"Hush, you." Jim waved her off.

"You're the one that called me up here!" Madison said to her father.

"I did? Oh, right. That was like half an hour ago!"

"The afternoon rush started early."

"I need you to take the boys for the rest of the day."

"No way!"

"What I think you meant there was *Yes, sir, boss, sir,*" Jim said.

"Dad, no. I've got plans. I'm clocking out in like twenty minutes."

"But I have to get down to the construction site," Jim McElwees all but whined.

"Unbelievable!" Madison scoffed, but nevertheless took the child from Norris's lap and moved to the couch.

"You're my favorite, Maddie," Jim said with a grin, standing up and grabbing a pair of keys out of a bowl of what appeared to be mostly breath mints. "I mean that!"

"Twenty bucks," Madison answered coolly, raising Green Sweater high, which earned a delighted coo out of the little gargoyle. "Per hour until they're off my hands."

"They're your nephews!"

"They're your grandchildren." She shrugged in return.

"That's three times your rate here," Jim tried to haggle, an attempt that was betrayed by the fact that he had already put on a faded red cap that carried an older logo for the Bone Yard in blocky white-threaded letters. "It's extortion!"

"Again, I can also just leave," Madison countered.

"Unbelievable."

"Sitting here . . ." Norris singsonged under his breath.

"Yes, why is that?" Madison asked her father. By the look Jim McElwees gave, he had sincerely forgotten about Norris's presence.

"Norris Kaplan! He wants the busboy job!" Jim answered after a beat, snapping his fingers at the recall. Call it a hunch, but Norris suspected that in a drawer somewhere were a lot of used day planners gifted to him by employees, family, and friends. "But he's still in high school . . . I worry we might become a little too fast-food of a joint if too many of our employees have SAT note cards peeking out of their apron, y'know."

God. The SATs: another fun American milestone he now had to worry about.

"I do all my SAT prep online!" Norris chimed in. "And, unlike some, I would address you with the proper respect due from an employee to an employer."

"Kiss ass," Madison inserted.

"I was hoping to see a few applicants," Jim said, clicking his tongue. "Maddie, should I see a few more prospects?"

"We did get a lot of applicants . . ." Madison mused as she picked a toddler-size blanket from the floor, shook it once, and placed it around the sleeping twin on the couch, throwing Norris a smirk as she did. Oh, she was enjoying this.

"But I have practice on Tuesdays and Thursdays this semester, so you need someone to cover those shifts," Madison added. "Not to mention, we're always swamped on Fridays with Julio gone."

"Hmm. That's all true, I suppose . . ."

Jim McElwees's eyes narrowed at Norris. He felt as if the man was taking inventory of every cell in his body through sight alone. Every secret, every incognito-mode porno browse, every nasty thought; the man could read all of it right then and there, Norris was sure of it.

"Fine," Jim eventually said with a short nod as he unexpectedly grabbed and shook Norris's hand.

"I'm, like, employed? Just like that?"

"I don't have time to meet all these kids, and she's got a good eye for people, my girl," Jim explained, nodding to Madison before exiting the room. "Leave your email or phone number or something. I'll be in touch. . . . Honey?"

"Yes, I'll tell Mom you'll be late," Madison preempted. "*No, I won't tell her it's because of construction stuff again, so she doesn't kill you.*"

"You're going to be the favorite till the day I die, Maddie!" Jim shouted as he barreled down the stairs. "Day I goddamn die, I tell you!"

And just like that, Norris was left alone with Madison and the twins; gainfully employed. She was smirking at him, ready to collect some gratitude. Norris liked to believe that he was pretty good at reading people's intentions but at the moment, he was drawing a blank at what had motivated this strange act of kindness.

"Thanks for the job," he offered, confused but grateful. Each paycheck was a step closer back to home, even if it would just be for a couple of weeks.

"Nepotism for good." Madison shrugged, casting Norris a once-over meant to convey that he was nowhere as pleasant of a sight as the baby.

"Sorry for . . ."

"Calling my best friend a bitch and using my name as a synonym for all vapid, brain-dead cheerleaders of the world?"

Madison continued casually, eyes still on the baby.

"Right. That." Norris sighed. "So, is that it, then? Did you hire me to make my life hell or something?"

"Hmm, I hadn't considered it," Madison said. "Interesting idea."

Norris scrutinized her. Something about the fact that she had a baby in her hands made her all the more terrifying. Like one of those lean lionesses that nuzzle with their cubs, with antelope blood still drying around their mouths.

"Oh, calm down," Madison finally said, rolling her eyes. "I'm mostly kidding. We just need all the help we can get, that's all. Dad will put off hiring someone for another two months if I let him."

"Mostly kidding?" Norris asked, eyebrows raised.

She glanced at the clock and got up from the couch on which she'd pretzeled herself. "Follow me," she continued, putting the baby down and covering him with a blanket before picking up a baby monitor. "I guess I have time to give you the grand tour before practice." She snatched Norris's résumé from her father's desk on her way out of the office. "C'mon, Canada."

6

BULLIES

HUNTING GROUNDS: Favors areas where prey is contained, seeks moments of chaos to pounce.

VOICE: The song of the bully is frequently monosyllabic.

SPECIES TRAJECTORY: Skirting that thin line between future mall cops and future car salesmen with problematic home lives.

In the space of a morning—five minutes, really—life in Austin had gone from a drag to absolutely untenable. To quote the great Martin Luther King Jr. at some unrecorded point in his life probably: "Eff this. Eff absolutely everything; I want to go home now."

It had started with Anderson High's east end staircase getting repainted a brand-spanking-new layer of burnt orange, the sort of superficial change parents loved to see but that was a hassle for anyone who actually used the staircase every day. Because of this unnecessary spruce up, the waves of students were forced to navigate the fifteen-foot-wide space in a single file to avoid the wet paint. The whole thing was a tedious bottle-neck process that managed to leave stray shoe prints across the shiny new steps and, in return, orange-painted footprints in nearly every hallway of Anderson High. Every day, more and more students grumbled about their ruined sneakers and orange-stained toes. (Incidentally, there were a lot of sandal wearers in the student body.)

"Can't you move any faster?" sighed the exasperated guy right behind Norris. They were all so tightly packed that Norris could smell the cinnamon of his gum.

"Yes, we're all choosing to be here because we could really use a hug right now," Norris muttered.

He was already in a crabby mood, having just come out of a brutal chemistry quiz, courtesy of Goade's sadistic streak. By his estimation, it would be another fifteen minutes before he made it to his locker in this body traffic, which meant he would probably be late to his next class.

Norris had just pushed his way another couple of steps when he heard the rumbling of what sounded like an incoming Zamboni, one floor above. Crap. The only people that seemed to revel in this mess were, of course, the walking bags of Frankenstein's spare parts that made up the football team.

"Hut! Hut! Hut! If you can't keep up, you're going to get stuffed! Hut! Hut! Hut!"

Norris immediately recognized Hairy Armpits's distinctive half whistle.

They found the whole thing endlessly entertaining and had

taken to barreling down the paint-free pathway in football formation, chanting "Hut! Hut! Hut!" as they pushed smaller lifeforms forward, forcing them to either throw themselves down the remaining stairs or jump out of the way and right into the wet paint.

"You guys are such assholes!" a girl shrieked a few steps behind Norris, signaling that his own shoving was imminent. Up until now, he'd managed to stay on the edges of their pile-on, but apparently his time had finally come. He clutched his chemistry book and braced himself as he was violently pushed into the wall, receiving a mouthful of hair from the kid directly in front of him.

"Don't mind them, folks," Norris's mouth suddenly said way too loudly. "They're just foraging for berries and shelter. Fire's going to be a real game changer."

An audible series of chuckles erupted around Norris. Just a few steps below him, the herd came to a stop.

"Yo, what did you say, Canada?" Hairy Armpits asked, turning back to lock eyes on Norris while the nearby chatter dwindled down to an attentive audience.

"Um . . . fire," Norris repeated in a Neanderthal drawl. He could have stopped there. Really, if he had any control over that stupid mouth hole of his, he would have.

"It cooks meat, provides warmth," his mouth continued like it tended to do whenever it was put on notice. "It also did wonders for personal hygiene with the whole boiling water thing, but I don't want to spoil the surprise."

A predictable "oooooh" was heard somewhere behind them.

In Norris's defense, it had really been a brutal quiz, and nothing could sour his mood faster than the thought of a C looming over his transcript.

The following five seconds happened both instantly and in slow motion:

Hairy Armpits blinked twice, sniffed once, and smirked.

The boy to Norris's left instinctively stepped out of the way.

Norris felt a hand grab his T-shirt collar like it was a Kleenex, immediately followed by a firm shove backward.

Ow.

He was sent tumbling back, and in the process, his foot slipped on the paint that he could only hope had already dried for the day.

He lost his balance fully, slamming his elbow against the sharp edge of the step against which he fell.

He felt his head, neck, T-shirt, lower back, and backside wipe through a thick layer of the paint that, nope, was most definitely not dried yet.

Ow again.

Hairy Armpits turned back and resumed his hut-hut-hutting as if the entire interaction had only been the most minor of inconveniences. There was less laughter than Norris expected; just a sea of pitying glances as an acidic embarrassment immediately began to flood his stomach. Most students had sidestepped him and gone on their way. The worst were those who hung back to offer him a hand, faces dripping with pity.

Eff this. Eff absolutely everything; I want to go home now.

"Are you all right?" a concerned girl asked.

She was looking at Norris like he was a wounded puppy, which really wasn't helping.

"I'm fine, really," he managed, blinking furiously at the hand/pity claw extended to him. There absolutely wasn't the prickle of tears behind Norris's eyes. While his mouth sometimes slipped beyond his control, he could at least control his tear ducts.

"It's just some paint," he concluded before making his way down the stairs and to his locker as quickly as he could.

It occurred to Norris at that moment that Hairy Armpits probably would never give this moment a second thought, whereas, for Norris, it was already congealing into something rock-hard in his chest. It would definitely be one of those repressed high school wounds that only decades of living on a yacht made of nachos would someday come close to healing.

As Norris began the long walk to his sub-basement locker, he could feel the eyes on the back of his head and all over his back, noticing the paint streaks, chuckling at the dumbass who had either slipped or been pushed. It was in his hair too, Norris realized. He would probably need a close-cropped haircut to get rid of it all, since black hair was basically a sponge.

It was the Austin airport all over again; dozens of eyes trying to decipher him. He hated this school, this city, this state, his dad for being all-around shitty, his mom for being selfish and well-adjusted and probably laughing her ass off with her unending slew of new friends at her work at this very moment. The suckiness of living in Texas, of attending this giant shopping mall of a school along with its special sun-freckled breed of assholes: it was all there for him to hate as a visible streak of orange paint drying at the back of his head. The countdown in his mind was advancing at molasses pace. Spring break might as well be a decade from now. Norris realized that for the first time ever, there wasn't a drop of sweat on him; his blood was running cold.

He quickly threw his backpack into his locker and began to rummage for a spare T-shirt before remembering that today was laundry day—meaning that the handful of spares he always had in the back were all currently moist and wrinkled in his hamper back home. Fantastic; the one time he needed one most. He slammed the locker door as loudly as he could, only to come face-to-face with Liam Hooper, who stood there watching him with that vacant stare.

"Dude!" Norris snapped. "You have *got* to stop doing that!"

He really was in no mood today. Liam watched him for a moment before quietly extending a single sheet of paper to Norris. He immediately recognized his slanted chicken scratch of hastily written chemistry notes; the orange-shaped footprint in its center was new.

"Thanks," Norris grumbled taking the paper. "Sorry for snapping. Rough morning."

"I saw," Liam noted with a frown. "Your shirt is stained."

"I'm aware, thank you. Anything else?"

"Your hair. Your hair is also stained."

"Dude, are you messing with me or something?"

Liam's face broke into the slow smile of a goddamn sloth.

"Maybe a little," he finally said. "Patrick isn't a bad guy. Before last year, he was skinnier than me. I think he's just a little . . . sensitive about his new physicality."

"Who?" Norris frowned.

"Patrick Lamarra. The, um, guy who just tossed you down a flight of stairs like last night's lasagna after a glass of hot milk."

"Oh . . . I call him Hairy Armpits."

Liam raised both eyebrows, still smiling. "And you really can't imagine why he might want to kick your ass just a little bit?"

Okay, fair point, but Norris certainly wasn't about to concede it.

"Want to hang out later?" Liam continued.

"Like, with you?" Norris asked. This again? He'd given Liam the brush-off once before, and in his experience people didn't come back for second helpings.

"Is that a crazy suggestion for some reason?"

"No. . . . Yes?" Norris said, awkwardly flailing a hand in the air. "I've just been pretty good at making . . . lasting first impressions on people so far in this country."

"Yeah, that's an understatement."

"Dude!" Norris snapped.

"What?" Liam asked.

"Well . . . nothing. It just felt like an interjection was needed there," Norris grumbled. "For my ego."

Liam chuckled, leaning against the lockers to watch the hall like a monk studying a waterfall.

"You might be kind of a dick," he said. "But I'm sure we all seem like dicks to you too."

He threw a look at a passing row of students who snickered at Norris's burnt orange'd backside.

"Everyone's a dick by someone else's standards."

Norris closed his locker and turned to Liam. Just who was this weird teen monk?

"Anyway, we should be friends," Liam concluded. "I think that ship might have already sailed for you and Patrick."

"Jesus, you must really want to learn how to ice skate," Norris said flatly.

"It's not just the hockey," Liam sighed, shifting his schoolbag from shoulder to shoulder. "You're not making this easy, man."

"I don't know what *this* is, man."

"It's just, well . . . I've been watching you a little and, I kind of get it," Liam said, making what amounted to an uncomfortable amount of eye contact. "Being so lonely all you can think to do with yourself is walk around to kill the clock."

Something twinged in Norris's chest; a needle prick somewhere between his heart and his lung. This was not a conversation he was entirely equipped for.

"But that's not a good way to live," Liam added. "Trust me."

"That's a weird thing to say," Norris said, clearing his throat. "You're being weird and intense, weirdly intense, and for all you know I could just be aiming for twenty thousand steps a day on my pedometer app, so you're also being presumptuous about my state of mind or what have you."

"My bad then." Liam chuckled again without malice. "So what do you say? Want to take a break from that pedometer app lifestyle and hang sometime?"

Let the record show, Norris Kaplan said yes.

7

THE BETA CHEERLEADER

HABITAT: Middle-to-upper range of the cheerleading pyramid.

HOBBIES: Kissing the asses of those at the top, carrying bags, stitching up uniforms.

PREDATORS: Occasionally preyed on by its own kind.

LARVAE FORMS: Permanent swing-pusher, "good listener."

ADULT FORMS: The beleaguered assistant, sober-sorority-sister hair holder, always a bridesmaid, never a bride.

The Bone Yard trafficked in big families and truckloads of UT students—as in literal loads of humans that traveled by truck beds—and the output they left behind in terms of greasy, balled-up napkins could clog a national pipeline. A lot of parents kept their kids on leashes on weekends, a practice Norris strongly supported.

Four hours into his first shift, Norris discovered that the key to excelling at the job was not to think about what he might actually be touching at any point in time. He had no qualms about touching bones, still moist with saliva, or napkins filled with everything from barbecue sauce to chewed-up meat fat. He floated above his body watching himself pick through these battle zones, clearing plate after plate.

The evening crowd was on its last leg, with the kitchen already closed and a group of twenty-somethings lingering out in the back. Judith was on standby to come pick Norris up once he texted her. He foresaw himself sleeping well into the afternoon the next day. Thank God for the weekend.

"Can I help you?" Norris finally asked after a solid five minutes of Madison's glare burrowing into the back of his skull.

"Norris Kaplan," Madison said, tapping the brown, leather-clad employee schedule. "Norris Kaplan, Norris Kaplan, Norris Kaplan."

Norris raised an eyebrow. Maybe her cheerleader brain had suddenly become stuck on repeat.

"Why are you signed up for so many shifts?" she asked accusingly.

"Well, *Madison*," Norris answered slowly. "The basic principle here is that at the end of all of this, let's face it, underpaid labor, there's supposed to be a paycheck. More shifts, more paychecks. It's a thing."

"Are you saving up for some kind of glandular surgery?" she said, whispering sympathetically. "I hear they can inject Botox under the skin to, y'know, stop the sweating. My aunt Livvie did it when her hot flashes started getting really bad."

"I really don't like you," Norris said, armpits instinctively clenched.

"I'll grieve quietly."

Madison removed her apron and joined Norris in the sitting area to realign the tables that throughout the day had inched out of their rigorously enforced pattern.

"No, really. Are you saving money to make a break for it back to the Great White North?"

Yes. "Something like that."

Norris had been stalking fares online and realized that flights were nearly double around spring break. He needed to start saving ASAP.

"What are you doing for spring break?" Norris asked, though he really had no idea when this had turned into an actual conversation. Or when she'd started flipping chairs onto tables alongside him.

"There's a competition out in Milwaukee," Madison said. "So my spring break will be spent on a bus with Mer having us rehearse every night in a crowded hotel room, while a bunch of the girls are having stress breakdowns."

"Shocker," Norris mumbled. Meredith struck him as someone who would one day pinch her heavily made-up child during a beauty pageant.

"Still, you must really like those things to spend your entire spring break doing that. That's, I don't know, commendable."

"The winning squad gets a ninety-thousand-dollar national college scholarship. Even split across the squad it amounts to a pretty penny. Colleges are expensive."

Norris's confused face must have given something away.

"It's a restaurant; not a gold mine," Madison said with pursed lips. "And as it turns out, college savings tend to dwindle by the fifth child. Another perk of being the youngest."

Norris couldn't imagine how a sprawling family and crowded dinner table could be burdens, but then again, he didn't have to grow up inside a sprawling family and around a crowded dinner table. There was clearly more to this story, going by her tone, and Norris felt it best to shovel some dirt onto that grenade of McElwees family drama.

"My friend Eric and I are going to Whistler," he offered. "For spring break, I mean. That's what I'm doing. It's this ski resort near Vancouver."

"Guys and spring break, I swear," Madison said with a sigh, looking grateful for the topic change. "It's like Christmas for little kids, except instead of trying to peek under the tree, you're all trying to put your erections into something drunk."

"Whoa, pronouns. Do I look like one of your protein-shake-and-vodka-chugging jocks?"

"Please. Football players, swimmers, theater kids. All guys are the same," Madison said. "Even in Canada, I'm guessing some coeds will be getting pelted by ice-bead necklaces by you and your friend."

"Hardly," Norris scoffed. "Eric is gayer than Christmas."

"Oh."

"What's that supposed to mean?" Norris asked.

Madison leaned into the leg of the chair she'd just flipped over and turned to face Norris with a blank expression.

"Well," she started. "Your friend is obviously going to hell for being a godless heathen, that's all."

"Excuse me?!" Norris exclaimed, indignant.

Madison held his stare for a second before bursting out laughing. It was a booming cackle that turned a few heads their way and confirmed that she was definitely Jim McElwees's child under that one hundred twenty pounds of prototypical cheerleader.

"Jesus, your face!" she said, doubling over. "Anyone ever tell you that you're kind of a martyr?"

"I don't—"

"What," she continued, smirking, "you thought everyone in Texas was a backwoods homophobe, is that it?"

Norris shrugged, caught off guard by his own sudden discomfort.

"Well, not *everyone* but, statistically . . ."

"Dude, this is Austin!" She laughed. "Livvie and her girlfriend were one of the first couples to get legally married in all of Texas a few years ago. It happened in the back, right here. Dad doesn't spare expenses when it comes to family weddings."

Norris scanned the softly lit tables, imagining the scene. It sounded kind of nice, actually.

"Not to mention that a good third of the squad is definitely on the questioning end of the spectrum," Madison continued matter-of-factly. Norris noticed all her chairs lined up and that his work had been cut in half without him ever asking.

"Look, I'm going to level with you: I'm trying to make head cheerleader this semester," she announced, with one hand on the counter and the other on her hip.

"Hmm. Have you considered being aggressive?" Norris suggested, taking on a cheer-like pattern to his voice as he clapped along. "Be, eee, eee, aggressive?"

Madison just stood there staring at him. Norris noticed she didn't so much roll her eyes as fix them on people until they felt uncomfortable. It was working.

"Do you want this job or not?"

"Your dad already hired me," Norris said with a grin, feeling her burning desire to suddenly throw him off the premises.

"Believe me, he won't bat an eye if he never sees you again," Maddie scoffed.

"True, but you gave me the tour, which means you intend to keep me around."

She glared.

"What I mean is that it's a lot," she powered on, glaring a very specific frequency of hatred at Norris. "I need help. Between the squad responsibilities and dad being, well, you saw the other day, and my sister's wedding coming up, and the prom committee, and God, key lime season is just around the corner, it would really help out to have some time set aside to practice and work on squad plans."

Key lime season?

"What does that have to do with me?"

"I need someone to, y'know, pitch in. Go beyond the requirements of the job description when we really need someone to take a look at the gutters, or fix the Wi-Fi for Dad's office, or be on the phone for eight hours with the cable company. Plus, you being at Anderson means I know your schedule, which would make my life so much easier for scheduling last-minute shifts and—"

"You've got to be kidding me. Forget it!"

"Oh, come on!"

"I'm not going to be your lackey—"

"—professional assistant and schedule alleviator," she corrected.

Who was this monster?

"Not going to be that either, you megalomaniac. Find someone else to pick up the slack while you slowly take over the world and come up with intricate *squad plans*." He stretched those last two words because, c'mon, that couldn't be real.

"What happened to you needing this job and always being willing to go the extra mile?" Maddie raised a brow at him.

"Yeah, *mile*, singular. This is an extra Saskatchewan! This can't be the only restaurant in Austin in need of a busboy," Norris said, ready to wash his hands of the Bone Yard and the insane family that ran it.

He was on his way out, back arched and proud, when Maddie said the two words that could stop him in his tracks in that moment.

"Aarti Puri!"

Goddammit.

"What about Aarti Puri?" Norris repeated suspiciously, trying to sound as uninterested as possible. Maddie leaned back with one arm on the counter and linked her fingers in front of her, looking at him with a newfound coolness.

"You like her, right?"

The tone of her voice confirmed what they both already knew; she had the upper hand again.

Norris updated himself for a possum-like defense, no eye contact or discernable motion. Unfortunately, Maddie did not give up and walk away and simply let out a delighted little laugh.

"No need to answer, by the way. That wasn't actually a question! There was a trail of drool from the bust of Stephen Austin to your locker—and I'm guessing to the nearest box of Kleenex as soon as you rushed home."

The last thing Norris needed was for rumors of some creepy crush by the weird foreign kid to get back to Aarti before she even bothered to learn his name.

"I could help you with that, y'know," Maddie continued. "In exchange."

"From what I can gather she hates you Madisons," Norris surmised. "In a unique and deeply personal way. Nice try, but you can't help me."

Maddie remained unflappable.

"Aarti and Ian dated for three months, maybe four, last semester," Maddie began to recite. "Before that, she dated Oliver, art kid, president of the photography club. He graduated last year.

There was apparently a thing with Seth Ezer at Sallie-Ellen's birthday this summer, but I don't have corroboration."

"Do *you* have a thing for Aarti or something?" Norris questioned. "How do you know all of that?"

"She's very pretty," Maddie acknowledged with a smirk. "And also strictly a social butterfly. A week here, a week there. A photo here and an art project there."

"Art project?"

"Yeah, that's her thing. She used to be an art kid," Maddie continued. "Wow, see how out of the loop you are? She likes parties and excitement, and a little bit of drama if we're being honest—things that I'm guessing you can't provide. You need me, pal."

Norris thought for a moment.

"That's the deal: take it or leave it," she continued.

"And if I leave it?"

She started to answer but was distracted by the buzzing of her phone, which was suddenly in her hand in the blink of an eye.

Maddie shrugged before returning to her frenetic texting, elbows anchored on the wooden counter. Norris watched her fingers move across the phone faster than he thought was physically possible. He suddenly felt like his Haitian grandfather must have, looking at him typing on his old laptop: obsolete and processing some youth revolution that had left him behind. It was the typing speed of people who received more than three texts a day.

Norris couldn't repress a snort. "Squad drama?"

"We're having a party."

She sighed in a frustrated tone as if Norris was one of the twins kicking off a blanket.

"Look, if you want a shot at Aarti Puri, you're going to need some assistance. Just like I need some assistance." She slid the apron his way, smiling like it was a check with too many zeros.

"An official Bone Yard apron," Norris mused.

"Dad usually waits until a couple of months to give those out to new employees, but he just texted me to make sure to give you one. Congratulations; he must really like you."

Norris raised an eyebrow. "Why?"

"I cannot overstate how much I do not know," Madison said. "Maybe he's secretly really into black guys."

Norris snorted despite himself. It wasn't a high bar, but Madison McElwees might be the most interesting cheerleader in all of Texas.

"So." She smirked, eyes sparkling with self-satisfaction. She knew she had him.

Goddammit.

The handshake was surprisingly firm and to the point. Madison was someone used to backroom deals or maybe just to being introduced to a lot of strangers as the mastermind behind a puppet regime that consisted of high school politics and local eateries.

"So," Norris said with a throat clear. "How do we do this, exactly?"

"Step one," she said. "I had a shift Monday afternoon after school?"

"Yeah?"

"Now *you* have a shift Monday afternoon after school." She grinned. "See how that works?"

Before Norris could protest and pull out of the entire deal, she quickly added, "And in exchange, there's a pool party this weekend. Do you have a cell phone?" Maddie asked before snatching Norris's phone out of his hand the moment it was presented. Norris could see that she was entering a new contact listed under *M*.

"I'll text you the address. Aarti will be there. You can make a good impression. Or at least an impression. It doesn't even have to be a good one."

Norris, suspicious, eyed his phone upon its returning. *McE, Maddie.*

"Um . . . No offense, but Aarti doesn't seem like the type to frequent cheerleading parties. As far as I can see, she has all her cognitive functions and stuff."

"Imagine if you were *trying* to offend me, Canada," Maddie said with a smirk. "Trust me, she'll be there."

8

HOUSE PARTY

ATTIRE: Black T-shirt, jeans, weekend Jordans.

GOALS: (1) A meaningful exchange with Aarti Puri, (2) not getting hurled down a flight of stairs.

SPECIAL ARTILLERY: Year-old condom from health class in wallet, because optimism plus preparedness is like teaming up Superman and Batman.

"Remember," Judith said as the car's navigation system announced that they had arrived at their destination. "Same rules as back home."

"No drinking, no drugs . . ." Norris recited listlessly, eye on the house in question. "No calls to your phone tomorrow morning and text you by eleven for pickup. I know, Mom."

She'd given him the exact same speech at his first sleepover at Eric's. They had been in the fourth grade at the time. To make matters worse, this spirit-fingered gathering was at Meredith's house—a fun fact Norris had learned only a few hours ago via text. Maddie assured him there wouldn't be any pig's blood over the doorway.

The address Maddie had given him had taken them to the deeper suburbs of Pflugerville and onto a street with impressive two-story homes. The neighborhood was at least one full income bracket over their own garden of apartments, and Norris recognized a few of the cars from the school's parking lot parked alongside the overcrowded street. There weren't that many turquoise Beetles around, thank God.

"You have a job, and I'm already dropping you off at pool parties." Judith smiled, touching the back of his neck and folding the flipped-out tag back out of sight. "Not so bad, this Austin thing, huh?"

"Right," he said, hurrying out of the car. "I'll text you later. Bye, Mom."

He'd omitted the deal he'd struck with Maddie, the flip side of which was that she had the misconception that he wanted to attend this . . . situation.

The party was in full swing through the door, and the ground was booming as Norris rang the bell.

NotMeredithNotMeredithNotMeredithNotMeredith—

A small and very chipper Asian girl with auburn streaks in her hair answered, a lipstick-rimmed Solo cup in one hand. She eyed him for a second and her smile widened.

"Hi," she greeted. "Anderson or Trinity?"

She didn't seem to associate any previous bad experiences with Norris. Thank God.

"Hi!" Norris matched, smiling as widely as he could and hoping his face/soul did not crack. "Maddie invited me."

"Maddie M.? That makes you Anderson then." She smiled, leading him in. "Sorry, we're keeping a tally." She motioned to a gigantic disarray of fluffy white towels. Norris imagined they'd started the day neatly folded by some poor mother or, more likely, maid. He guessed that this party's embryonic form was a pool party that had now been going on for hours.

"Drinks are in the kitchen, pool's in the back, the boys are barbecuing on the hour, bathrooms are upstairs—already clogged, ew—and Meredith and Maddie should be . . . somewhere around here." She then laughed for no reason.

It felt like he'd stumbled into a rerun of *The* O.C. or some other nineties show with angsty midtwenties models cast as kids escaping Austin's pummeling sun in bikini tops and basketball shorts.

He could hear water splashing and girls' shrieks from what he assumed to be the pool in the backyard and didn't have to wonder if there was even one adult present on the premises in the middle of the afternoon. This was the other half, he realized. Kids who had never spent a single moment of their lives not fitting in. It was the sort of party he thought existed only in the minds of screenwriters trying to aggrandize the high school experience—to make kids in basements feel like their *Mario Kart* parties and stolen beer cans from their dad's garage minifridges lacked meaning, which to be fair, they might.

Norris took a deep breath and went in.

Twenty-nine minutes and two hot dogs later, Norris still hadn't seen Maddie or Aarti. As far as he could tell, the party combined kids from two different schools that seemed to share a football field. It was a Canadiens and Quebec Nordiques situation. One landmass; two designated NHL teams.

So far, no one had mocked or insulted him, and he'd made chitchat with a guy whose *Rick and Morty* T-shirt had caught his eye. He might have learned the kid's name, but he chose to disentangle the moment the conversation stopped flowing naturally.

Norris took a lap around the house, catching bits of scintillating conversations as he moved.

"It was a frozen hot dog she made out with," some girl said. "Frozen, that's the sick part!"

"I hate when they do that," someone was whispering to a friend in the corner. "When you know they hate you and . . . Hi, Brittany!"

It wasn't that he didn't know what to do at parties. He just found them viscerally boring: like getting dressed for a big night out and then spending your evening in an intermission lobby, bumping against people you vaguely recognize and fumbling to align conversation topics for brief windows of validation. He refused to believe that this was the meter by which people measured their lives. He was getting bored, Aarti was still nowhere to be seen, and Norris thought it was a good time to send Maddie a text calling off their "deal." He didn't want to get invited to parties; he wanted a chance to talk to—

"Are you doing that thing where you pretend to text in a corner of a party so people assume you have plans at another, much cooler party?"

As if summoned by the mere thought of her, Aarti's voice over his shoulder startled him.

"Worse: weather app," Norris blurted, proud of his quick recovery. He pocketed the phone and tried to appear nonchalant as he turned to face her.

The black of her hair had already begun to peek through the red dye, and this time, instead of Parisian, she had a whole Los Angeles thing going: oversize sunglasses framing her hair, cutoff jeans, and a baggy sleeveless T-shirt, all of which looked both secondhand and very expensive, like those celebrities caught at the gas station who still managed to look unattainable. She was better dressed than everyone else at the moment. Norris was kind of in awe of her ability to move across the globe through wardrobe change alone.

"I was beginning to think you were a ghost," he said with a throat clear.

"Now that you mention it"—Aarti smiled—"an Indian exchange student did fall down a well fifteen years ago."

"Man, I hope not," Norris said. "I'm screwed if Anderson turns out to be a horror movie high school. The black guy always dies first."

She laughed, which somehow made her eyes sparkle even more than usual. God, how wasn't every guy in school after her 24/7? Or maybe they were—to Maddie's point, he just didn't know.

"Come on," Aarti said, already walking ahead. A few people were giving her odd looks as she squeezed past them, leading Norris to a door that led to a concrete basement filled with unmatched couches and a pool table, pushed to the side.

"The best thing about Meredith's parties is that only about half of those in attendance know that her house even *has* a basement," Aarti said. "Which means that booze is always untouched."

The crowd was sparser and seemed less magazine chiseled than the above swim and football teams. She navigated them to a corner of the basement where a guy was manning the makeshift bar and currently trying to spin a bottle in an attempt to impress a couple of girls but failing miserably.

"Dennis!" she said, leaning both forearms on the table and turning what Norris might assume—he was the sort of pervert to look—were Bs into Cs.

"Can you pass us the rum? And a couple of Cokes."

The boy behind the counter, presumably Dennis, was shirtless, with hair still wet from the pool.

"ID, please."

"That never gets old, Dennis," Aarti said, rolling her eyes as she grabbed a couple of red Solo cups.

"I'm hilarious," Dennis confirmed, reaching under the makeshift bar.

"New kid?" Dennis said, shooting Norris an inquisitive look as he handed her the Cokes and a handle of rum.

"Norris," Aarti confirmed. "Norris Last Name, meet Dennis Meyer." Without waiting for either party to acknowledge the introduction, she followed up with a not too subtle, "So, Dennis, have you seen . . . him around?"

Dennis shook his head, almost sympathetically. Norris reviewed his memory of Maddie's social geography lesson.

"No, sorry. I've seen his girlfriend, though. She's on the second floor with the rest of the cheer squad," Dennis continued.

"Fantastic." Aarti sighed.

"Is there going to be drama?"

"Not from me."

"If there is drama, can you two make it happen in a kiddie pool filled with Jell-O?"

Aarti rolled her eyes and grabbed Norris by the forearm, dragging him away. "You're a prince, Dennis."

"Actually, let's sit on the couch," Aarti suddenly said as they headed back toward the stairs, grabbing him by the forearm and moving them across the space.

"Couch it is," Norris agreed. He sincerely did not care; an underpass would be okay if it meant spending more time with her.

They settled into a nearby couch, and Aarti brought her legs up under her, taking another look around the room. She seemed intent on keeping an eye on the staircase that led back to the ground floor.

"By the way, it's okay if you don't drink," Aarti said, nodding over to his untouched red cup.

"I drink," Norris quickly said, and then proved it with a large gulp.

Of course, Norris had drunk before. The drinking age in Quebec was three years under the one in America, which meant that he and Eric had started to chip away at that underage rite of passage at an even younger age. One of Norris's many "sorority house behaviors," according to Eric, was that he didn't particularly like the taste of beer.

They both sipped their drinks in silence for a moment, watching the room. All things considered, the basement was where Norris should have been all along. It was where all the misfit toys of the party had naturally retreated. The two girls sitting on the stairs were retaking their umpteenth selfie and, at the pool table, a kid from math class smeared an unsubtle booger along the wooden table.

"Gross," Aarti commented, catching Norris's grimace. That she was also a natural people watcher was the latest in an apparently infinite series of similar qualities.

"How many beers is that finger accidentally going to slip into throughout the night?" Norris pondered with a grimace. Aarti's reply was interrupted as two more girls threw her a long look and then turned away the second Aarti made defiant eye contact back.

Norris was beginning to realize that for all these kids, life in Austin hadn't started nineteen days prior. They were all in the middle of their own dramas and lives that he had simply been dropped into without a road map.

"I'm sorry for bogarting you, by the way," Aarti said throwing another glance at the stairs. "Sitting with the girl getting dirty looks from people can't be fun."

"Right, I had a pretty packed schedule of awkwardly standing in the corner and trying to guess the Wi-Fi password on my phone."

She smiled again.

"I have to say . . . I did not expect to see you here," Aarti said. "Doesn't seem like your type of crowd. The jocks and cheerleaders."

Norris shrugged. "Is it yours?"

She took an assessing look around the room. "Not particularly. I still haven't found my tribe. Going on seventeen years now. I just didn't . . . I don't know. I didn't want them to think . . ."

"That this Ian drama had you huddled under a blanket in bed, eating ice cream with your hands?"

She laughed. Norris smiled. God, he wanted to make her laugh again.

"So," she said, taking it upon herself to change the topic as she finally turned to face him. "Has anyone given you a tour yet?"

"Of Meredith Santiago's house? No . . . but I'm guessing there's at least one trap room where you have to cut off your own arm to get the key to the exit."

"Of Austin, ass."

"You mean there's more than school, restaurants, and football fields?"

"You'd be surprised."

"Well, you'd be the right person to know then. You, um, skip class a lot," Norris noted in a tone he hoped wasn't too accusatory.

It really wasn't any of his business. "You can't think it's all that great either."

"Been keeping track, have you?" she asked with a quick smirk. Norris shrugged as nonchalantly as he could.

"I keep up with the assignments," she went on. "I just have better stuff to do with my time than track the speed of Mrs. Garrett's nose hair growth."

"It's growing pretty fas—"

"Aarti!" someone interrupted. A boy was perched at the top of the stairs, looking at the two of them, unsure of what he was actually seeing. "Jesus." He tumbled down the stairs to approach them.

"Hello, Ian."

Something about his aura of unearned self-confidence almost caught Norris off guard. He was tall enough, blond enough, trim enough, and all those enoughs together averaged up to handsome by high school standards. Sort of. In a boring, homegrown sort of way. Norris would bet money that his family owned a golden retriever named Bailey. Not that he was intimidated, of course. Not one bit.

"I can't believe you're here," the guy grumbled.

"These parties are open doored, if I recall," Aarti answered coolly. She was looking at him as if he were some outfit she disapproved of in a magazine: tacky. "Or did your girlfriend make you the designated bouncer tonight?"

"You haven't answered any of my texts," Ian said in a low, almost hurt voice, still only focused on Aarti.

"No, I haven't," she said with another sip of her drink. "I'm under no obligation to answer your texts, Ian, because I'm not your girlfriend. You already have one of those, remember? Even though you told me—swore to me—that you'd broken up. And just like that, I'm the town ho, macking on another girl's boyfriend."

Despite her detached demeanor, Norris was close enough to notice the new tension in Aarti's back.

"C'mon," Ian said, bringing his voice to a whisper. "Don't be like that. I told you, it's com—"

"Yes, complicated," Aarti acknowledged. "I know just how complicated."

Everything about her answer felt rehearsed, and suddenly their placement on this specific couch, right in the line of sight of whoever happened to be passing in front of the door upstairs, made complete sense.

"Who is this?" Ian asked instead, finally granting a measured look of concern at Norris.

"I'm Norris," Norris said with a quick and empty smile.

Ian looked at him with a . . . sneer? The guy was actually sneering at him. All that was missing was the pack of cigarettes rolled into the sleeve of his T-shirt.

Seemingly done with his evaluation of Norris, he shifted his attention back to Aarti. "Aarti, can we just please talk? Please." There was something pleading in his voice that seemed to work.

Aarti turned to Norris, looking torn about leaving him even though she was already standing up.

"Um, are you going to be okay, Norris?" she asked. "I won't be too long. I just need to deal with . . . this."

"Oh yeah, sure, I'm good." Norris smiled tightly. "No babysitter needed, really."

Ian scoffed and Norris got a sudden, powerful urge to lock the guy in Meredith's torture chamber and start peeling his skin away with a razor. No, not a torture razor either—an old shower razor that really needed you to dig into the skin.

Norris watched as the two of them disappeared up the staircase, already engaged in hushed whispers. Ian made a move to put his hand on the small of her back as they went up, which she swatted away, though not as fast as she *could have* in Norris's biased opinion. And that is when he finally got it: she'd invited Norris down here exactly for this to happen.

Texas was turning him into a freaking idiot.

Norris was left on the couch alone, and suddenly, the thought of eating ice cream in bed with his fingers seemed downright appealing.

9

HIGH SCHOOL FLIRTATIONS

OBSERVABLE CHARACTERISTICS: Fidgeting, awkward body language, strained laughter, giggling, neck-straining in an attempt to make eye contact.

COMMON PLACES OF OCCURRENCE: Hallway lockers, the cafeteria, sticky-floored basement of a keg party, empty classrooms, janitorial closets.

Instead of finding another corner of the party to bury himself in, Norris claimed the couch for the following hour. It was not at all on the vague chance that Aarti might make good on her word and come back looking for him, which she hadn't, by the way. A second rum and Coke seemed unwise, so Norris occupied himself by scribbling in his notebook instead. He had taken to carrying it around everywhere with him; the thing had proved to be something close to useful after all. It was thick but pliable and fit into his back pocket pretty well. There was no way he would actually use it to diarize like Kolb had suggested, but it was perfect for jotting little doodles and thoughts as he had them. The notebook had become his own personal field guide, a spot for his observations of everything and everyone that had crossed his path since arriving in Texas.

No one looked out of sorts and pathetic while writing something down, Norris told himself, a fact that was coming in particularly handy now in the basement of a party that he could not wait to leave. According to Judith's text, she needed another hour before she could make it up through the late-afternoon traffic to pick him up. Doodling on the couch felt safe.

"Pouting alone at a party; very hot."

Norris quickly shut the notebook, hiding the outline of a skate he had absently been tracing, and looked up to a vaguely annoyed Maddie, staring down at him with crossed arms. Her hair was curled for the evening, and there were bathing suit straps peeking from under her top.

"Shouldn't you be holding court upstairs in the VIP section?" he mumbled.

"I should, but all the girls are asking me about the brooding hot black guy in the basement."

"I—wait, really?"

"Of course not, you toddler!" Maddie cackled, plopping down onto the couch next to him and pulling out her phone to text as they talked. She had the casual white girl confidence of someone who did this, exactly this, every weekend.

94

"Dude," she said, eyes on her phone. "You need to do something. Anything. You're scribbling names into a notebook in the middle of a party. That is 'Tell an Adult' behavior."

"It's not names, it's—"

"Whatever it is, Canada, it's not a good look. And it's not going to get you the attention of a certain girl in earrings I would very literally kill someone for."

"I saw her, y'know," Norris sighed. "And Ian."

"Of course I know," Maddie said with a frown, still texting. As if the notion that anything could happen on the premises that she would not know was ludicrous. "I also know that Elisa and Ian got into a fight last night, which is probably why he started to hit up Aarti again. He's from the 'Cake and Eating It Too' school of dating."

Norris's head was spinning. Was this all he had to look forward to in this stupid country? Elisas and Ians and whispers and gossip and stupid slut boy Ian always being able to burst through the door and command Aarti's attention? He really missed Montreal.

"I don't like to be used," Norris sighed. "It's . . . decidedly unfun."

Maddie smiled sympathetically.

"If it helps, I can tell you that Aarti really liked Ian," Maddie said. "Moving on from someone you really like takes time. But honestly, Ian is kind of a big slut—don't tell anyone that I said that."

"Well, I'm not sure I'm cut out for—"

Maddie suddenly leaned into him as if to listen to something Norris was currently whispering and then threw her head back, laughing loud enough to get a few nearby folks to look their way.

"Are you having a stroke?"

She rolled her eyes and nodded over to the foot of the staircase, where Aarti was standing with a raised eyebrow, looking a little confused at the moment.

"Don't stare, moron," Maddie said before laughing again in a way that actually looked sincere. Lightly shoving at Norris's shoulder was a nice touch. The sudden thought that all cheerleaders were functioning sociopaths crossed Norris's mind.

"You're very rude for a basic white girl."

She pinched him—hard—and Norris's resulting yelp might have sounded like a laugh. When he looked back up, Aarti gave him a smile and raised her cup to him as a salutation, which Norris returned with an awkward little wave as she went back up the stairs. "She left!"

"Don't worry; that's good," Maddie said, instantly pulling away from Norris's close proximity and returning to her phone.

"How is that good?"

"You gotta learn to play the game a little, Canada," Maddie answered. "People like what they can't have. It's a rule of dating in these parts."

"Yeah, well, I'm not from these parts." Norris sighed before getting off the couch, notebook in hand, and going after Aarti. He was already exhausted by all the games. It was almost seven, and the upstairs crowd had increased to include the kids who had been outside when he'd gotten there and the new arrivals for whom this was the second stop of the night and who hadn't been interested in the poolside portion of the day. There was booming music vibrating through the floor as Norris pushed his way through, returning a stray fist bump to someone he didn't actually know as he looked for Aarti. Judith would be there soon; he had to act quickly.

"Hi," Norris said, finding Aarti on the outside porch as she leaned against the railing, a new beer in hand. Everything this girl did seemed like a still from an indie comedy with A-plus cinematography, Norris thought, definitely not looking at her butt.

"You and Madison McElwees were having a good time in there," Aarti noted with a tired smile.

"I just started working at her restaurant, that's all," Norris said. He didn't like games, but he was beginning to think that Maddie knew what she was doing, and it couldn't hurt to make Aarti a little jealous, right?

"So, how did things work out with Ian?"

"They didn't." She sighed with a note of finality before going on to add, "He wanted us to keep hooking up while he continued to date Elisa. Do you believe that?"

"I sincerely do," Norris replied. The outside heat was already seeping into his T-shirt.

"Fair enough. Well, anyway, ibidee, ibidee," she said bitterly.

"That's all, folks. Another one bites the dust."

"You really liked him, huh?"

Aarti shrugged.

Just then Ian and Elisa came out of the house. Elisa made a show of tightening her arm around Ian and throwing Aarti a vicious glare as the happy couple literally walked through them.

"Enjoy the bucket of crazy, dude," Ian muttered, strictly for his benefit. "You're welcome to it!"

"Yo, Ian? Enjoy the herpes medication, dude!" Norris suddenly yelled out, causing Elisa's eyes to widen as they walked to a red Honda. "Remember: remission isn't just a gift for yourself—it's a gift for your partner too!"

Aarti and Norris watched Ian make a show of angrily slamming his door and screeching his tires as he drove off.

"You really don't mind people not liking you, do you?" She chuckled, half-accusatory, half–something else. Amazed, maybe.

Of course I mind, Norris thought with a twinge. "Not really," he lied. "Not much I can do about it."

A moment passed.

"So what was the plan, anyway?" Norris started. "Ian, the guy that you like—"

She grimaced.

"—the guy that kind of screwed you over by telling you he was breaking up with his cheerleader girlfriend and then, after some back-seat spoils, changed his mind . . ." Norris revised.

"Am I getting it mostly right?"

She remained silent, her arms now crossed in front of her chest. Norris was dangerously close to entering his rant mode, as Judith called it, and the heat wasn't helping.

"Enter this jerk," Norris said pointing a thumb at his own face, plastering the biggest grin he could muster. "New kid, roaming the party with no one to talk to, and with an inborn ability to piss off people that could probably fight off Magneto . . . and also, black."

"That doesn't matter!" Aarti said, offended. Now it was Norris's turn to give her that look. One of Norris's biggest pet peeves, growing up in Canada, was the people telling him that his race didn't matter to them and giving themselves preemptive credit to do or say whatever they wanted. He didn't know her that well, but Aarti was smart enough to know better. Especially being a brown girl herself.

"It doesn't not matter and we both know it, Aarti."

"I'm sorry," she said after a beat, her hands now fidgeting with one of her many rings. "I don't always consider people's feelings, all right?"

Norris acknowledged the statement with a tip of the head, not really knowing what to do with himself now. An apology wasn't really on the list of outcomes he'd expected. He'd just known he had to say something.

"So, can this complete curse word of a girl at least give you a ride back to your place to apologize? I just called a cab, and I'll cover the detour."

"No thanks. My mom's picking me up."

Then Norris heard himself say, "But how about you give me your number?"

Suddenly, and without much historical precedence: balls.

Aarti blinked at him, and as the moment stretched on, Norris felt like an old photograph developing in Aarti's mind. An image suddenly forming. As if this was the first time she was actually seeing him come into focus through the whole "black Canadian" smoke shield.

"Sure," she finally said with a slight twinge of a smile.

Her car pulled up just as she finished entering her number into his phone. He had to suppress a grin as he watched her type. Her contact name simply amounted to an emoji: 😈.

"That makes complete sense," he noted with a smile.

Norris tried as best as he could to suppress the giddy snort he felt when Aarti kissed him on the cheek and stepped into her cab. Instead of battling his way back into the increasingly drunk crowd, he quickly texted Maddie while Aarti's cab pulled away. He doubted that she'd waited for him in the basement anyway.

Norris: I got her #.

Maddie: Congratulations. Successful evening! I'd wait a few days to text her, make her sweat a little bit. Oh and you also need to cover my shift on Wednesday, btw!

Norris slipped his phone back into his pocket with a smile. Against all odds, allowing himself to become the Moneypenny to Maddie McElwees's overextended James Bond had worked.

He wanted to type **thank you** or at least a string of exclamation points, but he didn't; he and Maddie weren't friends. Still, all things considered, this first social foray into Austin life hadn't been as bad as he feared. Not one bit.

One might even go so far as to call it a success.

10

MALE BONDING

IDENTIFYING CHARACTERISTICS: Prearranged meeting, typically in a sports facility or other odorous setting. Structured around activity that involves not being able to talk for long stretches.

STAGES OF ENCOUNTER: Initial greeting, assessment of each other, awkward period, eventual breaking of ice, final decision on whether another meeting will occur.

I t was only eight a.m. but the sun was already bright and high through the Kaplans' kitchen windows. As far as Norris was concerned, "bright and high" was the only position the damn thing ever occupied in Texas. He'd gotten used to sleeping well into the early afternoon on weekends since arriving in Austin, which made this whole thing an early morning state of affairs.

Not to mention that he was still a little hungover from the party. Norris's greatest secret as a red-blooded teenager was that deep down, he was the lightest of lightweights. He'd drunk exactly nine times in his life, and all nine incidents had left him with a massive hangover the next day. Even a beer made him giddy, according to Eric. Luckily, having no other barometer to compare him to, Judith always assumed that the occasional morning grogginess was just a natural stage of living with a pubescent body. Norris didn't feel like he needed to correct her.

"Don't yawn in his face when he gets here," Judith chastised, rinsing the frying pan before the egg grease could harden.

"Why not?" Norris asked, swallowing a second yawn. "Yawning is a valid response to being up this freaking early."

"He'll think you find him boring," she continued. "People pick up on those things."

"Jesus, Mom, it's not a date."

"I know that," she said, looking over her shoulder to give him an eye roll. "It would be so much easier if you were gay. Plenty of literature there. Podcasts. Support groups, even."

"*Mother.*"

"I'm teasing. It's just exciting to, y'know, see you actually start to fit in here!"

"I'm fitting in fine," Norris said, thinking of the new contact in his phone. He'd checked it this morning, just to make sure it was still there. His hands were itching to text Aarti, to say something clever, but so far Maddie's advice had worked and he was playing it cool—or at least, trying to. "You and Eric act like I'm some vicious monster. Like those ostriches at the zoo they warn you might beak your eyes out if you try to feed them."

"Well, I've always trusted the peer-review system," Judith added, a smirk to her voice. Norris might have gotten it from her and not his dad, after all. He was ready to unleash the perfect reply when his train of thought was derailed by a burst of three quick honks outside their door.

"Nice car," Judith commented, glancing out the window, and Norris peered outside to look. He nodded in agreement; it *was* a nice car, a new-looking silver Land Rover.

A few years ago, all Norris wanted was an Xbox 360. It seemed like every other kid in his class had gotten one over the holiday break. Eric had one. Julien Tilbault, that throbbing asshole, had one. It was all anyone at their school could talk about, which, in turn, made it all Norris could talk about at home. And then, one day, it was waiting for him on his bed after school. Norris was over the moon, clocking in twenty hours of gaming a week and coming as close to a gamer as he ever would, until over the following weeks—months, really— Norris noticed a change. Their meals had become more basic, and they were often just reheating leftovers. Their cable package had shrunk down to just the basic channels. It was the moment when Norris realized that, despite all his mother's impressive degrees, they were in "The Lower Half." And he loved her for protecting him from that realization for thirteen years and that damn Xbox was still carefully put away after each use.

"I didn't know he was rich," Norris commented, eyes still on the car outside their building. Part of him suddenly felt self-conscious for living in an apartment. So far, everyone at this school seemed to have big houses in the suburbs. With a car like that, Liam probably had a full compound somewhere.

"Hurry up!" Judith said, pushing him toward the door. "You don't want to keep your new friend waiting!"

As Norris and Liam pulled out of his driveway, Norris suspected which of the two halves Liam and his family inhabited. Still, money wasn't a topic polite people discussed.

"So," Norris whistled over the click of his seat belt. "You're rich, huh?"

Liam looked at him for a beat, hand freezing on a very leathery steering wheel. It was the usual blank Liam look, but his rapid blinking betrayed an attempt to gauge the proper answer—this was Liam Hooper taken aback.

"Um, I don't . . . Yeah, sorta, I guess," he eventually said. "Is that okay?"

"Sure." Norris shrugged as casually as he could. He hadn't meant to make him feel bad. "I didn't mean to, like, wealth-shame you."

"Right."

"I mean, I'd love to be rich. We're not, obviously. Apartment building and all," Norris's mouth continued. "I would absolutely use it for evil. Not active evil, but definitely morally gray evil."

"Right," Liam simply said as they came to a red light. "So, good morning."

"Good morning."

Judith had clearly gotten into his head. So far, it wasn't going too well with this "socializing" business. Norris cleared his throat and shifted the sports bag resting on his knees. It was then that he caught a glimpse of something in the rearview mirror that made his heart skip and realign.

"Are these your skates?" Norris exclaimed, reaching for the back seat because *No frickin' way* . . .

"Yeah, why? No good?" Liam suddenly sounded worried. "I ordered them online."

"Jeez, these are . . ." Norris took off the plastic protector, revealing freshly sharpened blades.

". . . really, *really* good skates," he finished once the lust that overtook his heart had been quelled. If Liam wasn't a civilian, he might even smell the blade; that fresh titanium had a way of hitting Norris where he blushed.

"Are you all right there?" Liam asked.

"I'm just considering if I can get away with killing you and running off to Mexico with these skates," Norris said nonchalantly, fingers drumming against the blade.

"Well, I am currently driving," Liam noted with a frown, eyes still on the road and giving the matter all the seriousness it deserved. "You'd probably get hurt in the crash."

"You're right," Norris acquiesced before nodding over to his window. "Do you mind pulling into that gas station parking lot for a second?"

Liam snorted, and an invisible tension gave way. As they continued to drive to the undisclosed ice rink, Liam became more talkative. Norris learned that he was exactly as weird as he first appeared, and that this wasn't necessarily a bad thing. He wasn't into hockey in the National Hockey League sense of the word and therefore had no opinions on any of the teams. He likewise did not despise Texas with the fiery passion of a hundred suns, which admittedly limited Norris's range of topics. This newfound passion for ice hockey was only the latest thing on Liam's long list of growing interests this new semester. He was also president of the Irish Student Organization, which was A) a thing and B) had a "small but very involved membership," although Liam wouldn't divulge an exact number. Norris suspected the number to be one.

Mostly he didn't feel the need to fill every lull in conversation with chatter, for which Norris was rather grateful.

"We're here," Liam said as the car pulled into a warehouse-peppered corner of the city, separated by plots of tall dry grass. They might as well have been in a different county altogether.

As Liam reached for his bag in the back seat, Norris noticed the hint of a tattoo under his raglan sleeve. From that angle, it looked like a semicolon. Norris was about to point it out when Liam suddenly pulled his sleeve farther down.

"Ready?" Liam asked, clearing his throat. Norris nodded, lips pursed and raising his own skate bag in answer.

It was only once they reached their destination that Norris realized he had been deceived. Lied to. Betrayed. Whatever it was unscrupulous Texans did to overly trusting northerners.

"This is not an ice rink!" he huffed as soon as they stepped into the chilled warehouse. His wet pits from time spent crossing the giant, deserted parking lot were already drying.

"What do you mean? Of course it is," Liam said, already

sliding onto the ice. His dirty sneakers left a dark streak trailing in his wake. "Ice" was a generous term for what was, in Norris's eyes, no more than a glorified layer of air conditioning frost over concrete. The ceiling was high and every sound they made reverberated around them.

Almost as soon as they stepped onto the ice, Norris could tell it was going to be a long day. The thing with Liam's skating was, well . . . it was hard to say. Some people skated driven by the fear of falling, their bodies stiff and motions constricted for fear of losing their footing. Norris was used to drawing people out of that stiffness one push of the blade at a time, steadily building their confidence. Not to brag, but David Laflèche, who ended up the star of Norris's team, could barely make it across the ice before Norris gave him a few pointers—in exchange for a full term of calculus notes two days before an exam.

Liam was the exact opposite. The moment they hit the ice he began to propel himself forward, landing stomach first across the makeshift rink in one swift motion that almost qualified as graceful.

"Slow down! You have to—"

Norris couldn't get through his thought before Liam was literally up and at it again, this time swinging his arms to increase his momentum. At the rate he was now going, he was headed straight for the—

With two quick kicks across the ice, Norris planted himself directly in Liam's path. He grabbed the taller boy by the forearm and spun them around the ice once, taking most of Liam's momentum onto himself. After two spins, Norris released his hold and let Liam fall lightly on his butt.

"How did you do that? That was awesome!"

"I'm the understudy for *Negro on Ice*," Norris said, scratching at his cheek in mild awkwardness. "Small show but a big following." Even back in Montreal, he was often the only black kid. By Norris's estimation, something about seeing a black ice skater was akin to seeing a teacher outside of school deciding between ice cream flavors at the grocery store: a few blinks were in order.

For the next hour Norris coached Liam through balance, edge control, and—most important for Liam—how to fall without killing himself or innocent bystanders. The taller boy's enthusiasm never flagged. Well . . . what passed for enthusiasm in Liam. It was hard to tell with him. Norris was able to forget about everything for a while: about how much he hated Austin, the sticky suckage of sweating through at least three shirts every day, the orange paint he was *still* finding in random places. (Seriously, how?) It all faded away on the ice. He didn't want to admit it, but he was actually enjoying himself.

It seemed that Liam felt the same way. "Maybe we can do this every week," he suggested at the end of the hour, as they glided off the ice. "Like for an hour or so?"

Norris didn't even balk. "Sure," he agreed. He was surprised to find he was smiling.

11

HALLWAY ENCOUNTERS

A BY NO MEANS COMPREHENSIVE LIST OF OBSERVED
BEHAVIOR IN AN AMERICAN HIGH SCHOOL HALLWAY:
- Bullies shoving smaller, nerdier prey against their lockers as they pass; worse still, actually placing them inside their own lockers.
- Couples that make out on the staircase. On the literal staircase. Like, spread horizontally across the stairs.
- Army cargo shorts—guy seen casually picking his nose and wiping it behind a combination lock.
- Stressed-out kids with rolling backpacks to carry all their books with them at all times who will either end up rich and successful or as supervillains. No in-betweens.

Norris still spent a fair amount of his free time at Anderson High walking around. In a past life, he might have been some vicar walking around his parish all day, nodding to passersby and doling out good will. Or, in the case of this lifetime, complete indifference. It was strange how pleasant of a ritual it had become.

He looked forward to these strolls whenever the day started to drag, and liked hearing the echoes of chatter and lectures happening behind closed doors, or peering into the open-doored classroom and occasionally spotting a familiar face, or row of heads diligently taking notes. It made him feel both apart from and of this gigantic new ecosystem he'd been thrown into.

Today, a few days after skating with Liam, Norris had an ulterior motive for his walk—he was hoping to bump into Aarti. Since the party Norris had yet to make any substantial move with her. Maddie's instructions were to "play it cool, Canada," which to Norris meant killing as much time as possible to avoid thinking about the cool, interesting girl he really stupidly wanted to text or call or email or telegram. Walking was the only thing that seemed to work.

But this morning, he didn't find Aarti. He found his chemistry teacher instead.

Mr. Goade was seated against a locker, inhaling the wettest, cheesiest cheeseburger Norris had ever seen in his life, a brown to-go fast-food bag at his side. Norris was beginning to think that the man had stacks of unhealthy snacks placed around the entire campus.

"Goddammit," Goade said, wiping his mouth with a fistful of brown napkins when he noticed Norris approaching him with a grin and both hands stuck into his pockets.

"Hi, Mr. Goade," Norris all but sang.

"Is this a Canadian thing?" Goade sighed, pulling himself up from the floor with his free hand. "Stalking the premises constantly like a nut?"

Norris ignored the question in favor of nodding to Goade's meal, wet and sticky with orange cheese and meat molasses. "What on earth are you eating?"

"Chicken, bacon, both pig and turkey, and sausage patty in the middle," Goade said, almost proudly.

"Does it taste like you're running around a farm and biting a bunch of different animals in a row?"

"I can't believe I felt bad for you on your first day." Goade scoffed, locking eyes with Norris and defiantly swallowing the last chunk in an impressive bite. "They should build a wall to keep you northerners out."

Norris pretended to gag at the sight.

"Don't you have an office?" he asked. "Four walls that would safely contain . . . this beautiful sight?"

"No, Kaplan. I do not. The teachers of this fine, hyperfunded institution share a bull pen. And my lovely wife has very publicly made my coworkers aware of the very strict, plant-based diet plan she currently has me on. Allegedly for my own good."

"You guys share a bullpen?" Norris snorted. "Like, journalists with hats and notepads in old movies?"

"You would know that if you ever visited my office hours."

"Don't need 'em." Norris shrugged. Goade's eyebrows seemed to concede that point to Norris. Two quizzes into the semester and Norris was officially a solid A-minus chemistry student. Two for two.

"Look, I carpool to work with the wife and, bless her, but she has the nose of a hound, so it's either deserted hallways or bathrooms, and that's just too sad," Goade said, crumpling the napkins, wrapper, and brown bag into a ball before discarding it into the nearest garbage can.

"This is plenty sad, dude."

"Let me have my delusions, Kaplan." Goade sighed as he walked away. "You need them, the older you get. You'll see."

"They have a salad menu too, y'know!" Norris shouted at his back.

Goade stopped in his tracks, glanced to both ends of the hallway, and slipped a quick, crude gesture to Norris before resuming his walk. Norris liked to believe himself unflappable, but something about his chemistry teacher flipping him off in a deserted hallway thoroughly tickled him. He laughed to himself as he continued his stroll. Goade had a bad reputation among the students—detached, moody, a deceptively hard grader and, now, diet cheater—but in a very short time he had cemented himself as Norris's favorite new teacher.

Norris was about to return to his locker in time to gather his books for American history when Aarti appeared out of nowhere and sidled up to him without missing a beat in the increasing deluge of bodies that filled the hallways once the bell rang.

"How did you know how to find me?" Norris asked, genuinely curious.

She smiled.

"I don't want to alarm you, but you might be a tad more predictable than you'd like to think."

"That is the meanest thing anyone has ever said to me," Norris said over the midday chatter as they walked in tandem in a sea of backpacks and elbows. He grabbed the math book she was carrying, though probably a beat too slow to qualify as naturally chivalrous. Effortfully chivalrous, maybe? Anderson High's go-to mathematics oeuvre was a freaking backbreaker, containing all the material for Geometry, Algebra I, and Algebra II. The all-in-one tome was one of the school's cost-cutting measures.

"Thanks," she said. "I cannot wait to burn this thing when I graduate."

"I might throw mine up at the sky like a graduation cap," Norris mused. "Take out a small plane."

"So there's a movie I want to see," Aarti said. "It's at the Violet Crown. Opens this Friday."

Norris tried very hard to push down the flicker of joy that danced in his belly. Was Aarti Puri asking him out on a date?

"Sounds cool," he said as casually as he could manage. Maddie would advise him to play hard to get at this stage. "But I have a shift at the Bone Yard on Friday."

"Oh, come on," she wheedled. Norris had a feeling Aarti was used to getting her way. "The movie's not until eight. I'll pick you up and leave your virtue unsullied by the end of the night."

"I mean, feel free to touch it a little bit, if you want," Norris coughed in the very worst attempt at flirting that had ever come out of his mouth.

Aarti, mercifully, laughed it off. "I'll consider gently massaging your virtue. How's that?"

"Right," a voice said out of nowhere. "Perfectly normal conversation happening here."

Maddie was staring at the both of them with a raised eyebrow, looking like she really wished she had just kept walking. She was in full orange-and-black cheerleader regalia and had a sports bag under her arm. Her hair was up and particularly shiny, cascading in meticulous curls from the center of her head. Norris had caught a glimpse of the other uniformed cheerleaders around school all morning, which meant they probably had an exhibition performance that afternoon.

"How long have you been standing here?" he asked with a frown.

"Gently massaging your virtue," Maddie answered flatly. "Quick question: Can you switch your Saturday shift with Julio's Sunday?"

"Sorry, hanging out with my mom Sunday," Norris said with a quick glance to the single xeroxed sheet scotch-taped to his locker door.

He did Judith's PowerPoints for her in the morning, and in the afternoon, they did groceries together, getting anything Norris wanted as compensation for his advanced IT skills of resizing arrows and searching online for the photos her lectures required.

"But," he teased, "if Julio can spot my Wednesday afternoon shift, we might be able to work something out."

He'd been putting off an English paper for two weeks now

and would definitely need a full day to bang it out.

"No, that won't work. . . . He's going out of town." Maddie sighed. "Okay, wait! How about . . ."

With the reflexes of a ninja, she snatched a dangling sheet from Norris's binder and scooted past him to grab a stray pencil from the top shelf of his locker before beginning to scribble furiously on the back.

"My education!" Norris gasped.

"Shh." Maddie tut-tutted. "Okay, if you can take my shift tomorrow, five to nine, I'll take Tuesday, Julio can switch with Maggie, the new girl, and we'll push her orientation to Sunday, which covers you. . . ."

Her finger moved around as she spoke, like a gifted detective solving a crime scene. She was a very specific sort of savant when it came to juggling the personalities and schedules of the Bone Yard employees. And to be fair, three employees never showed up for the same shift when Maddie did the scheduling whereas the same definitely could not be said of her father.

"Yes!" Maddie exclaimed, showing him the sheet of neat little blocks in a loosely drawn grid. "Okay, that works!"

"That was impressive," Aarti commented. Norris had almost forgotten she was there.

"Oh, right. Sorry about that!" Norris cleared his throat and straightened his back with a note of formality. "You guys know each other, right?"

The two girls shared a bemused look at the introduction before Maddie laughed out loud. Aarti contented herself with a smirk.

"What?!"

"We've been in the same school since the fourth grade, Canada."

"Maddie and I have bio together, dude," Aarti added, with her signature fake smile. "We're the best of besties."

"Well, pardon me for being a well-bred gentleman."

Maddie rolled her eyes and turned away, something she did whenever she had no time for what qualified as "Norris nonsense" during their shifts together.

"How did you do on the bio test?"

"I skipped it." Aarti cringed in response. "Mrs. Marek rescheduled it for me. Is it going to be brutal?"

"Not that bad, actually. It's literally all chapter seven stuff. Don't even touch chapter eight."

"Okay, good to know. Thanks!" Aarti smiled. Maddie smiled back and after an extended beat gave Norris a nod of acknowledgement.

Before Norris could say anything, she was already on her way, pom-pom strings dangling from her sports bag.

"She's got spirit, yes, she does," Aarti sang.

"What does that mean?"

"That I should definitely study chapter eight," Aarti added wryly, still watching Maddie go.

Norris frowned.

"What? No," he said. "She wouldn't do that."

She looked at him for a moment.

"If you say so."

"No, really," Norris insisted, feeling a sudden need to defend his friend. "She wouldn't. Extracurricular gymnastics aside, she's actually one of the few people in this entire school that doesn't make me want to set my hair on fire."

"High praise." Aarti smiled. "Should I be jealous?"

Hardly. Although . . .

"Would you be jealous?" Norris continued, closing his locker. She seemed unimpressed at the prospect.

"Nah, I don't really do jealous." Aarti shrugged. "It doesn't look good on me."

Norris scoured his brain and there simply was no scenario under which bringing up Ian was a good idea in that moment, so he didn't.

"Right," he said instead, realizing that the hallway's foot traffic had drastically decreased and that most students had found their way to class already. "I have to go."

"All right," Aarti added. "It's a date."

Norris nodded, trying for casual, but in his head, he couldn't stop repeating those three beautiful words.

It's a date.

12

ABSENTEE DADS

DENSITY: Based on average North American divorce rate of 45 percent, plenty of them to go around.

RESOURCES: "Nine hundred Canadian dollars less per month until offspring reaches age eighteen."

NESTING HABITS: Predisposed to desert their first nest.

PRONE TO: Late-night ice cream and hockey-highlights viewing behind Mom's back, affairs, broken promises.

It was nearly a month into his career at Anderson High before Norris and his dad could coordinate an actual webcam session. Their first attempt had been the night of his arrival in Austin. Norris had rushed to his computer and spent a good couple of hours idly waiting before giving up on that gray icon ever turning green. Around eleven that night, just as he was getting into bed, he'd finally gotten a text: **Sry, Reggie fever!**

The next time, it was a rash, and the time after that, his dad had been called in for a double shift at the hospital, leaving

Norris with a call from a very apologetic Janet.

"Felix feels terrible about bailing on you," Janet had said, leaning into the camera's frame behind the empty desk chair without sitting down. There was a stain on her shirt, and Norris could hear cooing in the background.

"It's fine."

"Are you liking Texas?" she asked distractedly.

"Nope."

"That's great! Your dad will be so upset he missed you!"

"It's fine, Janet."

It was understandable. Work or new baby, Norris knew his dad was spending a lot of time elbow deep in fecal matters that weren't his. Felix Kaplan was a nurse technician who had recently transitioned from a hospital in Montreal to a senior center in Vancouver, where he was still getting his bearings. The sudden move from Montreal, four months before their own, was stated as being necessary to be closer to Janet's family. This was both a valid excuse and complete bull; Janet had a way of skirting that line.

"I'll tell him to text you! Bye, Norr—!" Janet had said, cutting herself off midsentence with a click. His father's text didn't come for another day and a half.

Norris knew that disliking his, urgh, *stepmother* was a cliché and that as far as stepmothers ten years younger than your mom went, he could probably do worse than Janet, but he couldn't help it. Janet had a gap between her front teeth, wore bright makeup, and had talon-like nails that were covered with intricate

120

designs. Massive chest aside, he did not see the appeal. Plus, she'd called him "Maurice" for their first few interactions, a fact she now made up for by using his name as much as possible—*Norris, Norris, Norris*—which was just obnoxious. Then again, maybe it was all just genetic loyalty. The fact that Basic Janet had been the preferred alternative to the half of Norris's own genetic makeup that was Judith caused him to naturally dislike her.

When they finally managed to check in, Norris's father looked exhausted, still in his green scrubs with what Norris could tell was an ID lanyard around his neck. His kitchen's light was too bright, and with the late-afternoon sun coming in from his window, Norris could barely make out his dad's features under the pixelated reflection of his shaved head.

"Nice room, kid! How is the rest of the new place?" Felix asked through a yawn that was quickly masked by a smile.

"It's fine."

"It looks pretty big from here," Felix said. "You're on your laptop, right? Give me a tour."

"Um, mom's studying in the living room."

"Ah. Maybe another time, then."

"The apartment is fine, Dad. It's the zip code that's the issue."

"C'mon, it can't be that bad. Find a rink yet?"

"Yeah, Dad," Norris answered. He flashed back to Monk Liam scrambling on the ice. It was going to be interesting, that was for sure. The kid was pretty good, but still just as weird.

"Did you know Austin is consistently listed as one of the top ten cities in all of North America?"

Norris made a point of rolling his eyes for the camera. "Those lists are written by people whose brains collapse because a row of food trucks have Christmas lights dangling from their counter." His father just smiled absently. "How's the brood?" Norris asked, nodding to the bassinet he could see right at the frame.

"He's good. Although, honestly? I forgot how much of a sleep killer these things could be," Felix said, rubbing his eyes. "I'm too old for this."

Many in their extended family agreed, Norris included, so he said nothing.

"Did you get the last pictures?"

"I did." Norris nodded. "Very baby-like, with baby-like features."

Norris had no idea what it meant, that he now had a half brother, more than a decade younger than him and one country away. He wondered if he would even see it, him, *Reggie*, more than fourteen times in his entire lifetime. Probably not.

"You, on the other hand, were a quiet baby."

"Oh yeah?"

"Smart too; always watching. I would wake up, and you'd be staring right at me and smiling."

Norris suspected this wasn't true but liked the story nonetheless. He was about to ask for more details when his bedroom door opened.

"Honey, I can't access my work folders," Judith said in a frustrated tone, dangling a laptop on her arm.

"Can you take a—oh."

122

"Hi, Judith," his father said in that sweet and measured tone meant to hide months of contentious fights and the plate he'd received across the head that one time—one of the Kaplan household's most dramatic moments.

"I'm sorry, I didn't know you were on a call. Hello, Felix."

"Hi! How is the new job?" Norris's computer answered in false cheerfulness.

"Good. Yours?"

"Good."

A protracted silence followed—Divorced Decorum, Norris called it. He simply couldn't help himself.

"Call it a hunch, but I think you two have had sex before."

"Jesus, kid!" Felix chortled.

"Your son," Judith said accusingly.

"Your son," Felix answered in kind. Years ago, Norris remembered this being a bit of theirs.

"All right, logging off," Felix said with a preemptive wave.

"Dad, wait, I—" Norris looked over to his mother hesitantly. What he was about to say would not make her happy, but he wanted a confirmation on the record, and it wasn't often these days all three of them were in the same room, webcam or otherwise.

"I can still spend the summer there, right?"

It all happened in a split second, but Norris counted three exchanges of glares: one from his mom to his dad, one from his dad to someone offscreen to his left (Janet, of course), and the last one from Felix to the bassinet at his side. Norris could imagine what Janet was probably frantically mouthing just out of sight. How long had that gap-toothed Fantine been standing there?

"Yeah . . ." Felix began. "We can definitely talk about that then, kid."

This clearly wasn't enough for off-camera Janet.

"The thing is with work and the baby . . . I wouldn't be able to spend much time with you, y'know? And we wouldn't be able to visit Montreal too often."

"That's okay," Norris said quickly. "I can call or Skype with people from your place."

"Well, you can do that from Texas, can't you?" Felix asked.

"I guess, but—"

"Excuse me, but our child's not a package, Felix," Judith chimed in.

"Oh yeah, how was the overnight shipping to Texas, Judith?" Felix replied without missing a beat.

Uh. So, that's where Norris got it.

"You know what, Felix—"

"No, but please educate me, professor."

"Guys?" Norris said. "It's going to be really hard to repress memories made at my age, so can we not?"

Felix and Judith shared a guilty look through the camera. Reminding them both of the effects of divorce on an only child's fragile psyche was one of the easiest ways of defusing these things. Not to mention that new computer he had gotten for his last birthday.

"We might, I don't know . . . We might be able to make it work," Felix said after another moment. "Things might have calmed down by then. I'll let you know. It could be fun."

"Okay!" Norris answered. The fact that his dad was resolutely avoiding breaking eye contact with the camera told him that this executive decision was being made above Janet's clearance.

"Good!" Felix said with a grin. "There, everyone's happy! I have to go, but I'll talk to you next week, kid."

"Bye, Dad."

The icon went gray again, relegating Norris's father to a simple silhouette. Whatever was passing through Norris's face at that moment, Judith felt the need to rub his shoulder, awkwardly dangling the laptop on her arm. It was infantilizing, but Norris also didn't want her hand gone just yet.

"Summer is still a ways off. I'm sure it'll work out by then," she said soothingly.

"Liar," Norris answered, though he still made no move to shrug her off his shoulder.

When the Kaplan marriage ended after fourteen years—roughly ten of them pleasant by Norris's calculations—Felix Kaplan had made a point of telling Norris over and over again that he was not going away. Every time they saw each other, every phone call, *I'm not going away.*

I know you're not, Norris remembered answering. And then, as these things tended to go, Felix had gone away. Little by little, weekends had turned into weekly dinners and "check-ins" that came without any concrete dates, except when it came time to announce that he would now be a big brother, whatever that meant. The prospect of father and son spending two months under the same roof, with a six-month notice no less, was now a "maybe."

"Your dad really is very busy these days, and babies are no picnic, believe me."

"Babies: hard. Got it," Norris said, shrugging off his mother's hand. He cleared space on his desk by pushing crumpled water bottles, socks, and stray sheets to the floor with a slow, encompassing arm swipe.

"Let's have a look," he continued resolutely. "Did you remember to turn on the Remote Desktop app at work?"

13

DATING ADVICE

DEFINITION: The act of another person trying to help improve your sorry, sorry excuse for game.

COROLLARY EMOTIONS: Pity, shame, total abject despair.

"It's a mask," Maddie said dismissively, elbowing Norris's phone out of her way. "Move, Canada."

"I know it's a mask—I'm asking what you think the mask *represents*," Norris grumbled. Over the past few days, Norris and Aarti had entered into a loose texting exchange leading up to their date, which happened to be tonight. It was a neutral platform that let Norris into a whole new side of her. He learned that she used *lol* fairly often, but Norris would occasionally get a *hahah* out of her and that extra *h* felt like genuine laughter. He imagined Aarti sitting on her bed somewhere across the greater Austin area, holding her phone with both hands and giggling at his weird observations about the school.

The closer he got to their actual date, the more compelled he felt to reread their stream of exchanges, trying to pinpoint some added bit of insight he might have missed the first time.

"Sounds like a valid question for a therapist."

"I should let you deal with this mess alone," Norris muttered, nodding over to the crates.

"We have a deal," Maddie reminded him with all the compassion of a repo agent to a carful of tiny orphans.

"Our deal involves you providing emotional and technical support in dealing with all this Aarti stuff!"

"Oh my God, it's just an emoji," Maddie said distractedly. "She obviously likes you, so tone down the crazy and you'll be fine."

She was clearly more focused on the crates of lightbulbs she was carrying than on deciphering what was, to Norris, the useless, more cryptic cousin of the hieroglyph. Why couldn't people just use words all the time?

"I'm just wondering if it meant something all along."

"It didn't."

"Also, should I feel weird that she's the one picking me up tonight?"

"You should feel weird about not having a car living in Austin," Maddie said, and Norris could hear the smile in her voice even though her face was currently obstructed. "Picking up a guy at a steaming bus stop isn't as romantic as you think."

"Well, I don't have a car, okay!" Norris began to sputter, hearing his voice pitch higher. "Not everyone can just borrow their dad's Rolls. That's discrimination, Madison. Discrimination against pedestrians!"

"Oh my God, I'm kidding!" Maddie threw him a pitiful look. "Look, take it from a bitchy cheerleader," she said, patting his shoulder. "What you're doing with Aarti is working. We save the mind games for people we actually like. Her texting you at random intervals, adding weird emojis to your exchanges, that's all her version of pulling your pigtails. She likes you. Breathe. Now please help me with these lights before you go, or I will throw one at your head."

No fewer than twelve crates of lightbulbs had been set out on the Bone Yard tables. Big Jim took these lights *very* seriously; all had previously been packed with military precision. Every conceivable form of electric illumination known to man was represented—Edison bulbs, café globes, tiny LEDs, and curtains of icicle lights—plus, a few token boxes of standard string lights that seemed too generic in this insane assortment. It had taken a lot longer than expected, but eventually, all the lights had been unboxed, untangled, and were now being arranged across the back of the Bone Yard's seating area.

Norris ran the lights, passing the cords to Maddie, who looped them over hooks and wrapped them into loose knots to avoid cutting the current when the time came.

"What is this for, again?"

"My sister's getting married soon, and we're busting out all our holiday lights for the occasion." She sighed. "It's ridiculously early to be setting up, but in the unlikely event that, like, one of the approximately million lights is out, Dad wants to know."

"Does Austin have a citywide blackout every time a Mc-Elwees ties the knot?" Because, really, it was a ridiculous number of lights. Norris's arms were killing him, but even if they didn't have a deal, he would feel horrible leaving a coworker to deal with installing all of these by themselves.

"If Dad got his way, they'd probably strobe in time with the wedding march whenever one of his children got married," she laughed, climbing down from the ladder. "Okay, kill the lights in the kitchen. I've got the overheads. Ready?"

"Ready for . . . ?"

"This," Maddie announced, and flipped a switch.

And in an instant, the Bone Yard completely disappeared behind a wall of stars. The lights ran floor to ceiling; some of them faded gently in and out, while others threw a soft, steady glow. Still, it was an obscene amount of electrical voltage that turned the place into a fairy-tale wonderland. If there was a PETA for energy consumption, they'd definitely be on the receiving end of some red paint right now.

And in the middle of it all stood Maddie, shining almost as brightly. "It's cheesy," she breathed. "But I love this place when it's like this."

"Definitely the nicest fire hazard I've ever seen," he agreed.

Norris had to admit there was a definite appeal to it all. The whole place looked like a postcard. He pretended to examine some lights so she wouldn't catch him staring too hard.

"Oh hush, Canada. It's going to be beautiful."

"Is this a big deal for your parents, then? A bird flying out of the nest, as it were?"

"Everything is a big deal for my family. Mostly because my family *is* big. Holidays, weddings, christenings . . . A McElwees celebration is considered incomplete if there are less than twenty family members present. And forget about booking a hotel: that's a grave insult, on par with not complimenting Aunt June's potato salad." Maddie inspected the lights, jotting notes on her legal pad.

"I shudder to consider the consequences of *that* oversight," Norris drawled.

"We have more than our fair share of eccentrics, but I freaking love my family, y'know?"

I miss my dad, Norris thought in spite of himself. Luckily, his mouth managed to remain shut in the moment. Maddie didn't need to know about that stuff.

"I know, I know, I'm boring as hell. Whatever, Canada. I still can't imagine living far away from here and missing out on things like this," she admitted.

"You get used to it," Norris said without thinking, which earned him a look but, fortunately, no comment.

". . . I just meant that, um, leaving Montreal sort of felt like that."

"I'm sorry," she said sympathetically, and Norris thought it best to leave it at that.

As they packed up the empty crates, taking the extra care to turn off the proper fuse-box switches so as to not blind the entire restaurant should a kid accidentally turn on the lights, Maddie told Norris all about her sister, her future brother-in-law, and the various branches of House McElwees. Big Jim and his daughters, of which Maddie was the youngest, were at the center of an insane family tree. There was Aunt June's (in)famous potato salad; Cousin Ricky, who had been struck by lightning three times; Gallow, the family dog who'd swallowed two different rings on two different instances and was now banned from being in the official wedding party; and Great-Uncle Oscar, who still wore his army uniform to formal and informal occasions alike. A few odd cousins had spread beyond the confines of the state, but for the most part, the McElweeses were rooted Texans, generational occupants. They would all be in attendance at the wedding. Maddie was nervous about her bridesmaid speech, and everyone was nervous about Pastor John's stutter. The hors d'oeuvres were so good that Maddie always snuck away a tray.

They finally put away the last box of lights and, almost in unison, checked their phones. What was supposed to be a loose pre-date evening, researching fascinating facts to casually drop in mid-date with Aarti had turned into a quick two-hour shift at the Bone Yard because, Maddie. The entire back of the restaurant had even been closed off during prime dining-out hours because as Norris was learning, marriage was very serious business here.

"She's running late," Norris noted, checking his watch and then the giant wooden clock behind the restaurant's bar, just in case one of the two wasn't working at the moment.

Maddie hopped onto the counter, phone in hand as always.

"Good," she said. "Gives us time to review. Ask a lot of questions. When you get too into your head, do something to get out of it. Seriously, padawan, I'm not training a Jedi who is going to invite his girlfriend to come watch him play video games someday."

"Not my girlfriend yet . . ." Norris mumbled, unfolding his apron.

"Baby steps," Maddie said, picking a stray piece of lint off his shoulder for him. "Be confident, but not pushy. Open doors for her, only *yes* means *yes*, like all those pamphlets and flyers they've been shoving under our eyes since the third grade, even in Canada, I assume—remember them. Oh, and pay for everything."

"But what if she—"

"—even if she already offered to split it, yes," Maddie pre-empted. "It gives the date a little something extra, to quote the great Elle Woods. It's a movie ticket and dinner; you can afford it, you cheapskate."

"Gee," Norris said flatly, feeling his nerves act up again. "Any notes on my outfit, while you're at it?"

"Oh my God! So many notes," she laughed. "What's with all the black T-shirt and jeans combos? I get the minimalist appeal, but after two months, you're really pushing 'classic' to its limit."

"I was kidding."

"I know, but I've had that one in the chamber since the

moment I met you." Maddie smirked as she gave him a look-over. Norris realized that she hadn't checked her phone in ages.

"Aarti's all about fashion anyway. Your makeover is coming the second the two of you are official."

"What are you doing tonight, anyway?" Norris asked.

"I have a date with Meredith and Patrick."

"Oh," Norris said. It hadn't taken long for him to learn that Meredith—dreaded head cheerleader Meredith—and Patrick—he of Hairy Armpits fame—were actually a couple. They were perfect for each other, in Norris's view. "That sounds . . . kinky and unchristian?"

"Ew, no. What's wrong with you?"

Norris only shrugged, throwing another look at the Bone Yard's parking lot through the blinds-down glass door. He liked hanging out with Maddie, but at the moment what was wrong with him was the prospect of being stood up and having a cheer-leader as audience to it all—even if it was just Maddie.

"Mer is telling her parents she's hanging out with me, so we're going to be watching movies upstairs together. That way she's not lying to her parents. Meredith's parents aren't too keen on her dating Patrick. . . ."

"Austin's local car hood–shitter? No kidding."

"He was drunk."

Norris just gave her a look.

"Okay, yes, that incident was pretty gross—but Patrick might surprise you. He's occasionally really sweet. He was a big teddy bear when we dated."

"Wait, wait, wait, wait—you guys dated?! You and Patrick?! Patrick and you? Ma-trick? Pat-ison?" Norris laughed. "I can't picture it."

"I was still stuffing my bra," Maddie said. "I wouldn't exactly call that a love affair for the ages, but . . ."

Her face took on a wistful quality.

"One time, I remember tumbling off into the rafters at an awful exhibition night event for new recruits. Right into the old football coach, the poor guy. I didn't actually make the squad until my third try, y'know? But anyway, people would not stop laughing. I was mortified and about to burst into tears. In front of the entire fifth and sixth grades. Like, I would have never lived it down, you don't even know. But Patrick started this Maddie chant. 'Maddie, Maddie, Maddie!'"

"And people actually joined?"

"Oh, people will join any chant if you pitch it right." She grinned. "Anyway, I had hurt my ankle in the fall and thought I would be on the sidelines all night for this Bats Bonanza thing, but Pat picked me up and gave me a piggyback ride the entire evening. He said he was the luckiest guy in all of Texas. He had just gotten his linebacker growth spurt." She smiled to herself. "That first gigantic, overwhelming crush. It's a heck of a thing, huh?"

Norris didn't feel the need to add anything, but he could relate. He might never actually forget the smell of his first crush, Anne Marie Villeneuve's, hair. He had often hung around the water fountain near her locker, hoping for a glimpse of her.

"He's only ever been a throbbing asshole to me."

"You can't always see people well through other's eyes, Canada," she added after a laugh. "Who they are when there are other people around isn't who they are when they're alone."

She then widened her eyes dramatically at him. "Exhibit A."

"Oh, so I'm Exhibit A?" Norris exclaimed, bringing an outraged hand to his chest.

"To some people." She smiled. "The dickish Canadian guy with a chip on his shoulder."

She was definitely talking about Meredith's opinion of Norris. Maddie's best friend had perfected the art of rolling her eyes in annoyance at Norris's very presence, and truth be told, he was quite proud of his ability to grin and compliment her on whatever item seemed to be giving her the most insecurities at the moment.

"So," Norris pressed. "Why did you and Patrick break up if he was such a charmer, anyway?"

"Meredith really liked him." She shrugged.

"Um, what?"

Going by her tone, Maddie apparently thought that those four words made a full story.

"So, you just . . . what? Stepped aside?"

"More or less."

Her voice had changed, nearly imperceptibly, into a tone he hadn't heard from her yet. It was gone again in an instant, but it prompted his next question.

"Wait. When did that happen, again?"

"Hmm." Maddie pondered. "Last year . . . give or take a month."

"*What?!*" Norris's outrage surprised him. "And they started dating, like, right under your nose?"

"Oh no. Meredith felt horrible about it. It took a few weeks for her to believe I was actually okay with it."

"I don't know if that makes you a saint or a martyr."

"It's fine, Canada. Guys are a dime a dozen." Maddie shrugged. "Best friends aren't. It's not like Patrick and I were ever going to get married or anything."

"Yeah, but still, that's your best friend and your boyfriend. Jesus, dude."

Norris couldn't imagine what it would feel like to walk in on Aarti making out with Eric, if Eric was straight, obviously. He was pretty sure it ended with him sobbing under an overpass in the rain like one of those Super Bowl puppy commercials.

The thing about Maddie was that for all the balls she always seemed to be juggling—the restaurant, the cheerleading squad, Norris himself, really—she seemed to take the back seat in her own life. Norris had stopped wondering where she found the time to do anything else when he realized that maybe she *didn't* do anything else. She was the opposite of Norris with his very healthy focus on his own life.

"Can you drop it, Norris?" she insisted. "I'm fine. Really."

She smiled, almost sadly. Norris thought about how exhausting it might be. To always be the peacekeeper, the good sister, the obedient daughter . . . At first he'd assumed Maddie went to the top of the pyramid, but he'd been wrong. Now he saw it. Maddie had to be in the middle of the pyramid because she was the only one who could hold it all together.

A set of car lights suddenly lit up the front of the restaurant.

"That would be your date," Maddie said, sounding relieved to get rid of him.

Even the rhythmic honk brought a smile to Norris's lips. Aarti would never not make an entrance a day in her life.

Overture, curtain, lights, then.

"Um, have a nice night, Maddie, okay?" Norris said before pushing open the door.

"You too, Canada," Maddie said.

14

THE MANIC PIXIE DREAM GIRL

IDENTIFYING CHARACTERISTICS: Quirky yet flattering sense of fashion; accessories conveying an interest in the arts and travel.
HABITAT: Unknown; suspected hidden lair somewhere in Central Austin.
PREY: Sexually inexperienced, generally awkward North American teenage boys.

Aarti had picked him up in a dark blue Honda, obviously borrowed from her parents for that evening. It wasn't the latest model, but Norris didn't need to look it up to know that this was likely the best-rated American family vehicle, whatever year it was plucked from. Immigrants, his own parents included, had a way of always opting for the safest, most average option. The best way to fit in to this land whose roads they were borrowing. From the moment she'd lowered the window in the Bone Yard's parking lot, Norris's throat had been stripped dry of all moisture because, sweet holy mercy, did that girl know how to make an impression. They were now driving to the movie theater, and Norris, after hesitating on whether to compliment her on her earrings or her hair or her dress, had opted for all of the above by complimenting her on "the entire situation," which he instantly regretted.

"My entire situation?" she asked, an eye on the road.

"Yeah, you know . . . the hair and dress and stuff. You look good? But not in an objectifying way or anything. Just . . ."

She'd let out a laugh, not seeming to mind his choice of words in expressing himself—which, let's face it, definitely boded well for any long-term dating prospects.

Still, fifteen minutes into this drive, Norris couldn't classify Aarti, which was somewhat vexing. Knowing where people fell made it easier to know how to act around them, especially as far as Anderson High hatchlings were concerned. He'd stepped on enough land mines there already to last him through prom. (God, there would definitely be a prom, wouldn't there?) As far as Aarti went, Norris could tell there were definitely shades of Manic Pixie Dream Girl involved there, depending on which movie was being referenced.

Her interests were all over the place. She'd gone through an anime phase, a tennis phase, and now she was into local politics. She hoped to take a year off before college and disliked millennials with the fiery passion of a millennial. Norris could definitely relate there. Still, she was easy to talk to, smart and quick and not shy about that fact. Unfortunately, all of Aarti Puri's good qualities were dwarfed by the fact that the girl drove like a freaking *maniac*.

"Jesus!" Norris screamed as the small car and its inexplicably manual transmission came to another stilted stop, right there in the middle of Lamar Street.

"I'm sorry!" Aarti laughed. "Oh my God, I'm so sorry!"

A string of honks came flying from behind them. Why was she laughing, that strange creature?

"It's a nervous tic," she said, cheeks flushed with laughter. "I always cackle in nurses' faces whenever I have to get shots. It's so embarrassing."

"Right, um, so, you do . . . know how to drive, right?" Norris noted as casually as he could manage, bringing a hand to steady himself on the car's ceiling after another brusque stop.

"I know how to drive!"

Something about her tone instructed Norris to badger the witness. "Do you know how to drive this car?"

"That's a, uh, learning process," Aarti answered, wrestling against the stick shift and jolting them forward one more time before the car mercifully resumed smooth progression.

"There we go!" Aarti exclaimed happily.

Their new pace wasn't enough for the van on their right given the bejeweled, red-fingernailed middle finger that appeared in the driver's window when it drove around them.

"Doesn't the learning usually happen before the driving? I hear that's a thing. Like, a state-mandated thing," Norris ventured.

Sure, the alluring pretty girl might get offended and leave Norris by the side of the road, but that really didn't seem like too bad of an alternative to being driven around by someone who was still "figuring out" the potential death trap they were both sitting in. *Black Ice*, the Quebec province's series of driver's ed videos, known for its spectacularly gory depictions of fatal car crashes, had profoundly marked Norris the previous year. The puddle of vomit he'd left in Eric's backpack could attest to that.

"Boring linear thinking," Aarti dismissed. "And actually, I asked for the stick shift."

"Why?" Norris asked.

"Oh! Well, it's a good skill to have," Aarti answered in a tone that conveyed she had said these exact words before. "It's a big world. A lot of countries only have stick shifts, and I don't want to be caught unprepared later on, y'know?"

"Future world traveler, huh?" Norris asked.

"Future world conqueror, Canada."

Norris leaned back into his seat and grabbed onto the side of the passenger window as subtly as he could. She sounded confident in her abilities, which had to count for something. In a weird way, she reminded Norris of his mom—a thought he didn't want to mine any further in order to keep his brain from collapsing into a horrifying abyss.

They finally—safely—pulled into the parking lot of the Violet Crown, an indie theater. Norris had learned that movies were a big part of Austin's culture. On top of the annual film festival that overtook the downtown area, and all the national chain theaters, there was also the local Alamo Drafthouse, a chain of hipster-ish movie theaters with monthly sing-alongs and eighties classics where shadow servers brought you food midscreening, as well as the historic Stateside at the Paramount theater down-town, and finally the artsier Violet Crown, known for its higher amenities and cinephile vibe. Everything about the lobby looked modern and hip, with fake wooden paneling, floor-to-ceiling windows, and to Norris, it felt like the lobby of some fancy Berlin hotel, complete with low purplish lights.

"I'm so excited to see this movie," Aarti said when he handed her one of the two tickets he'd purchased, having followed through on Maddie's advice. For his part, Norris was mostly excited to see what excited Aarti. "Trust me, you're going to love it," Aarti added. "The director is a visionary!"

Norris did not, in fact, love it.

The movie was sheer nonsense. Or rather, it was a nonsensi-cal documentary about a woman in a small Switzerland town near Geneva who spent her life perfecting her own breed of ori-gami paper art and then had died in anonymity. If that sounded dry, flat, and uncompelling in a sentence, one hundred and forty minutes of screen time did nothing to heighten the narrative. The second leg of the film was concerned with the beauty of the tiny miniature *Paper Family*—the translated title of the overall ordeal—she had built for herself.

There were dozens of montages of her shelves filled with white angels, purple birds, and small, faceless dogs. Not to men-tion the cupboards that contained hundreds of folded figures, meticulously "put away in grief." Presumably, because the word *grief* was more poetic than *storage maximization*.

After the screening, Norris and Aarti lingered in the cinema's café, watching various clusters of hipster university students and middle-aged couples step off the escalator and head into the screening room they had just left for the late-night show. Norris realized that they were probably the youngest attendants of the night.

Aarti was monopolizing the large pharmacy-size bag of sour candy that he'd purchased for them, fishing out a single Sour Patch Kid at a time and putting back any green one she accidentally pulled.

"So? Out with it: What did you think of the movie?" Aarti pressed, as Norris knew she would.

"I . . . liked the camera work," Norris said neutrally, catching a discarded green candy before it could fall back into the bag.

"The camera work?"

"Very steady," Norris mused as he chewed. "Very straight, stable perspective. They definitely had a tripod."

Aarti let out a laugh. "Oh my God! You hated it!"

Norris paused before admitting, "Deeply," with the fire of an anonymous internet commenter.

"I can't believe you! It was so sad and moving!" Aarti said. "She never found her tribe."

"Her what now?"

"There are dozens, no, hundreds and hundreds of people who are into origami," Aarti explained, revving up for one of the high-minded debates that made her eyes shine even more brightly than usual. "She died alone, surrounded by fake paper people in a town of actual people that were dying to get to know her. She could have given them away or taught people how to do this amazing art. Instead, she was just miserable and—"

"See, that's what bugged me," Norris interjected. "How do we know she was miserable? How did that filmmaker know? She might have been really happy alone, doing what she loved in privacy. For all we know, she wouldn't have changed a thing about the way she lived!"

Aarti looked at him for a moment.

"You can't possibly believe that."

"Some people like to be alone," Norris offered. "The fact that people see them as being a kicked puppy for that doesn't make it so."

"I think that's what people tell themselves when they end up alone," Aarti said. "Plus, we're both assuming that she was a good person. She was probably a shrew."

Norris laughed. "Where are you getting that?"

"Because being alone is an unnatural state," Aarti said with a frown, dropping a green candy only to pick out another green one twice in a row. "Chances are she made people close to her leave. When you push people away, they leave. All that's left of you is the beautiful tragedy of your solitude. That's what the filmmaker was trying to capture, I think."

Norris nodded along, trying to hide his violent disagreement.

"Dynamite camera work." He simply grinned.

"Oh, fuck you," Aarti scoffed, throwing a lonely yellow sour candy at him. "Are you excited for your big spring-break fling, then? You're going back home, right?"

Norris nodded, grateful for the change of subject. At long last, spring break was coming up. "Back to Canada, yes, but not Montreal. British Columbia. Me and my friend Eric are going to his uncle's condo, near Whistler Blackcomb, the ski resort."

"What, just the two of you?" she asked, raising an eyebrow. "For the entire week."

"Yup!" Norris confirmed enthusiastically. He'd been counting the days down in his notebook and was starting to get positively giddy at the prospect. Bags were already packed. Eric had been emailing him photos of Whistler's slopes curated from the web for the past week. For the longest time, it had been an abstract concept that would never come, but in a few weeks, Norris would be breathing in lungfuls of crisp, frozen air again.

"That's cool." Aarti smiled, but she didn't seem very impressed. "I guess you can hit the town for some house parties and there will be some college kids cutting loose around that you can connect with."

"I guess," he said.

"Gotta take advantage of a week without adult supervision, right?"

Norris wanted to make an argument for just spending time with your best friend; he wanted to ask more questions to gauge if going out to parties was the only way she could picture having fun.

But more than that, he wanted to kiss her.

Before fear could talk him out of it, he reached across the

small table and took Aarti's face in both hands and leaned toward her. The artificial, grainy sugar of the Sour Patch Kids stung Norris's lips, which didn't stop him. As he kissed her, he could taste the candy on her lips and, more important, feel her smile against his lips. The rest of him felt like he was being electrocuted. If he had to go, this was how he wanted it to happen. No regrets on that front.

"Uh," Aarti said, leaning away after a long moment, still grinning. Another thirty seconds and this might have been considered a full make-out session. *Out in public!* Norris imagined his mother chastising him.

"What?"

"Vague undertones of Quebec maple syrup," she said thoughtfully.

"I hear it's an acquired taste," Norris suggested.

"I didn't say I hated it."

Her eyes were doing that thing again, drawing him in, making Norris lose himself in them. Did she enjoy the kiss? Had he used the right amount of pressure? To be fair, Norris had gotten the whole kissing thing down fairly early. Hours of watching every clip of every rom-com available online and fiercely making out with his own forearm sitting alone on his bed back in the sixth grade, before kissing another human being had become an actual land mine in his daily life. Since then, he'd kissed girls here and there, and done more than kiss a few.

But nothing compared to kissing Aarti Puri.

15

THE BRO REUNION

ACCEPTABLE DISPLAYS OF AFFECTION: Fist bump, loose back pat, presents?

EXPECTATIONS: Your friend, exactly as you left him a few months ago, all inside jokes and lengthy arguments rebooting precisely where you left them.

WORST-CASE SCENARIOS: All chemistry has disappeared, one of you has joined a new Caucasian Enthusiasts Association, "I brought along all my new friends from school now that I don't have to babysit you at the loser table; I hope that's okay."

Spring break finally arrived, and, after a lot of hugs and disclaimers, and packing, and digging through still-packed boxes in order to get ahold of his thermal underwear, Norris found himself 39,000 feet above Texas—a welcome buffer between him and the Austin heat. Judith had been in the thick of grading midterms and had a three-day window to turn around three lecture sections, or roughly 244 students' assignments. Picking up the slack on her department's undergraduate workload had apparently been an unadvertised requirement of her new position. Norris had left her at the kitchen table, where he practically had to place his head under her lips for their customary goodbye kiss.

"Call me when you land," she said, her face twisted in disdain as she crossed out a particularly offensive paragraph in the essay she was reading. "Say hi to Eric for me—don't leave his uncle's condo in a mess—and don't break anything! Furniture, appliance, or bone."

Solid advice.

His latest text from Aarti had been a photo of the outfits she was planning for a gallery opening that evening. No one would ever call Norris fashion forward, but he agreed with her that the middle one, a dark red sweater that could double as a dress and ornate purple leggings, was probably the most "Aarti" of the looks she had photographed laid out on the bed.

😺 texted:

Send me your snow suit options! Curious 2 see u in ur natural habitat

Norris: I only have the one snow suit

😺: Are u one of those guys that only buys new clothes when the old ones get too small

Norris: Or get ripped.

😺: You tragedy

Norris: I try

He had made it to the Vancouver airport, only halfway to Whistler itself, and already he missed Aarti.

"We've got to go, Kaplan," Eric greeted him suddenly, popping out of absolutely nowhere and grabbing Norris by the arm. How did people keep doing that?

"What the fu— Hello to you too!" Norris exclaimed. He hadn't expected a tearful reunion, but maybe some acknowledgment that they hadn't seen each other in so many months?

"Yeah, yeah," Eric said, dragging him through the Vancouver airport without a hint of slowing down. "We have ten minutes to get to parking lot E before they charge me for another hour."

His tone reminded Norris of when they went to the faraway sandwich shop for lunch back in Montreal and needed to hightail it back to school to avoid late slips.

"It was a good flight, slept the whole way, thanks for asking," he said, falling into a half dash with Eric toward the luggage carousels.

"There!" Eric said, reaching for Norris's familiar red-checkered luggage the second it passed through the thick, dirty plastic curtains on a stream of luggage.

"That's yours, right? Why didn't you just carry it on the flight?" Eric demanded, popping the handle on the bag that had carried their science projects on presentation days for two years.

"Three pounds over the carry-on limit," Norris sighed, finding a seat and removing his backpack. *Burn in hell, TSA.*

"What now?" Eric asked impatiently.

"I'm putting on my coat, Jesus," Norris snapped, pulling his bundled winter coat out of the bag.

"Well, why didn't you do that before?"

"Texas: hot. Canada: cold," Norris explained slowly. "And can you chill out? Because I'm not doing this for five days."

That was when Norris finally saw it.

Oh. My. God.

"Oh my God!"

Eric must have heard it in his tone. His best friend's hand twitched as though his first instinct was to hide . . . it.

"We don't have time for this." Eric tried to distract him, refusing to make eye contact like a misbehaving child. Too late.

"Listen," Norris giggled as he zipped up his coat. "I don't care if there's a Zika outbreak at the Hudson News. This *will* be properly acknowledged."

"You are such a pain in the ass," Eric groaned, melodramatically bending his knees and throwing his head back. "Honestly, America can fucking have you!"

Now that he got a chance to take a longer look, *it* stood out so much more given that nothing else was different about Eric. He was wearing his same old go-to purple hoodie with a Collège Français volleyball T-shirt peeking out at the collar. It was the factory line definition of Eric, right down to the pubescent baby face that would always look four years younger than his actual age. *In another reality, we would be hugging hello,* Norris thought. But in this one, there were at least fifteen minutes of relentless mockery to squeeze into the eight minutes left between wherever they were *now* and parking lot E.

"Eight minutes to parking lot E," Norris prompted. "Out with it. Explain that thing in your ear, please."

"Yes, fine, I got an earring," Eric confessed theatrically, turning his head to defiantly place it in Norris's direct line of sight.

"Well, it's obviously ridiculous," Norris concluded, unfolding a beanie and stuffing it over his head. "But then again, I predicted you missing me would lead you to act out and rebel in some way. Common among teenagers."

"Whatever, Marc-André likes it," Eric complained through a smile as he snatched Norris's luggage and walked away. "And you're paying for the extra hour of parking if we're late."

The first day in Whistler was a quest for survival. The condo—despite having fresh towels and a kitchen stocked with every packaged snack a bachelor might imagine two teenage boys could want—lacked one critical component: Wi-Fi. After casually searching every surface of the apartment for a Post-it with the network and password, then ransacking the entire space for a router, the pair came to the realization that Eric's uncle lived an internet-free lifestyle, deviant that he was.

"I can't eat, dude!" Eric proclaimed. "It's Maslow's hierarchy of needs. I can't eat until my other, more urgent needs are satisfied: Wi-Fi, shelter, Wi-Fi again!"

"You're telling me," Norris groaned, joining in his friend's anguish. "Aarti is halfway across the world, and my mom will kill me if I run up the international texting bill!"

Eventually, the pair agreed to trek eight blocks through two feet of rising snow to a coffee shop they spotted on the drive in. Norris at least needed to let Judith know he'd arrived safely in

Whistler. Something about trudging through snow with Eric at a pitch-black six p.m. in the evening, both cursing the wind under their breaths, filled Norris's stomach with a fuzzy sense of nostalgia. *Who says you can't go home again?*

Norris immediately pulled up his inbox the moment they settled into the coffee shop.

(4) new emails.

Judith Bien-Aimée: *Hi, sweetie, hope you landed okay!*

Madison McElwees: *Hi Norris, can you switch schedules with Julio on the 17th? He needs to buckle down on his thesis. Hope the maple is pouring up north.*

Dad: *Happy spring break! Have fun in BC. I attached a photo of your little bro.*

Liam Hooper: *Hope all is good in Canada. I've had a few people ask about our hockey sessions and I've been thinking. . . . Might be time to expand?? Talk more when you get back.*

Uh.

Liam's "hockey team in Texas" pipe dreams aside, Norris was disappointed by his inbox. He immediately deleted his father's email because really, all babies looked the same to him and he liked keeping his inbox lean. It wasn't that he had been expecting a flurry of new messages; he had never been, and would never be, that popular. Still, a check-in from Aarti—or another outfit update, even a random emoji—would have been nice. Weren't they dating? Wasn't regular contact kind of the point?

"So," Eric began, numbering the topics they'd already covered on the drive over on his fingers. "New girlfriend, my monk-like replacement, a squad of feral cheerleaders, restaurant job . . . am I missing anything?"

"That's plenty!" Norris laughed. "So, out with it: Marc-André is not, in fact, straight?"

Eric's lip twitched. "He's, um, yeah . . . He's good."

"How did you two even get together in the first place? I'm gone for less than a term and Collège Français sprouts a second gay guy for you? Who has my old locker, no less?"

"I told you." Eric shrugged, still smiling. "We just started hanging out and talking. I can't really pinpoint it."

"Talking about what?"

"Movies, parents, hockey a little bit, you," Eric listed after a moment of ruminating.

"Me?"

"He asked if you were my 'boyfriend or something' considering the amount of time I apparently spend talking about you . . . I guess your best friend ditching you halfway through the year sort of stays on your mind as far as conversation topics go."

Norris frowned at that. "Eric, I didn't ditch you. My mom—"

"I know, I know," Eric said, raising a hand. "We don't need to do the whole hugging, crying, and learning thing. It wasn't rational. It's passed, don't worry."

The idea that Norris had hurt his best friend in the process of leaving bothered him. He realized then that he'd never asked about it in all their chats. To him, having to move to Texas had been his problem. He'd never even considered the ripples it would cause for his best friend.

"You've gotten gayer," Norris noted after a long comfortable silence. Eric gasped and moved an exaggeratedly limp wrist to his chest, feigning dramatic outrage.

"Oh, shut up," Norris said. "I just mean . . . I don't know what I mean, actually."

"Is it the earring?"

"The earring is part of it," Norris mused, a thought forming on the outskirts of his mind. Eric just seemed . . . calmer. More confident. More *himself*, maybe? "Wait, did you come out? As in, *out* out? To everyone?!"

Another thing Norris and Eric had always had in common in a school that catered to mostly white and Catholic families was that dread that at any point their entire existence might get reduced to a single-letter word. N-word. F-word. Norris never judged Eric for wanting to avoid that if he could.

"No . . . Yes? Sorta?" Eric said. "Andréanne doesn't want to be my beard anymore. She's dating Morissey now. I know: it offended me to my core too."

Back in fifth grade, Jean Morissey had popped a pimple in

155

class and then wiped the pus against her desk, thinking no one had seen. However, even from across the classroom, Norris and Eric could barely contain their mutual urge to vomit.

"I was at the dinner table and my dad was just *drilling* me about chicks, and that I should hurry up and tap some ass because otherwise kids would start thinking I was a . . . y'know. I just got so sick of it. And you weren't there, and I just told him that his son is a 'one of them.'"

"Jesus fuck, dude, congrats! I guess. . . . Do you congratulate a coming out?"

"Gift certificates are preferred."

"Did he have a heart attack, your dad?"

Eric shrugged.

"There were a couple of rants," he admitted. "Seventeen-day silent treatment."

Norris didn't feel the need to ask why none of this had been disclosed in their text chats. There was plenty he hadn't shared with his best friend too, simply because he didn't see him every day and his life now needed exposition. His exchanges with Eric were too rare and precious to get bogged down in all that grim detail; Norris preferred to enjoy them. Eric was basically a white gay version of himself, so it made sense that he'd have had the same impulse.

"But I actually think he's coming around now," Eric added with a smile, as they gathered their stuff and headed out of the coffee shop. That was enough laptop-ing for the time being. There were mountains to be enjoyed. "Mom bought him a stack of books on how to cope with a gay child. Thin ones; big fonts. He definitely thinks I'm here having gay interracial winter sex with you, but he still drove me to the airport, so y'know, baby steps."

"The earring does look good." Norris grinned, earning him a shove back into a fresh snowbank on their way back to the condo.

"Shut the fuck up, Kaplan."

Norris didn't say it, but the outcome could have been far worse. Eric's dad was a raging ass. Whenever he gave Norris or other kids from the team a ride home, he was never short on nasty comments about new minority-owned stores or families. All Asians were Chinese to him and black was a communal noun. *Vous autres, les noirs* ("You blacks") was a common preface to many of the man's fascinating observations about the specific way black drivers misbehaved on the road or about P. K. Subban, the lone black hockey player on the Canadiens at one time. He also wasn't a fan of Quebecers who did not know the native French, even though his wife was from Toronto and his son one of those bilinguals—forgetting his Quebec roots by mostly speaking English now. Norris had often wondered what the man said about him or his mother after begrudgingly dropping him off at home.

"So, you've told me about Liam. Have you made any other friends down there?" Eric asked.

"Nope," Norris said swiftly. "Not a one. I think it's the biting I do. The guidance counselor says it's off-putting to classmates, but I'm like: they could wear oven mitts."

"Kaplan."

"A couple." Norris sighed and then continued as Eric glowered him into submission. "I work with some cool folks at the restaurant. This girl Maddie . . . I wouldn't really call her my friend, but she helped me out a bunch with the Aarti stuff. And Liam's super-chill. He sounds like he's always high out of his goddamn mind, but he's, um, he's really good people, actually."

"That's good." Eric grinned. "Glad to hear it. All that and a lady friend that takes you to indie movies and drives like a maniac. Dang. Maybe Austin, Texas, was where you belonged all along."

"I wouldn't go that far. . . ." Norris protested, but as they walked on into the sparkling snow, he couldn't help but think that Eric might have a point.

16

HOMECOMINGS

ESTIMATE REQUIRED TO FULLY UNPACK ONE WEEK OF CLOTHES: Three weeks.
ALLOTTED TIME TO CATCH UP WITH MOM: Forty minutes, tops.
CATCHING UP ON HOMEWORK: TBD.
CATCHING UP WITH PSEUDOGIRLFRIEND: As soon as possible.

G *ah. God. No. Why?*
The Austin sun was right where Norris had left it, which was to say, high and bright. It was as if it had been hitting the gym, unfiltered cigarette clenched between its teeth, waiting to give Norris the pummeling of his life. His sweating was back with a vengeance.

"You have to make sure to bundle up! Your body is adjusting from Vancouver weather to *this*," Judith worried, one hand on the steering wheel and the other instinctively tugging Norris's open shirt collar closed. "That's the perfect recipe for catching a cold. Winter is over here."

"When was winter?" Norris coughed.

"That one and a half weeks of rain, I think," Judith said, as they sat in a particularly clogged artery of traffic on their way home from the airport. "That was the winter. Did you and Eric have a good time?"

"Yeah, it was really fun." Norris nodded. "I missed him," he added uncharacteristically. It just kind of slipped out.

"I know," Judith said pointedly, raising a momentary eyebrow at the fruit of her loins. "Élaine called me to check on things for this Whistler getaway. We spent a few hours catching up. I miss her too."

"You still talk to her?"

"I left friends in Canada too, Norris," Judith reminded him. "She's happy for Eric and Marc-André."

"I didn't think Eric had told her yet," Norris noted. "About the boyfriend, I mean."

Judith rolled her eyes.

"You kids always think you're so good at hiding things. We made you, for Pete's sake. . . . We know you! As for whether I still talk to her: not as much as I promised myself I would." Judith ruminated. "It's hard to make time. Work. Life. *You.*"

"Please," Norris scoffed. "Name an easier kid. Like, a single one."

Judith thought for a moment. And another. Norris assumed the topic had been dropped, but eventually she answered, "Steve Urkel."

Dammit if he hadn't missed her.

He had missed someone else too. Norris's next thought was of the badly wrapped present currently nestled in his backpack and the person he couldn't wait to give it to.

"Mom, can you give me a ride somewhere after we drop off my bag?"

Aarti wasn't the easiest person to pinpoint, even now that he was back in a land of cell service and Wi-Fi. When she didn't answer a text announcing his return, Norris waited a few hours before following up. It worked; moments later, he'd received a dropped pin to her location and the mask Norris now considered her standard signature. 😺

The pin led them to a monastery-like building near Judith's department, north of the University of Texas campus, known for views that captured most of Austin.

"Do you want me to come get you after?" Judith had asked as they pulled up to the gentle slope. Even driving, Norris had to admit that the view really was killer.

"No, I'll be fine, Mom," Norris said, mouth going dry the moment he spotted Aarti by her camera and tripod, apparently filming something. "I can bus it home."

"So, that's the girl, eh? She seems really pretty. From a distance," Judith mused, invasively leaning into the passenger seat to ogle Aarti who, thank God, had her back turned to the road.

"Mom."

"I'm sure the front of her is very pretty too," Judith continued. "I would love to meet her."

"Nah, it's a real Harvey Dent situation up close, believe me," Norris quipped as he got his backpack and quickly got out, slamming the car door shut. One step at a time. Judith could meet Aarti when she officially became his girlfriend. Maybe next weekend.

"Bye, Mom."

She drove off behind him, and Norris took a moment to admire Aarti as she set up her shot.

"I know you're there," she called out, but he could hear the smile in her voice. She turned, pushing her red hair away from her face and for a second, Norris was speechless.

"How was Whistler?" Aarti asked, greeting Norris with a kiss on the cheek and a happy but somewhat distracted hug.

"Good," Norris answered, regaining speech. "Snow, mountains, snow, mountains. It was fun, but I can't believe I actually missed Austin."

"Really?" she derided. "You were gone for less than a week."

Norris shrugged.

"What did you end up doing around here?"

She wearily motioned to the camera. "This. All over. Please kill me."

They sat down on the grass, and Aarti began to fill him in on her week. She had apparently been filming this vista every day for the past three days and planned on collapsing the footage into a supercut, focused on highlighting the traffic. It was a new project of hers, as she was "hitting a wall with photography."

The whole camera thing would almost be a Manic Pixie

cliché if it weren't for how single-minded and focused she was about it. She knew the difference between lenses, where to order them, where to fix them around here, could time-stamp movies from the graininess of the film alone, always seemed to have an endless supply of SD cards in her bag, and maneuvered the handle of her high-tech tripod like a weary mechanic. To Norris, there was something ridiculously hot about her expertise. He wished he was as focused about, well, anything.

"You're pretty awesome, y'know."

"I'm aware. Always happy to hear it, though."

She smiled brightly, covering her eyes from the sun's glare and looking up at him with a smile. They both leaned in for a quick kiss on the lips. Norris smiled and joined their hands for a moment only to have her untangle them as she stood and returned to the camera, moving the focus wheel to the right and then back to the left for seemingly no reason.

"You're very touchy today," she teased, now tinkering with the lens. "Was there something in Canada's water or something? Fluoride and neediness?"

Norris's face must have fallen for a moment since she quickly followed up with "I'm kidding, I'm kidding. Sorry, I'm kind of distracted here. I spent all of spring break looking at portfolios, and mine is just garbage. Like, immature high school nonsense."

She sighed heavily, a finger through her hair, shaking her head at the camera.

Norris didn't know what to say. She seemed genuinely distraught, but he wasn't sure whether his being here was even helping. He just wanted to find a way to make her smile.

"I almost forgot," Norris said. "I got you this." He fished the gift out of his backpack and watched with anticipation as she began carefully peeling back the paper.

"A snow globe," she said as she finished unwrapping it. "Cool, thanks."

"I figure that if I couldn't bring back actual snow, it was the next best thing." Norris added, "It's not the same as bringing back a souvenir from one of your own world travels, but . . ."

"But you figured I was a generic-airport-souvenir kind of girl?" she asked.

"What? No, I just—that's not at all—"

"Look, I'm sorry. I don't mean to be an asshole," she added, drumming her fingers alongside the globe, trying to see into it. Finally, she looked up at him, seeming to decide something. "I've been thinking it's time to tell my parents that I want to pursue photography in a real way. Like, go to art school instead of Harvard kind of way, or even skip college entirely kind of way. It's going to shock the hell out of them, and then it's going to make them really furiously mad."

"Do they really not know?" he asked, hoping for an encouraging tone. "You take photos all day long. You love movies, lengthy, boring ones. They know you. They must know this is your thing."

"You should get it." She frowned, looking up from the globe. "Your parents are immigrants too."

"That doesn't matter."

It was her turn to give him *that* look. The one he made such

164

a specialty of unleashing on people who pretended to be dumber than they actually were.

"It doesn't not matter and we both know it." She echoed the exact words he had once said to her.

She sighed and moved away from her camera to a nearby bench, where Norris joined her.

"Imagine telling your mom you didn't want to go to college, that you were considering dropping out of high school and getting a GED to free up time to work on your . . . hockey," Aarti challenged. "How would that go?"

Norris quickly played the 15,043 arguments that could ensue from him walking into their kitchen with that statement. They all ended with the same outcome: him getting ready for school that next morning. A complete nonstarter.

"Poorly," he simply said instead.

"Poorly." Aarti nodded in agreement. "Well, that's what's waiting for me. And I need to do it sooner rather than later."

"Why?"

"Because college is around the corner," Aarti said. "And to them, this . . ." She waved over to the camera and Norris noticed her nails were now orange. Had she gone through all the colors of the rainbow in the time he had known her?

"This is just a fun high school extracurricular. It's cheerleading or hockey or mathletes. Something to write an Ivy League application essay about."

"I get it," Norris said quietly. Because he did. When you were the child of immigrants, you weren't just you; your success was also your parents', your cousins', your relatives' still struggling for life in Haiti or India, wishing they were you. It was your job, your preordained celestial existence or whatever, to make the most of it.

She turned to him. "So, how do I tell them I want to do this? Really do it?"

Norris had no idea.

"I don't know." A beat passed. "Do you want to grab something to eat?" he offered. "Maybe talk some more?"

She shook her head. "I have to finish this."

"Right. Okay." Norris smiled.

"Thanks for the snow globe."

The kiss Norris received on the cheek was chaste and polite, the receipt for an airport snow globe. What had happened to the undertone of maple syrup? Had he done something wrong?

As he walked away from her and prepared for the long wait at the bus stop, he couldn't help but feel that Aarti didn't just want to be alone . . . she wanted to be away from *him*.

17

THE DATELESS EVENING

DOING YOUR HOMEWORK? Check.

SALVAGING THE DECREPIT REMAINS OF YOUR HOCKEY FANTASY LEAGUE? Check.

COMPLETING ALL THE CROSSWORD PUZZLES IN MOM'S LATEST STACK OF MAGAZINES? Check.

DOING SUDOKU? Hard pass. It's freaking math disguised as entertainment.

BINGING TWO BACK SEASONS OF DEGRASSI: THE NEXT GENERATION? Check.

> @Eric53 is online.
>
> @Norrtorious—Hey, how's it going?
>
> @Eric53—What's wrong?
>
> @Norrtorious—Why do you think something's wrong?
>
> @Eric53—"Hey, how's it going?"
>
> @Eric53—Bitch, plz.
>
> @Norrtorious—M'fine. Just bored here.
>
> @Eric53—I'm just going to keep saying Bitch, plz.
>
> @Norrtorious—What are you up to tonight?

@Eric53—Date with M-A. He's picking me up and shit.

@Norrtorious—Chivalrous.

@Eric53—He made a point of telling me his parents are away. . . . Was that a code for sex? Am I about to have sex tonight?

@Norrtorious—¯_( )_/¯

@Eric53—Do I want to have sex tonight?!

@Norrtorious—Lol, how am I supposed to answer that?

@Eric53—This is really stressful. Where's Aarti?

@Norrtorious—Some fashion show she's photographing. I'll join her in a few.

@Eric53—She sounds way too cool for u, lol.

@Eric53—Is everything ok?

@Norrtorious—Of course. Go spread the gay agenda.

@Norrtorious—I'm fine, really.

@Eric53—If u say so. International text it up if ur having a meltdown or something.

@Norrtorious—No meltdowns, lol. Go.

@Eric53 is offline.

Norris wasn't sure why he had lied to Eric, exactly, but he didn't want to get into the Aarti stuff. Instead, Norris scanned his small list of contacts for some alternative to this entirely unwelcome feeling in his chest.

His dad hadn't been online in five days, according to the time stamp next to his grayed-out icon. Of course he hadn't. On an impulse, Norris clicked Edit and changed the icon's name from "Dad" to "Canadad." He stared at the name for a moment before saving the change that felt both important and completely insignificant.

A few days ago, Norris could not wait to be back in Austin. Now he was saddling up for another Saturday evening on his own, confused by Aarti's sudden coldness.

He scrolled through his phone and unearthed a two-day old email from Maddie. Upon closer inspection, it contained a forwarded invitation to a movie event at the Alamo Drafthouse by some "Oliver McMahon" for Saturday . . . which was tonight. She'd highlighted the last line of the email in yellow:

Invite your Canadian. He was chill at Mer's.

Had he even talked to an Oliver at that thing? The swim team guy with the *Rick and Morty* T-shirt, maybe?

Either way: hard pass. Hanging out with a bunch of jocks smuggling brown-bagged bottles of tequila into a *Rocky Horror* sing-along sounded entirely too exhausting at the moment.

"There's actual dinner on the stove," Judith noted from Norris's doorway, putting on sparkling red earrings. She nodded to the empty microwave cup sitting on Norris's desk and raised a disgusted lip at the processed cheese glue around its rim. "Soup Joumou."

"With noodles?"

Let it be known that—antislavery insurrection against French colonial rule aside—the best thing Haitians had ever done was spicy pumpkin stew. Norris's favorite recipe on earth, right over a standard La Belle Province poutine without too much gravy.

"Dumplings," she corrected with a smile, feathering her hair in his mirror. She had a new wig on: one with auburn highlights that, while obviously still a wig, also gave her a sharp modern look. Norris's mom never favored hair extensions or wigs that could pass for real hair like some of her Haitian friends preferred. For Judith they were hats, and strictly matters of fashion. Some days her natural short, natty gray hair fraying around the edges was her go-to look; on others, she would wear a replica of Beyoncé's pixie cut. To say nothing of the headscarves. His mother was kind of a boss when it came to self-assurance on that front.

New wig. New earrings. Her dress, an old one from Canada normally saved for family events and weddings, was freshly pressed. And nails painted a glossy dark purple that matched her lips.

"Are you going on a goddamn date?!"

"Language," she warned.

"Shouldn't I be—I don't know—consulted?" Norris sputtered. Emotionally fragile child of divorce, et cetera. He knew it was coming but figured he had at least a year before she asked him to install a dating app on her phone.

"That's quite the thesis statement, babe." Judith snorted. "Want to break down that argument for me?"

"No, it's fine." Norris quickly reconsidered. "Have a good time."

Norris didn't really mind. She definitely deserved a nice guy after the northern gap-toothed bimbo situation. Judith, however, was still looking at him, as if she were counting the typos on his face.

170

"What?" he asked.

She smiled, stepped into the room, and kissed his head, wrapping her bare arm around him. "It's just dinner. I met him at a panel for new faculty. No one is taking you on a family bonding fishing trip yet, babe."

She smelled like perfume. He could never decipher the specific scents past that first whiff. They all smelled the same to Norris: alcohol, softly lit commercials, and old magazines.

"Hmm, want to talk about it?" Judith asked softly. "The mystery girl that this is definitely not about? I can postpone."

"I really don't, Mom," Norris assured her. "Go."

"Text if you go out. I'll be back by midnight."

"Cool."

"Or," she continued, "at the latest, eleven a.m. tomorrow morning, if he doesn't have his kid this weekend."

She blew him a kiss before closing the door.

#@&*$Y)#Y#$()$&)#???!!!!

Screw *Rocky Horror*. Short of a full lobotomy to erase his mother's parting blow from his mind, Norris thought of the next-best Saturday evening plan.

"Hey," Liam's voice answered after four rings. "Welcome back."

"She didn't look twice at the snow globe," Norris explained as best as he could, his frustration echoing around the empty rink as he missed the net for the third time in as many tries.

"So your relationship with Aarti Puri is doomed because . . . she didn't look twice at the snow globe?" Liam repeated verbatim, chin on his hockey stick as he watched the wayward puck glide to a stop across the rink. Norris skated backward to make space for Liam at the pucks they had lined up for drills.

"When you say it that way, you make me sound like a moron." He groaned.

"Apologies," Liam said quite unapologetically, skating forward to ready himself at the nearest puck.

Liam's original Saturday night plans had involved "working on his night garden," which he had not minded postponing. Once at the ice rink, they had fallen pretty seamlessly into the regular pattern of their practices. It was nice to spend time with an Austinite who seemed to vaguely enjoy his presence. His stance had definitely gotten better.

"If I may," Liam started after clearing his throat as if he was about to jump over a blinking land mine. "You and Aarti seem to be . . . very different people."

"What's that supposed to mean?" Norris asked. Him, bad; her, good? Her, pretty; him, something fished out of the bottom of the lagoon? Her, life of the party; him, neighbor who calls the cops with noise complaint at exactly nine thirty p.m.?

"I just mean that you might have different expectations for relationships, based on your personalities. That's always either really easy or really messy."

"Loosen your back; it's not golf," Norris casually instructed, taking in Liam's posture as he aligned his stick with the second puck.

"Maybe you giving her a gift turned her off," Liam continued

172

as he followed Norris's advice. "Because she had different expectations for where you are."

"Don't you have any advice?" Norris sighed. "I was really kind of hoping for some sage wisdom here!"

"Distractions distract," Liam eventually offered, letting his second and third pucks fly. This time, they only narrowly missed the net.

"And practice pays off," Norris noted. "Dang, dude! Your stick control is a lot better."

"Thanks." Liam smiled proudly. He had shed most of that fear of the ice that kept beginners tiptoeing. "I basically did nothing else for all of spring break. Well, I wrote half a musical, but that doesn't really count."

Norris circled the ice, absentmindedly collecting stray pucks they'd shot all over the rink and sending them into a single corner.

"Who have you been practicing with?" He kept his voice casual.

"Patrick and a couple of the guys," Liam admitted. "I told you in the email. People are interested."

"You mean Hairy Armpits?" Norris scoffed.

"Patrick," Liam gently corrected. "He seems decent. Austin has plenty of hockey fans as it turns out."

"Well." Norris whistled. "It looks like you don't need me anymore."

"I mean, I wouldn't say that. . . . Even if there are enough players interested to form a team, we'll still need, y'know, a captain. Someone to run drills and all that stuff."

Norris turned to find Liam staring at him.

"No."

"Why not?"

"A *team*?! We don't have enough players, for one." Norris hedged. "By the sound of it, you've only got a handful of players, which isn't actually enough. And as for the captain thing, forget it. This is just for fun. . . . I'm not an actual jock, dude."

"You're a little bit of a jock," Liam mused. "If we're going to boil individuals down to a single label that encompasses the whole of their being . . . between the hockey and the skiing and the fact that you spend a lot of time with cheerleaders trying to figure out how to successfully date 'hot chicks,' your closest category is, well, jock."

"You're a very mean person." Norris sniffed. "Like, cruel."

Liam smiled and resumed his pitch.

"We need an actual captain and it can't be me. I can barely stand in these things. If we had eighteen players . . ."

"Twenty." Norris sighed. "Two rotating goalies."

"If we had twenty players," Liam continued undeterred, motioning to the open rink, "then you'd be okay with opening this up?"

"Sure, dude," Norris relented. He couldn't stare at that naive optimism and self-starter-ish-ness too long without getting blinded. "Find twenty Anderson High guys that want to join a hockey team and yeah, I'll teach them to lace up their skates."

"Bless your little jock heart." Liam grinned.

Norris couldn't help but laugh. He'd meant to issue an impossible challenge, but he was beginning to think that Liam was a few steps ahead of him and already had a full team recruited. He knew Norris too well.

But that was okay by him, he realized. Liam was going to be his teammate, and that was one label Norris was actually comfortable with.

18

THE CHEERLEADER TABLE

LOCATION: Dead center of the cafeteria, surveying the kingdom, exactly halfway between the performers and the athletes.

HEAD OF THE TABLE: Meredith Santiago.

RIGHT HAND: Maddie McElwees.

SMALL COUNCIL: Trish, Viola, Elisa.

SEATING: By invitation only. (Don't worry about it; you're not invited.)

DIET: Prepackaged salads; sushi trays.

TOOLS: Phones out and lined up; heavy-duty glass water bottles with color-coordinated silicon sleeves; sports bags at all feet.

Aarti Puri had officially become a conundrum.

Not Norris's girlfriend, not his crush, but a conundrum. *Webster's Dictionary*'s kind of conundrum.

> *Conundrum: A question asked for amusement, typically one with a pun in its answer; a riddle.*

Conundrum: A confusing and difficult problem or question.

Conundrum: 😼

The middle chunk of his now well-creased notebook was filled with scribbles and stray sketches of anything that fell into his line of vision. It was a good way to keep busy and stop his brain from tossing and turning over what had changed with Aarti, and why she'd suddenly gone cold. He'd sent her a few jokey texts, a few inquiries about her photography, and some stray observations about life at Anderson High, but her answers were all of the monosyllabic kind. (See: *lol, no updates there, y'know, ha, cool.*)

It could all be fixed, though, he knew; he was one clever text away from turning things around. The trick was just in finding the right message. He was staring at his phone, trying to line up the right words, when a voice addressed him, breaking his chain of thoughts.

"What?" Norris snapped, annoyed.

"Um, don't snarl at us," Meredith retorted with a raised eyebrow. "You're the one who practically plowed down our table!"

He looked up to find a whole tableful of cheerleaders, mid-lunch in the cafeteria. *Shit.* She might have had a point.

"It's a temporary state of affairs," Norris managed, as he sank down into the seat next to Maddie. "I'm just sending a text, all right?"

"Why do you need to sit down for that?" Meredith asked.

"To reduce the risk of typos," Norris explained. "*General* autocorrects to *genital* in the blink of an eye."

"Is your mother exhausted at all times?" Maddie asked rhetorically, smiling as she moved her bag to make room for him at the small, crowded table.

Norris considered. "She does sigh a lot."

"Maddie? Does your new bestie have to sit with us?" Meredith demanded after her umpteenth sigh went unanswered.

"Hi, Meredith." Norris grinned. "I love your hair today. Shine and bounce! Getting both right is really tricky, I hear."

He'd discovered fake politeness to be far more effective when it came to Meredith Santiago than any insult he might think up. His enthused waves whenever he walked past her along the halls always left her in an infuriated state that was simply delightful.

"Maddie! Do something!"

"We don't actually own the school tables, babe." Maddie rolled her eyes affectionately, snatching one of Meredith's fries. Norris could not possibly imagine what she saw in that friendship, or how it ever saw the light of day for that matter. When the conversation moved on to prom, and how Patrick was already asking about the color of her dress so he could get a matching bow tie, Norris decided then and there the girl was either a complete saint or deranged. The thought of Maddie smiling sadly as these two neck suckers made out around her was enough to prompt Norris to go in for another compliment hammer blow.

"You know, Meredith, have you ever thought about . . ."

Norris had made the mistake of looking up for a split second and caught a glimpse of Aarti walking into the cafeteria, camera strap around her neck. She made eye contact with Norris, smiled tightly, and kept on walking.

"Ah," Maddie noted, following his glance. "That explains it. Trouble in paradise?"

Norris sighed. "You could say that. Snakes in every bush and we're officially out of apples."

"What happened?" she asked, looking concerned.

"Oooh, I smell dish," Trish interjected, leaning into Maddie and Norris's end of the table with a predatory smile. "Who broke up? Who hooked up? Don't keep it to yourself."

"Is this about *her*?" one of them asked, nodding to Aarti's table. Norris was about to get up and go join her when Maddie shook her head, subtly. The message was clear: *rushing to her side is not a good idea right now.* Instead, he focused on Maddie as if she were the most fascinating thing in the world.

"Is the village bike at it again?" Lucy was intrigued.

"Who has the slut banged now?"

"Honestly, can we stop with calling other girls whores and sluts?" Meredith said, rolling her eyes. "Because we really don't have a leg to stand on throwing a fit when someone carves our name on a bathroom stall . . . Lucy."

Lucy said nothing in reply, suddenly finding her own salad fascinating.

"So what were you two whispering about then?" Trish was relentless.

"No dish," Maddie dismissed. "I hate that expression. Norris is just bemoaning the fact that Anderson doesn't have a hockey team. Very Canadian concerns."

"Y'all aren't actually going to start a team, are you?" Meredith asked, resigned to address Norris directly.

Norris was surprised she knew about Liam's hockey team pipe dreams, but then again, she'd probably heard it from Patrick.

"Doubtful." He shrugged. "Hockey gear is kind of expensive, and that rink is too small for an actual team."

Norris was forcing himself to be a pessimist about the whole thing to avoid any disappointment down the line when it didn't actually happen. It was a strategy he'd been using for much of his life, actually; nothing hoped for, nothing lost.

Norris leaned closer to Meredith, eager to change the topic. "Now that I have you, I've been meaning to talk to you about Patrick, actually. I assume you're the one responsible for the . . . personal grooming complaints."

"His grooming is fine," Meredith snapped.

"As a rich, verdant field where hobbits and other fairy-tale creatures can establish a colony, sure," Norris said. "But as the armpits of a dude with an infinite collection of tank tops? It needs some severe landscaping. Like, advanced deforestation."

Two of the cheerleaders down the table, Trish and Viola, burst out laughing.

Diplomatic as always, Maddie used the occasion to take a very long sip of her drink, but Norris could swear she was smiling.

"I mean, he's not wrong, Mer," Lucy said. "It's . . . notice-able."

"Thank you, Lucy!" Norris exclaimed. Somewhere along the way, Norris had learned too many of their names. *Holy crap*, all *of their names*.

"He's Greek on his mother's side! They're hairy people!" Meredith cried defensively, ratcheting Norris's laugh up to a cackle. The next time he looked over, Aarti was gone.

"Are you okay?" Maddie mouthed from across the table, eyes filled with concern. Norris felt something stir in the pit of his stomach. That girl needed to stop caring so much about others. It was goddamn disconcerting.

Norris nodded as the conversation around them merci-fully moved on to ranking the complete lack of hair on the swim team (some of the members also shaved off their actual eyebrows for aerodynamic purposes, Norris learned). Despite the direction of the conversation, Norris chose to spend a nonpainful lunch hour eating with a table of cheerleaders because, screw it, why the hell not? What else would this state throw at him? When the bell rang, Meredith was the first one to stand up, throwing Norris a withering stare that said "Don't ever sit here again," which meant that Norris might now have to become the squad's first male cheerleader just to spite her.

Five minutes later, Norris closed his locker door, books in hand and notebook in his pocket, only to find Maddie staring at him, pink sports bag at her feet.

"Spill," she instructed, checking her watch. "Now. I have Mechanics with Goade in five minutes, which means I have roughly twenty minutes to talk. What's happened with you and Aarti?"

"It's fine."

Norris had no reason to blame her for the current state of things with Aarti. All Maddie had done, in her own quid pro quo way, was try to help.

"Canada!" she pressed. "I can't help unless I know what's wrong here."

"I told you, it's nothing. . . ."

"Do you think you're a good liar?" she asked, checking her watch again. "Because you're not. Your face is like a pop-up book for every feeling in there."

"Look," Norris began. "I'm just not sure there's anything to be done at this stage. . . ."

"Canada! We're talking about dating here. I'm the genius janitor, there's a complex equation on the chalkboard after hours. . . . Give me some chalk and let me solve it!" she continued, undeterred. "I'm a surgeon, this entire thing is an open patient; hand me the scalpel, dude!"

"All, right, all right! Jeez. No more metaphors, please."

So Norris told her everything, as best as he himself understood it. He watched Maddie's face transition from sympathetic to earnestly, genuinely confused.

"A snow globe?" she repeated, untying her ponytail and retying it in the exact shape it previously held. "Please be kidding."

"How is that a dealbr—"

"Did Aarti Puri ever mention having a specific interest in snow globes? Is she the sort of girl who screams 'snow globe' and 'Hello Kitty' stationery to you? Did she, at any point, request a snow globe from the great land of Kah-na-dia?"

"I was being a thoughtful boyfriend!"

"She's not your girlfriend yet!" Maddie said, raising her voice an octave higher and reaching forward to grab his nipple through his T-shirt and twist.

"OW!" Norris yelped and jumped back, almost dropping his books in the process.

"Did you actually just give me a purple nurple?" he accused. "Are you twelve?"

"It was earned. All right, at least I'm getting a better picture here." She exhaled sharply. "You're that guy, Canada. The guy who thinks he's purchased the deeds to a girlfriend the second he holds a car door open."

"Well, I don't even drive, so in my case, it would be to motion toward a city bus."

She smiled at him. "Look, you still like her, right?"

Norris nodded in spite of himself. He did. At this point, life would be much simpler if he didn't, but even the brief second that he'd seen her in the cafeteria had been enough to make his heart skip a stupid beat. Arrhythmia was giving a confirmation that there was still some active liking in his blood stream.

"Well, then we're going to have to double down." She nodded confidently. "I'm going to teach you everything I know.

Friday—you're covering Julio's morning shift Sunday, by the way—hope you didn't have any other plans."

"Would it matter if I did?" Norris sighed.

"Nope." She smiled. "See you there!"

19

THE FIRST HOCKEY PRACTICE

MASTERMIND: Liam Hooper.

PROVEN SKILLS AS POTENTIAL CAPTAIN: Rich parents, self-starter-ish-ness.

RECRUITMENT TACTICS: Definitely: flyers. Maybe: word of mouth, online message boards, bathroom stall graffiti, who knows? Liam is persistent.

POOL OF PLAYERS: The greater Austin area.

EXPECTED PROFICIENCY LEVEL: "Ice is slippery."

LIKELIHOOD OF PAIN: High.

In hindsight, Norris really didn't know Liam at all.

He'd once decided to scribble everything he knew about the guy in his notebook as he did with most people who crossed his path often enough in Austin, Texas. Liam was white. Liam was rich—not just in comparison to him and Judith, but in the official summering-is-a-verb sense of the word. Liam had a powerful, intense stare and a low, soothing voice that might one day make him a spiritual guru or a very intimidating drug dealer's henchman.

But mostly, Liam had an innate, natural ability to convince people to join his cause. (Which again boded well for either drug dealing or spiritual leadership conferencing.) That was probably why the guy had somehow managed to convince eighteen people to show up at their first official hockey practice.

"How?!" Norris had asked, walking into the warehouse with his skates around his neck and a stack of traffic cones for their usual session, only to find a few clusters of guys and four girls, in mismatched attire, all waving to Liam. Some were already circling the ice while others stood on the edges, awaiting instructions, looking excited but uncomfortable.

"You're never alone in your interests," Liam had said. "You just got to dig a little further."

"That sounds like the rallying cry of perverts across the internet."

"Or hockey fans in the greater Austin area." Liam smirked proudly. Norris was on the verge of congratulating Liam when a voice bellowed at them from across the ice.

"Yo, finally! Where have you guys been?"

Patrick "Hairy Armpits" Lamarra barreled toward them, skates already improperly laced.

"No!" Norris said, stopping dead short and turning to Liam.

"He was by far one of the most enthused people," Liam said. "He might surprise you."

Patrick stopped himself by using Norris as a speed bump.

"Are you ready to do this, my dudes?" he exclaimed, bumping his gloved hand against Norris's head.

"Give him a chance," Liam preemptively mouthed to Norris before turning to give Patrick a knowing nod.

"Right," Patrick said, catching on to Liam's look and turning to Norris, chin slightly raised. "Listen, Norris, we're good, right? I probably shouldn't have gotten physical that time. . . . Y'know, at school."

"You mean that time you shoved me down a flight of stairs?" Norris really had no incentive to make this easy for him.

"Right, that," Patrick said, his tone more whiny than uncomfortable. "Bygones or whatever? I'd really like to play with you guys. If you'll let me."

Liam was quietly observing the exchange. He seemed invested, so Norris thought it best to simply go along with it.

"Bygones or whatever." Norris sighed. "Let's just do this."

Liam grinned and pulled a whistle out from under his jersey, giving it three sharp blows.

"All right, folks, let's gather around! Welcome to our first official hockey practice!" He seemed to have the whole leadership thing down; if he had been serious about Norris captaining the team, Norris hoped it had been forgotten.

The scrimmage—their first real attempt at an actual seven-on-seven hockey game—was fast, messy, and would have had half the players benched halfway through the first period had it been any legitimate hockey league. There were only two periods, clocking twenty minutes each. Collectively, the sixteen players involved broke about thirty-six rules. Despite their teams' ill-defined positions, Norris mostly played defense and made sure to go easy on the rougher skaters, still looking a bit wobbly on their feet. A handful of them were surprisingly agile. Norris had to admit that even Patrick had a certain flair to his skating, tracing loose loops around the thin ice.

Norris only had a passing knowledge of some of the other players. He learned from the half-time chitchat that Brett, a nineteen-year-old, was from Boston, as was his cousin, who was also his roommate now that the two were in college. A few more were college aged. Apparently, Liam had placed an online ad for interested players under the Activities Partner section of a popular local classified website. Norris was starting to think that a friendship with Liam would end with the two of them in some serial killer's basement somewhere because Liam wanted to take a chain-welding class with an expert.

Keeping count of the goals quickly became meaningless for the purpose of their scrimmage, and Norris stopped keeping track at five to three. There were no dressing rooms to speak of, so practice ended with the sweaty, smelly players dousing themselves in deodorant in the corner.

Norris and Liam took care of the nets and traffic cones and stray pucks, watching from afar as the team—jeez, their team—came together.

"Thanks to our boys for bringing us all together today!" Patrick cheered as they all headed out of the warehouse.

Afterward, everyone grabbed a bite to eat at a nearby traveling taco stand and gobbled up the food in the skating rink's air-conditioned lobby. Norris would have normally excused himself from all extraneous socialization, but Liam was his ride home. Plus, he had seen that particular taco truck around Austin, and it was also highlighted in one of Judith's pamphlets—and he really was starving.

"My ankles are kind of killing me," Pat-reek admitted with a mouthful of cheese, shrimp, and jalapeños, reaching down to rub his ankles as they ate.

"You need better skates," Norris begrudgingly counseled. "These are too big for you."

"These are my cousin's. Skates are so fucking expensive."

Norris sighed. "I know a couple of websites that have good deals on skates," he said, pointing to Liam's blades. "They won't be as good as Liam's, but you can find some decent blades. I could send you some links or whatever."

"Nice, dude! Thanks," Patrick said, elbowing him in the side.

"We were just wondering . . ." one of the players whose name Norris could not remember asked. "Do we have a name yet?"

"Not yet," Liam said. "It shouldn't be a unilateral decision."

"Not the Bats," Norris said quickly.

"Agreed," one of the guys said. "Everything in this town is Bats or Longhorns. We need a third animal on the field."

By the end of the meal, Norris somehow had a dozen new names on his phone and their animal avatar was still undecided, locked somewhere between the Austin Rolling Dices and the Austin Winterbringers.

The buzz from practice was starting to fade, and Norris's muscles were falling asleep. It would be the best soreness to wake up to the next day, but he was getting ready to pass out after a good shower. Liam was driving Norris home, for which Norris was grateful. His forehead was already glistening in Austin's late evening heat—no pummeling sun but still eighty degrees in freaking March.

Norris opened his mouth to complain—about his sore muscles, about the heat, about the fact that he was now committed to spend actual time with Patrick "Hairy Armpits" Lamarra at least once a week—but as he looked around at the group, joking around and laughing as they recalled the best moments of their first team practice, he closed it again and smiled.

20

KEY LIME SEASON

NUMBER OF INDIVIDUAL PIES PRODUCED PER DAY: Thirty to sixty.

CARDBOARD BOX ASSEMBLY SPEED: Twenty-five seconds.

KEY LIME JUICING SPEED: Four average-sized key limes per minute.

NUMBER OF CURRENTLY BAND-AIDED FINGERS: Three.

CREAM-WHIPPING SPEED WHEN PICKING UP KITCHEN SLACK: Hummingbird on five cups of coffee.

RISK OF DEVELOPING CARPAL TUNNEL SYNDROME BY AGE EIGHTEEN: High.

Spring at the Bone Yard came with yet another tradition, something that Austin had no shortage of between UT Longhorns gear, the music festivals, and annual film events that peppered downtown. In this instance, apparently, it all came down to key lime pie.

"As in: condensed milk, sour cream, lime juice, and graham

cracker?" Norris asked incredulously.

He had arrived early to find a sweat-stained Jim McElwees installing a *very* hand-painted placard under the Bone Yard's sign: Key Lime Days Ahead, framed with neon limes and an acid-green pie.

"Don't forget the whipped cream," Big Jim answered, tapping the board and confirming himself as the proud artist. "Special homemade recipe. None of that canned nonsense!"

"Cool," Norris commented. "Is this, um, seasonal?"

"Through the spring and the summer! This bad boy is our ice cream truck. In the summer we deliver it around town. People love it! Give the people what they want—in a timely fashion and at their door—and you can charge eighteen dollars a pop! Free life lesson for you, Nor!"

No one could say that Big Jim's zest for life wasn't infectious. *Ha. Zest.* Norris had smiled and gone in assuming that this simple menu addition would not change much in his life, unaware of how utterly wrong he was.

"*Ha,* is that what he said?" Maddie scoffed, adding the seventeenth case of limes to the backup storage. Norris followed her lead and placed the eighteenth case on top. Julio was right behind them, carrying number nineteen.

"Let me tell you how it usually goes." She launched into her explanation. "Spring rolls in and we get about five dozen of these things delivered in three days, because Dad bulk orders. Every year he bulk orders. He has an old bandmate who farms them in Fairview. He thinks he's getting a deal, but really these are standard prices. I've checked online."

"Every year we tell him." Julio sighed, picking up the narrative. "And every year he forgets."

"It's Key Lime Spring. Key Lime Prom. Key Lime Graduation. Summer finally rolls around," Maddie continued, sending a quick text without missing a beat. "And our delivery guys always bail by the end of the summer because their band has gotten a new gig, or because the heat is just too much. Plus, the smell of baked-in lime and sugar gets to you. Believe me."

"So by the end of the summer," Maddie said again, "we're drafting servers and busboys to pick up the slack and do delivery in the morning and evening. Not to mention that these things rot. They rot real bad. Half of these will go to waste. That's usually when Mom and Bobby come in here to try to salvage what they can."

Bobby was the twins' father and one of the brothers-in-law. He stopped by the Bone Yard occasionally, and Norris had met him a few times: pair of sunglasses hanging from his V-neck and a college ring. Norris knew the type and had slipped back into the kitchens before receiving an unsolicited fist bump. Working at the Bone Yard meant slowly falling into sync with the McElwees clan's extended family tree. Norris knew who married who, who still called Big Jim "Mr. McElwees" and who called him "Big Jim," "Pop," or "Sir," and what the distinction between each title meant. Bobby was a "Pop," but, as far as Norris could tell, that had been a premature claim on his part.

"These are long, limey days, Canada," Julio concluded, with the gravitas of an old sailor who had seen some shit in his days and looked at a sunny day knowing the storm was ahead. "Long limey days indeed." He tied his apron and headed into the main seating area.

Maddie grinned at Norris as she began to juggle two stray limes.

"Believe me, by October you'll be so sick of these you'll see them in your nightmares," she warned, eyes focused on the half-steady loops she was attempting to create. Whenever two dropped, she automatically grabbed two more from the nearest case. "Mushy, sweetened, gained-ten-pounds-in-six-months nightmares."

"Wait, what?"

"They're . . . really good pies," she admitted, bouncing a lime at Norris with her arm. "You'll see."

"Stop dropping all those limes!" Norris admonished as two more rolled to the ground.

"I only dropped four," Maddie replied.

"Listen, Madison," Norris quipped, stopping another one before it rolled too far. "Nobody likes a pretty girl who can count, all right?"

"Just hand me your phone, all right?" She sighed. "Let's do this."

Norris didn't quite know why he'd agreed to this, but as they'd been working, Maddie had somehow made a pretty successful argument for giving her full access to his previous exchanges with Aarti, which meant his phone. After making sure his browsing history was clear of any recent embarrassing and/or pornographic searches (like most red-blooded teenag-ers, he had a healthy curiosity about these things), Norris handed over his phone and walked to another corner of the back room, leaving Maddie to process like an android pro-cessing data. Her back was arched and her thumb took long, vertical swipes through his past month of pseudoromantic history.

"Well, there's your problem, right there," she eventually noted, eyes still glued to his phone. "You're trying so hard! Every-thing you send her is a snarky joke—I don't want to alarm you, but some of this stuff just borders on cheerleading squad–level cattiness, by the way. It's stressful to receive that stuff! Espe-cially in writing. You're barraging the poor girl with Ping-Pong balls she has to whack back."

Your goddamn mouth, as Judith had warned him. Only in text form.

"I never meant to do that!" Norris moaned. "How do I fix it?"

"Cut through the bull and say something real."

"Like what?"

"Aarti," Maddie began to recite as she swiftly typed on his phone, keeping Norris at bay with her foot as she scooted back onto the counter.

"I am so horny for you. I want to squeeze your tits and your butt and then have you squeeze my butt and my nipples as we dissolve into a human meat puddle together, XOXO."

Norris snatched his phone back, tripping over himself and hitting the counter to read the actual text Maddie had typed.

HI, AARTI

LOOK, I KNOW THINGS ARE KIND OF WEIRD AND YOU'RE UNDER A LOT OF STRESS WITH LIFE, ETC. BUT I'D LOVE TO TAKE YOU ON ANOTHER DATE IF YOU'RE UP FOR IT. SOMETHING REALLY SPECIAL! NO EMOTIONALLY MANIPULATIVE SNOW GLOBES WILL BE INVOLVED. OR, IF YOU JUST WANT TO BE FRIENDS, THAT'S COOL TOO.

"You cheerleader," Norris snarled as Maddie batted her eyes whimsically.

"Trust me," she sighed, jumping off the counter. "That's a lot better than this endless stream of quips you've been vomiting at her."

"I thought girls liked funny guys?"

"Girls also like six-packs, but I don't see you hitting the gym," she sneered. "It's aggressive! Like, 'Aren't I funny! Notice my humor! Laugh! Laugh, I say!!'"

Norris was still grumbling when the response from Aarti, the fastest he'd ever received, arrived with a ding: **OK** ☺

Chastened, he was forced to admit Maddie was—as always—right. Clearly Aarti had been scared off by his eagerness, and the apparently obvious effort he'd been putting into his carefully crafted, carefully timed responses had only been pushing her further away.

So. He had another shot with Aarti. He looked back at the text Maddie had penned for him.

"'Something really special'? What does that even mean?"

Maddie shrugged, jumping off the counter. "Whatever you choose to make it."

Norris groaned, racking his brain. Another dreary documentary was not his idea of a magical evening. He and Aarti clearly weren't aligned there.

"So a candlelit dinner or something?"

Maddie shook her head in visible disgust.

"Well, no: not that. So cliché. Is the inside of your head an ABC Family sitcom?" she asked. "For some reason, this girl likes you. Your entire . . . thing, it works for her. So, as counterintuitive as that is . . . I would say to be yourself on this one. Take her on a date that only Norris Kaplan could take her on." By her tone, that instruction was the worst advice she'd ever issued in over sixteen years of advice giving.

A Norris Kaplan date. That would definitely require some diary mapping.

"So," Norris said, exhausted with talking about himself, which might be a historical first. "Um, how is our deal working out on your end?"

"What do you mean?"

"Are you getting more time to sleep, eat, successfully lead cheers?"

Their shifts hadn't been overlapping lately because of all her practices and gymnastics and whatever it was that cheerleaders actually did to prepare for the leading of cheers.

"Um, good," she said, almost sounding coy. "It's going pretty . . . well, great, actually."

Maddie took a look around the room and leaned into him, suddenly quieter.

"Coach Armbruster said that she wants to make me squad

captain next year, officially, which also comes with insane college scholarship opportunities. Like, I could get a free ride. Or something close to it."

"Maddie!" Norris screamed excitedly, shoving her lightly. "That's freaking awesome! Congratulations!"

True, Norris had no idea what being squad captain actually entailed. He pictured something between a crown and a whip being bestowed upon Maddie by Armbruster, the gym teacher, as dozens of freshmen cowered in the corner.

"Yeah," Maddie sighed, palming a lemon.

"Wait, why aren't you more excited?"

"Well, I mean, this has kind of been Meredith's dream for forever. . . ."

Norris nodded; he unfortunately knew far more about the Anderson cheerleading squad than he ever could have predicted, and seemed to remember Meredith waxing poetic on all the things she'd do for the team when she was captain. "This is so much bigger than that, McElwees. We're talking money, sister!"

"I feel like a bad friend," she eventually admitted with a sigh, resting her head against the stack of crates. "She's definitely going to kill me."

"Please, you're like the best person in all of Texas," Norris said with an eye roll. "It's kind of annoying, truth be told."

"Mer's just not always the easiest person when it comes to these things," Maddie admitted. "She banished Ellie from our table—in the second grade, mind you—for wearing her hair the same way as her at her birthday party. She actually said that: 'You're banished.' What kind of second grader even knows the word *banish*?"

There did not seem to be any animosity at the memory; just a sort of wonderment at her best friend's quirks. Norris sighed. Meredith Santiago's emotional well-being was not something he'd ever planned to spend any energy considering, let alone preserving.

"Y'know, if you shatter the amulet she always wears, she'll just dissolve into dust and all your problems are solved."

Norris received a soft kick to the shin as Maddie turned to throw her arm over a case of limes. It wasn't like her to be this dramatic.

"Look: you haven't done anything behind her back, right?"

Maddie shook her head violently. Of course she hadn't.

"Well then, there you go." Norris shrugged. "Besides, you apparently stepped aside for Patrick. . . . She can give you this win. At worst, she will lose her tiny—ever-so-tiny, we're talking pebble-size—marbles for a couple of hours, sure. But she'll come around. No banishments. And at some point, you have to accept the spotlight instead of just being in the background clapping for Meredith."

She undid her ponytail and redid it again, slightly tighter than before, clearly stressed by the situation.

"Or," Norris continued, leaning in and lowering his voice. "Use your newfound status to broker an alliance with the theater kids, borrow a few ships from the swim team, and strike before

Meredith even knows what hit her. Keep her younger siblings as hostages and, should the remaining Santiagos get any ideas of insurrection, exterminate their lineage."

She stared at him for a moment.

"Have you tried stopping yourself two sentences short?" she suggested, rolling her eyes on the way out. "I feel like every facet of your life would benefit from it."

"You're too nice," Norris commented. "That's your problem. Like, just stop worrying about everyone else's feelings all the time. Being selfish sometimes is good too."

She raised her eyebrows, unimpressed. "You should consider a career in politics. This inspirational crap belongs on a hat, Canada."

"I'm serious, Maddie," Norris insisted. "You have to be selfish sometimes. Not always—please don't ascend to Meredith levels of awfulness—but, like, put yourself first sometimes.

"What?" Norris mumbled when she stared at him too long, as if he'd grown a second head. "You're not the only one who wants your friends to be happy."

Maddie smiled at the word *friend*, as if she'd caught him at something embarrassing. But in truth, Norris didn't mind how easily the word had come. Liam had been in it for the hockey, at least at first, but between securing him this job and all the help with Aarti, Maddie had been kind of a weird gift from the gods, delivered to make his life easier, in the same chronic, compulsive way she seemed dedicated to making all the lives around her easier.

"Thanks, Norris," Maddie said, all traces of smirk and sarcasm gone. She pulled him in for a hug, and Norris found himself settling into it for a moment before remembering himself and ducking away. "Now help me with these pies."

21

THE BIG DATE

APPROXIMATE TIME TO PLAN THE MOST IMPORTANT DATE OF ONE'S HIGH SCHOOL CAREER: Four days.

APPROXIMATE TIME TO GET READY FOR SAID DATE: Twenty minutes.

APPROXIMATE TIME TO ANXIOUSLY PUT THE SAME "MIDNIGHT NAVY" T-SHIRT (MISTAKEN FOR BLACK UPON PURCHASE) ON AND OFF BEFORE FINALLY LEAVING THE HOUSE: Two hours.

"School? Seriously?" Aarti said, following Norris into the now-emptied halls of Anderson High. Unlike his own tattered sneakers, her heels created an echo around the hall in a way Norris hadn't anticipated.

"I promise: I am categorically *not* going to murder you," he found himself reassuring her for the second time as he led them down the east gate entrance. The fact that he had to remind her of that twice couldn't bode well, but it was the only school door still unlocked at this hour. They had roughly twenty minutes to get settled before lockdown, and a full two hours after that before the cleaning staff made their first sweep. Norris had spent enough hours roaming these halls to know them very well.

"Really? Because 'new foreign student lures local teen into school after hours' seems like the start of a horror story that ends with my beautiful murdered body dumped in a creek." Aarti laughed, looking around the halls like she expected a masked accomplice to jump out at any moment.

Norris had spent days trying to figure out how to deliver on the special evening that Maddie had promised. Creative and personal. The personal was easy; Norris just hoped that what he had planned qualified as special. And not in a bad, murder-y kind of way.

Aarti wore short-shorts and an open jacket with a peacock bedazzled on the back. Her hair was still slightly wet at the tips, meaning that she either dashed off in a hurry or spent a good hour in front of the mirror perfecting every aspect of this look. Norris could never quite tell which, but his mouth always instantly dried up when he saw her.

"So, you have dates in Canada, right? You're familiar with the concept?" she asked dryly, replacing a stray lock of hair.

"We're still waiting on iPhones, but yes. Yes, we have dates . . . Exhibit A. Ta-da!"

Above them, framed on the ceiling in all its glory, stood Coach Bombay, a pile of hockey urchins behind him. Pool ripples reflected quavering blue across the tagline "He's never coached.

They've never won." On his sharklike wanderings during free period, Norris had discovered where the AV club hoarded their equipment. Norris had "liberated" a projector for the occasion, setting up his all-time favorite movie to project onto the ceiling of the Anderson High Olympic-size (of course) swimming pool. He figured if Aarti couldn't appreciate *The Mighty Ducks*, well . . . he'd cross that bridge.

"Is that a hockey movie?"

Blasphemy.

"*The Mighty Ducks* is a hockey movie the same way *Citizen Kane* is a snow globe movie."

"Really? You want to bring up snow globes right now, Kaplan?"

"Touché."

Their footsteps echoed around the empty facility as Norris led Aarti to a prime viewing location in the bleachers. In a basket were blankets, some recently, if not freshly, microwaved popcorn, and beer.

"Okay, this is actually kind of cool," Aarti admitted. "But seriously: the second you try to murder me I am pushing you into that pool with the plugged-in electrical equipment and leaving your body to be violated by the swim team."

"Well, there goes my carefully planned homicide for our second date," Norris retorted, dripping sarcastic regret.

Aarti laughed, and Norris felt himself relax a little.

She must have felt the chemistry too because they barely paid attention to the movie once it started playing. It wasn't that Aarti couldn't appreciate fine hockey culture. It was that they were both far more interested in talking to each other than watching the actual movie. Norris shared the broad strokes of his parents' divorce, and the fact that even though he was bilingual, his brain still defaulted to French, his first of the two languages, when counting or doing math. In return, he learned that Aarti had seen an episode of *Law & Order* at age four and gone through a phase of leaving stray hairs everywhere so her DNA would be trackable if she were to be kidnapped, which lasted until she was twelve.

"We've never lived anywhere else either," Aarti said when Norris revealed that Austin had been his first move. "Well, like maybe two years in Chicago, but I was barely out of the womb, so it doesn't really count for me."

Norris grimaced. "Can't imagine why anybody would willingly come here. It's barely fit for cockroach survival. . . . Although some of the residents might qualify."

"Right?" Aarti laughed. "But compared to the rest of the state, it's not that bad. Austin isn't full-on, *real* Texas. Seriously, the state tree might as well be a cactus covered in NRA bumper stickers."

Norris shuddered. "That sounds like some sort of Orwellian dystopia. With sand."

"You have no idea. If you'd moved anywhere else in Texas, you'd be walking around with cowboy-boot footprints permanently imprinted on both ass cheeks." She paused, as if to figure out how to make her next inquiry.

"I always meant to ask you . . . why didn't you stay with your dad?"

Norris couldn't repress an eye roll before launching into *that* saga. "Dad transferred to a hospital in Vancouver right before we moved. With the new wife and a kid, he doesn't really, quote, 'have room for a teenager,' unquote."

Norris pushed down his irritation at the topic as best as he could, choosing to focus on Aarti instead.

"Standard child-of-divorce baggage. Had to pay extra to check it at the airport."

"Everybody's got their thing." Aarti nodded. "My parents were total world travelers before getting jobs in academia and tying themselves to this patch of dirt."

There was a bitterness to her tone that Norris hadn't heard before. "So does this mean you haven't had that talk with your parents yet? About what you really want to do with your life?"

"Not yet." Aarti looked away, lost in thought. "I remember the first museum we visited as a family. My dad marveled at the classical Impressionist painters but scoffed at any experimental art or photography—he kept saying that anyone could do that nowadays." She shook her head, then seemed to return to herself. "Hey, I didn't tell you, but I actually got a mentor."

"Oh yeah?"

"I'm going to be shadowing, or I guess it's technically an unpaid internship, but I'll be helping out this photographer at her studio downtown. Alayna Kerr? She's phenomenal. She's from Guinea-Bissau and has taken all these amazing photos, met all these people; it's freaking insane. She's, like, barely twenty-five!"

Her eyes were almost sparkling as she spoke.

"How did she end up here?"

"The great melting pot," Aarti said, opening her arms forward dramatically. "I'll be able to go to her studio during free periods, and not having to spend my entire day here keeps me from, y'know, burning this entire school to the ground sometimes."

"I'd start with the gym locker rooms—that way, even if the fire department stops the flames from spreading, you'll still have thrown a wrench into the entire high school football–industrial complex."

Aarti tossed back her head with a burst of laughter.

Something about the sound short-circuited every electrical impulse along Norris's spine. He liked making her laugh. More than that—liked that *she* liked him. Aarti was worldly and cool and, somehow, his misanthropic streak appeared to have found a welcoming audience, which was more than he could say for . . . well, anyone except his parents and Eric, really.

The time was passing so quickly that Norris was surprised when the movie ended. At some point, she'd snuggled up to him, and after playing possum for a few seconds, he'd exhaled and leaned into it.

"If you try to quiz me on any of the finer plot points, I will absolutely fail and argue sabotage," Aarti said as the credits rolled. For all of Norris's carefully planned larceny, smuggling, and breaking and entering, *The Mighty Ducks* had proved to be little more than an elaborate soundtrack. Had they really talked through the whole movie?

Aarti's chin fell sharply onto his chest, but Norris honestly could not care less if she was piercing his skin with a screwdriver right now. They lay there, staring at the lit-up roof of the pool.

Could he . . . ? Dammit, yes: he could and he would.

3 . . . 2 . . . 1.

Somewhere between heartbeats, Norris leaned down and kissed Aarti. It was weirdly more nerve-racking and intimate than kissing her at the movie had been. Aarti's mouth tasted like tea with too much sugar in it, which was the only way tea tasted good anyway. The solid nineteen minutes of making out that followed were a very specific form of awesome. Norris's nerves soon faded away and something about the making out felt incredibly familiar, as though they had been doing this for years now and would for more to come.

Just then, the pool doors burst open, and Norris instinctively recoiled from Aarti.

"Aw," a gravelly voice echoed around the pool. "Young love, ain't that sweet?"

Mr. Goade, in a disturbingly tight and small swimsuit and flip-flops, sounded more amused than disapproving at the sight.

"What was the movie?"

"Um . . . *The Mighty Ducks.*"

"Ah." Goade nodded approvingly. "Fine cinematic achievement. I know you're still relatively new, Norris, but you do know you are not allowed to be here at this hour, right?" he commented, taking in their setup.

"Um, neither are you," Aarti said, looking away and covering both eyes with her hand.

"Also, why are you naked?!" Norris blurted out, opting to cover the sight of Goade's body from the neck down with his hand. "Please address the nakedness!"

"I'm obviously not naked on school premises," Mr. Goade said calmly. Through his fingers, Norris could see the chemistry teacher place by the bleachers the small duffel bag he was carrying, alongside a frayed gray-green towel, which he was taking his time spreading out. A distant part of Norris admired his lack of body shame. "If you two would stop the theatrics, you'd see I'm working a bathing suit."

"No, that's a freaking Speedo, dude!" What the hell was wrong with this country?

"These are brand-new swim trunks," Goade said, now sounding a little defensive. "Maybe a little snug . . ."

"If it takes a V-shape like that, it's definitely a size too small, Mr. Goade," Aarti said, still looking away, stifling her laugher.

"Noted, Miss Puri," Goade said, actually stretching. "Although, unlike certain parties, I actually have a key to this building, granting me access after hours. Cheaper than a gym membership these days. And just what exactly might those bottles contain?"

"Canadian soda," Norris quickly lied. "Imported."

"Canadian soda," Goade casually repeated as he slowly stepped out of his flip-flops and lowered a very retro-looking pair of swim goggles from the top of his head. "Tell you what?

I'm going to jump into this pool and take exactly five laps, as recommended by my asshole of a cardiologist. Afterward, I will be tempted to take a sip of this Canadian soda. Unless you two lovebirds find a way out of here before I'm done."

Norris and Aarti exchanged quick looks. There was definitely no making out left to be had at this swimming pool.

"Say no more. We were just heading out. Right, Aarti?"

"Yes, right. Lap away, Mr. Goade," Aarti quickly added, already grabbing the nearest beer. "We'll be out of your hair in a second."

They left the projector on a bench outside the AV club for someone else to deal with, and it wasn't until they were safely at Aarti's car that they permitted themselves to laugh, doubled over against the passenger-side door.

"So how does a half-naked chemistry teacher rank, date-wise?" he asked.

The ten additional minutes of car-leaning makeout and giggles that followed were answer enough for Norris.

22

MCELWEES FAMILY TREE

ORIGINS: Irish? Presumably Irish. Sounds Irelandish.

DISTINGUISHING TRAITS: Bright blue eyes, freckled arms, skinny (with one exception), booming cackle of a laugh.

PATRIARCH: Jim McElwees (the exception).

MATRIARCH: Mia Jeanine McElwees.

DAUGHTERS: Livvie Carroll (thirty-four), Mindee (thirty-one), Marion (twenty-six), Malcolm (twenty), Madison (sixteen)

INCOMING SON-IN-LAW: Robert "Bobby" Posnanski.

GRANDCHILDREN: Gale and Cactus (note: everyone understandably prefers to call them "the twins." I mean, good God).

"Your father is an insane person," Norris bemoaned to Maddie as he rolled his apron into a bundle and discarded it over an old stack of laminated kids' menus under the counter. Key lime season was, in fact, as brutal as advertised. Even with a giant family wedding looming days away, Big Jim still found a second pocket of energy to double down on the pie promotion.

"Energy, people! The limes are delicious this year, the graham cracker crust is hand mixed. Let's make some magic and then make sure there's one on every table of not only the dining room, but also the greater Austin area."

The Bone Yard currently was in its postlunch haze anyway, so it was all hands on deck in managing the output of key lime, cream, and graham cracker that had become their lives. Because he always reimbursed the gas, Big Jim considered these delivery runs to be a quirk of the job; sort of like making fresh coffee whenever the pot was empty. Julio swore Jim was so obsessed he once saw him take a bite out of an actual lime, which sounded ridiculous at first, but Norris was beginning to find it increasingly believable.

"You come from insane stock. Test your kids for the recessive insanity gene."

"You don't get to play innocent now," Maddie said as she grabbed the first stack of pie boxes from the delivery counter, a ring of keys around her finger. "You were adequately warned."

Norris snatched the second half, along with the printout of the delivery schedule, and followed her out to the parking lot. The past few weeks had, as promised, been a key lime nightmare for all Bone Yard employees. Forty to sixty pies were produced every day and Austin's demand was only rising. Norris had already gotten an outrageous number of paper cuts while folding sheets of lime-green cardboard into boxes, and just that morning Judith had leaned into Norris by the microwave, taken a whiff of his head, and asked if he accidentally used lemon-scented floor cleaner as shampoo.

To make matters worse, the delivery situation was still in flux, and in the late afternoons, it often came down to whoever was available to make the local rounds. The fact that he didn't have a driver's license meant that he was consistently the one charged with the car-to-door portion of the delivery; the only benefits were the occasional at-the-door tips he got. Julio and Cheryl were both "sick" to study for their University of Texas finals. The backup delivery team more often than not consisted of Norris and Maddie these days. In fact, between closing the restaurant on Tuesday, Friday, and Sunday evenings and this key lime situation Norris was spending as much time in Maddie's car as Liam's. They'd been having more practices than ever as they prepared for their very first game. Norris had been skeptical at first, but Liam had found them a local league that seemed legit, with an actual website that did not appear to have been crafted by a lonely murderer in his basement as a ploy to bring his victims into the light.

"You really need to get a driver's license," Maddie noted as they pulled into a residential area of East Austin filled with small one-floor homes and front yards littered with toys, bikes, and plastic cars. Norris grabbed the box and went up to deliver the order. Two minutes later, he was back.

"Godammit!"

Norris slammed the door to Maddie's car and settled into the passenger seat with a scowl on his face.

"Prank order?" Maddie preemptively guessed.

"Prank order. I even heard giggling behind the door." He checked the scribbled name on the dashboard's delivery log. "M. Ockhurts? Max Ockhurts, maybe? I can't even make it out. . . ."

"Mike," Maddie decoded with a groan. "Mike Ockhurts. *My cock hurts*. C'mon, Dad: How did he not catch this one?"

Stunts like these weren't altogether unprecedented at the Bone Yard. Big Jim's dream of One Pie in Every Home for the Greater Austin Area meant that he was likely to fall for these sorts of things. Anyone who expressed a passing interest in advertising his pies got a stack of express-shipped flyers at their door the same afternoon, detailed descriptions of ingredient sourcing over the phone, and he had even entertained the idea of mailing freeze-dried pie slice samples around town before his wife and daughters put an end to that costly plan. His optimism when it came to his key lime pursuit was charming enough to Norris but also one of the few things that drove Maddie—who was otherwise made of Teflon when it came to dealing with her father's antics—up the absolute wall.

"And of course this was a cash order," she moaned. "God, why is that even still an option? . . . Credit cards only! Even food trucks are going paperless these days! To deliver to someone's home without insurance is just bonkers. You're asking to be prank called."

Norris nearly jumped back when she then reached into his lap midrant. "*What* are you doing?!"

"Using every part of the buffalo, Canada. This has been in the car all afternoon," she said, moving the box to her own lap and pulling out two wrapped sets of plastic utensils from her glove compartment. "If it's not eaten soon, it'll go bad. Also, I'm starving."

"You want to eat this here?"

"Why not?"

The question came with an unwrapped fork dangling toward him, and Norris actually had no valid counterargument. Not to mention that he was feeling a little peckish himself. Dealing with key lime nonsense at every shift still didn't negate the primary characteristic that the damn things were freaking delicious. Mouthwatering, really.

Norris sighed as he took the fork. They spent the next hour parked in front of the house of what was sure to be an increasingly panicked phone prankster as they fell into an easy rhythm of reaching into the key lime box. Norris liked talking to Maddie. His mouth occasionally took over, but he never got *that* look from her, like he'd accidentally stumbled onto a spell that turned the ground into quicksand; or the entire world. Maybe that was why so many people liked her; she gave them room to fumble.

"And how are things with Aarti?"

"Good!" Norris exclaimed, and realized that he meant it. Ever since their date at the pool, he and Aarti had been spending more time together, and he was starting to feel more relaxed around her. He'd even eased off on the overly clever texting Maddie had called him out on. "Regular texting. Second base, if you want to bring baseball into the equation. Things are really, really good." He knocked on the wooden panel as punctuation.

"Oh," Maddie said, looking more confused than Norris would have liked at the assertion that he wasn't blowing things with Aarti.

"You sound surprised?" Norris said. But Maddie's face remained pensive.

"No. That's great, Canada. Really." She smiled, though it almost looked wistful. "I knew you had it in you."

For her part, Maddie caught him up on the various goings-on of the squad, which Norris was content to just nod along to. When it was his turn, Norris talked about his own family; his nominal cousins who lived in Haitian pockets all over the map, who he didn't really keep in touch with, and all the disgusting memes that he still received from his hockey team back home.

"Is it weird to still be hearing from them, but not be part of the team anymore?"

Norris shrugged.

"A little, but it's okay," he admitted. "I have a new team now, which helps. And I can definitely live without all the gross stuff guys feel the compulsive need to share.

"Like, imagine getting this at two in the morning!" he said, bringing his phone close to Maddie's face to show her the last one he'd received from an old teammate, Antoine.

"Pig creatures!" She gagged once she understood what exactly she was looking at. "Jesus, we're really late. We should head back."

She was right. Norris looked back to the house where the porch light was now turned on and two adult silhouettes were definitely staring at them from the living room window.

"Yeah, we should go before I'm arrested for loitering while black. And key lime intoxicated." He nodded. "By the way, don't think I don't see through your obvious ulterior motives for coming with me on these deliveries."

Maddie froze. "Is that right?"

"Yup," Norris said confidently. "You can't fool me. Big McElwees wedding ahead. A million family members in town: Do I even have to ask how the McElwees household is coping?"

Maddie moaned and then groaned, maybe both at the same time. "It's a nightmare, Canada."

Norris laughed. He was pretty sure that every surface of the Bone Yard was currently covered in beaded lights, ready to be unleashed for the event.

Maddie went on to explain the household insanity as they drove on through the orange-lit streets of Austin. The main thing about the McElweeses was that there were a lot of them. A bucketload, as it turned out; spread out all over Texas and beyond. Norris's first thought upon seeing the framed photo of the whole clan in the Bone Yard's back room, all dressed in purple-and-gold turtlenecks for the whimsical portrait had been that he was looking at the very blond cast of a wacky sitcom. *The Tackies* on ABC Family.

Maddie herself was youngest of five despite the fact that she steered the ship like a true matriarch-in-training. Mindee and Malcolm would sometimes stop by the restaurant to say hi to their dad. Norris secretly thought it was probably to ask for money.

Beyond that, Norris was only roughly acquainted with the older, non-Maddie McElwees children. Marion (named for their grandmother, according to Maddie) was the one getting married. She was nice enough, in her midtwenties, and still lived in town with her fiancé, which meant that Norris got to see her in person every few weeks at least. She was tall, a former varsity tennis player of Anderson High herself, and now worked in law but wasn't a lawyer. Livvie was the eldest, definitely in her early thirties and mother to the twins. She had an efficient hairdo and lived in Houston with her wife and their three kids. Big Jim had sent them a stack of seven pies when key lime season had started.

This was without accounting for all the cousins and off-the-stump branches of the McElwees garden that were coming into town for the wedding. There was apparently even a family newsletter. The family discount was working a double shift at the restaurant as more and more "_____ McElwees" (Joe, Lynn, John) dropped their last name when the check came, expecting the number to magically turn to zero.

"More cousins keep arriving every day too!" Maddie said, guiding the car into a convenience store parking lot, Maddie's offhand "Let's get slushies" the only explanation. Maybe the sudden, random craving was a stress thing, but Norris wasn't complaining. "It's not a giant house like Meredith's! I keep tripping over sleeping bags in the morning, and Dad actually got whiteboards up to keep track of bathroom rotations. It's like a summer camp nightmare that won't end. Why is booking a hotel room a family slight, anyway? We love you, glad you're in town, have

218

some cake on the wedding day, but, like, please poop elsewhere for the preceding week!"

"That's definitely a Haitian thing too," Norris mused. The bored-looking clerk barely looked up from his phone as Norris and Maddie entered the otherwise empty store; fewer than five minutes later they were back in the car, slushies acquired.

"My mom gives up her bed whenever my aunt Rose visits us," he continued, no longer tired. "It's just this unspoken thing that *has* to happen. My mom hates it. She grumbles every time she visits. Meanwhile, she's buying new sheets, new pillows, even leaving a little mint on there too. Last time, she kept placing hotel flyers on the kitchen table, but Aunt Rose just wouldn't take the hint. Like, why would she? Her sister literally breaks out the silverware for her when she visits! So it's two whole weeks of Mom going insane, overcompensating by turning the bed every other day, and Aunt Rose leaves thinking she can't wait until the next time she visits."

"Jeez, I can't wait to get to college, to at least have my dorm room as a buffer." She sighed wistfully.

"That's as far as you're going, then?" Norris inquired after a long, loud slurp. "The University of Texas?"

Maddie raised a listless arm from the steering wheel, giant slushie straw still in her mouth, and made a half fist extending her forefinger and pinky outward, somewhere between rock and roll and devil worshipping. Hook 'em Horns; the universal sign of solidarity for the University of Texas football team. The gesture was almost second nature to her—as it was to anyone who spent more than a few weeks in Austin. In the past four months, Norris had seen it from elderly little ladies in plastic visors and drunken businessmen in wrinkled business suits.

"And what's wrong with UT, you snob? Doesn't your mom teach there?"

"Nothing, it's a great school," Norris fumbled. "I—just—you're going to be here forever? Down the street? That's it?"

She shrugged, not seeming particularly offended, thank God.

"That's a whole lot. All my friends are here. My family. I want to see the world, sure, but that's what vacations are for. I don't think I would consider anywhere else home," Maddie said, as if pondering the question for herself. "Don't think I could, to be honest."

"But how do you know?" Norris pressed. He honestly would trade a pair of NHL playoff tickets for a fraction of Madison McElwees's self-assurance and confidence in how life was going to turn out. Most days, Norris could barely picture life past his next meal. His longest-term goal thus far had been the trip to Whistler.

"I just do," Maddie added as they pulled toward his building. "We're here."

How many rides had she given him for her to know the way to his place by heart? Norris was beginning to feel like a freeloader. She looked at him for a moment as they pulled up to his building.

"Right. Thanks for the ri—" Norris began, unbuckling his belt.

"Wait! Er, I have something for you," she said, pulling a white envelope with a pearly lace ribbon around its flap from her purse. Norris knew what these envelopes were. The last time he had seen it, it was stacked with 184 identical replicas in a cardboard box on Big Jim's desk.

"A wedding invitation?"

"Yeah, I was thinking you might want to come. Y'know, if you want. You're a member of the Bone Yard family, Canada."

Norris smiled at the piece of ornate card stock. It was a very nice invitation. Norris had actually never been to a wedding before.

"And I know you're not a church guy, so you can totally skip that and just show up to the Bone Yard after for the reception. It's basically going to be a very well-dressed picnic."

Norris nodded gratefully; Liam had already scheduled practice that Saturday, but he should have enough time to shower and change before the reception.

Something about the invitation coming free of any stipulations, quid pro quo, or additional shift to cover felt important to Norris. *A guest of the family.*

"Thanks, Maddie," he simply said, preferring to avoid unnecessary mushiness that might embarrass both of them.

23

THE DRUNK FRIEND

IDENTIFYING CHARACTERISTICS: Slurring of speech, rude suggestions, misplacement of phone.

OTHER FACTS: Society dictates not leaving the drunk friend in a ditch. Typically occurs with the least-liked acquaintance, because of course.

WARNING: Vomit could be splattered upon you at any time.

Practice that Saturday was, dare he say, good.

Norris had been watching the team with trepidation, with just a few weeks to prepare for their first-ever game, but he was having trouble finding fault with their play. Shannon had proved to be a natural on defense, Brett was an excellent goalie, and even Patrick—who *of course* wanted to play forward—was making good progress with his stick handling. If Norris weren't predisposed to assume total nuclear fallout at all times, he might even say they had a good shot at winning their game.

Norris and Liam finished picking up the equipment and joined the rest of the team in the parking lot, only to realize that Patrick had manifested a case of beers. Though he was tempted, Norris abstained from the proffered can; he needed to go home, shower, change, and make it to the reception for the McElwees wedding. He was surprised to find he was actually kind of . . . *excited*? to head to the party the whole Bone Yard crew had spent months prepping for. All in all, he thought, this was turning out to be one of Norris's most successful Austin days.

That was the exact moment Patrick chose to projectile vomit everywhere.

Patrick was, as it turned out, already quite shit-faced. Neither Norris nor Liam had a handle on exactly how many of the beers he had drunk, but out of a case of twenty-four, at least seven had gone to him.

"No worries, folks. Lamarra is just down with a cold!" Norris said, because nothing could diffuse a budding team like one of the key players projectile vomiting Lone Star all over one of his new teammates.

"No wonder he was so loose on the ice," Norris grumbled, putting a groggy and barely coherent Patrick on the back seat of Liam's car and beginning the unfun process of patting him down for a cell phone–shaped lump. The posthockey, post-vomit smell likewise wasn't amazing.

"Who drinks seven beers before four p.m.?"

Norris had noticed that there was a recklessness to how

223

American teens drank. At Meredith's, around the school parking lot, before prescheduled hockey practices, they did it because someone told them they couldn't. Maybe the same thing was happening back in Montreal too, and he had simply missed that window there.

"You're assuming that he hadn't been drinking before practice," Liam said, throwing an almost knowing look into his rearview mirror to the back seat. "That's not seven-beers drunk."

"Did you find his cell phone?"

They pulled out of the warehouse's parking lot, waving to the car of one of the other players who honked them goodbye. Liam's turning on of the ignition had barely elicited a whisper from the top-of-the-line engine.

"No!" Norris groaned. "Patrick, buddy, where's your cell? We need to contact your girlfriend, parents, a really nice neighbor. . . ."

With a dramatic amount of effort, Patrick gestured toward a window, and whatever that actually meant, it was clear that there was no phone to be had on the premises. Phone, elsewhere.

"Goddammit." Norris sighed. He climbed off Patrick and into the passenger seat as nimbly as possible at the first red light. Things had gone too well today; Stephen Fuller Austin's ghost was awake and demanded penance.

"What do we do with him?" Liam asked. "We have to help him."

"Do we? He did push me down a flight of stairs," Norris said.

"You were being a little bitch," Patrick mumbled out of nowhere.

"Dude," Norris snapped. "We will leave you by the side of the goddamn highway!"

"No, we won't." Liam sighed, not even letting Norris have his bluff.

"I wish I remembered his girlfriend's address. . . ." Norris trailed off, trying to remember the route to Meredith's, and failing. This was likely Meredith's mess anyway; dating her probably required constant lubrication.

"My house isn't an option," Liam said solemnly.

"Why not?"

"Trust me," Liam said. "It's just not. My parents wouldn't . . . react well to me bringing a drunk guy from school home."

"No shit," Patrick snorted from the back seat, suddenly drunkenly alert again. "Hey, Mom, I know I had a full mental breakdown last year, but here's a drunk-ass dude for your couch." He then laughed to himself.

"What do you mean?" Norris asked aloud to the rearview mirror.

"I get it, man. Life's hard. It's cool!" Patrick's drunken hand reached over Liam's head and attempted to pat it, grazing his ear twice instead.

"Patrick, buddy, I'm going to need you to shut up right now," Liam said calmly.

"Wait, is that true?" Norris asked.

"Ignore it," Liam quickly answered, purposely avoiding looking Norris's way. "He's obviously incoherent."

Liam was now driving in a way that seemed equally stressed and nonchalant, all clenched jaw and occasional glances to Patrick through the rearview.

"Right. Um, well, I have a Haitian mother," Norris countered. "She will ship me to Haiti before letting me fall prey to your decadent American ways."

That might have been an exaggeration, but Norris really wasn't ready to have Liam Hooper (of the multiple-sports-utility-vehicle-household Hoopers) and Patrick (who until very recently was Hairy Armpits in all his stories to Judith) look around their tiny apartment. He just wasn't.

"Well, we can't just drop him off at a hospital," Liam said. "I mean, can we?"

Only one other alternative came to mind.

"Take a left on Guadalupe," Norris instructed with a sigh of resignation. Goddammit.

It had seemed like a good idea at the time . . . which might one day be the title of a Norris Kaplan biography.

Norris and Liam had snuck through the back with Patrick in tow, both carrying one heavy drunk arm around their neck because, of course, he'd lost the use of his legs once they pulled into the Bone Yard's at-capacity parking lot. Norris never again wanted to be anywhere near Patrick Lamarra's post–hockey game armpits. The smell of Axe Chocolate could severely alter the local wildlife.

Even during peak post–Longhorns game frenzy, Norris had

never seen this many vehicles in the parking lot. Maddie hadn't been answering her phone, probably in the middle of a toast during his three calls, but they had no other option. Julio had been the one to open the door and had been dispatched to go get Maddie for them without telling anyone.

Norris could hear the sounds of the festivities coming through the back. Laughter and chatter rising into the early evening air, heavy with the scent of food, and clattering of utensils Norris knew so well by now. The wedding was in full swing.

"Hmm," Patrick moaned, breathing hot, drunk-ass air into Norris's neck. "I know here. . . . Why are we here?"

"The last resort." Norris sighed.

"Maaaddie!" Patrick suddenly said, his head bursting forward, startling both Norris and Liam.

"Um . . . . hi, guys?" Maddie greeted them, appearing in front of the back entrance of the Bone Yard. She looked unsure of what it was she was even seeing. Her dress was the same turquoise color as those worn by a handful of other women that Norris had seen, with a black ribbon around her waist that matched the one in her hair. *She looks beautiful*, Norris thought, before shaking the thought away.

"Maddie! Hey, girl," Patrick slurred. "Mad. Eee. Mah. Dee."

"Hi, Pat," Maddie said, as if to a toddler, giving Patrick—her ex-boyfriend, Norris reminded himself—a hesitant once-over before turning to Norris for an explanation.

"His owners didn't tag him," Norris said, jutting his shoulder

227

and causing Patrick's head to sway from his shoulder to Liam's. "Very irresponsible."

Maddie had no ponytail to undo and retie slightly more tightly, as she normally would. Her hair was instead curled and assembled in a complex sculpture that didn't really match her face. *Bridesmaid hair*, Norris thought. A little awkward and clearly not optional.

"This isn't what I had in mind when I invited you, Canada," she said.

"Hi. Madison, right? Look, we're sorry to bother you," Liam noted. "We didn't know what to do, and he's . . . very drunk."

"This is Liam," Norris continued. "He's sober."

"Neither of us knows where he lives, we couldn't find his phone, and you two are close, or were close, and I know you're in the middle of a big family wedding right now, but um . . ." Norris offered in a single breath. "Long story short: we demand shelter."

"I guess he is real." Maddie finally sighed with a skeptical look at Liam, stepping aside and waving them into the kitchens. "Welcome to the Bone Yard, Liam. We'll get Patrick upstairs, get him some water, and there's plenty of food. I can call his cousins after the speeches. Meredith is at her aunt's in Houston."

"Um . . ." Liam asked quietly as they maneuvered their way through the steaming kitchens, a few steps behind Maddie, "is there a reason why she just snorted at my existence?"

"Well, apparently, you coming up to me wanting to learn

hockey was a flimsy backstory," Norris explained. "She thought you were my imaginary friend."

"Interesting. I could be," Liam conceded. "I could be imaginary. Reality is a matter of optics."

Norris rolled his eyes as they followed Maddie through the kitchen, which was currently bustling. For the occasion of the wedding, the regular Bone Yard staff had been replaced by one of Austin's premiere catering services, which consisted of extremely focused chefs putting final touches on their masterpieces and a flurry of cater waiters from the catering service walking through and circling them with perfectly balanced trays of tiny food. The inconvenience of four teenagers—one thoroughly sloshed—did not seem to be a concern for them at the moment.

"So, drunken party crashers aside, how are the festivities going?" Norris offered as they followed Maddie.

"Let's see," Maddie said, throwing a quick glance to her phone. "One lost necklace, one baseless accusation of necklace thievery, two bridesmaids feuding, and one spilled tray of drinks in mason jars, which revealed the necklace to be in another family member's purse."

No wonder the cater waiters were keeping their backs stiff. As far as large emotional gatherings of large emotional people went, the McElwees family wasn't for beginners.

"Sorry to be adding to your plate," Liam said sheepishly.

Maddie smiled to him as if the two were already friends.

"Nonsense! Everything's right on schedule," Maddie said,

distractedly tracking for an opening in the foot traffic that would presumably let them get to the restaurant's second floor. "You did the right thing bringing him here."

"Nice dress, by the way," Norris said, without knowing why he said it.

"Thanks. We usually ditch the leggings and pom-poms for anything that comes with shrimp puffs."

"Very good. Blue, but also a little green, which is very good also, obviously."

Norris clocked the slow, deliberate rising of Liam's eyebrow.

"Turquoise," she laughed. "Remind me to include color palettes in our lessons."

Turquoise was her color; she looked wholesome in a way that could probably sell a thousand units of that dress in department stores around the country, to girls of all ages hoping for a similar outcome.

"Looking good from behind too, Madz," Patrick slurred, coming back alive. Maddie ignored him and pushed forward, gently moving stray guests who had wandered inside for the AC out of her way by touching a shoulder here and there with a Sears catalog smile, apparently unbothered by the fact that Patrick was openly ogling her.

"Madz and I used to date, y'know," Patrick said to Liam.

"A long time ago, dummy," Maddie said without any bite.

"We were good together, though," Patrick slurred, restless, which Maddie pretended not to hear as she collected half a dozen water bottles from a nearby table.

230

"All right, the coast is clear," she whispered as they headed up the stairs. Pulling the two-hundred-pound mass that was Patrick up the narrow wooden stairs of the Bone Yard required some readjustment from both Liam and Norris, and Norris slipped his arm to Patrick's lower back.

"Hands above the waist," Patrick slurred. "Don't be a fag, dude."

Norris abruptly released his hold.

"Oww!" Patrick mewled, tripping forward and falling into the banister, headfirst.

"Norris!" Maddie chastised, turning around at the crash. "He's obviously drunk."

"No, he's obviously an asshole," Norris corrected. "The drunk is just helping it come up to the surface."

The rest of the stairs were navigated in complete silence.

Maddie fished a set of keys out of her tiny turquoise clutch purse and handed them to Norris. "Dad's office is locked. No one should bother you there. I'll send water up soon."

Norris hated the idea that he might just be the latest in a string of people to take advantage of her generosity like this. He reminded himself that it wasn't technically him—it was Patrick's dumb ass.

They put Patrick down onto the sofa with as much gentleness as Norris could muster in his heart right now, which was absolutely none. Patrick winced as he was dropped, prompting Liam to throw Norris another dark look. This one, Norris happily returned.

"Please make sure he doesn't throw up on anything," Maddie implored.

"How are we supposed to control his intestinal floors?" Norris asked with crossed arms. Liam was right—he had rapidly lost all interest in Hairy Armpits's well-being.

"Obscure Canadian healing techniques?" She shrugged. "If he does, Dad will be able to smell it, and he'll piece it together, trust me. He turns into freaking CSI whenever underage drinking is involved. All our heads will roll." Maddie adjusted her dress in a mirror hanging from the wall and whacked Patrick upside the head on her way out.

"Ow!"

"You deserve that."

They'd been in the office for a few hours now.

Norris texted his mom to tell her he was at the Bone Yard and got a **be good** and lips emoji in reply. Maddie had a cater waiter drop off a few bottles of iced water and a tray of hors d'oeuvres for them, and an empty ice bucket, texting Norris that she was being held up. Before Norris could inquire, she sent him a photo of herself posing with six more women dressed in slightly different versions of the same turquoise dress, smiling brightly. Right. They'd crashed her family wedding after all.

Norris texted her that they had the situation under control and settled in on Big Jim's chair, throwing a look over to Liam who was thumbing through one of Big Jim's books on the history of the jalapeño.

232

"Hey, are you all right? You've been a little weird since the car."

Liam shrugged, without looking up from the book. "Don't worry about it."

A weird tension had developed between Norris and Liam since Patrick had made the comment about Liam having a mental breakdown. Norris had no idea how much truth Patrick's drunken assertion held and was waiting for Liam to say something about it, but he was pretty sure that if it weren't for Patrick's intermittent seismic snoring, they would be sitting in complete silence.

"You can leave, y'know," Liam offered. "I'll look after him."

Under the fourteen layers of calm and collectedness that made up Liam's epidermis, he could sense that Liam was angry with him. For what, Norris had no idea. This had been an unexpectedly trying day.

"It's okay. I'll stay."

"Why?" Liam inquired. "He's not your responsibility. And you obviously hate him."

"Do you really not have a problem with him being a bigot?"

"I'm not defending what he said."

"You're kind of defending what he said," Norris challenged. "Why are you staying?"

"He's a teammate," Liam answered. "That means something."

Norris exhaled in frustration. Liam definitely wasn't imaginary; Norris's imaginary best friend when he was six was a floating chaise longue, laughing at all his jokes. He would never invent someone this complicated.

They could hear the faint echoes of heartfelt speeches followed by rounds of clapping in the backyard. Norris had been curious to check out the reception before this entire mess.

Patrick began to stir in his drunken stupor and then quickly sat up with a hand tightly keeping his vomit-filled mouth shut. "Mmbathroom," he mumbled. "Mmbathroom mmnow."

Before Liam could do it, Norris rushed over to his side to hand him the empty ice bucket. Maddie's foresight was definitely impressive, Norris thought before suddenly stopping short, keeping the bucket just out of Patrick's reach.

Judith called these "teaching moments."

"Y'know, I've been on the verge of liking you lately," Norris warned, holding the bucket at bay. "But use that word again and I won't bother to pee on you even if you're fatally stung by a jellyfish and your life can only be saved by my pee."

"Norris . . ." Liam started.

"Sorry, Liam, but this is really between me and Pat here."

Patrick frowned in confusion, definitely looking the part of someone between stomach virus and food poisoning, but Norris wasn't buying it.

"You know what word," he said simply. "You might not care, but I'll never speak to you again, let alone play hockey or any other ice-based sport with you. Are we good?"

Patrick nodded frantically and a few wretches later the bucket was no longer empty. After downing all the bottles of water on hand, he returned to the couch, like a giant cat, wrapping himself in a nearby throw blanket with the Longhorn logo.

"Do you want to try calling your parents? Even if you lie about where you are?" Norris asked Patrick, putting a stray towel over the pungent bucket of bile. "They have to be getting worried by now."

"That'd be incorrec . . . incurr . . . wrong," Patrick slurred, wiping his mouth. "My parents are in fucking San Antonio, dude."

"Like all weekend?"

"Most weekends," Patrick mumbled, falling back into the sofa, snoring wetly again.

Norris and Liam shared a look. He had no idea what the home life was like that led to someone like Patrick Lamarra, but it couldn't be a fun one, all things considered.

"Um, I need some air," Liam suddenly said, standing up. "The vomit is getting to me. . . . I'm going to go for a walk. I'll be back."

"O-okay," Norris said, left alone with Patrick's snoring and the bucket of vomit. It seemed like a fine metaphor for the turn this day had taken.

A half hour later, Liam was still missing in action. Norris had sent him a text but hadn't received any replies yet. He did however receive a new text from Aarti. It consisted of a dish emoji and two brown heads, one male one female and then a question mark. As it turned out, tiny drawings was one of her favorite means of communication. Something about the photographer in her liked to see how people interpreted them. Norris kept a loose log of all the obscure ones she'd used with him in his notebook and what their meaning had turned out to be. She seemed vaguely disappointed whenever she had to actually translate them into words when he was stumped. This one, however, only amounted to "brown people eating" in Norris's mind. To be fair, it had been a long day. Was she asking him to grab a bite to eat?

Norris thought about looping her into the situation for counsel, but no matter how much he wished he could see Aarti, it felt like too many questions to answer. A hockey practice turned into wedding siege, being sequestered with a vomiting football player, Liam being weird. Norris didn't quite know where to start.

"So, how are we doing up here?" Maddie asked, coming into the room and startling Norris out of his reply to Aarti. It wasn't urgent; he could get back to her later.

"Good enough," Norris said, putting his phone away. "Um, did you see Liam down there?"

"No, but I was loading gifts into the cars, so I might have missed him," Maddie explained, kicking off her shoes and making the sound all girls and women made when removing uncomfortable heels.

"You're too nice," Norris noted with a sigh.

"Where did he go?" She frowned, rubbing her heels.

Patrick yawned and scratched at his belly. The guy had a

236

remarkable ability to bounce from moments of tension to this weird, aggro cheerfulness—the human version of an expressive set of dog ears.

"The wedding crowd is starting to thin out," Maddie said. "I'll wait until the happy couple has been dismissed and drive Patrick home."

"Thanks, Madz." Patrick smiled at his ex-girlfriend.

Maddie smiled back and Norris found himself annoyed again, like he did whenever he tried to imagine the two of them making out the way Meredith and Patrick did in basically every doorway of the school.

"Although, I don't need supervision." Patrick groaned.

"Yes, you do," Maddie and Norris agreed in unison.

"Yo, did Liam really bail on us?" Patrick asked, stretching from the sofa and looking around like a kid just waking up from a nap. "That's rude."

You projectile vomited this afternoon, Norris considered bringing up.

"No. I don't know, maybe," he said instead, cracking open a water bottle. For all he knew, Liam had really left. He seemed genuinely upset, though, at what, Norris still had no idea.

"What happened?" Maddie inquired, bringing her legs up on the sofa. She looked earnestly curious but understandably exhausted.

"No clue," Norris said, although that wasn't totally true. Things had been strained ever since Patrick's comment in the car. "Actually, he's been weird since this guy said something about, like, a mental breakdown?"

"Oh, it's *that* Liam!" Maddie exclaimed before turning to smack Patrick's arm.

"Wait, what?" Norris asked.

Maddie shrugged. "I hadn't realized that your convenient friend that you hang out with when you're not roaming the halls alone was, y'know, Liam-Liam. Anderson is a big school, but something like that doesn't happen without everyone hearing."

"Hearing about what, Maddie? I'm so confused."

Maddie looked genuinely remorseful.

"Dude tried to off himself," Patrick said.

Tried to off himself?

"Maddie, is that true?"

"I don't—" Maddie paused, interrupting herself. "You're his friend, Norris. Isn't that a question for Liam?" Her tone was measured. Norris could tell this would be her final word on the matter.

"This is your fault, Patrick!" Norris snapped at Patrick, feeling the need to blame someone for the situation. "Why did you have to go and out him as a Prozac popper in the car?!"

"Wellbutrin, actually," came Liam's cool voice. It was the exact same tone he always had, and his face matched it. If he wasn't standing in the doorway, holding a couple of plates, there would be no way to tell he'd just overheard Norris being a complete asshole.

Shit.

Fuck.

Shitfuckcocknuggetasshole.

"Hi," Norris quickly said, followed by "Hello, hey, what's up!" Greetings were now incantations that might hopefully rewind time in five second bursts.

"Are you ready to go?"

"Yeah, yeah, I think so," Norris said, looking around for something to do. Anything but make eye contact right now.

"I figured we deserved some cake," Liam said with pursed lips.

"Thanks, dude!" Patrick said, snatching a piece of cake and biting into it like he hadn't just expelled a bucket of viscera.

"Thanks for hosting us, Madison," Liam added. "It was very welcoming of you."

"Um, y-y-yeah, of course," Maddie said, throwing Norris a glare. "It was great to officially meet you, Liam. You should stop by more often."

"I'll be in the car when you guys are ready to leave." Liam nodded tightly before exiting the room. "Take your time. The cake's really good."

All three watched as Liam put down the cake slices and exited the room with a stiff back.

"Dude," Patrick said disapprovingly, mouth full with cake. "Way harsh."

"How bad was that?" Norris asked Maddie, hands over his face. Eviscerating Patrick wouldn't help in this situation. This one was on him.

"Go talk to him," Maddie urged, her voice channeling so

much concern that it was rapidly filling Norris's stomach with bile. He could use his own bucket right now.

"You're being too nice, it's freaking me out."

"Go talk to him, you northern hillbilly."

"Better," Norris replied, as he headed out to the car.

24

THE DREADED HEART-TO-HEART

POTENTIAL LIAM HOOPER REVELATIONS TO BRACE FOR:
"My parents are going through a divorce."
"I have a crippling porn addiction."
"I've been having an affair with Mrs. Kolb."
"I've been having an affair with Mr. Goade."
"So, you know squirrels? I kind of find them sexy. Always have."

Norris found Liam in the driver's seat of his car, in the back of the Bone Yard's parking lot. After knocking on the glass, he was granted a seat in the car, where Liam was apparently content to sit in silence, which to Norris was a very specific trapdoor at the bottom of hell. He would rather plan fifteen dates for Aarti or mud wrestle Ian than deal with this level of guilt and awkwardness.

"Maddie is going to drive Patrick home," he said, settling into the car. "His car is still at the warehouse, so that's one less hassle for us."

Why was he so bad at this? Norris wanted to apologize, but he also felt as though Liam had gotten too close, grabbed his hand, and shoved it deep into his guts. This was all way too close for comfort.

Even under controlled laboratory circumstances, Norris was known to occasionally say something that left people wide-eyed and stunned. Or, in the worst cases, always accidental, genuinely hurt. Only afterward, in that awkward silence that would stretch from minutes to days, would he realize what had happened. Sometimes it came weeks later, when Norris would notice that a social media contact had unfriended him after some perceived slight he himself barely remembered. And at that point, it was better for everyone to just move on rather than go into flailing damage control for people who no longer wanted anything to do with him. After all, Norris couldn't control their feelings.

But somehow making up with Liam felt more important than all that.

"Look, I'm really sorry," Norris finally blurted out. "My mouth . . . I flap it sometimes. It's a thing. You've been nothing but nice to me since I got here, and that was a dickish thing to say. Truly. I didn't mean it."

"I know," Liam answered calmly.

"Oh." Norris frowned.

"What?"

"N-n-nothing," Norris stuttered. "I just thought we were going to do the thing where you pretend not to know what I'm talking about for a while before, y'know, delving into it."

"Oh," Liam noted. "Did you want me to?"

"No, no, no." Norris grimaced. "Let's just wax this patch of chest hair."

"Well, I assume you're talking about the Prozac-popper comment."

"That was . . . incredibly insensitive, and I'm sorry." Norris sighed. "I really didn't mean to make light of the whole . . . situation."

"I know." Liam nodded.

"And let's not forget that Patrick was really the one being the throbbing dick on this one. I was more . . .'"

"Flaccid?" Liam chuckled.

"You know what I mean! Mine was accidental. No intent to cause harm, man."

Liam was still looking forward, head leaned back. "The people who cause the most harm never really intend to," he offered.

"Fair enough." Norris shook his head.

"Look, I didn't expect you never to hear about it. . . . I guess maybe part of hanging out with the new kid—no offense—was the fact that you weren't looking at me like a mental patient, which was . . . nice."

"I don't think of you that way, dude. You're, like, an aggressively chill human being," Norris assured him. Although he had more questions about Liam's past, Norris knew they were irrelevant to the friend sitting next to him right now. Petty curiosity he did not need to indulge in.

"So, um, what happened exactly?"

Liam turned to him. "I still don't know," he admitted. "I broke up with this girl, Laynie. She went to Trinity, but . . ."

Norris mentally thumbed through the Rolodex of names he had heard at Meredith's house, the faces he'd seen and maybe been introduced to, but no Laynie popped up.

". . . I got over the breakup. That part was fine, I wasn't heart-broken or anything," Liam continued. "But after that, it just got harder and harder to get out of bed in the morning. School, parties, constantly imagining what people were thinking about you. Not wearing the same shirt two days in a row because someone might notice and tell someone else. Even though you could probably wear a burlap sack, considering how little people actually pay attention to each other. . . ."

Norris kept his eyes on the glove box in front of him, as if to look directly at Liam would be to break whatever bond they were making.

"Anyway. I would get up, eat breakfast with my family, and pretend to stay back to take a dump or something, then just go back to bed. And then eventually, anywhere that wasn't my bed felt like it was some disappointment waiting to happen. School, even showering . . ." He turned to Norris. "Like, what was the point of any of it, y'know?"

Oh God. Please don't be an actual question. Please don't be an actual question. Please don't be an actual question. . . .

"Don't worry." Liam chuckled. "Even Dr. Leidwinger doesn't have the answer to that one. I'm told there isn't one."

"So . . ." Norris began, stretching the word with the carefulness of someone stepping over a quivering bear trap. He didn't want to say the wrong thing and snap the bear trap closed, but this whole thing—talking about feelings—was new for him. Back home, he and his friends usually talked about hockey, school gossip, television, movies, end of list. Even he and Eric had rarely ventured into this kind of territory before.

"So. Pills." Liam exhaled, picking at the leather on his steering wheel. "Lots and lots of pills. I was brushing my teeth, I think for the first time in days, and I saw a bottle of aspirin. My mom has sleep issues, so I just imagined what her bathroom pharmacy had to look like. . . . And then, I really couldn't stop imagining it. Her pharmacy. The answer to all this bull . . . I felt like a dick after since she blamed herself so hard."

Liam shook his head as if to shake away the thought.

"Anyway, my little sister found me. She'd left her clarinet, so the nanny drove her back during lunch hour. Apparently, there was a puddle of puke at the bottom of my bed, which was the only way she . . . Well, anyway. The gist of it is that I have my own row of prescriptions now." He smiled wryly. "But not Prozac."

Well. Fuck.

"Is that what your semicolon is about?" Norris nodded over to Liam's forearm, currently covered by a plaid shirt.

"Yeah," Liam said, pulling his sleeve up to reveal the tattoo in full. A beam of streetlight appropriately fell right onto it, highlighting the fuzz on his arm. It was upside down from this perspective but could be read correctly from Liam's, which, he supposed, was actually the point. It was also much bigger than Norris had originally thought.

"I wanted a reminder. It kind of signifies 'new chapter,'" Liam explained. "Sort of putting all that other stuff behind you while still acknowledging what happened. Saw it online and it just kind of made sense. I didn't think my mom would sign the release for me to get it, but she did."

Liam was looking at him expectantly.

"Jesus, dude" was all Norris could muster. He didn't quite know how to approach any of this.

"I really don't mean to put any of that on you, by the way," Liam said. "I wanted to pick up where I left off and come back to Anderson, but then . . . Well, there's really no starting over. By the time I came back after winter break, everyone had heard. People I never even talked to. Middle schoolers stepping into high school for the first time. Teachers. The coach didn't think it was a good idea for me to join a varsity team 'in my state' and that I should focus on healing, whatever that means."

"That's . . . intense," Norris admitted weakly. His brain was out of witty repartee by this point.

"Everyone's face falls when they hear my name. Yours didn't. I mean, you were still looking at me like I was a freak, but for entirely different reasons." Liam smiled.

"Well, you did have a flyer with my face on it," Norris reminded him.

"True."

Neither of them said anything for a moment. It was an

unspoken half time in this emotional relay race Norris had been drafted into without notice. Norris couldn't relate, but he could remember all the eyes that had been on his Habs T-shirt on the way to Austin. It was small and silly by comparison, but he still hated the feeling of being looked at, being judged. People he'd never seen before coming to their own conclusions about who he was. He imagined all those people knowing something intimate and personal about him.

"How are you doing now? Are you still . . . depressed?" Norris asked.

"Yeah." Liam shrugged, eyes back on the Bone Yard. "It's not as bad as it used to be."

Norris had been waiting for the happy ending. The high five that would put this Very Special Episode behind them, so they could never talk about it ever again.

"But you still struggle with it?"

"Sometimes." Liam shrugged again noncommittally, leaning back in the driver's seat and staring at nothing in particular. "Not enough to try that again—therapy actually helps there—but yeah, sure. I don't know if it will ever completely go away. Anyway, if it all freaks you out, we don't need to be friends. You don't have to feel bad for me or anything."

"I'm not your friend out of charity," Norris eventually said. "I think you're cool. And weird. Like, fifty-fifty."

"I'm glad to hear that. But you also don't have to start acting like being my friend is some sort of, I don't know, responsibility. You're not my support system or whatever. Just a dude I like hanging out with. I get why you might not want to, that's totally your choice, but it's important that you know that."

There was a firm openness to his voice that Norris thought would make Liam a good father one day. Where that thought came from, he couldn't say.

"Why?" Norris wanted to know. "In case you hadn't noticed, I'm kind of a big headache." Eric and his mother aside, most people eventually came to notice that.

"I guess mostly because you're never not yourself," Liam explained. "For better or worse, there's something about that that's, I don't know, refreshing?"

Norris had absolutely no idea what that meant. For all he knew, Liam had dropped some serious hallucinogens before he got to the car, but at least there was no longer a huge invisible vise around their two heads. Liam was just Liam again. *Eric would like this guy*, he thought.

"Do we hug?" Norris asked after gathering his stuff. "This feels like a huggy moment."

Liam smiled but seemed hesitant. "I would say yes, but . . ."

"But . . ."

"You're a very sweaty person, and you haven't showered since practice, so . . ."

"Oh my God. Fuck you," Norris hissed as he pulled Liam in for an admittedly gross, sweaty sideways hug anyway.

25

MEETING THE PARENTS

**POTENTIAL SCENARIOS WHEN MEETING YOUR NEW
GIRLFRIEND'S PARENTS:**

"We heard you kissed our daughter in a public school pool;
prepare to die."

"We heard you kissed our daughter in a public school pool;
we just wanted to take your measurements for the wedding
attire."

"Who are you and what are you doing in our house?"

When Norris had finally capitulated and asked Aarti for a translation of the mysterious emoji that she'd sent him at the McElwees wedding, her answer, while straightforward enough, had opened a whole new slew of questions for Norris. Enough for him to reach out for a trusted second opinion.

"What does it mean?"

Maddie had glanced at his phone in the middle of the staff-wide process of unbundling the wedding lights.

"Well, the words are pretty straightforward."

"'My parents want to have you over for dinner. Free this weekend?'" Norris read aloud again. Hoping to unlock some hidden meaning.

"So?" Norris wondered. "That's good, right? I mean . . . that's . . ."

"Boyfriend territory," she'd agreed, looking vaguely annoyed at the fact that he was texting instead of helping.

Liam had later concurred by text.

So had Eric. Norris had briefly thought of reaching out to Patrick for his fire-bad-tree-pretty type of simple jock wisdom, but thought better of it. They were now on texting terms according to the slew of random hockey factoids that Norris's phone occasionally buzzed with.

Apparently, the takeaway was that Aarti's parents wanted to meet Norris, which was how Norris found himself on the Puri doorstep, ringing the Puris' doorbell.

"You're wearing a tie," Aarti noted when she opened the door. She stared at Norris for a moment, unsure of what she was actually looking at.

"What, were you expecting a black T-shirt again?" Norris asked, surreptitiously adjusting his sleeves by pulling down on the cuffs with his forefingers.

"I mean, I've literally only ever seen you wear one thing," she admitted as she stepped aside to let him in, closing the door behind her before giving him a quick peck on the upper lip. "Like you're Fred Flintstone or something."

"I Windsor knotted this sucker too." Norris grinned, straightening his tie. It had taken a few different online tutorials, but he had managed a pretty good one, all things considered. Aarti's hair was down and pitch-black this time around, an artificial shade of her natural color.

"Thanks for doing this."

As if he would ever say no to her. She had told her parents Norris was important enough to meet; there was no way he was passing on that.

"You're nervous," Norris teased as he stepped into the small but impeccably appointed house.

Despite a deceptively large entryway, the rest of the house was smaller, almost on the cramped side. Every piece of furniture was carved and heavy, as opposed to his and Judith's suite of Swedish assembly-line particleboard.

"Hardly," Aarti said. "I just don't like these dinner engagements." She turned and abruptly yelled down the hall, "He's here!"

Some Hindi-language show on television or on the radio that Norris hadn't consciously realized was playing from the kitchen was instantly lowered but was not shut off. The trial of meeting Aarti's parents would apparently be a musical.

It wasn't long before Aarti's parents appeared. Mr. Puri had a . . . contradictory appearance. Half of him was casual and laid-back, but there was a stiff undercurrent of foreign propriety. It came out in the details: dress shirtsleeves crisply folded, hair obviously dyed and carefully slicked back, the fact that his house slippers were made of leather. This was someone raised to believe that the role of a host carried certain responsibilities. Norris's dad had the same mannerisms; his took the form of a gold watch he always slipped on when the doorbell rang. It was something specific and proud that this new life would never shake out of them.

Norris had been instructed to linger in the parlor while the table was being set. Apparently, arriving fifteen minutes early had not been the sign of respect he intended, but a scheduling inconvenience. *Shit.*

The Puris' shelves consisted almost exclusively of religion and science fiction. The lowest shelves were stuffed with trinkets and thick rubber-banded manila folders wedged between reference books: basic English, Webster's dictionaries, not one but *two* editions of *Immigration and Citizenship*. These were the foundations of the higher shelves but still worth displaying. Books were clearly a source of pride in this home.

Norris found himself lingering on the two shelves that contained fourteen hardcovers of all seven Harry Potter novels. The cover art grew from cute kid to lanky grown man in both English and Hindi, charged with saving the world on Hermione Granger's coattails. He didn't know that Aarti was a Potterhead.

"These are mine," Mr. Puri said, suddenly materializing behind Norris with a smirk. *Goddamn leather slippers.* Norris had no idea how long he'd been standing there, watching his reading habits be scrutinized.

"Really?" Norris choked on his own breath.

"We have to hide them when Aarti's grandmother visits from Calcutta. Western sorcery, blasphemy, blah, blah . . . I get where she's coming from, but that doesn't stop me from delving back into Azkaban on nights I can't sleep."

"We're ready!" echoed from the kitchen.

"I'm a Gryffindor," Mr. Puri added on their way out, pointing to a red-and-yellow scarf neatly folded over the second row of fantasy books, which Norris now understood to be his.

"Um, yeah, same. Gryffindor too." Norris smiled.

Slytherin, actually, according to the last online quiz he had bothered to take. But he wanted to impress Aarti's father, not become the Draco to Mr. Puri's Harry Potter.

He bit down the thought as he followed Mr. Puri into the dining room, where everything was set out.

"It's very nice to meet you, Norris." Mrs. Puri smiled at him, pouring water into small copper cups.

Mrs. Puri, for her part, was *definitely* Aarti's mom. A few specific touches, like her earrings and gold bangles, confirmed to Norris exactly where Aarti got her talent for accessorizing. Her hair was longer and knotted twice over, but a few wrinkles and lines aside, she was basically Aarti's slightly shorter carbon copy. This also made her kind of stunning. MILF would be gauche, but "Mother I Would Like to Read with Under a Tree" might qualify. She was elegant and contained in a way Norris imagined that only women who had once lived in London were elegant and contained.

"What does your father do?" Mr. Puri asked as they settled

into the meal. "Is he an engineer? I've been meeting a lot of Haitian engineers lately. Austin's tech boom, they say."

"Dad—" Aarti started.

Oh please, Norris thought. *No daddy issues to sidestep here. Bring it, Mr. Puri.*

"My dad's a medic, actually," Norris replied. "He's back in Canada, though. My parents have been divorced for a few years. I still see him fairly often. It's a very friendly situation."

"Right, right, sorry about that. Aarti had mentioned that. Your mother is a professor, is that right?" Mrs. Puri asked, staring at him with her daughter's focused black eyes. Her accent was a smidge heavier than her husband's.

"Um, yes." Norris nodded. "Antilles literature and Haitian diaspora are her main jam. She just started at UT. That's why we moved here."

What do your parents do? Why did you move here? Norris had decided to include the answers to three questions he knew were coming in every one of his replies, in order to expedite the interrogation portion of dinner.

"How are you liking Austin?"

"It's very hot, but I'm learning to like it," Norris said between bites. "Aarti introduced me to a few cool spots, and then I started working at the Bone Yard, the barbecue restaurant, and there's a hockey rink where I occasionally play with another friend from Anderson."

How did you meet our daughter? What do you do with your time? What are your academic aspirations? Boom, boom, boom.

An air of approval passed between the Puris, but Norris wasn't done yet.

"This food is really delicious," Norris added as a finishing blow. "Thank you for inviting me."

Put me in the family will and grant me your daughter's hand in marriage, bitches.

"Thank you, Norris." Mrs. Puri smiled earnestly. "It's chicken tikka masala." She sounded out each syllable, probably unaware that it was a staple of every Indian takeout menu Norris had ever glimpsed. Part of him suspected that it wasn't something that was served often in this house, the same way Judith always made a few specific Haitian dishes whenever they had non-Haitian guests over for dinner back in Canada.

Norris leaned in to Aarti and whispered, "Beginner's Indian food, right?"

"Can't you taste the training wheels?" she whispered back, causing both of them to chuckle.

"So, Norris, do you plan on going to college here in the States as well?" Mrs. Puri broke in from across the table, signaling that this wasn't the sort of table where two out of the four participants could engage in any lengthy side discussion.

"Which college would that be?" Mr. Puri quickly asked.

"Aren't you leading the witness there, Dad?" Aarti rebutted calmly. "Just *which* college? Like there's no alternative."

"There isn't."

Norris caught something passing between Aarti and her father, untold previous arguments squeezed into a glance.

"Um, maybe I'll go back to Canada," he answered slowly. "McGill was always the plan. We'll see now. I mean, I don't think college was ever not an option. My mom would kill me."

Mrs. Puri smiled approvingly at Norris with a mouthful of chicken. She seemed to agree with the sentiment he had expressed. Aarti, not so much.

"Hear that, Aarti?" her father prompted.

"I want to see the world, Dad," Aarti shot back. "Isn't it hypocritical for you of all people to say no to that?"

"You see the world by studying, *dear daughter*," her father answered. "Me, your mother, Norris's mother, how do you think this happened? We studied, we got visas, and doors opened so we could come here."

"And I want to see the rest of this America you all worked so hard to reach," she stated in a way that sounded half-rehearsed, half–sudden realization. "We've been in Texas all my life. There are forty-nine other states right here!"

"We were in Chicago until Aarti was two," Mrs. Puri corrected to Norris, as if they were watching reruns of a show she had seen before and felt the need to point out plot points.

"Object permanence was kind of a game-changer, Mom," Aarti retorted. "We're citizens of this country, not tourists. You two worked so hard to get us here—for me, yes, I know—and we've seen one tiny corner of it. Isn't that insane to you?"

Um.

Despite her words, Aarti's voice was earnest, not angry. Mr. Puri's expression was neutral, but he was listening to what Aarti had to say. It was weird to see a calm disagreement where neither party seemed to be getting angry.

"There's so much right here," Aarti continued. "I want to see the Appalachian Trail, New York, California, Salem, Alabama . . . fuck it, even Canada! It's all a train ride away!"

"Thank you," Norris whispered to no one in particular.

"You want to go to Alabama?" Mr. Puri asked as if trying to formulate a diagnosis.

"Why not?"

I mean, brown skin, Norris thought but did not say.

"Alabama is not going anywhere, Aarti," her mother reassured her, and Norris remembered his own mother's words about Canada when they first arrived: "You can see all of these things with a degree in your hand."

"After that, it will probably be graduate school, and then finding a job, and then giving you both grandchildren." Aarti glanced to a wall with dozens of golden framed photos containing brown-skinned, crooked-toothed babies, smiling women in beautiful iridescent saris, and proud men with gold watches. It created an unspoken altar. Their apartment had one as well, Norris realized. The wall of relatives—not the ones who had fallen off the map or been arrested for possession, but the ones you were supposed to compare yourself to and aspire to overthrow.

Aarti's back was so tense it arched, and her face was doing that thing Norris had noticed where—as far as he could tell—she was individually licking each of her top row of teeth looking for the right words.

Seeing her like this was somewhat unsettling to Norris. Sure of herself was Aarti Puri's default setting.

"I want to be a photojournalist," she finally declared on the exhale. The silence that followed implied that this was a new episode and not a rerun after all. "I don't want to be pre-miserable in premed."

Norris watched Mr. and Mrs. Puri share a look.

"Concerts, protests. The country is a political mess these days: plenty of websites pay a lot for photos of people on the ground at rallies, demonstrations, and—"

"God," Mr. Puri exclaimed after a moment to take in the information, turning to his wife with a weak laugh. "Darling, we raised a white girl!"

Mrs. Puri shook her head in weary affection. Let the record show that Norris did not snort. Not one bit.

"Dad!" Aarti gasped, genuinely frustrated and losing some of the untouchable maturity that had slipped into her voice moments prior. "That is such a prejudiced—"

"*Guest,*" Mrs. Puri interjected. The silence that fell confirmed once and for all who really sat on the Iron Throne in this household. The topic had to be changed, period.

Conversation redirected itself to discussing the intricacies of bringing out the tikka without overpowering a four-person serving. Aarti still looked vaguely annoyed, but her back was loose and she'd given Norris a weak, if victorious, smile. She'd said what she wanted to say. That was something to celebrate.

He reached under the table and gave Aarti's hand a light squeeze before returning to praising her mom's use of herbs and spices.

26

THE HIGH SCHOOL GIRL'S ROOM

OBSERVABLE CHARACTERISTICS: Awkward bed sitting, excessive sweating, attempts to hide excessive sweating.

APPROPRIATE COMMENTARY: "Wow, your room is really cool!"

INAPPROPRIATE COMMENTARY: "Wow, I've been trying to get up to your room for a long time!"

Norris's vocal offer to help clear the dishes was expectedly dismissed. He and Aarti were each served a small cup of gold-tinted tea that was slightly bitter but not altogether unpleasant. Norris got the impression that this was a customary post-meal lull in this home and tried to pace his tea sips to match Aarti's, who had an eye on her phone the whole time. Norris watched as Mrs. Puri silently opened the patio window and her husband brought two cigarettes to his mouth, lighting one and then the other. He handed one to his wife as the two began to do the dishes in tandem.

Secondhand smoke aside, it was an easy, domestic gesture

that made Norris feel like an intruder. He was grateful for the out when Mrs. Puri eventually turned to Aarti and, presumably, excused them both in Hindi. Aarti nodded and signaled for Norris to follow her. As they made their way up the narrow, carpeted stairs, Norris heard the radio turn on in the kitchen. He wondered how many decades and across how many countries the pair had spent doing their dishes in this exact fashion.

"The tragedy of the Puri family, ladies and gentlemen," Aarti said as she let herself drop onto her bed.

Norris stood at the doorway, looking in with some apprehension.

"I liked your parents," he said, imprinting as much of the small and colorful room as he could at a cursory glance. Her messiness was different from Norris's. Her messiness was meticulous. Each pile of clothes was color-coordinated and the packed shelves of magazines and trinkets all seemed to have an ongoing theme. Music and concert swag. School stuff. Photography. Maps. Lots and lots of clothes. Unlike Norris's generic blue bedding, rented furniture, and rolled-up posters that he still hadn't bothered to put up, this room could not be anyone's but Aarti's.

"They like you too," she said, pulling a pile of stray blouses and T-shirts into a makeshift pillow under her chin. "Your mother is in academia. Your pants aren't dragging around your ankles; you're one of the tribe now! A model immigrant."

It did not feel like a compliment, going by her tone.

"Isn't that a little racist?" Norris asked half-jokingly.

260

"Hmm, race aware," she reassessed after a beat. "You think my dad just interrogated you over dinner because 'new black guy at school' was reassuring enough?"

Fair. Norris wasn't dumb enough to think there wasn't some audition element to this dinner invitation.

"That's my brother, Rohan," Aarti preemptively answered, following Norris's gaze to a framed selfie of Aarti and a slightly older Indian guy with bright eyes and slicked-back hair. "Junior at Dartmouth."

"Impressive." Norris whistled. "You look alike."

Norris noticed the additional space she had cleared on the bed as an invitation for him to join her and awkwardly positioned himself down on one arm, lying at a literal arm's length to avoid looking too comfortable should the Puris pop by their daughter's bedroom. The pillowcase he found himself lying over didn't smell bad, but Norris bet it hadn't been changed in at least a week. Judith would change them. God, *why* was he thinking of his mom right now?!

"So what's the big Puri family tragedy, exactly?" Norris asked to jolt his brain out of itself.

"What isn't?" Aarti asked, inching closer. Norris couldn't help but think that part of her was enjoying his discomfort in the moment. "Two amazing world travelers, top of their classes, and here they are decades later aspiring to nothing more than tenure, Hawaii vacations, and for their daughter to give them grandchildren by age twenty-five. It's freaking medieval."

None of these things sounded particularly bad to him. Well,

maybe the creating-a-small-human-from-scratch part; that was just a horror movie.

"They've settled on America," he suggested.

"They've just settled. Wasn't the point of working so hard that their kids would have slightly more options on how to live *their* lives?" She let out a frustrated sigh. "Anyway . . . I'm just glad I finally told them. Thank you for, you know, helping me. Whatever happens next, at least it's out there now."

"You're welcome." Norris gazed at her, feeling, for once, perfectly at ease. God, she really was beautiful.

Aarti seemed to sense his change in mood. "What are you thinking about?" she asked.

"Nothing, just . . . I think this is the first time I've, like, lounged on a girl's bed."

He probably shouldn't have said that.

"I probably shouldn't have said that."

"It's okay. You're sweet," she chuckled, moving closer. "Guys around here like to pretend they've been porn stars since age nine. It's exhausting."

Norris was caught between a burning desire to ask her if he was the first boy to ever lie on her bed and the fact that her hair smelled really amazing. Something about her eyes—especially this close—always made Norris lose sight of the rest of the world.

I could be a really good boyfriend, Norris wanted to say. The best boyfriend. Some real Magic Carpet Ride boyfriending.

"You're my favorite thing about this country, y'know" was what Norris's mouth decided on instead.

Aarti smiled. "You know, instead of college, you should come with me when I get out of this town," she said. "You would definitely need a driver's license, though."

"Well, sure," Norris started. "But where would I go? From what I've heard, this country is not kind to black high school graduates."

"We could solve crimes," she offered. "For a small stipend each time, of course."

She smirked at him. The moment went on a little too long. They both became aware of how close they were; how horizontally positioned; on a bed. A very comfortable bed.

"Dude, I'm not going to have sex with you right now!" she laughed, causing Norris's head, ego, and the faintest hint of boner to all simultaneously pull back. "My parents are downstairs."

"What? No!" Norris stuttered. "I wasn't thinking that. Like, at all. How very dare you!"

In the process of moving back, Norris's arm slipped off the edge of the bed and he slammed his head against the wooden bedpost. A) *Ow.* B) He would happily do it again too if it kept Aarti laughing this hard.

"So, you were at Maddie's McElwees's sister's wedding?" Aarti asked, staring at him sideways with her head on the pillow. Their fingers interweaved and Norris smiled as she drummed her fingertips alongside his.

"Yeah," Norris answered. "It wasn't planned. We just had no idea what to do."

"Didn't you have an actual wedding invitation, though?"

"I mean, yes, she'd invited me, technically, but I'm pretty sure she wasn't expecting us to come in through the back door with a drunken Patrick."

She nodded a few times, as if trying to put a picture together in her mind.

"You've been hanging out with cheerleaders and football players too much. You're turning into a jock-y little drummer boy," she finally said. "They've got you on Patrick Lamarra watch."

"He's not that bad." Norris shrugged. "You just have to load up on pee pads and chewsticks."

Norris wanted to change the topic but didn't exactly know why. He felt settled in a way he hadn't since moving to Austin. He had Liam, and somewhere to play hockey on weekends. Work was great too. And Aarti? Aarti was right here. It was almost surreal.

"So, have you heard about prom?" Norris then asked. He had clocked a few posters around school, and that had been enough for the idea to burrow into his brain.

"Of course," Aarti said dismissively. "Better get used to it. Every year, for every high school grade . . . it's obscene. Other schools only have it for seniors but we're not that lucky at Anderson. Why?"

"We should go," Norris said as casually as he could.

"You can't be serious."

"No." Norris pondered. "Well, maybe. I don't know. Isn't it supposed to be a big thing for you Americans? I wouldn't mind seeing it."

"It's just a dance. God!" She laughed into her pillow, shaking her head at herself rather than Norris.

"What?"

"Nothing . . . just, now might be a good time to tell you that I'm not Madison McElwees, Norris."

"What's that supposed to mean?"

"Going to prom with the cheerleaders and football players," she said, affecting a vocal fry that Norris would have previously found hilarious. "That's not me! That's the prom queen you work with."

Pointing out that Maddie would probably forfeit the crown to Meredith or a nearby orphan did not seem like the right move right now.

"Maddie and I aren't . . . we're not anything. She's still hung up on her ex, and I would never be into a cheerleader. That's ridiculous. C'mon now."

"Right." Aarti rolled her eyes. "White girl, balancing at the top of the pyramid in yoga pants and goes to bed texting in a silk nightie. I bet you recoil in horror."

Norris knew this tone—upset, and hiding it through sarcasm. He had *perfected* this tone. He could run out a karaoke machine singing exactly in this tone. He really didn't want Aarti to have this nagging at the back of her head every time she looked at him. So Norris turned around and stretched his arm over her to reach his suit jacket, hanging from Aarti's desk chair. He quickly fished out the now-frayed little notebook, compulsively filled over the past few months, and handed it to her.

"What's that?"

Norris shrugged. "Proof that I'm not pining for Maddie Mc-Elwees."

In his notebook, he knew, there was a rather vicious string of sentences about her, back when she was still only referred to as "The Skinny Madison" instead of just Maddie. His opinion of her had changed since then, of course, but he wanted Aarti not to worry.

"I take it back: I'm dating an artsy diary keeper. You're an emo in sheep's clothing."

She flipped onto her stomach and began to read.

She did not seem overly offended, smirking and flipping through the notebook, looking utterly fascinated. She occasionally snorted or chuckled at a description of this or that person. Somewhere along the way, he'd filled almost every page. The flight to Whistler and back. The day he'd boringly chronicled every item of Longhorn attire that walked through the Bone Yard. Another time, he'd tried to keep track of Goade's diet, and had only come to the fact that the man should by all account be dead of scurvy.

"'School assemblies,'" Aaarti read aloud. "'A fuck dungeon by any other name. What is this? Hell. Hell. I am in hell. Maybe if I keep acknowledging that I'm in hell it will be enough to qualify as a glitch in the hell matrix and the whole thing will crash. Hell. Hell. Hell . . .' Wow, both sides of the sheet."

Okay—Anderson High conducted a downright cartoonish number of assemblies. Every other morning since the semester began, Norris had found himself corralled into the obscenely large auditorium and forced to sit through a series of meaningless announcements. Parking pass updates for seniors, the rest of the football season, student council elections, the upcoming football season, College Day for juniors, next year's football season. Norris suspected that these gatherings were a form of Valium for the student body on days it did not have any actual football to look forward to. Like when a recovering drug addict discovers a love for jogging four hours a day.

"Oh my God!" Aarti burst out laughing, pointing to another page. "What is this?"

She held up a page to him that featured a pretty solid facsimile sketch of Ian, arms and legs spread out like a boxered version of Leonardo da Vinci's *The Vitruvian Man*, which they'd learned about in history class, with various arrows pointing at his body. Aarti gave him a knowing smile.

"The girl I liked was obsessed with this prick."

"Understandable," she conceded. "What's this one?"

"Oh," Norris started. "I tried to trace Patrick and his friends' genome back to the missing human genome." *It was done in boredom*, Norris meant to add. He mostly liked Patrick now.

"Oh my God!" she exclaimed. "You have two, three . . . four! Four pages for Meredith Santiago!"

That one, Norris mostly stood by. He would die on that hill.

Aarti laughed out loud, throwing her head back at a random page.

Norris forced a smile, slightly regretting the choice to hand over the notebook. He'd just wanted to make her feel better.

"Can I, um, can I get it back?" he asked, reaching for the notebook, suddenly nervous.

"Actually, I take it back: I'm dating a mean girl," Aarti said as she handed it over.

"So, prom?"

She looked at him with a soft smile. "Pass."

"Oh, come on!"

"There are so many other parties that are worth the effort; I'm not going to go to a glorified gymnasium dance."

"You'll crash Meredith Santiago's basement to see your ex, but you won't go to an actual dance with someone you're actually dating? What kind of logic is that?"

She frowned at that.

"I mean, you should go, if you want. It would definitely give you some fodder for this." She flicked the cover of his notebook and got up to turn on some music. "But it's just not my scene, Norris. Sorry," she said with a definite resolve that Norris knew better than to try to push past. Aarti Puri would be a photographer one day; Aarti Puri would not go to prom with him—with him or anyone else.

27

THE FIRST HOCKEY GAME

CONFIRMED NUMBER OF PARTICIPANTS: Nineteen (six-on-six game with goalkeepers, one referee, and two alternates on both sides).

EXPECTED PROFICIENCY LEVEL: Some surprisingly good players, two who might be Quebec-level.

POTENTIAL TEAM NAMES: Desert Penguins, Austin Improbables, Emergency Room Riders.

POTENTIAL TEAM SLOGANS: "It seemed like a good idea at the time."

ACTUAL EXPERIENCE ICE SKATING OR PLAYING HOCKEY: Optional.

"It's a dance!" Norris said, slamming Liam's trunk with his foot.

When Norris was a kid, the cereal he always wanted was the one Judith would categorically not buy. The actual cereal didn't really matter—tiny Norris was never in it for the sugar or the toys. He just wanted whatever she told him he couldn't have. If she refused to buy the super fiber brand that tasted like cardboard, Norris would whine endlessly and clutch the cereal box to his chest with tears in his eyes in the grocery aisle. Needless to say, as soon as Judith figured that out, Norris became a very regular seven-year-old. The point was that the prom thing had been on his mind since the previous weekend, even as he and Liam approached their first-ever league game.

"Like, what's the big deal in just going? There are no strings attached."

"Hmm," Liam hummed in that way Norris now knew meant he had some razor-sharp bit of insight, which he was just waiting for permission to share.

"Go ahead," Norris said with an eye roll as he dangled multiple boxes on top of his sports bag.

"Just like there weren't any strings attached to that snow globe?" Liam asked, carrying the other half of the boxes.

"I've decided that I don't like you," Norris finally concluded as they reached the warehouse.

"Really? I find you to be a very charming guy."

The biggest surprise of the day was the stack of boxes Liam had hauled out of the back of his car. Brand-new gear. Helmets in a few different sizes, pads, a portable blade sharpener, and a handful of middle-of-the-road Bauer hockey sticks. A few of the guys' sticks had looked extremely flimsy the previous week.

"That's a lot of equipment to just hand out, dude!" Norris said, looking down at the loot they'd just dropped off on the sidelines as the other players busied themselves with warm-up drills around the ice. "Like, you could buy a car. A small car, secondhand, but still . . . you could be mobile!"

"I have a car."

"A small boat, then! Where did you get the funds?"

Liam stared at him blankly, tilted by the weight of the boxes he was carrying.

"Right," Norris remembered. "Rich."

"It's amazing how much money my dad will throw at the problem that is me these days." Liam grinned.

"If I ever meet your parents," Norris continued, "I want to talk to them about these beans I've got that really would make an amazing investment."

"We do own a few farms in Wisconsin," Liam said. "Maybe we can trade you the beans for the biggest cow we've got."

That was how they both seemed comfortable talking about these new heavy topics that were now part of their lexicon—in a dry, glib way that put neither of them on the spot.

"Come on," Liam said with a nervous glance at the other team, which was filtering in through the doors. "Let's do this thing."

The team was endlessly grateful for Liam's gifts, changing into them right there on the ice. Maybe it was the excitement of new gear, but there was a buzzing feel of anticipation as the referee arrived and called captains for the coin toss. Liam and Norris went together, and after winning the toss, chose their side.

And then, with a nod to his teammates, who stared back

solemnly, and a blow of the whistle, they were off.

The game started awkwardly, with a few missed passes that Norris attributed to nerves, but soon they hit their rhythm and were passing nicely. Patrick even got a decent shot off that the other team's goalie was hard-pressed to block. All in all, they were doing well and holding their own in a scoreless second period when Norris overheard one of the guys from the other team say, looking straight at him, "I didn't know they taught black people how to play hockey."

"What did you just say?" Norris asked, because he genuinely thought he'd misheard.

"Whatever, don't go hood on me. I'm just saying, black people have football and basketball, which makes sense, but hockey, that's Icelandic shit, man. Not your lane."

Quickly moving past the fury and embarrassment boiling in the pit of his stomach, Norris cataloged the guy's face for a launching off point and settled on the crooked teeth peeking through thick, gingivitis-inflamed gums. These would do just fine.

"Hey, man, cool it," Liam said, sliding to a stop near them and having overhead. "I don't want to have to have the ref kick you out."

"Dude, c'mon," the guy said before he skated off. "Homeboy's not offended, right? No need to get all PC."

And, sure, Norris could have let it go. Or laughed it off. But that was an alternate-reality Norris—one who existed in a world where Batman used an arrow and Superman had a shaved head.

"Yeah, no sweat, man." Norris smiled brightly at the other guy's retreating back.

"Are you okay?" Liam asked.

"I'm good." He nodded. "Really!"

In truth, that asshole demanded a swift and thorough humiliation, and Norris was, in turn, vicious. The second period continued and, in three quick motions, the puck was stolen and the enemy landed on his butt. The guy's hand-eye coordination did not let him do more than carry a tiki torch. Every time the opportunity presented itself, Norris made sure to let the unknown asshole get ahold of the puck first, before effortlessly stealing it from him, with the biggest, blackest grin. He realized he really had missed not playing with a hand tied behind his back. A few moments later, Norris did it again, to the chuckles of a few of the other players.

"You're fucking cheating, you piece of—"

The guy scrambled to his feet, face and eyes red, gut peeking through his T-shirt that was at least two sizes too small, under his oversize, unzipped hoodie. Fine Aryan specimen, that one.

Norris was nevertheless taken aback when he threw his stick to the ground and started to step toward him. Up close, there was actually a sizable height difference between them, and the other guy loomed a good head over his own five ten. On the other hand, Norris had not been in a single fight in his hockey career. And after eight years of playing the sport, there was something kind of cool about it taking place in Texas.

Before he could even bring his hands up, the shoulder check

came fast and surprisingly vicious, sending the other guy sliding perpendicularly before he could reach Norris and causing a few visible winces to be heard around the ice.

"Like I said," Liam said, coming to a near-wobbly stop afterward. "Cool it."

It was a penalty shoulder check; no doubt about it. No referee would have been fooled.

"What the hell?!"

The guy looked from Liam to him, where most of his frustration seemed to lie, and back to the line of players behind them. As he left, he hurled a litany of insults back at them. His language was . . . colorful. Full of color. A complete Crayola box set of color.

The uncomfortable thing when these things happened—because Lord knows this wasn't the first instance of casual racism Norris had encountered as one of the only black kids at his elementary school—was the expectation of a reaction. Norris never wanted to be the black guy who escalated things. In his head, he always imagined his mother shaking her head disapprovingly at him from the sidelines should he get into a fight. So he mostly just did this. Stayed quiet and waited for things to calm down . . . A thoroughly un-Norris approach to life, according to Eric.

"Holy shit! Did you see that?" he heard Patrick whisper at his side. "Our boy's a killer!"

"It was a complete accident," Liam said, sounding genuinely guilt-free. They all watched the other player exit the premises before resuming the game.

Norris scored the first, and only, goal early in the third period, which caused a small round of clapping to erupt from the sidelines. Norris looked up to see a few of Anderson's cheerleaders, Meredith and Maddie at the foreground, burst into cheers.

"Holy shit, dude," Norris noted, wiping sweat from his chin. "We've got fans."

"We?" Liam grinned, coming to a perfect stop next to him.

In truth, Norris wasn't totally surprised to see them there—Patrick and Meredith were disgustingly inseparable, after all—but it still felt good. Aarti hadn't been interested in coming to his game, and Judith had inquired a few times, only to be reminded that no matter how much he loved her, she was his mother, which meant that her public appearances in his social life had to be limited and scheduled well in advance. So, needless to say, the handful of girls cheering and giggling for them on the sidelines was a strange sight but a welcome one. When had he turned into an actual American cliché?

And when, exactly, had he started liking it?

They won the game, 1–0. Not a proper whooping, but Norris was excited all the same, and his reaction was nothing compared to his giddy teammates'. After fist bumps were exchanged, Norris noticed Liam and Maddie chatting by the side of the rink. The postgame crowd had dwindled and the rest of the players were already filing out of the warehouse. Meredith and Patrick had immediately devolved into an impromptu make-out session as soon as Patrick had stepped off the ice, hair still damp with sweat. Meredith and Norris exchanged the right amount of judgmental glaring as he skated past them to join Liam and Maddie. Something about seeing the various, very purposely compartmentalized aspects of his life chitchat together made him inexplicably anxious.

"You're good, Canada!" Maddie greeted him. "I was just telling Liam here that you're a really great skater," she complimented him.

"Thanks. And just to be clear, Carey Price is a really great skater." Norris grinned. "I'm somewhere between Wayne Gretzky and Kristi Yamaguchi."

"But humbler, right?" asked Maddie.

"Better looking than Gretzky too," Norris added. "Thanks for coming." Lord knew she had a packed schedule. "I know it's not a football game."

"Definitely not football," she agreed. "But, y'know, I can see the appeal."

Liam was eyeing them both with a muted expression, his eyes darting back and forth between them as they spoke.

"Stop that," Norris said, pounding Liam's head lightly with his glove. "Are you ready to bounce?"

"Can't drop you off tonight, sorry," Liam said. "I have my Late-Evening Gardening class. Already running late."

Ugh. Norris was too exhausted for the bus, and Judith would be another hour at least. His life was a series of acute sufferings.

"Is that code for something?" Maddie whispered.

"Code?" Liam answered with a frown.

"It's an actual class," Norris finally explained.

"Oh." She smiled without missing a beat. "Sorry, it just kind of sounds like—"

"Like he's going to be lighting up all the joints, yes," Norris agreed. "I told him."

Alas, Liam was perhaps the only person in the world for whom a night-gardening class wasn't a lie.

"Tonight we're doing Moth Traps." He grinned.

"I'll give you a ride," Maddie said, twirling a ring of keys around her fingers. "I have Dad's convertible today, so the posthockey . . . boyroma isn't a concern. And some old learner's permit pamphlets I still have from middle school, because really, it's time."

"That's a lost battle." Liam waved them off. "Good game, coach. See you at school."

"Not your coach!" Norris shouted off.

"Madison!" Meredith shrieked, startling them both.

Jesus.

"Me and Patrick are going to, um, hang out in his car, okay? He'll drop me off."

"Sounds good, babe!" Maddie waved back.

"Something was definitely perforated just now," Norris said, still holding his ear.

"Be grateful." Maddie smiled. "Last year she sang the national anthem at homecoming."

"Is the local wildlife still recovering?"

"Wow," Norris said, discarding his gear into the back seat with a stunned look.

"I know," Maddie preempted. "Shut up."

Of course Big Jim had a convertible. Norris had expected something out of Malibu Stacy's pink cartoon dream house, so the patches of rust against the formerly burnt orange Beemer that awaited them in the parking lot, complete with chipped white leather seats, had been a bit of a shocker.

"It's the McElwees last-resort vehicle when everything else is in use," Maddie explained, sunglasses on and roof down.

"So, does it get hard?" Norris asked. "Meredith and Patrick humping on every available surface?"

"I told you already, Canada," she said. "I'm over Patrick. That's ancient history. I'm not much of a piner."

Her face was unreadable through the sunglasses, but to Norris, she seemed to be telling the truth.

"Are you coming to prom?" Maddie inquired, as if she too had access to his innermost thoughts. *Creepy.*

"Um, I—"

"I know it looks lame from the sidelines, but it's always loads of fun. Everyone's hot in their dresses and tuxes, there's photo booths, bad music, bubble machines. It's a whole production."

Nothing, absolutely nothing, in this state was ever done small; Norris had learned this by now.

"You and Aarti should really come," Maddie continued. "We have a key to homeroom, don't tell anyone, and someone always starts a second party there once it gets late enough. Last year someone made pizza, and someone filled water guns with craft beer. The entire second floor was sticky for finals."

God save him, that did not seem unfun.

"Prom is not really Aarti's thing," Norris finally said.

"Ah," Maddie answered diplomatically. Norris was grateful that she didn't push further.

"Yeah."

They drove on in silence for the rest of the way.

"Well," Maddie suggested as they pulled in front of his building. "You should come with us then. It's not limited to couples; this isn't Utah. It'll just be a good time. You and Patrick are sort of friends now, and believe me, Meredith is never as pleasant as when she has a crown on her head when she inevitably wins prom queen. You did sort of miss out on the wedding after all."

Huh. Well, that was a thought. And Aarti had told him that he could—no, should—go.

"That actually sounds . . . really fun." Norris smiled.

"Shut up," Maddie said automatically.

"No, I'm being serious."

"Seriously?"

"Seriously."

And like that: Norris Kaplan was going to the prom.

28

THE AMERICAN PROM

DEFINING CHARACTERISTICS: Suit and tie, dancing, selfies, cheesy decor.

FOOD SOURCES: Bowls of unhygienic snacks right next to bathrooms, snuck-in flasks, punch bowl spiked by someone wearing sunglasses indoors.

EXPECTATIONS FROM EVERY MOVIE EVER:

1. Balloons. So many balloons.
2. Record-scratch speeches to a cheering student body that artificially comes together as a family for one night.
3. Magically learning all the moves needed for a synchronized dance number.

There were, as it turned out, many rules to Behaving Like a Gentleman in a Prom-Like Setting, and Judith wanted Norris to soak up as many of them as possible before the event in question. As much as he tried to explain to her that he wasn't an escort and that it was definitely, definitely a group thing, most of her rules seemed to be focused on treating Maddie with respect. He was to never let Maddie's glass be empty. They were to dance at least twice; more so if Maddie requested it. By her own account, she hadn't raised a "poorly socialized little hoodlum who checks hockey statistics on his phone while that poor girl sighs looking at the dance floor." Norris had a hard time imagining Maddie waiting for a guy, any guy, to invite her to dance, but considering the stakes, he didn't altogether mind their new postdinner kitchen dance lessons . . . Prom date. Friend. Dance Partner. Norris could manage one of these, at best, so the prospect of juggling all three became more and more overwhelming.

After realizing that her son was now A) constipated and B) trembling at the prospect of the dozens of tiny ways this evening might end up being a disaster, Judith now overcompensated by sitting on Norris's bed—presumably guarding it so Norris wouldn't jump in and pull the covers over his head—and complimenting him on his dapper haircut, winning personality, and good looks, as Norris fidgeted in front of the mirror hanging from his closet door. His neck had definitely gained weight since the last time he'd worn this shirt, for one of Judith's conferences back in Montreal. Freaking key lime pie leftovers. Why the heck was he so nervous? And why did he feel guilty? He'd told Aarti about it, and she'd of course promptly made fun of him.

😺😺 **Enjoy the bowl of punch and pamphlets on STDs at the door, Friday Night Lights ;)**

"You're going to have so much fun!" Judith said. "People always say your generation is all phone app orgies and lipstick parties, but a prom just sounds so . . . I don't know . . . traditional! Every movie from America I saw as a child had a prom. I always wanted to go to one."

"Mom. Please never—and I can't stress this enough—never say the word *orgy* again. . . . Don't even say *corgi* anymore because they kind of sound the same."

Norris's reflection moved his pocket square a little to the left, and then a little to the right, and then the same amount of a little to the left again, only now it no longer aligned with the button of his shirt. Something about the bulkiness of his notebook and pen in his breast pocket made it impossible to fit correctly.

"Dammit!" Norris snapped, pulling the vile piece of fabric out entirely. "What's the point of this thing anyway?!"

"Language," Judith soothed. "It's a pocket square. Like a handkerchief."

"So if she has to sneeze I'm supposed to hand it to her?"

"Correct."

"And then, what? I stuff it back into my jacket all mucus-y for the rest of the night?"

Judith laughed. "I think it's just decorative."

Decorative was all the permission Norris needed to crumple the pocket square into a ball and discard it to a corner of his bed.

"Norris! That cost . . ." Judith trailed off. It might have been a little much but in two hours, Norris would be at a Texan high school prom, of all places: a pocket square was his line in the sand.

"Never mind. You look great without it." She sighed, standing up. The part of Norris that was hoping for a last-minute grounding deflated. She smiled, though Norris couldn't possibly see at what.

"Lord, look at you. When did you turn into a man, exactly? Tuesday? It definitely wasn't Monday. Monday that was still my little boy standing in front of me." She beamed.

Norris let her redo his tie, unsure of what to say to that. He never knew in those moments where Judith, or Felix for that matter, seemed fascinated by his very existence. Then again, Norris supposed he would never see himself as the two of them saw him.

"Chin up," Judith ordered. "This Madison seemed very . . ."

"White?"

"I was going to say *nice*, but sure, let's go with that. Is her family nice too?"

Norris nodded without moving his neck, which as it turned out wasn't very easy to do.

"They're great. And yeah, she is," Norris agreed. "Um, very nice."

And pretty. And smart. And fun. And popular. And the boss's daughter. And one of the two real friends Norris had made in this entire country.

"Hey," Judith said, snapping Norris out of it. She poked at

his temple gently. "Stay out of there."

Maybe it was something about her tone, or the simplicity of the directive, but Norris resolved to do just that. At least for the rest of the day. Judith wondered if they should take a photo, and Norris even went along with four different mother-son configurations before pointing out that Judith was officially running late for her faculty meeting.

"Shoot! Don't spill anything more than seltzer on that suit," Judith said, laptop already in hand and purse straps at her arm. "Your father will sense it in Canada: *I wouldn't have bought him such an expensive suit if he was just going to ruin it.*"

The instances were few and far between, rare slips of the motherly mask Norris would occasionally glimpse, but she always puffed her cheeks when mimicking Felix. Norris wondered if this was how she'd seen the man for the last leg of their marriage: a fat and slow-witted pile of disappointment, weighing her down despite the tall frame and easy charm the rest of the world saw in his father.

"No eating spaghetti with my fingers. Got it." Norris smiled.

"Sorry I can't drop you off, but there's no missing this meeting. There's sixty bucks on the table for cab rides there and back. Text me pictures if you can, and remember, home by one a.m. and t—"

"Tip the driver, yes, Mom, I know. Go. You're really late."

She kissed him on the cheek again before dashing off, another inscrutable soup of expressions on her face. Apprehensive pride? She clearly wasn't used to Norris having much of an active social life, which was fair enough: it was a brave new world for both of them.

After checking his phone for an Aarti update for the umpteenth time, Norris made his way into Anderson High's banquet hall, which was, in fact, a full-on party space. Between the tablecloths, silverware, and air filled with silver, white, and black balloons, the space felt nothing like the familiar school hallways just a few yards away.

He was decidedly overdressed as far as the guys went. In his mind, proms, even those of the junior variety, were black-tie affairs; but Austin being Austin, that mandate still allowed for a lot of wiggle room for both chaperoning parents and students alike. Some were true southerners, dressed to the nines for the occasion; flowers in hair and boutonnieres for the men. Others wore more subdued attire, which was still pretty impressive—pageantry of churchgoers and all that. The third contingent were very literally dressed for an average neighborhood barbecue. Was that guy wearing sand camouflage cargo shorts? Jesus.

"Tuxedo!" Patrick exclaimed upon spotting Norris, giving him a knuckle sandwich, which Norris now accepted as Patrick's way of saying hello. "Looking baller, man!"

"Thanks, Patrick."

His armpit hairs were currently contained under layers of cotton seersucker for the occasion, topped by way of a lime green bow tie. . . . A lot was happening. Patrick held up his drink.

"Coconut water." He nodded. "Trying to cut back."

"That's good, man."

"Not sure if I ever thanked you for helping that day, by the way."

"Teammates." Norris smiled.

If Norris were a better person—no major realignment, just like 4 percent better of a person—he might have completely put the staircase and F-word incidents behind him like Patrick genuinely seemed to have. He treated Norris like a proxy member of his tribe now. Norris got nods in the hallways, fist bumps after hockey drills, and disgusting meme photos from around the web that he suspected Patrick enjoyed sending to every one of his contacts. Still, that 4 percent still occasionally felt like a canyon. They would get there, eventually. Probably.

"Flying solo tonight?" Patrick asked.

"I'm meeting Maddie here, which I don't even think means anything . . . basically, just that we're going to, um, interact with each other near balloons."

"You didn't even pick her up?" Patrick grinned. "Who said Canadians were polite again?"

"It's not a date! Like, I'm not on a date here with you, after all, so by that measure, nothing that takes place here can—"

"Dude, c'mon, what do I care?" Patrick said with a harmless chuckle. "Maddie's the one you need to apologize to."

"I'm sure she barely noticed with all the excitement going on," Norris eventually said, looking around at their chattering, excited classmates. Only about half the junior student body was present, but those who came were clearly here to have a good time, laughing and taking selfies with this person and then the next. All the recognizable faces from Anderson High belonged to the expected kids that Norris associated with Maddie's extensive social circle; the cream of the Bats varsity crop. It was . . . nice.

"Y'know, Madz is a real sweetheart," Patrick said solemnly as they navigated toward an empty table. "She's always been. So don't be a dick to her, all right?"

"Excuse me?"

"Just, I don't know, man, treat her right. That's all," Patrick continued. "Big-brother spiel over."

Norris's face must have betrayed his intense confusion since Patrick felt the need to go on.

"Look, I swear I'm not bringing the hammer down on you or anything. It's mostly for my sake. Meredith wanted me to say something. Maddie and Mer; Mer and Maddie. One's unhappy, so is the other. And then my ear gets talked off until I'm comatose."

"Right," Norris simply said. "No being a dick to Maddie. Got it."

"Good!"

Patrick patted his back again, having recognized one of his football teammates and preparing to join a small pack of seersucker-ed bros. Norris chose not to follow and settled for the holding pattern of standing by the snacks table. He slid his phone out of his currently very pleated slacks. There were no new texts from Aarti, which was to be expected.

"A tuxedo, Canada?" Maddie said, startling him with a quick kiss on the cheek. "You're making it too easy."

"You're, um, wow, stunning" was the only thing Norris could think to say. Maddie's dress was less revealing and less ostentatious than the pageant taffeta constructions that some of the other girls were wearing but perfectly suited to her. She looked so good it took a moment for him to realize that the shade of orange was dangerously close to burnt orange—his previous rage color.

"Hmm, stunning, uh?" She tilted her hip forward with a smirk at the compliment. "According to Derek and Marco from the swim team, I'm looking both *choice* and *tight*, so *stunning* is definitely a step up."

"I mean, both are also appropriate in this case," he said with a grin. Something weird was happening to his chest.

"Liam didn't come?" she inquired, looking around.

"Not really his scene," Norris answered. It was a position that had been deduced from the **not really my scene** text Norris had received when the invitation had been extended. According to the photo Liam had sent earlier, his scene tonight was a woodworking workshop across town.

"Fair enough. Elisa and Sarah both passed on it too," she said, screaming over the music that was kicking off through the loudspeakers. "I'm glad you came, though!"

Luckily, Norris soon found himself dragged out of his own head and onto the dance floor, trying to keep up as best as he could with Maddie, Patrick, Meredith, Trish, and a bunch of the girls from school. Credit where credit was due, Patrick was busting a severe move.

Norris's biggest secret was perhaps the fact that he truly, sincerely loved dancing. The opportunities were few and far between, but something about Maddie's embarrassed squeals and Patrick's cheering, and the school's more than acceptable soundtrack turned the dance floor into a true friend; they understood each other. It was a beautiful, supportive friendship filled with motions and lights and girls in shimmering dresses laughing from the sidelines. His dancing had evolved into a shapeless waddling that put him at one with the universe.

"Noooooo," he whined, as he felt himself being dragged out of the gym. Okay, fine, part of the deepest recesses of Norris's soul might actually really enjoy dancing when he could turn off the self-conscious part of his brain. The occasions to do it without looking like a fool and/or ass were few and far between, but it just made him happy. The last time had been almost two years ago, at one of Judith's old friend's weddings.

"I need some air," Maddie laughed, still dragging him.

"Where, why? The dance floor is that way!"

"Yes, I am removing you from the dance floor; the dance floor is not your friend."

"The dance floor and I are starting a hockey league together."

She laughed again.

"Where are we going?"

"To get some air," she insisted, leading him by the hand. Had he ever held hands with Aarti? Actually held hands publicly? She didn't seem the type.

🐱 **Are you going to screen her a movie at the pool too?** 🐱 🐱

"That was truly shocking," Maddie said, shaking her head. "Like, upsetting."

Norris still felt like dancing and kept moving around her.

"You loved it!"

"Stop moving!"

"Never!" he cried, still dancing as they exited through Anderson's double doors.

Buzz. Norris paused on the front steps as his phone vibrated with another text from Aarti.

🐱 **Did she pick you up for your date the way I always do, since you don't drive?** 🐱 🐱

Norris shook his head, sitting down on the steps of the school. He stared at his phone in frustration.

Maddie slid down to a seat beside him. "What's going on? Aarti?"

Even though it was probably weird to talk to a girl you were on a date with about another girl you were dating, after months of talking to Maddie about Aarti it felt all too natural, and so he told her the whole thing—about Aarti's flat-out refusal to go to prom, about her telling him *he* should go, ending in her jealous messages the moment images of him and Maddie presumably hit social media.

Norris slid his phone into his pocket with a frustrated sigh.

"Whatever, I don't need to respond to her right now. She could've come if she wanted, but she didn't. I'm not going to spend my night texting her. That'd be kind of pathetic."

"I'm proud of you, Canada," Maddie said, watching him, a smile on her face.

"Because I'm out here, socializing like a real live American boy?" Norris snorted. "If this keeps going, I might buy a Chevy and take it to a levee, whatever that is."

"Because you're finally above all her mind games, Norris!"

"Says the mind-game whisperer."

Maddie shook her head.

"You know, I was happy to help you get together with her because it's what you wanted, but . . . can I be truthful here? . . . It's really not supposed to be this hard."

"What's not supposed to be this hard?"

"Dating!" she exclaimed before pointing to two classmates who Norris recognized but did not know, giggling into each other's ears as they traipsed toward their cars.

"See?" Maddie narrated. "He likes her, she likes him the exact same amount, and—"

"And isn't that convenient?" Norris said with a sigh, still eyeing the couple. The guy had been holding on to the girl's purse all night too. It was sweet.

"Something like that," Maddie said wistfully. "I'm not saying you're not a walking bag of neurotic nonsense sometimes, most of the time, but Aarti's been messing with your head for months now, and . . . honestly? You deserve better."

Norris raised an eyebrow, surprised. He'd never heard Maddie say anything negative about . . . well, anyone, really. She had a sharp tongue, sure, but she seemed to genuinely like everyone who crossed her path, Aarti Puri included. "Meow," he said with a smile. "I can't say I dislike you getting all cheerleader catty on my behalf."

"I'm serious," Maddie replied. "You've been seeing her basically since you got here, and for what? Are you even officially boyfriend/girlfriend?"

Norris shook his head. If there was one thing he felt pretty certain of, it was that Aarti Puri didn't take being someone's girlfriend lightly. It was one of the things he liked most about her—that she was so un-pin-down-able. It was a quality, though, that was slightly less charming five months in. "No, she's not my girlfriend."

In the distance, someone let out a cackling laugh. Norris found that he wasn't in any particular rush to get back to the dance.

Maddie was looking at him again. She was doing that a lot tonight. She had a way of lolling her head from side to side when considering a prospect, like pros and cons were accumulating in her head.

"What?"

Finally, she tipped her head, seeming to decide something. "I have to do everything myself," she said, shaking her head with a little smile and grabbing him by both shoulders. "It's my plight in life."

The next thing Norris felt were Maddie's lips against his. Kiwi-lime lip balm. Something tropical and yummy. Maddie was kissing him! Wait, why was Maddie kissing him?! And yet Norris's next thought, elbowing the first out of the way, was that . . . he really, really liked it.

He could feel her smile against his lips, and maybe he was smiling too. There was nothing frantic, messy, or desperate to it. It felt familiar and giddy and another uncertain thing all at once.

Somewhere along the way, Maddie had come to know him, and Norris knew her too. There was something about kissing someone you knew that quieted the part of your brain that ever felt anxious or small.

"Um," Norris whispered. "Since when?"

"Your interview, probably," she said with the collected smirk of someone used to an entire crowd repeating her every syllable upon command. "I remember thinking, God, this sweaty disaster boy is kind of cute when he's not vomiting pure nonsense at you."

"That was, like, the first actual conversation we ever had."

"I'm aware," Maddie said.

She'd gotten him the job on the spot. No reference checks when all she knew of him was that he was prone to calling her and her friends bad names in hallways . . .

"So," he said, ". . . the whole time?"

"Pretty much."

"Why didn't—"

293

"You liked someone else, Canada." She shrugged in a decidedly Norris-like way. It didn't come off like an accusation; more like a sad fact.

She laughed out loud, slipping an arm under his. "It's fine," she said. "Really."

"I really like kissing you," Norris said. "And I like dancing, and I like balloons, and you came to our weird, ridiculous hockey game, and you're nice and kind, which may sound lame, but is actually really rare, and did I mention the kissing?"

She smiled. God, she was pretty. Had she always been this gorgeous? "What about Aarti?" Her tone got serious again. "I'm not a thief, Norris. And unlike Mer, I try not to chase the drama. I can't stand it, honestly."

Aarti. Right.

The spark that Norris had felt the first time he'd seen her at school still hadn't subsided. It was still there—a jolt that shook him whenever her name popped up on his phone. After all these months, after meeting her parents and clocking so much time together, he still felt like he'd just approached her to introduce himself at a crowded party. His mind was permanently racing to find ways to keep her attention in him alive; blowing and blowing on the spark to make it grow, and competing with the Ian-shaped hole that occupied more and more space in his mind these days. Sure, it might all be in his head, it might have all been a prison of his own making but it felt no less exhausting these days.

"Like I said, she's not my girlfriend," Norris finally said, though he felt a twinge of guilt even as he said it. Aarti might not technically be his girlfriend, but he also never thought he'd be the type to go around kissing someone else. "Besides, you kissed me," he pointed out. Not that he minded, because he definitely did not.

"Someone told me to learn to be more selfish."

"Sounds like a very wise, tall, and handsome person," Norris agreed, and leaned in again, happy to be resuming the kissing.

29

THE AFTER-PROM PARTY

DEFINING CHARACTERISTICS: Complete lack of parental figures, wall-to-wall bodies thrashing, joints in bathrooms, sex in cars, party crashers, extensive property damage.

FOOD SOURCES: Kegs, coolers, ransacked liquor cabinets—nothing solid.

EXPECTATIONS FROM EVERY MOVIE EVER:

1. Secrets revealed, tempers flaring.
2. Fistfights. Someone is inevitably punched across the face. Please, God, let it be Ian.
3. Hissy fits. Someone is inevitably left publicly shamed. Please, God, let it be Meredith.
4. Strict dance laws are likely to be upheaved.

After Meredith's perfunctory coronation as prom queen for the second year in a row, Maddie, Meredith, Patrick, and a few others decided to check out an after-party currently taking place at a nearby golf club. Apparently, plenty of the kids who could not bother with the actual jock-y prom crowd (which Norris categorically did not see himself being a part of) were already there in jeans and shorts, getting properly trashed without adult supervision.

Norris and Maddie rode in the back of a crowded pickup truck, surrounded by laughter and shrieks—the sort of car filled with teenagers he had always rolled his eyes at before. Right now, he couldn't help but feel like he had been missing out, especially while holding Maddie's hand. His lips were still tingling from their kiss. Again and again, he found himself catching her eye at the same time she was looking at him. *This could be something*, he allowed himself to ponder.

That was, of course, until they got to the golf club, where the party was in full swing around them. Norris froze dead in his tracks before he could even feel the room's air-conditioning.

"What's wrong?" Maddie asked.

"Aarti," Norris simply said, looking straight into the crowded space. Maddie followed his eyes to the middle of the dance floor, where Aarti and Ian were making out *hard*.

"Oh," Maddie said softly.

It was the sort of making out that needed the qualifier. Standard making out implied lips and tongues and nothing more. The current display involved esophaguses and pancreases (*has anyone ever used the plural of* pancreas *before?* he wondered distractedly). Ian and Aarti were making out *hard*, groping and pulling. Even people around the pair were taking unfavorable notice, and like them, all Norris could do was contemplate the sight. He felt restless, angry, and sad all at once. Nothing was rising; it was just a slow boil of emotions sitting hard and heavy in his belly.

Before he knew what he was doing, he had marched over and interrupted the make-out session. "Norris, no! Bad idea!" Maddie cried, hustling after him. That was the thing about Aarti; his legs always seemed to be moving toward her before his brain could catch up.

"Really, Aarti?" he asked, startling her out of the kiss. She looked back defiantly, shocked but entirely unapologetic.

"What are you doing here?"

"Dude," Ian said. "Fuck off! Every time we turn around, you're there. What the hell?"

For all the online stalking, this was Norris's first up-close look at Ian. It really was impressive how much blandness could be squeezed into a single human being.

"Don't you have a girlfriend?" Norris asked.

"None of your business, man!"

He was right. Norris really knew nothing of the Ian and Aarti drama; he was on the periphery of Ian's life in the same way that Ian was on the periphery of his.

"Guys, I don't want to hurt any feelings here, but neither of you has the physique to pull off the aggro showdown that's about to happen here," Maddie joked, trying her hardest to diffuse the simmering tension. "So, let's all calm down and breathe before we embarrass ourselves."

Aarti rolled her eyes at Maddie's words. Rolled her eyes *hard*.

"Christ, were you born with a hall-monitor badge around your neck? Let them at it. What do you care?"

"Norris." Maddie turned to him, trying her best to ignore Aarti's taunt. "How about we just get out of here, hmm?"

Norris could feel Maddie tugging at his arm, but he really didn't want to move. There was an urge in his stomach to hit.

"Aren't you being just a little bit of a hypocrite here, Norris?" Aarti said, arms crossed in front of her. "You're wearing a tuxedo! You were at prom with someone else."

"Yeah," Norris retorted. "Because the girl I've been dating for *months* wouldn't go with me! And by the way, if you think going to prom is too much of a cliché, rushing to Ian's side whenever he snaps his fingers, hoping he'll leave his girlfriend, is straight out of the daddy issues playbook."

That one earned Norris some "oohs" from the crowd, which felt both good and terrible.

"I don't owe you an explanation for anything I do, Nor," Aarti said. "We're not exclusive!"

"Oh, enough with that crap!" Norris said, maybe a little too loudly. They were now gathering an audience. "What does that mean? Honestly! Are we a freaking commune of hippies? We're sixteen! What's so wrong with dating one person and—"

"Canada, stop!" Maddie said, stepping in and employing the authoritative tone of hers that could command a kitchen full of grown men at the Bone Yard. "This is so not worth it. Let's just go get some air, all right?"

"Sidekick Barbie to the rescue," Aarti said. "Accessories

include cell phone, barbecue sauce bottle, and Meredith Santiago's tampon case."

An uncomfortable sensation formed in Norris's stomach at her words. He felt something roiling.

"What the hell is your problem?" Maddie asked Aarti.

"Oh, that wasn't me, babe," Aarti said, her voice low and detached and taking on a new edge. "That was just my favorite line from your entry in Norris's field guide."

"What are you talking about?"

"The little yellow diary he keeps? You must have seen it around. All he does is write in that thing. His most intimate thoughts about the vapid, stupid, or ridiculous people that come his way."

Aarti laughed, turning to Norris for a moment. "What, you only showed it to me then? I should be flattered."

In that moment, everything became startlingly clear. When he looked at Aarti, he didn't see the artist or the dreamer; he only saw the role she was currently playacting: complete bitch. Playacting, because it was definitely an act. She was very good at being nasty when hurt, Norris thought. In that moment, she reminded him of himself.

"You're the worst of the bunch," Aarti said with a sneer before turning away and heading for the exit.

Norris was getting exhausted. This was too much. Their voices were starting to blur. "I don't feel well."

"Hey," Maddie said, resting a hand on his cheek. Why was she being so gentle with him, after what Aarti just told her?

"You're looking kind of pale."

"I am?"

"Well, no, actually," she said. "But that always seems to be something people say to someone who doesn't look well on TV."

Norris chuckled uncomfortably. "Look, what she said, that's not— I mean, I categorically don't think that of you, okay?" he pleaded in a hushed tone. The crowd was dispersing, leaving him and Maddie alone. "Please believe that."

"Hey, I know, it's okay. Really." She brought him in for a hug, and Norris melted into her embrace. No wonder people were always hugging her around school; she gave really good hugs. Her hands reached around his waist and then up against his chest. She gave his lapel a tug.

"I'm gonna go give my dad a call, so he doesn't worry," Maddie said.

"Okay," Norris said. "Are you going to come back?"

"Of course." Maddie smiled, but something about it felt off.

A few moments went by and then it all came together in a sickening rush. Norris patted himself down. *No, shit, no, no.* The notebook was gone.

Maddie had swiped it during their hug.

Maddie was nice. Maddie spent her days caring for other people. When her father needed someone to take over the reins, she was an assistant. When any of her friends needed a shoulder to cry on, she was there with a smile. When her church needed money for new pews, she was the one stapling flyers around the school. When an abrasive new foreign kid needed a job and dating advice, Maddie was there.

That's what Norris told himself as he rushed outside, looking around for Maddie. There was nothing she wouldn't forgive in that notebook. Right?

"She's at the gazebo" Norris heard out of nowhere.

Meredith was climbing up the hill, arms fully gloved, ridiculous tiara perched on her head and meticulously braided locks circling her head. She held up the hem of her taffeta dress, the fringes already muddy. "I was looking for a place to pee and she just ran out. . . ."

"Thanks," Norris mumbled as he caught up with Meredith and headed for the gazebo at the back of the expansive golf course.

"Do you want me to come wi—"

"No!" Norris all but hurled back.

This would be fine! He would cover a week of shifts for her to make up for it, and they would go back to doing their thing. Norris and Maddie. All he had to do was talk to her, and everything would be okay.

Norris found her seated on the lit-up gazebo, reading the notebook intently. Unlike Aarti, who had contented herself with skimming a few entries, she had a frown on her face and seemed to be absorbing every page. She looked up to him and returned to flipping through, reading aloud the headlines of Norris's scribbles. "'The Taxonomic Differences Between Swim Team and Football Team' . . . 'Teachers Most Likely to Start a Drug Cartel on the Side' . . . Oh, here it is."

Shit.

"'The Beta Cheerleader,'" she read aloud. "'Just blonde, just talented enough to flip to the middle of the pyramid. Hobbies include kissing the ass of those at the top.'"

She gently closed the notebook and put it down on the gazebo's seat.

"I should be flattered I got my own page, right?"

"That was before I got to know you," Norris sputtered. "It's a first impression and nothing else! You've totally changed my mind!"

"Oh, have I, Norris?" she said. "Did I redeem all basic white cheerleaders in your complex little mind?"

"Come on, Maddie, that's not fair. Haven't you ever realized you were wrong about anyone before? I wrote all that a million years ago. It's in the past."

"It's *not* in the past." Maddie shook her head, holding up the notebook as evidence. "It's in your tuxedo pocket. It's coming out of Aarti's *mouth.*"

"Maddie . . ." Norris began, desperately trying to defuse the hurt in her voice that was gutting him in the moment. He didn't know what to say.

"All I did was be nice to you, Norris," Maddie said. "From what I can see, all *everyone* did was be nice to you. *Basic white cheerleader. Coven of bitches. Prozac popper.* That wasn't a slip. That's the real you, isn't it?"

"No! I don't . . . I don't know." For once Norris was at a loss. *Was* it the real him? He'd felt badly about it, sure, and in the case of Liam, he'd made sure to apologize. But he still couldn't help thinking those things, and half the time, he still couldn't stop his mouth from saying them. "I guess I . . . I guess I do judge people."

Didn't everybody? All the time, always?

"I'll say." Maddie gestured at the notebook as she snapped it firmly shut. "But guess what: you may turn your nose up at the cheerleaders and the jocks and the prozac popper, you may sit in your room cackling over our predictable habits, but the rest of us are just trying our hardest to make it through each day being who we are. And I'll tell you right now—you are as profoundly basic as the rest of us, Canada. Actually, no. You're worse. Because at least the football team fuckboys aren't pretending to be better than everyone in a hundred-mile radius."

"Maddie," Norris pleaded. This was a misunderstanding. This was getting out of hand. "You know I'm better than the football fuckboys."

"Right," Maddie said after a moment, eyeing him up and down and taking in the whole of his being. "You know what, you deserve her."

He didn't even have to ask who she meant. Of course she meant Aarti, the girl he'd spent all year admiring and pining for; the girl whose side he'd rushed to at every opportunity, just like he'd accused her of doing with Ian, in the most pathetic, clichéd of ways. The girl who'd, the second she thought she was on the brink of not getting what she wanted, responded with outright cruelty.

She was right, Norris thought. He and Aarti *did* deserve each other. And the person he didn't deserve was the kind, generous person sitting across from him, looking like she was doing everything in her power not to cry.

"Maddie . . ."

Norris turned to see Meredith hovering at the doorway to the gazebo. She took a step toward Maddie, making an attempt to put an arm around her best friend's shoulder. Maddie shrugged it off.

"No worries, babe. I'm fine," Maddie said, throwing a bright smile at Meredith. She looked back at Norris in a way that very much felt like it would be the last time, and then started to walk back toward the golf club, framed by the late-night fountains.

Meredith was staring at him like he was a flavorless piece of gum, chewed gray and found at the bottom of very expensive shoes.

"I thought you cared about Maddie."

"I do care about her!"

"No, I care about Maddie," Meredith all but hissed, obviously trying very hard not to shout. "Everyone back inside cares about Maddie. You—I have no idea. Liked that she was nice to you? Maybe it fed your ego, I don't know. And I really don't care."

"I don't . . . know" was all Norris could think to say. He was exhausted from the ups and downs of this seemingly endless evening.

Meredith scoffed. "Sixteen years and she's finally wrong about someone," she eventually sighed. "Go home, Norris."

A moment passed, and then another. The night was hot,

because that was how nights were in this place. Hot and oppressive. Norris felt as though any ball he tried to throw upward would immediately be brought down to the ground by the density of this heat. The very weight of being in Texas.

Maybe that was all he'd been doing all along: distracting himself from being in this place. His legs were no longer wobbly and had instead hardened into cement blocks as he trekked back toward the clubhouse.

Two girls chuckled upon seeing him, then quickly turned their shoulders to him. There was no one to give him a ride home, he realized. Norris was exhausted and really no longer had any reason to pretend that he belonged there, anyway.

But he didn't want to go home yet. He just wanted . . .

What did he want, exactly? He wasn't sure.

One thing he did know was that it was a perfect occasion to try a long-held theory of his, which was that any black guy in a passable tuxedo can walk into a fancy kitchen. No one even noticed Norris as he waltzed into the clubhouse, through the passing waitstaff, and grabbed a bottle of champagne from an opened case. He quickly shoved it his jacket on his way out through the course's parking lot, Meredith's words ringing in his ears.

Go home, Norris.

30

THE DRUNK DIAL

THE THREE KEY FORMS OF THE DRUNK DIAL:
1. The Lonely Drunk Dial
2. The Angry Drunk Dial
3. The Weepy Drunk Dial

Call 1: Eric

"Hey," came Eric's voice. "Here, someone wants to say hi."

"Hi, Norris," came the anonymous happy voice on the other line. *Who the fuck is that?*

"Who the fuck are you?"

"Oh, I'm Marc-André," the voice introduced itself. "I've heard a lot about you."

Oh, for fuck's sake.

"Yes, hi. Eric now, please. Cool, thanks."

More shuffling. Eric came back on the line.

"Are you in danger?" Norris asked.

"What?"

"Is this a dangerous situation for your personal safety?"

Eric laughed. "You called me, asshole!"

"Oh."

That's right, he had. Jesus. Bloody goddamn hell, how drunk was he right now?

"Are you on a date right now?"

"Um," Eric said. "Yeah, kinda. Are *you* in active danger?"

This entire state was a goddamn war zone, so yes, he very much was.

"Norris?"

"No," Norris managed after a moment of assessment. His blood sugar couldn't be amazing, and he was pretty sure he would be constipated this week, but there was no *active* danger. Apparently, the human body started to break down at age forty, so he was still ahead of the curve on that score.

"Are you sure?" Eric repeated his question.

"Why do you keep asking me that?"

"Because you called me."

"That's a little didactic. Darmactic. Dramatic." Words were hard tonight.

"Well, you don't normally call," Eric pointed out. "Even when you lived here, we didn't. Or, you didn't. You text and you email, but the voice-to-voice thing isn't your forte. Norris Kaplan 101. So, what did you call me for?"

Am I an asshole? Did I totally just fuck things up with the most amazing girl I've ever met?

"Pocket dial."

"Oh, bull-shite." His best friend didn't believe him for a

second. "Tell me what's wrong. Is this Aarti-related?"

"Nothing's wrong," Norris denied. "I'm at the prom with my friend Maddie. Her friend's having some sort of drama."

"What about Aarti?"

"What about her?" Norris echoed, defensive. "Man, that is the oldest of news."

"If you say so . . ."

"Oh, for God's sake." Norris hung up, quickly opened his camera, and took a selfie of himself brandishing the champagne bottle. *Hmm . . .* He rubbed his eyes, straightened his collar, and snapped another. Then another. And another. Eventually he captured one that looked decent enough. His eyes were less red in this shot. It was enough to assuage Eric, thousands of miles away and about to get laid.

Norris typed quickly:

Legit pocket dial. I'm totally fine. Go bk to your date!

Eric's reply came a few seconds later:

K. Let's chat tomorrow. Nice tux.

When had Norris turned into such a good liar?

Call 2: Dad

Austin, for all its many flaws, had a crap ton of active pay phones. Good pay phones too. Ones you could easily step into if your own phone's battery was in the red and your reception nonexistent in this part of the city. A part of Austin that Norris actually didn't recognize. From the soreness in his feet—stupid dress shoes—he had walked for quite a bit. Almost two hours.

No, that couldn't be right. The clock was a liar. For a moment he strongly considered the possibility that he might have walked all the way to Houston, which confirmed that he was definitely still tipsy. He was exhausted and restless all at once. Stupid Maddie. Stupid Aarti.

Anyway, the point was that Norris still remembered and appreciated pay phones. For the longest time, he'd gone without a cell phone back in Montreal. He might have been part of the very last generation of kids to remember life without one. It wasn't until the fourth grade that he'd walked into school one September to find every other kid suddenly connected to the world wide web and constantly checking their black screens for updates of the three to nine people they probably each knew at that age. Much like the Xbox, getting one from Judith had mostly been a matter of fitting in, something he'd wasted an obscene amount of energy trying to do over the years before realizing that it wasn't for him. In the end, he really was an origami person after all.

The stray pay phone he stepped into had been flooded by a streetlight, otherwise Norris might have walked right past it. Luckily for him, it was both trash- and urine-free, save for an empty soda cup and lipsticked straw forgotten over the console. Maybe they were making a comeback among the cool twenty-somethings this town seemed overrun by—retro technology that allowed you to live without constant notifications and alerts and a GeoPin so that everyone always knew who you were and what you were doing. Norris could definitely see the appeal to that.

There was only one number he'd bothered to memorize. Months ago, when he thought he would be dialing it every day, and it felt important to know by heart in case of situations like . . . well, situations like these.

"Oh, hello, deadbeat!" Norris hailed when his father picked up.

"Norris?"

"Correct, yes: Norris. Nor . . . iss."

"Are you okay?"

"Nohr-hissssss," Norris repeated, stretching out his name. "By the way: stupid name. Like, definitely the wrong call. Do you know how many people squint at me and then think 'Morris'? I'm going to have to deal with that all my life, fuck you very much."

"Noted," came the voice on the other line. "Anything else?"

Norris thought for a long moment. "*Butane* is a really funny word."

"Are you drunk?"

His father sounded more amused than anything else.

"Mm. Little bit, maybe," Norris conceded. "And see? That right there: What kind of shit dad gets a call from their only child in a different country, sauced out of his mind, and finds that 'musing?"

"I'm in a different country, kiddo, like you said. Are you safe?"

"That's not the point. We're never going to live in the same house again, by the way."

There was a pause on the line, some light shuffling. A phone

311

passing from one shoulder to the other.

"I'm sorry about that."

"Oh, so you know already? Right, *obvi*. I guess I thought I'd be unleashing some profound wisdom on you, but of course you already know. Your oldest kid, sixteen years in, just flies off to America and you'll never see him again, but whatever. You have a shitty little sequel in the works, so what do you care, right?"

"Obvi?"

"Yes, Dad. I hang out with cheerleaders and football players now and use the word *obvi*. I like a good abbreviation. It's elegant. Saves me time."

"Where is your mother?"

"They're all going to hate me after tonight anyway, so I guess I should say I used to hang with cheerleaders and football players."

"Where is your mother?" Felix repeated.

"On a date, probably."

Silence. Norris could almost hear the frown on Felix's brow.

"Aren't you going to say anything?!" Norris snapped. "Jesus! How—"

His father cut him off. "Where are you?"

"'M cold," Norris answered. Tee-hee, *butane*.

"That's not what I asked," Felix said, his voice taking the tone it did when Norris came home late from the ice rink and hadn't bothered to call. But that was all before. . . .

"Somewhere that's cold," Norris doubled down. *Because, really.*

"I'm fine," Norris said, rubbing his face. He was sick of Felix's voice, of the fake concern, of the way his head spun when he tried to look for a street sign. He was in Texas. Felix was in Vancouver. What was the point of this? Of any of it?

"Forget it," Norris said. "I'll get home fine. It's all fine."

"Norris—"

"Go look after the kid who still cares what you think," Norris lashed out. "Or maybe get a head start on that third family for when this one blows up in your face. Bye, *Felix*."

There was something soothing in the dial tone when it came. It rang at the exact frequency of the throbbing migraine in the back of his head. Norris wondered why he hadn't hung up sooner.

Car lights blazed over him, searing his retinas as a siren screamed. The overwhelming sensory assault of blue and red and loud, Jesus Christ, so freaking loud, made Norris feel even sicker.

"Hey," a low, manly voice came, stepping out of the car and pointing a flashlight at Norris. Definitely not helping the retinas situation. "Are you all right there?"

Norris took a deep breath, trying to align his thoughts as best as he could in the moment.

"What the hell do you want, assface?" was all that came out.

31

THE TEENAGE MISCREANT

CHARACTERISTICS: Wise mouth paired with little thought. Overly
confident thanks to alcohol consumption.
MOTTO: "Do your freaking worst, universe."
MISCREANT KRYPTONITE: The mother.
ATYPICAL OFFENSES: Mouthing off to a white cop. (Hands-down
the dumbest.)

There was a specific scent to the police station holding room,
as it turned out. To Norris, it smelled like a specific person—
some guy named Clyde. Clyde smelled like bureaucracy that
hadn't showered for a few weeks and coated its thinning hair in
Crème de Despair every morning. Clyde's rising stench lived in
every corner of the small gray room Norris had been put in, in
the mold that had amassed in the corners of his table, in the peeling gray paint of the door, which really did not seem that solid,
all things considered.

His stomach was killing him. Too much alcohol, not enough

food. Norris wanted to make a run for it; he wanted a time machine; most of all, he really wanted his mom.

Are you all right there? Where are you going, kid? Where are you coming from? How old are you? Are you drunk? Where is your ID? Canada? Don't lie to me now: How old are you?

There were clear correct answers to these questions, and Norris had apparently failed to provide a single one of them. His mouth's answers were closer to pointing out the fact that the officer's shoes were brown and his belt appeared to be black under the car's tail lights; to the fact that America definitely had a gun problem; and that really, if you thought about it, this whole thing was the fault of some asshole named Ian.

So, now Clyde.

Norris had apparently looked petrified enough, arriving at the station—head pounding—that the officer had put him in this separate space of confinement. Part of it, he thought, was due to the fact that the holding area he had walked past was currently at capacity. The officer had driven them to a small county station nearby rather than what Norris imagined to be Austin's central station somewhere downtown. Norris had walked quickly behind the officer, but he'd looked in long enough to see two white fraternity bros in popped collar dress shirts, sleeping it off on each other's shoulders, a Latino guy with his hands tucked into his hoodie pocket and his head sunk low. He looked like he'd been crying. But mostly, Norris had glimpsed enough to make out at least five black men; one wore a suit and two appeared homeless. Either that or film-festival hipsters.

"Your mother is here," the policewoman offered as she opened the door. From her voice, Norris thought she might have a cold.

She escorted him to another area and slid behind a desk, stamping something. They had all his information. Norris Harrison Kaplan, seventeen, Canadian. Intoxicated. More words that Norris couldn't make out upside down from his side of the counter.

"Excuse me, ma'am, where is my mother?"

She looked up at him. "I'll take you to her in a bit. Just need to process this. Protocol for minors."

It wasn't a cold, Norris noted. Her voice just naturally sounded like she needed to clear her throat.

"Is she really mad?"

She stopped writing again and looked up at him with a frown. "That's . . ."

"What?"

"Nothing." She waved it off. "That's just the first time I've ever heard someone ask that question here."

She pushed herself off her chair, shaking her head with a wry smile.

"Yes, kid. She's fucking pissed."

Judith had been silent since the station. Normally Norris was an expert on all her silences: Grading Silence, Studying Silence, The-Man-I-Married-and-Followed-to-Canada-Just-Left-Forever Silence . . . but at the moment, Norris couldn't gauge whether this was the calm before an unspeakable storm or if she was simply ignoring him beyond the bare necessities of retrieving his body and ferrying it home. Plus, he was still tipsy.

"'M hungry," Norris complained, his face crumpled against the passenger seat window. His head was killing him and his stomach felt like it was rotting from the inside. Judith kept driving, eyes on the road. Her face was unnervingly calm. The only sign that she was seething were her hands clenching the steering wheel; every time an orange highway light flicked by, Norris could make out the veins in her grip.

"Mom," he tried again. "Tonight was ridiculous, 'm aware of that, but 'm really freaking starving here. I didn't actually have any food at the prom, and I don't feel—"

His phone vibrated on the dash: "LIAM." The blue light flooded the entire car, further punishing Norris's brain. Everything felt like another ingredient for the soupy headache simmering right behind his eyeballs.

"No," Judith said icily.

"It's Liam," Norris whined, which felt like a valid and coherent explanation. Liam had done nothing wrong. Liam was still one of the *good* Austin people. Norris picked up the phone, if only to text back, when his mother's hand moved through his to snatch the phone and slam it back down onto the dashboard. Twice. It was a miracle that it didn't shatter.

"You paid for that phone, y'know," he grumbled.

Judith turned up the radio in response, unleashing a new level of Top 40 torture to Norris's pounding brain. *Okay . . . calm before the storm, then.*

* * *

"The drunk thing I can understand." Judith finally spoke, dropping her keys into the key bowl and turning on the range-hood light, rather than the insanely bright overhead. It was her first act of mercy all night.

"Teenagers drink. Teenagers lie. They get moody for no reason and sulk in their rooms."

"Mom . . ." Norris started to explain before catching her eye and thinking better of it as her voice crescendoed.

"They won't stop talking about some girl for weeks, ask you to dry-clean their suit before going to dinner at her house, then never once bring her over or offer for you to meet her! God forbid you even dare broach the subject. Oh no. Just put the food on the table and pick them up when they text, like you're a taxi. But that's okay, because Norris is a good one, right? You're so lucky, Judith! Norris is so mature; Norris gets good grades; Norris doesn't do drugs; Norris knows better than to get mixed up with bad people. . . ."

This wasn't just about the alcohol. Even sober, Norris wouldn't have been able to track what the hell she was talking about.

"You would *never* get a call at two a.m. that Norris has been charged for disorderly conduct, Judith." She pointed a finger at him. "Norris would *never* be arrested for contempt of a law officer, Judith! *You didn't raise a fucking moron, Judith!*"

"I didn't *do* anything!" Norris snapped, loudly enough for it to echo through the apartment. He could get loud too. "You weren't there! That cop was a fucking asshole!"

Ow.

In hindsight, it was weird that Norris had never been slapped. Not that he'd ever deserved it, but considering the aghast looks on Maddie's face and Aarti's tonight—even Meredith's—he'd kind of been expecting one for a while now. He had zingers ready for those occasions when the shadow of a slap might loom overhead. But not for his mother. His own mother had slapped him. A full-on *The Young and the Restless* slap.

"What the hell, Mom?!" Norris barked, eyes red and cheek stinging. "Are we just doing physical abuse now?! Want to get a branch and turn it into a switch while you're at it? Jesus Christ!"

"Shut your mouth," Judith roared. "Shut your goddamn mouth. You're smarter than that, so don't play dumb, Norris!"

"Why are you so mad at me?" Norris shouted back. The neighbors could definitely hear them now. His throat was dry, but he didn't care. "I'm sorry if I interrupted one of your dates, or whatever, but I DID NOT DO ANYTHING! Ground me for leaving the prom, ground me for drinking, but I didn't drive, I didn't have unprotected sex, I didn't even get high! You *know* that! You're supposed to be on my side here, Mom!"

"NO!" she hurled back. "Not on this, Norris! I can't be!"

"Why the hell not?!"

"You know *damn* well! Trayvon Martin," she began. "Tamir Rice, Cameron Tillman, so many others that I can't remember all their names anymore!"

Norris knew too well. It was almost a ritual, even back in Canada. They would sit as a family and watch quietly. "Be smart out there," Felix used to say.

"You're not a handsome blue-eyed little Ken doll who's going to get a slap on the wrist every time he messes up. That, tonight?" she said, pointing to the door. "Do you know what that was? Do you?!"

"I—"

"That was a fucking *coin flip*, Norris. That was the coin landing heads." Her finger dug into his chest, punctuating every other word she was saying, spittle flying at his face. "Heads. A good one. Officer Miller, who has four sons, and luckily, mercifully, thank *Jesus* saw someone else's kid back-talking him tonight."

She exhaled, her breath Thai-food hot against his face.

"Tails." Her voice broke. "*Tails*, and I would be at the morgue right now identifying you! With some man lecturing me about your blood alcohol level and belligerent language and how you had it coming."

The last poke was to the middle of his forehead. Norris stared back, tight-lipped and doing everything in his power to keep his eyes unfocused. He couldn't bear to actually *see* her right now. Not like this.

"Am I wrong? Hmm? Tell me I'm wrong here, Norris."

She shoved Norris's head aside as if she couldn't think of anything else to do and finally stepped away. Her fingers dug into her hairline, under the wig. She turned back to him, and she had never appeared older to Norris.

"You're not Liam. Or Eric. You don't get to be." She quivered, chest heaving as though she just ran a marathon. "And that's unfair, and I'm sorry, baby. I really am, but that's the world. It was for your dad, it is for you, and it will be for your son too, so you might as well get used to it. You . . ."

320

She started to leave the kitchen but turned back one last time. His mother was openly crying now.

"You're a statistic waiting to happen, and not only did I raise a kid dumb enough not to realize that . . . I brought him to the middle of Texas, of all places. Mother of the year."

Her bedroom door slammed.

And the bathroom door behind it slammed too.

Norris went to bed. He wasn't hungry anymore.

32

THE POSTPROM HANGOVER

CHARACTERISTICS: Dry mouth, sore feet, headache, regret, and more headache again.

ANTIDOTES: Water, window shades, deep-fried pancakes, waffles, and chicken, all topped with syrup. As much greasy food as the human body can physically handle.

Norris's sleep was the heavy, all-encompassing quicksand that restores and drains with equal measure.

He slept through his first urge to pee, past his second urge to pee. In the brief, fleeting moments where awareness came knocking, he swatted it away. How much was a mattress? He could probably get another. He slept until the sun beating through his open windows no longer bothered him. There were dreams, brief flashes of coherence, and he slept through those as well. The dream of himself naked at Anderson High: he slept through. The dream of him holding a crying infant: he slept through.

He slept until his brain could no longer ignore the screaming agony between his ears. Was this what being hungover was? Norris's mouth was dry, and he was officially starving. Wincing against the late afternoon sun, he stumbled into the kitchen.

There was a ghost sitting at the table.

"Hi, Dad," Norris said, because he couldn't think of anything else to say. He threw his mother a look, and she answered by placing a glass of ice water in front of his chair, along with two aspirins.

"Sit," she said softly, gently touching the spot she'd slapped a few hours prior. "We need to talk."

Norris obeyed, noticing an old sports bag he recognized by the door.

"How are you feeling?" his father asked with a look somewhere between pity, admonishment, and amusement.

"Like crap," Norris said, crushing the tablets between his teeth and chugging the bitter powder with a gulp of water instead of swallowing it because he still didn't know how to do that.

"What are you doing here?"

"Well," Felix said. "The thing about your teenage son drunk dialing you, and his mother calling you an hour later to tell you he's in jail—it's hard to get a full night's sleep after that."

Drunk tank; not jail, Norris thought but did not say.

"I thought you'd be more upset," he said sheepishly.

"Oh, I'm goddamn furious, kid." Felix smiled. "But I remember what a hangover looks like."

Judith raised her eyebrows as if to say *I'm sure you do*, which everyone noticed, but the table unanimously decided to leave unacknowledged.

"Anyway, the yelling comes later. When it will stick to your sober mind," Felix replied. "Six hundred dollars on a last-minute flight. Believe me; there will be yelling. Not to mention the hotel I'm going to have to get now . . ."

"We have a kid together." Judith sighed. "The couch pulls out."

"Thank you, Judith," Felix said. "I like to rest between my yelling fits."

He turned back to his son, thankfully still using his calm, sensitive-to-hangovers voice, and asked: "So, kid. What do you want to do?"

There it was again, the question Norris was seemingly being asked on all sides. *What do you want?* In this case, the specifics of what his dad was asking seemed pretty clear. *Do you want to stay in Texas, where you are so clearly failing at life, or come back to Canada and allow things to return to not-quite-how-they-were-before, but close enough?*

Norris thought back to his conversation with his mother in the Anderson High parking lot, which now felt like a full eternity ago; of the bargain they'd made that day. *You have to give it a shot. If we're going to pack it all up and go back home, which I'm putting on the table, then you have to actually try.*

But he had tried, hadn't he? He'd made some friends. He'd gotten a job. He'd started a hockey team. He'd gone to the *prom*, for Christ's sake. He'd given it the best shot he possibly could have, and what did he get in return? One relationship that could only be classified as a failure. Another that crashed and burned before it even began. He'd made a scene, said some rude things, narrowly avoided an actual fistfight. He'd probably lost all the friends he'd made, considering they were Maddie's friends and not his, anyway. He'd certainly never go to another prom again.

Norris had asked the universe, and it had come back with a resoundingly clear answer: trying, American high school–style, was not a good look on Norris Kaplan. Texas was not a good *place* for Norris Kaplan.

"Mom, Dad." He looked back and forth between their faces, which so mirrored his own. "Thank you for everything you've done for me. I think I want to go home now, please."

33

THE BIG GOODBYE

TO-DO LIST BEFORE RETURNING TO MONTREAL:

- Reduce Mom's rage to a simmering, functioning anger.
- Say goodbye to Aarti.
- Say goodbye to Liam.
- Say goodbye to Maddie.
- Make it through final exams.
- Pack up room.

Norris was honestly grateful for the distraction of finals rolling around. No Aarti, no Maddie, no friends or "friends" with loaded quotation marks and innuendos. Judith had never even gotten around to grounding him after that horrible night, but studying in his room was exactly where he wanted to be. Hearing Felix rummaging around in the cupboards in the kitchen reminded Norris of life back in Montreal with the added wrinkle of now also occasionally overhearing him on the phone with Janet right outside his window. That was definitely new, and Norris preferred to focus on his notebooks than on the nagging memories of the many times he'd heard his father laugh on the phone outside their old apartment. No one really believed Janet had been the first Janet.

By and large, Anderson High was an easy school. Not the people, obviously—walking land mines, each and every one of them—but the classes themselves were all fairly simple. It wasn't an indictment of the American education system, but there really wasn't much to getting decent grades there as far as Norris was concerned. Due to the massive student body, tests and assignments were tailor-made to be passed. It was a straightforward process of turning board scribbles into notes, notes into memories, and then vomiting those memories onto exam pages. Even Goade's reputation as taskmaster of "a sadistic final exam from the depths of hell," a description provided by one Hairy Armpitted acquaintance, had boiled down to a few tricky formulas from the take-home problem set. Norris was sure he couldn't have gotten less than a B-plus. He could live with that. His only worry now was how it would all transfer back into the Quebec grading system. He really didn't want to retake any of these classes; Austin would be best left as a closed chapter in his mind, a weird life hiatus he might remember in passing years from now.

@Eric53 is online.
@Eric53—So, you're coming back? Permanently?!
@Norrtorious—Yup. That's a wrap on Texas.
@Eric53—Ur mom's OK with dat?

@Norrtorious—I think she's just happy to get rid of me for a summer? I'm gonna be with my dad while mom arranges the details.

@Eric53—Dang. She's OK leaving Texas and her new job after just getting there?

@Norrtorious—She says she'll be able to get adjunct work at McGill with Texas on her resume now. She's staying thru August to wrap up her summer semester but we should be back to status quo by September.

@Eric53—And the GF?

Norrtorious—That's not a thing anymore.

@Eric53—And ur job?

@Norrtorious—See above.

@Eric53—Wat happened down there?

@Norrtorious—Oh y'know. A little misdemeanor here; police station shenanigans there. I'll fill you in in person.

@Eric53—WTF?

@Norrtorious—Dude, check the best bro manual; we're going to be living in the same country again; I'm going to need some goddamn enthusiasm here!

@Eric53—Of course I'll be glad to have you back, u drama queen. Do u have any idea how quiet the bus ride to school is without you? I'm listening to podcasts FFS.

@Eric 53 is offline.

Norris had planned on picking up his last check from the Bone Yard in person, saying goodbye to everyone there, and maybe even getting a moment alone with Maddie, but it had been pre-emptively left in his mailbox. The fact that there wasn't a stamp on the envelope implied that it had been an in-person delivery, which was as good as a slammed door to the face. Someone really did not want him anywhere near the Bone Yard premises, and for some reason, he couldn't stop imagining Meredith taking her friendship duties very, very seriously. The chewing gum left behind his locker's lock one morning also had a vague after-smell of morning-drills bitchiness.

Finals were a hectic time for everyone; some of the varsity teams were away for games, and there were various posters around the school tracking the championships that were just out of reach for the Anderson High Bats. For the remaining students, some teachers turned their last few classes into study periods so students stayed home. Somehow, it took days for him to catch a glimpse of Maddie with two friends in one of the second-floor dance studios. Norris lingered outside the door, with an apology on his lips. Seven letters, one contraction. That's all he had to say. It was up to her to believe him or not, but Norris needed to get it off his chest. Suddenly the studio doors swung open, slamming Norris against the forehead and into a nearby water fountain. Ow.

"Nope," Meredith preempted, visibly proud of her work. "Jesus! Are you here for my firstborn or something? It's not going to happen," she said, snapping her fingers at the hallway where she presumably wanted him to disappear off to. "Git."

"Did you really just say 'git'?"

"Short and direct one-syllable command; it's the best way to deal with guys like you. Look, whatever you're waiting out here for you're not going to get it," she added, arms crossed in front of her.

Norris looked back to the studio door's window, catching a glimpse of Maddie's ponytail as the girls therein performed a series of cartwheels, one after another. Something in his chest twitched at the brief sight. If she knew he was out there, she was doing a great job of ignoring it.

"I just want to apologize, all right?"

"How's this instead? You stay away from her and I don't set you on literal fire. Does that sound like a deal, Norris?"

"Whatever," Norris said before walking away. A lengthy exchange with Meredith was a price of admission he wasn't ready to pay. He wouldn't give her the satisfaction of telling her he was leaving Texas.

"Stop putting gum behind my lock, you psycho!" Norris called back behind him.

"Nope" came the satisfied reply, as the doors slammed again.

God, he couldn't wait to leave this cursed time zone.

Liam was one of the few people Norris would genuinely miss hanging out with. He was sure that whatever farewell they engaged in would involve Buddhist mantras about the journey ahead and how distance was an illusion anyway. Instead, Liam slammed his locker more forcefully than Norris would have thought the news warranted and immediately stormed off toward the student parking lot. At least he hadn't reneged on giving Norris a ride home.

"So, that's it?" Liam concluded after Norris was done summarizing the past few days. "You're just bailing?"

"Dude," Norris sighed as Liam held the door open for him. "Me and Austin . . . it's just not a good fit, all right."

"You're a poker, Norris."

"I'm a . . ."

"A poker," Liam continued. "Most people—heck, most living beings—have *fight* or *flight* as their two responses to crisis. You, Norris? You're a *poker*. You don't fight; you poke, and *then* run away. I don't know why. Maybe so you can feel rightfully victimized?"

It was almost flattering how upset he was by the news of Norris's departure.

"Look—"

"And honestly, you can't complain about life fucking you over because you have too many people caring about you, Norris. That's just . . . silly. This is *your* problem, not Austin's, not anybody else's. You made the mess; stay and clean it up."

"I didn't ask you to make me your little pet project," Norris finally snapped once they got to the car.

"See?" Liam said with a solemn nod as he started his car. "Poker."

"Look, I'm going to miss you. That's all." Liam had come around by the time they pulled up outside Norris's building after a

331

mostly silent drive home. To be fair, plenty of drives with Liam were silent. That laid-back demeanor was part of what had made him so easy to be around; the air never filled with awkwardness.

"This is me reacting poorly to the news of you leaving. That's all. You shouldn't internalize that. You understand your life better than I do."

"Um, y-y-yeah," Norris stuttered. "Thank you?"

That was the uncanny thing about Liam; his ability to voice these statements directly from his heart muscle thingy, stripped of ego or any voices in his head that might constantly worry about how they would sound to the world around him. Norris was envious of this quality; it made Liam seem almost invincible. He wondered how different the guy he had come to know this year might be from the one before the tattoo; the unhappy, miserable Liam he'd never met.

"Are you sure about leaving?"

"The Texas climate doesn't agree with me."

Liam laughed. "What does that even mean?"

In response, Norris raised both arms halfway up, revealing darkened armpits even through the fabric of his black T-shirt. One thing he definitely wouldn't miss about Texas was having to walk around with his arms clenched firmly to his sides.

"Dude, the AC is running!" Liam said, pointing to his car's console. "Are you sick?"

"I coined it. Geothermal allergy." Norris nodded. "I'm literally allergic to life here."

Liam laughed some more.

"So, have you talked to Maddie?"

"I don't want to be set on fire," Norris said. "It wouldn't be a great look for me."

"What?"

"Meredith."

"Ah. And Aarti?"

"I've tried, believe me." Four unanswered emails to Aarti, nine texts to Maddie. All unanswered. He had the receipts of his many tries.

Norris shrugged. "At some point, people ignoring you kind of means you should leave them alone, right?" Wasn't that the rationale behind restraining orders?

"Not always. Sometimes they just need time. You should say goodbye," Liam said. "People deserve that."

34

CLOSURE

**STRATEGIES FOR SURVIVING A GOODBYE WITH
EX-GIRLFRIEND:**

The "it was your fault for not just accepting the snow globe"
  route.

The "Godspeed, I hear Ian has genital warts" route.

The "I'm leaving so you can't be mad at me" route.

The "kick me once in the shin with whatever boot you want"
  route.

When the door opened, Norris smiled as best as he could.
"Hi, Mr. Puri. Is Aarti home?"

"Norris?" Aarti's father seemed genuinely surprised to find
him at their door. "Come in, come in!"

Norris knew he needed to make things right with Aarti but
hadn't been quite ready to ask Judith to drive him around on
his Make Amends Tour. He and his mother were somewhere
between silent treatment and tense détente. So Norris had

thought it best to simply bus it to Aarti's house, which had taken two transfers and a hike through the suburbs. His T-shirt's wet pits were definitely showing the trek, which in turn greatly limited his motions as he awkwardly shook Mr. Puri's hand. It was one of those no-big-deal-but-I've-seen-your-daughter-seminaked handshakes that avoided any direct eye contact, and for an excruciating second, Norris thought the man could smell it on him.

"We haven't seen you in a while. Keeping busy, I assume?" Mr. Puri asked, closing the door behind him.

"Yes, you know . . . sleep, homework, eating vegetables, community service. Lather, rinse, repeat," Norris stumbled as best as he could.

"Well, that's good," Mr. Puri chuckled. "Aarti is already at the exhibit, I'm afraid. Were you supposed to meet her here?"

"Exhibit?"

"Her photo exhibit," Mr. Puri said, frowning at a clock on the wall. "I'm very glad you stopped by, actually. I was just dozing off. Her mother would never forgive me for missing it."

"Yeah, it was a stretch. I thought I might be able to catch her before she headed out," Norris lied as he pretended to check his watch. That he had no idea what Mr. Puri was talking about was an understatement.

"I'll give you a ride if you want," Mr. Puri said. "Her mother is already there, helping her set up."

"Oh no, that's okay! Really."

"Oh, come on." Mr. Puri smiled in an unnerving way that showed a glimmer of teeth. "You're a friend of the family."

Before Norris could make a coherent argument as to why him crashing Aarti's exhibit could only be disastrous for all parties involved, Mr. Puri had stepped out of his slippers and grabbed a set of keys from a nearby bowl.

Of all the passenger seats Norris had ridden in since moving to Texas, Mr. Puri's was by far the most nerve-racking one yet. The man had the kind of mustache that led Norris to believe that, slim as it may be, there was still a definite chance that he was being driven into the desert to dig up his own grave for defiling the man's daughter. . . . Like, an 8 percent chance.

"So, how are the finals treating your mother?" Mr. Puri asked as they cruised along the small residential streets of Cedar Park. There was apparently no curtailing the awkward-small-talk portion of this show. "I bet she's got her fair share of grading."

And a spectacular disappointment of a son.

"Good." Norris shrugged. "She's always been a fast grader."

"Any summer plans?"

"Nothing concrete yet. Maybe some traveling home to Montreal."

Norris didn't want to get into it. His daughter could tell him once he was gone if she was so inclined.

"Same for us." Mr. Puri smiled. "Aarti's mother and I are going back to India for a few weeks; Rohan, Aarti's brother, has an internship in New York and we've arranged for her to stay with her cousins in Boston."

Norris couldn't contain his snort at this ongoing battle of wills between father and daughter.

"And I'm guessing she'll be getting a tour of a certain presti-gious college nearby in Cambridge while she's there?"

Mr. Puri gave him a quick furtive glance as they pulled into the downtown area. Norris could tell he was wondering if he was in the presence of a spy or an ally.

"Is it that obvious?"

"A little."

"Well, whether she wants to admit it or not, she's on her way to making for a really strong application," Mr. Puri said with the smile of exactly what he was in the moment: a proud parent born an ocean away. "I looked it up," he continued without prompt-ing. "And this photography business is actually a unique interest. Everyone plays an instrument these days. But our Aarti? Our Aarti, she does photos!"

The gallery was a small space, located on the second floor of a branch of the public library. The first floor was deserted and clearly an all-ages space with pastel book racks, large teddy bears that doubled as chairs, and low tables with round edges. On the walls were talking vegetables advocating for children to consume them. Norris and Mr. Puri shared an apprehensive look that, mercifully, was quickly proven unnecessary as they reached the second floor: a tall space with concrete floors, pummeled with sharply defined beams of light from a row of diamond-shaped skylights. It was as though they had been designed to hit a few specific white walls where framed photos and a few paintings were currently displayed.

"It's like the first floor is a decoy," Mr. Puri whispered as they joined the sharply dressed crowd, and Norris couldn't help but agree. The space wasn't quite packed, but there were more people than Norris had expected.

They found Mrs. Puri by a table of hors d'oeuvres chatting with a small, frizzy-haired woman who did a strange double take when she saw Norris. If Mrs. Puri was surprised to see Norris, her smile did not break as she gave him a lingering look that eventually turned into a warmer smile of recognition. She was wearing a sari that glimmered in the light and seemed perfectly at home in this sophisticated and posh gallery atmosphere.

"Mr. Puri!" the small woman exclaimed. "I was just telling your wife what an extraordinary talent your daughter is!"

Norris assumed her to be Aarti's mentor, Alayna Kerr.

"And would you be open to writing her a recommendation letter to that effect?" Mr. Puri immediately asked without missing a beat. "With those exact words, if you will? *Extraordinary talent?*"

Aarti's photos only made up a third of the exhibit, which was dedicated to "New Eyes," talent that Mrs. Kerr had been "lucky enough to be able to nurture." Something about it felt self-congratulatory to Norris. He wondered if Ms. Kerr knew Mrs. Kolb, Anderson High's adviser, who still made a point of waving to him in the hallways, almost six months into this soon-to-be aborted Austin adventure. He would probably have to tell her he was leaving too. The goodbye tour was getting longer.

It took a couple of laps of the space, but Norris finally spotted

Aarti along with the other two young artists who were being showcased that afternoon; a tall Asian man with a well-trimmed goatee and a middle-aged woman who Norris might place on the spectrum between Kolb-level enthusiasm and just plain drunk. The three stars of the afternoon were currently holding court in a small circle of artists, or people who at least dressed the part. Aarti was wearing a black dress and her hair was up in a bun, a strategic move to make her appear older, no doubt.

Aarti clocked him from across the room, and his awkward wave was evidently not enough, as she seamlessly returned to her conversation. Norris took the hint and continued to stroll through the premises, hoping to catch her again later.

Norris stopped at a large photo of a black guy he did not recognize. He knew nothing about photography, light, and angles, but he had to agree with her father: Aarti Puri *did* photos.

"I like this one," someone commented behind him, a plastic cup of red wine in hand.

"She's very young," their friend said of Aarti as criticism, or maybe praise, before both moved on to another photo. Though, one of them did give him a second look that confused Norris until he turned back to the photo.

Oh.

Dangling high enough that Norris had to tilt back to fully take it in was Norris himself, frozen in time and talking animatedly, arm dangling out of what he recognized as Aarti's car door. He didn't remember what he had been talking about when she'd snapped that particular image, presumably at a red light, but Norris's face was caught in a half grin, half smirk, that Webster's dictionary might define as *shit-eating*.

"*Guy Talking*," Aarti answered his unasked question, sidling up to him, her heels clacking under her. "That's the title. It seemed appropriate."

"Hi," Norris said. Clever repartee didn't seem right, somehow.

"Hello."

They both spent a quiet moment facing the image of *Guy Talking* rather than each other. Up close, Norris could make out streaks of navy blue dye in the black of her hair, which matched her nail polish and the highlights of her dress. He suddenly realized that his own jeans and black T-shirt ensemble, day in, day out, must have been incredibly disappointing to someone this fashionable.

"Um, congratulations," he eventually said. "This is all . . . insanely cool. There are so many people here. Actual human beings too; not Anderson students."

"What are you doing here, Norris?"

"Right. That. Um, I stopped by your house, but you weren't there. Your dad told me to tag along. . . . It kind of just happened. Is it weird? Should I not be here?"

"You have an invitation in your inbox."

"I do?"

She nodded, but she still hadn't turned to face him. This seemed to be a conversation she preferred to have with *Guy Talking*.

"You've had it for weeks. I just didn't expect to see you."

Norris was touched. The fact that she actually wanted him

here was opening enough for him. "Can we talk? Um, just really quickly?"

She finally turned his way, looking torn. She rolled her eyes and motioned for him to follow her toward the fire escape. A door marked Exit seemed like the right place for this conversation.

"Look, I'm really sorry," Norris immediately launched in the second the door closed behind them. "I know you were just jealous that I went to prom with Maddie and that's why you showed up at the after-party with Ian. And you're right, it was hypocritical of me to get angry because you were right to be jealous—I really did kind of have a crush on Maddie, but to be fair I didn't realize it at the time, and anyway I did ask you to prom and you turned me down. Regardless: I should have pulled you aside and talked to you, instead of causing a scene."

"That's not . . ."

"The good news is that I'm going back to Canada. Also, I have a record now, maybe? Well, a citation, whatever that is. The point is, there is some genuine street cred going on back there," he said, pointing back toward the exhibit and the photo of the hardened criminal she had unknowingly captured.

"You're going back to Canada?" she repeated, weighing the words as though she hadn't heard anything that had followed. "Like, for good?"

"Pretty much."

"Is that why you came here, then? To say goodbye?"

"Sort of." Norris smiled sheepishly.

The response of being shoved against the door was not what he had expected.

341

"Why are you upset?! That was a good apology!"

"Oh yes, because why would my first exhibit *ever* be about me when *you* could crash it and make it about yourself and your need to be absolved of any guilt before you up and leave the country?"

She seemed like she still had something to say, so Norris thought it best to remain quiet.

"You seemed so normal when we first met," Aarti noted. She picked at the tag that had slipped out of her sleeve and slipped it back up with a glare, daring him to bring it up. "Funny and cute, sure—"

"Thank y—"

"Shut the hell up," she cut him off, getting louder. "But normal was really the primary appeal here. And after all my shit with Ian, I thought I needed that. A nice immigrant—not Indian, but still immigrant—guy who my parents would swoon over. Someone who really likes me, and what's wrong with that? Just let yourself be wooed and dated, Aarti. . . ."

Her voice lowered again. "The point is . . . you're not normal, dude! You are as exhausting as every other red-foreheaded American guy with a faux-hawk, I swear."

The door swung open behind Norris, hitting him in the back. Clearly, Austin was ready for him to leave.

"Oops. Sorry about that," a man in his late twenties said as he pushed past Norris, phone in hand.

"Great photos." He distractedly smiled to Aarti before tumbling down the narrow stairs, enthralled by his own phone.

"Thank you so much!"

Aarti was now staring at him with crossed arms.

"Um, Liam says that no one is normal," Norris ventured now that it was clearly his turn again. "He says we're all just different flavors of fucked-up, hiding it as best as we can. I'm starting to think that maybe he was right."

"That sounds like an intense conversation."

"Actually, it was prompted by him finding a jalapeño in his cafeteria mac and cheese."

Aarti snorted.

"You weren't . . . actually in love with me, right?" she then asked.

Norris thought about it for a moment. There was the answer he wanted to give, the answer he should give, and in a third distinct column, some objective truth he might look back on one day, years from now and be able to perfectly articulate.

He thought back to the day they first met. It felt like so long ago now: Aarti waltzing into his life with her quick wit and her camera lens, facing off with a gaggle of cheerleaders, Maddie McElwees included.

"I liked the idea that I was interesting enough to hold your attention, maybe," he finally admitted. "You seemed different from everyone else here, in a good way, obviously. Also, you're ridiculously hot. Draws the eye."

But Aarti was more than a simple compliment away from letting this go.

"Why couldn't you just admit that you liked Maddie?" she

343

admonished. "Instead of making me simultaneously feel like I was in a shadow competition with the entire cheerleading squad, *and* feel like I was crazy for feeling that way? Fuck, Norris. That really sucked."

She was right; Norris had never taken the time to imagine what it might have all looked like from her perspective. How Maddie had grown from cheerleading drone to one of his closest/only friends in Texas. He'd spectacularly messed that one up.

"I honestly didn't know. I'm sorry," he said, drumming his fingers along the staircase railing. Those two words were all he seemed to have right. "I'm not . . . I'm not always superaware of the whole 'feelings' thing. My own or other people's. Watching you pine for Ian wasn't superfun either, if we're being honest."

The two of them had always been circling other people's orbits.

"God," she eventually groaned, finding a seat on the stairs. "We would have been a disaster if we'd actually gotten to be boyfriend and girlfriend, huh?"

Norris was exhausted at the mere thought of how they might chip at each other's insecurities for months to come. And how the only thing that had prevented their lives from becoming irreparably linked had been luck and a thin layer of polyurethane.

"Fucking nuclear," he concluded, joining her on the stairs, though staying a couple of steps higher to avoid close proximity.

"So, what's going to happen with you and Madison McElwees?"

Aarti had a way of saying Maddie's full name that, while not resentful, dripped with an intonation of "ooh la la." Anthropological interest, Judith would call it.

"I don't think much can be done there," Norris said, feeling sad all over again. "I'm leaving soon. Once a girl tells you that you're profoundly basic, it's time to take the hint, right?"

"She actually said that?" Aarti asked, a small smirk creeping onto her lips. "I have to admit that I do like her style."

"What about us? Can we be friends?" Norris asked after a moment.

"You're moving back to Canada."

Right. That.

"So, what am I going to say, Norris? No?"

"Actual friends, who write emails, talk about their lives, and all that crap?" he followed. Because whatever else could be said, Aarti Puri was heading for a really interesting life and Norris inexplicably kind of wanted to be part of it. Even if it was only at a distance.

"Sure. Friends." Aarti shrugged with a smile. "Permanent pause on the benefits, though."

"Now see, I strongly feel like that's the irrational part of your brain talking," Norris said. "I'm not leaving for another few days, and in the meantime, I will sacrifice my body if you need that emotional closu—"

Fourth hit in four minutes. Okay, fine: that one Norris had coming.

The two of them hugged, awkward as it was.

"I like your photos. Even though I'm sure my opinion isn't worth much right now."

"It's Canadian currency." Aarti smiled. "Less, but not worthless." She rejoined the exhibit.

On his way out, Norris caught a last glimpse of Aarti, chatting with a woman who kept animatedly shaking her forearm as if to pass on her enthusiasm. Norris almost wanted to track down Mr. Puri by the hors d'oeuvres and tell him that he and his wife had nothing to worry about. Their daughter would rule whatever corner of the world she set her mind to. She'd travel, write novels, film documentaries, hold exhibits, or just make more money than God on Wall Street. And Norris would always feel this weird, inexplicable pride that she had ever looked twice at him.

There was only one person left on his goodbye tour that he really needed to see.

Norris texted Maddie one more time.

Norris: Hey Maddie. Good news! I'm going back to Montreal. Can I please see you one last time to apologize? Love, Canada.

The reply came swiftly.

Maddie: No.

35

AIRPORT ANALYSIS

DEFINITION: The act of introspection that naturally occurs upon watching planes take off and land.

BENEFITS: Intense self-reflection, leading to life changes.

HAZARDS: Intense self-reflection, leading to life changes. Also charges related to last-minute flight changes.

The flight to Montreal was scheduled to depart on time, which, naturally, meant that they had to arrive two hours early. They had never traveled much when Norris was young, but he remembered that his father liked to leave plenty of time to get through security. Judith had hugged him twice outside the airport. Once in the car, stretching into the back seat to kiss his neck while reassuring him that she wasn't mad.

"I'm sorry, Mom," Norris had said, one last time.

"I just want you to be happy. You know that," she answered, as if he'd said the silliest thing.

They hauled their bags from the trunk, triple-checked passports, and made for the automatic doors.

"Norris!" His mother shouted through the passenger window. She unbuckled and left the engine idling to wrap her arms around him. "I love you." She turned to Felix. "You: look after our kid, all right?"

Only a mother could say something in a manner that was both heartfelt plea and unspoken threat.

Something had been nagging Norris ever since they left the apartment, and it stayed with him through security check. They stopped at Hudson News for overpriced bags of caramel M&M'S and mixed nuts: preventative measures against airplane "food." Settling in at their gate, the anticipatory exhaustion Norris always felt at airports washed over him as he watched hurried passengers ebb and flow in a sea of neck pillows and overstuffed carry-ons. There would be jetlag and cabin pressure, baggage claim roulette, followed by the transit shit show of catching a cab to look forward to, but that wasn't what weighed on him as he struggled to find a comfortable position on the ergonomically sadistic airport chair.

"Janet's going to be *thrilled* to have me hanging around for a few weeks," he quipped, trying to give voice to it. Maybe that was it: dread at living with Stepmommy Dearest, and her crying spawn, to boot.

"You're my son. She knows that." Felix waved it off. "I'm kind of looking forward to having my boys together."

No, it wasn't dread. Norris still couldn't explain that feeling in the pit of his stomach. It wasn't anger at his dad for trying to make everything sound so easy, or even guilt from his mother being bend-over-backward accommodating. It was something else. It was . . . sadness. A double-decker burrito-size sadness, right there in his gut.

"Are you going to miss your Austin friends?" Felix offered. His paternal sixth sense must have noticed something was wrong. "Your mom mentioned something about a sports team."

"Oh. That."

Norris pulled out his phone and found a picture of the players out on the ice. He tilted his screen to throw off the glare coming in the airport's beaming windows. Maddie had taken that picture during their first game.

"They've gotten pretty good," Norris said. "I mean, some of them. They can stand up."

"You know." Felix nodded. "The first thing I did when we got to Montreal was find that bar, Lakaye, since it was the only one that broadcast Haitian football. It was a way for me to feel connected to home, even in Montreal. I guess you starting a hockey team in Texas is kind of the same thing. Who's that?" His father pointed to the screen.

"Liam." Norris smiled as he began to narrate the next photo. "Liam Hooper. The dude I started the league with. Or, I guess he started it. Really I just tagged along."

Another photo of Liam.

"That's him fly-fishing. He has this bucket list of . . . stuff he just wants to do, and he kind of just does them."

"Sounds fun," Felix said.

349

Inspiring. That sadness-burrito wasn't getting any better.

"You always seemed like such a lone wolf as a kid. . . ."

"I wasn't a lone wolf, Dad," Norris said. "I just didn't have friends."

"Who's that?" Felix asked, clearing his throat like he always did when he couldn't joke something away, intrigued by the next photo that came up. They'd fallen into playing a game of swipe-and-tell now.

"She's cute! Is she your girlfriend?"

"Aarti? No. Well, we were kind of going out, not really, though . . . anyway that's over now."

"Do you know how to use prote—"

"Please stop talking."

"Okay," Felix simply said. "Were you nice to her? This girl?"

"I thought I was. But maybe I could have been nicer," Norris confessed after a moment.

Neither of them said anything for a while. Norris noticed that the M&M'S wrapper had been flattened into a sheet and folded around Felix's anxious fingers like a long ring.

"It feels like I've missed a lot in a really short window," Felix eventually admitted. "Your first hangover, your first girlfriend . . . I had speeches prepared for all of these."

"You did?"

"Well, I have one ready for your first time. I can tell you all about that."

"God, Dad." Norris groaned. "Please don't."

"Nothing graphic. You're never going to be a porn star, so

350

forget all that stuff your mother and I pretended you didn't browse when you got your own laptop. Just be in the moment, and pay attention to her needs, and—"

"I *will* scream," Norris warned. He swiped to a new photo to change the subject.

"Okay, okay. Who's that?" Felix asked. "Another girlfriend? Jesus, kiddo."

"No, not a girlfriend either . . . She worked at the restaurant with me."

"She looks nice." Felix observed. It was a photo someone had snapped on the dance floor at the prom, before everything had gone so wrong. Maddie was grinning with him. She looked happy. He looked happy.

"She is nice," Norris said. *The nicest*.

"She likes you," Felix observed, pointing to the screen. "You can definitely tell."

The thing was that Norris really couldn't. He had revisited the chain of events over and over in his mind but he just couldn't track it. When had Maddie become interested in him? When had Aarti figured it out? When had he started liking Maddie back? Was there an alternate reality where he didn't get into it with Aarti and Ian, and left the after-party as Maddie suggested, happily on her arm? That alternate reality felt both as likely and as impossible to Norris as the one he was stuck in right now. Nothing about moving back to Canada felt right in the moment: one more alternate reality away from the real thing. He tried to put the thought out of his head and shoved the phone into his pocket. She might have liked him when the photo was taken, but that was then.

"It doesn't matter, Dad. They're just photos."

"Here." Felix reached into his pocket, pulling out his own phone along with a wad of old receipts. He opened an album to show Norris.

"Cute," Norris offered. Babies were cute as a general population, but he did not get much out of individualizing them. Felix swiped to another photo of the same baby.

"He's fat," Norris couldn't help but note. "Still definitely cute, but watch out for those candy snacks or that thing will chub up on you so fast."

Felix laughed out loud. "That's you, actually."

"That fat-headed baby is me?"

"Your head was always this exact size," Felix said. "You just grew into it, thank God."

"There weren't smart phones when I was a baby," Norris pointed out.

"No, but I had all the old family albums digitized. Easier to carry around."

Norris just nodded. He hadn't expected that.

"It looks like you had a pretty good life here," Felix continued. "All things considered."

"I messed it up."

"I know I'm a shit dad," Felix said. "I know that. We all mess things up. It's what you do with the mess that matters."

Norris nodded, and on impulse, fished his little notebook out from his backpack. For some reason, he hadn't been able to part with it, even after all the mess it had caused. He casually flipped through it, wondering if Kolb knew what she'd started when she'd simply handed him the nearest notebook from a bin.

Flipping through the entries, Norris started to feel sick to his stomach. What had Aarti found funny in any of these? They were bitter rants, mean asides. This guy was homesick, insecure, bitter, and so fucking lonely he spent his lunch hours walking around without going anywhere. Patrick Lamarra might say the authorial voice behind this notebook was "kind of a little bitch."

"What's that?" Felix asked.

"Excuses," Norris answered after taking a moment to consider.

He wanted to tear out the pages, one by one, crumple them, and in doing so erase all the crap that this thing had caused him. But, as his father had said: It doesn't matter if you make a mess. It matters that you fix it. Maybe the whole point of approaching life as origami that the documentary had missed was learning to fold your sharp edges.

"Dad?"

"Yes, kid?"

"Can I please stay?"

36

MOVIE-MAGIC ENDINGS

THE FANTASY: Racing through airport turnstiles, total strangers helping in one's last minute quest for love, a final joyous embrace celebrating the validity of one's life decisions.

THE REALITY: . . . Not that.

All movies are lies. Period, end of sentence.

The dash to the airport thing—that romantic-comedy trope was always a single straight line. People cheered for the guy along the way; traffic moved fast enough for him to get there at a dash; security officers were won over by his heartfelt attempt to seize the moment and right his wrongs. Turns out that the reverse was a whole situation that amounted to two words: incredibly expensive. Norris had waited two hours too long to pull off the Band-Aid.

"Four hundred eighty-five dollar shipment fee?!" Felix exclaimed.

"Per luggage," the desk attendant added apologetically. "It's an international flight, sir."

Norris's two luggage bags had already been checked and processed through. The only way to get them back was for them to be processed to Canada and then flagged for a return at the Austin airport. Or, alternatively, Felix could drag the luggage home and ship it back to Norris.

"No," Norris said. "You already spent a fortune coming to collect my sorry ass. It's not worth it. Keep it there for me, please? If you have the space."

"Why?" Felix said with a raised eyebrow.

"You know, for when I visit, maybe? Underwear changes are nice."

Norris had a little brother out there. A tiny little human puppy that shared some of his genetic makeup, the poor little bastard. He wanted to see him someday.

"That'd be nice, son. Real nice . . ."

There was a beat of parental silence before Felix spoke again.

"I love you, son. You know that, right?"

"But I'm still paying for the ticket, right?"

"Oh, every last cent."

Norris smiled.

"Love you too, Dad. Thanks for, y'know, showing up."

"That's a given."

Felix's hug was different from Judith's. Stronger, yes, but also somewhat looser; fraternal but still present. Norris really didn't have time to analyze or gauge his parents based on forearm density.

"You're a given, kiddo." He nodded firmly. "Your mom and I will be on your ass no matter where you go to college or what time zone you screw up in next."

Halfway through the cab ride home, Norris decided on a stop before getting home to face the music with Judith. He'd waited too long to pull enough Band-Aids already today—and there was the distinct possibility that his mother would kill him the moment she saw him, considering she'd already discussed her exit path from Austin with her department head two days prior.

"Hey, Jim!" Norris said with an awkward wave, stepping into the restaurant and, of course, instantly catching the eye of the patriarch. He realized he had no idea how much Big Jim knew about the mess he'd made with Maddie.

"Oh, Norris!" Big Jim said, working himself down the narrow staircase from his office and sounding genuinely surprised. Pleasantly surprised even?

"What happened to Canada?"

"That's kind of not happening anymore," Norris started. "Wait, how do you know about this?"

"Well, ain't that why you quit out of the blue? To go back for the treatment?"

"Treatment?"

"Yeah, is the P-word infection okay?" Big Jim said, leaning into Norris with a concerned, hushed voice. "'Internal shaft boils.' Isn't the treatment only available in Quebec?"

Thank God there weren't any radioactive puddles around

Austin: Meredith would make a wonderful supervillain. Superman would be utterly screwed.

"The boils are better," Norris confirmed through a clenched smile. "Thanks for the concern."

Big Jim smiled back at him.

"Glad to hear it! She's in the back," he continued. "Don't keep her too long, though! We're short on the floor today."

Norris found Maddie, folding lime-green cardboard sheets into perfect boxes, slapping a Bone Yard sticker onto each new box with the distracted dexterity of someone who had been doing this all her life. Her head was bopping along to whatever was currently playing on her headphones. *Downward* was a good word for her expression—and overall mood—the moment she spotted Norris at the door to the storage room.

"What the hell are you doing here?"

This was already going better than he could have expected, considering he wasn't asphyxiating under Big Jim's headlock.

"Meredith told your dad I quit because . . . I had an infection that needed care."

Maddie hummed. "Who says it was Meredith?"

Norris faked a gasp that she instantly defused with ruthlessly dead eyes. She was in no mood for his shtick at the moment, it seemed.

"What do you want, Norris?"

So many things.

"I sat in a cab for forty minutes trying to figure out the best way to go about saying all this stuff, but I really can't think of another way of saying it than just, y'know, coming out with it. Well, actually I tried texting Liam for advice on the way here, for something romantic or whatever."

Norris took out his phone to read the evidence.

"All he had to say was, 'Light doesn't necessarily travel at the speed of light; the slowest recording of light speed was thirty-eight miles per hour.' Like, what does that mean? I sincerely think the guy is high all the time. Anyway, rambling: Of course I knew it was a date. A really important date. Y'know: prom. I think that's what was terrifying about it, maybe. This would be, could be, a real thing. And you could get bored of me just like . . . you could end up hating me. Or we could get along great. And all the options were equally scary to me. But scary in the best way, y'know? In fact, I think if we dated, it could be kind of, err, great?"

Maddie only blinked at him.

To be fair, that might have actually all been one breath.

"So would you please let me take you out on the awesome date you deserved? Because you're a really phenomenal person and, um, I would really, really like to prove to you that I'm not a completely unredeemable asshole. Because getting to spend time with you is a really good reason to not be an unredeemable ass-hole."

She looked at him for a moment, stack of key lime boxes still in hand. From what Norris could tell of her current facial expression, she might have been fighting off a smile or trying to remember the perfect monologue to eviscerate Norris that she and Meredith had no doubt rehearsed half a dozen times. It turned out to be neither.

"And also? I'm so, so sorry."

She stepped around the counter.

"Look, Canada. Norris." She smiled, carefully wrapping her headphone cords around her hand as to avoid any tangling of the wire. "I . . . appreciate the rantpology, but honestly? There's an abs-to-drama ratio for boys, and you would need a sixteen-pack for me to want to deal with your nonsense."

"I, um—"

"But thanks for the apology. I really appreciate it." She gave him a small smile and sidestepped him, grabbing an apron off the rack and flipping it around her neck.

"Use the service exit, all right?" she added with a wink. "Cutting through the kitchens is strictly for employees."

By the time Norris had made it back to the cab, a surcharge of twenty-five dollars had been added to his fare. Judith was waiting for him on the steps of their apartment building, phone at her ear, ranting in Creole. As soon as she clocked the cab, the phone was down in her pocket. Norris couldn't be sure, but he was pretty sure that she actually cracked her neck—a sure sign of an impending dragging of her ungrateful son.

All movies were *lies*.

EPILOGUE

Norris had never experienced true Texas sun . . . until now. All his sweating, all his suffering these past seven months had been from their excuse for winter and spring. July was another beast entirely. It was a dry, punishing heat that turned every other thought into a groan. One hundred eleven degrees of nonsense. Austin was in full drought, and the trickling rivulets around Red River were now dusty canals of hardened mud mixed with rocks and dead branches. The locals did not seem to mind; this was simply life in Austin. There were no evacuation notices, no noticeable drops in traffic or festivals, and no alternative work schedules. Occasionally Norris would spot a Stay Hydrated advertisement with an anthropomorphized water bottle under it, reminding people to twist its skullcap open six to eight times a day.

Norris's body had stopped sweating, perhaps in rebellion against these unholy circumstances. Judith was relieved.

"Your body has gotten used to it." She'd waved him off when he brought the matter to her. "Thank God! The electric bill was out of control with the daily wash loads."

For Norris, this meant that his body had reached a point in the microwave cycle where the cheese stopped bubbling and blackened into a crust, devoid of any moisture. Texas was over-cooking him.

To make matters worse, his days were spent exposed to the elements in a small, smelly car, floorboard now littered with mini–water bottles he amassed at every possible venue where they were handing them out for free. The Bone Yard's brand-new delivery car ("thirdhand brand-new," to quote Big Jim) came with less-than-reliable AC.

Norris slammed his door shut on the driver's side of the "Bone Yarder," which today was being a complete vehicular dick.

"How are you not dying?" he marveled, plugging the behe-moth, turn-of-the-century credit card machine into the car charger.

"I cracked a window," Liam answered. The best thing about Norris's position was the new employee who had joined the Bone Yard family on a whim, picking up Norris for a movie after work one day. It turned out that Norris wasn't the only one who could interview well.

"The window lets the outside air *in*," Norris pointed out. "That actually doesn't help."

"I like heat," Liam replied, checking one more delivery off

their list. He was in his summer tank top phase, no longer concerned with hiding his tattoo. His hair was longer, and verging dangerously close to a man bun. They would need to have a talk soon.

"It's really conducive to this new micromeditation I found online. It activates the spiritual essence."

Norris pulled the car (yes, he'd finally gotten his provisional license) out of the small office parking lot where they had just dropped off a piping hot tray of wings and lost the game of Rock-Paper-Scissors by which he and Liam decided who was in charge of making the actual trek to the door. "Please don't kill me when you finally snap."

"Why couldn't I stay in the car again?" Liam asked as they climbed the wooden stairs up to the restaurant.

"Buffer," Norris explained. "You're needed."

Maddie was holding court in her father's office with Meredith and Trish. Norris could hear their giggling chatter from the lobby as he and Liam snaked through a crowd of burnt orange–clad customers waiting to be seated. Navigating the family restaurant was second nature to him now; Norris would have missed it had he been unable to grovel his way into getting his job back. Not that he would ever admit it—especially not given how things currently stood.

The girls instantly fell silent when the door opened, turning to Norris in a way that definitely wasn't reminiscent of the velociraptors in *Jurassic Park*. Even though the AC was on full blast, all three wore bikini tops and short-shorts. Maddie swiveled back and forth on her father's office chair. Her smile dropped at the sight of Norris, which was par for the course these days.

"Three deliveries down: two debit, one cash, already put it in the till downstairs," Norris summarized.

"You're running late," Maddie noted coolly, glancing at the schedule on the computer screen.

"Car pileup on Guadalupe." Norris placed a stack of receipts on the desk. "We'll make it up on the next run."

She pursed her lips then turned to Liam, flipping from sour to sweet.

"Hi, Liam," Maddie greeted him. "How are you settling into the groove of things?"

Liam smiled, amused by the entire thing. *Dick.*

"Good," he said. "Settling. Grooving. Norris has been a good supervisor."

"Oh, he's not your supervisor. In fact, you outrank him. Feel free to get drunk with power." Maddie smiled acidly.

"Uh," Liam said, as if actually considering it.

"Great! It can be a lot to take in, so let me know if you need anything, okay?"

"Will do, thanks."

Big Jim and his wife were currently on a cruise at his wife's insistence (really an ultimatum), and Maddie was in charge. There had been grumbles that she was too young, but two weeks in, everything was running smoothly. She signed for deliveries, managed the employee timetables, and still had time to invent

fun ways to make Norris's "probation period" as goddamn puni-
tive as possible.

"By the way, Norris . . ." Maddie paused to sip her lemonade, staring at him over her sunglasses. "I'm going to need you to
make a stop in Pflugerville on your way out. Order of key lime
pies placed yesterday. I hope that won't be a problem."

"Since when?!" Norris sputtered. "I just drove past Pflugerville to get back here!" Norris snarked. "Why didn't you tell me
beforehand? This is such a waste of gas."

"Norris . . ." Liam warned in singsong. "Buffering?"

Maddie took another sip. "Slipped my mind."

"This is still your family's business, y'know," Norris said. "Is
sabotaging it worth making me miserable?"

"Oh yes," she replied.

Meredith was taking an obscene amount of pleasure in
watching this unfold. "You could always quit," she offered help-
fully.

"You could always give me another shot," Norris countered.
Really, she was being unreasonable.

Meredith snorted from her seat on the couch, which prompted
Norris to snort back loudly in her general direction. This would
be much better without audience participation.

"Who's that?" Norris asked.

Maddie shook her head and turned her phone around for
him to see.

"Diego," she said coolly. "New transfer from Trinity next
year."

"And apparently, smitten with our little Maddie here," Meredith added. "He couldn't stop talking about her after meeting her downstairs."

Norris took in the photo of a tanned, olive-skinned shirtless guy with a jersey wrapped around his head, glistening in the sun, baseball bat high and at the ready. It was the sort of candid that looked vaguely like a pornographic calendar. An eight-pack. Kid had an eight-pack. Norris also suspected Diego to be very profoundly stupid in person. "Clinical case study" stupid.

"Congratulations," he simply said with a grin instead. "He's really good-looking. Let me know if you need dating lessons."

Maddie's face almost—almost—broke into a smile.

"You're going to crack, y'know," Maddie told him, rolling her office chair over to the printer and handing Norris the new address.

"Watch me," Norris said. "Three hundred four days."

"What's in three hundred four days?" Trish asked, confused.

Maddie rolled her eyes. "Senior prom."

"He's actually insane," Meredith noted through her own sip of lemonade. Her nails were orange for the summer. "She's not going to prom with you again, you ridiculous person."

Witch.

Witch who Norris could no longer openly berate lest it cost him points with Maddie.

"Aw, actually I think that's sweet," Trish cooed.

Norris snapped his fingers at her in gratitude. "Thank you, Trish. I always liked you! What corsage do you think she'll want?"

"Depends on the dress," Trish considered, assessing Maddie. "She's gorg in anything coral."

"Don't encourage him." Maddie sighed.

Too late. Coral. Noted.

She hadn't said no. Norris had three hundred four days to turn those eye rolls and scoffs into a *yes*. Their first actual date would happen. He'd make sure of it. And if the *yes* never came—because there really was a healthy chance that Maddie would never look at him *that* way again—at least they were on their way to being friends again. Norris had received his first text from Aarti since she left for vacation just the other day, and between the photos of her fashion-forward little cousins and the updates on his "key lime delivery lifestyle" situation, "just friends" was a pretty good place to be. As far as Norris was concerned, that was closer to "everything" than just "something."

It wasn't the happy ending he wanted but, then again, there were no such things as happy endings. Happy endings were artificial things manufactured out of less-than-ideal circumstances. A divorce wasn't the end of family, nor was someone moving away the end of a friendship. These things could be endings, but only if you decided to make them so. Otherwise, things just added up and continued forward, across the map, in new shapes and iterations.

"All right, pin in the corsage discussion. Liam: onward," Norris declared, rubbing his hands together. "We have a stop in Pflugerville to add to the schedule."

"This is all . . . very mature," Liam noted as he and Norris packed the car with another row of steaming tinfoil trays, three key lime pies, and a cardboard box of utensils and fixings. Quinceañera in Cherrywood.

"Aren't you always going on about visualizing your desired reality or whatever?" Norris asked, wrapping his hand into his T-shirt to avoid burning it on the car door.

"Yes, but—"

"Well," Norris preempted. "Picture this: Me and Maddie, Meredith and Patrick, I guess, and you and your own date—Trish was definitely giving you hot-tub eyes up there—in a limo at prom, with a regional hockey trophy in the trunk. How's that for a picture-perfect American prom night?"

Liam's eyebrow quirked. He was getting pretty fluent in Norris-speak and Norris, for his part, had learned to align himself to Liam's wavelength. It wasn't that far-fetched.

The future—his future, in Austin, Texas—was only just beginning. Norris was looking forward to it. Diego and his eight-pack would be a footnote in history.

"Pretty good picture," Liam admitted.

"Got that right," Norris confirmed. "It'll be goddamn glorious."

THE END
But also, like, not really.
That's kind of the point.

ACKNOWLEDGMENTS

When I was young—and before you ask, I'm now at the age where I can feel that first imminent gray hair growing inside my chin—"acknowledgments" were typically just a string of names without context. They felt like a mandatory receipt at the end of my books that were only there because the patent holder of the book's binding glue demanded credit or something. Long story short, I never read them. Since I apparently get four full pages here, hopefully these will be a little less ™.

Mind you, that is still not enough space to go into details about everyone's contributions, so I will simply say that without all the names that follow, you would be holding a mess of xeroxed pages held together by ketchup and hope.

First, to Joelle Hobeika, Sara Shandler, and Alessandra Balzer, the best editors I could have asked for. I know writers who have panic attacks when their editors email them, but in my case, it's always a delight. With occasional dog pictures. They have been the Captain America, Iron Man, and Thor trifecta of this process. (In my head, I'm more of the Infinity Gauntlet of the situation. Important, but also kind of convoluted with too much backstory.)

To the other amazing folks of Alloy Entertainment, including Eliza Swift, Romy Golan, Matt Bloomgarden, Laura Barbiea, and, last but not least, Joshua Bank—five particularly awesome humans, including one Rangers fan who I'm still hoping will see the light. That's right, Josh: I'm using the acknowledgments of my first novel to take a potshot at your hockey team. This will live on in print. Habs forever.

Likewise, to everyone else at B+B/HarperCollins: Kelsey Murphy, Bethany Reis, Michelle Cunningham, Alison Donalty, Nellie Kurtzman, Bess Braswell, Ebony LaDelle, Gina Rizzo, Haley George, Andrea Pappenheimer, Kerry Moynagh, Kathleen Faber, Patty Rosati, Molly Motch, Rebecca McGuire, and Jenny Moles. Also to Maeve O'Regan at HarperCanada. Thanks for taking a chance on this story. (I wasn't kidding about it taking a village, y'all.)

To my agent, Leslie York, who signed an MFA runt who thought he was the next Jeffrey Eugenides writing short stories about people having metaphorical conversations on road trips, and still stuck with me while I, for lack of a better term, "found my chill."

To the loved ones who withstood all my groans from the other room, anxious texts, tweets, and toe nudges while I wrote this book and occasionally did everything not to write it because that's how it goes.

To the real-world inspirations for Aarti, Maddie, Eric, and Liam, who I'm lucky to still have in my life. This story is pure fiction—Norris and Ben would not get along—but the inspirations behind these characters are crystal clear in my head. All names have been changed, with the exception of Aarti's. . . . There really is an Aarti (not Puri) out there who finds the fact that she lives on as a "muse" hilarious. She is going to be insufferable after this. Oh, fun fact: Liam turned out to be a Harvard-PhD-program-in-neuroscience genius, now mapping brains all over.

To all my favorite teachers, from that high school substitute teacher who playacted the entirety of *The Shining* instead of teaching us to Elizabeth McCracken, Michael W. Addams, Rivka Galchen, and Jim Magnuson, who came much later but were as inspiring. You all made me want to keep trying to tell stories. This is getting long . . . should I stop? (Nah . . . but, like, you don't have to keep reading.)

To the kid who tried to set my backpack on fire in the seventh grade while I was wearing it because his dad told him that black people smell like weed when they burn. I wish I could go back in time and tell Young Ben that this kid would be aggressively balding by the end of high school and completely unGoogleable by 2018—which takes commitment to mediocrity—while he will get to write a real book.

To my dad, who, for all his flaws, used to make me smell his books and recite French fables for his friends when I was a kid and then looked at me like I was the best thing he had ever done.

We also now look exactly alike.

And I know she got the dedication already, but I'll wrap it up by yet again thanking my awesome, phenomenal mom, who left everyone she knew behind in Haiti and moved to Sherbrooke, Quebec, Canada, for a chance to give her son a better life. The same mom who never made me feel weird for spending my summers as a committed indoors kid, reading, doodling, watching way too much TV, and completing every single side quest in every single *Final Fantasy* video game. And later, when I said I wanted to move to New York City for college, she woke up at five a.m. instead of six to go over SAT flashcards with me. That incredible woman cannot be undersold.

Thanks, everyone.